Endurek

The Land of Talsar - Book 3

Heidi Likins

Endurek

The Land of Talsar - Book 3

Heidi Likins

Published in USA

ISBN-13: 978-1514892947

Praise for other books in the Talsar Series

A great read! Had a hard time putting it down. The adventures and challenges the characters faced kept me wondering what was going to happen next. -Karen

This intriguing story has the elements of allegory similar to the C.S. Lewis Narnia stories and some of the mysticism of Harry Potter, which blended together to create a novel that is both entertaining and thought-provoking. A take-away from reading this book is to reminder to analyze situations beyond first impressions.
                                        -Hemming Way

A masterpiece of writing! Veiled light is astonishing in all aspects. Ariyuna changes throughout the book through God, or how the book describes him as V'Arah. Thank you Mrs. Likins for your great wisdom. -Jason (12 years old)

Very well written and engaging. It will keep you on the edge of your seat and wondering what is going to happen next. It is full of good life lessons. -Ottercat3

Clever and imaginative characters. Tales that inspire while taking you on a fast pace adventure. Can't wait for the next book! - Faye

I really enjoyed this book because we learned to trust God and every time Ariyuna learns a lesson she gets a jewel and also builds her character. I enjoyed the magical land of Talsar. I liked it as much as the Hobbit. -Sophia (11 years old)

To Isaac

May the deceptions of this world

never mar the splendor of the eternal.

My deepest gratitude to the Displaced Modifiers
and to those who have faithfully
spurred me on to better things.

Jill Brown

Joanne Barringer

Mary Davis

Jim Hart

Andrew Likins

Isaac Likins

Donita K. Paul

Carol Reinsma

Faye Spieker

Vikki Walton

N
W   E
S

Yuratag Mountains

Red Peaks

Lake Kassar

Maaz
Marsh

Surtak

Dorben

Belgutai

Tegus River

Dundaad

Magsa

Altan Forest

Batu

Talsar

Forest
of Mist

Temgulun

Cheren River

Bat'Uul Mountains

Vachir

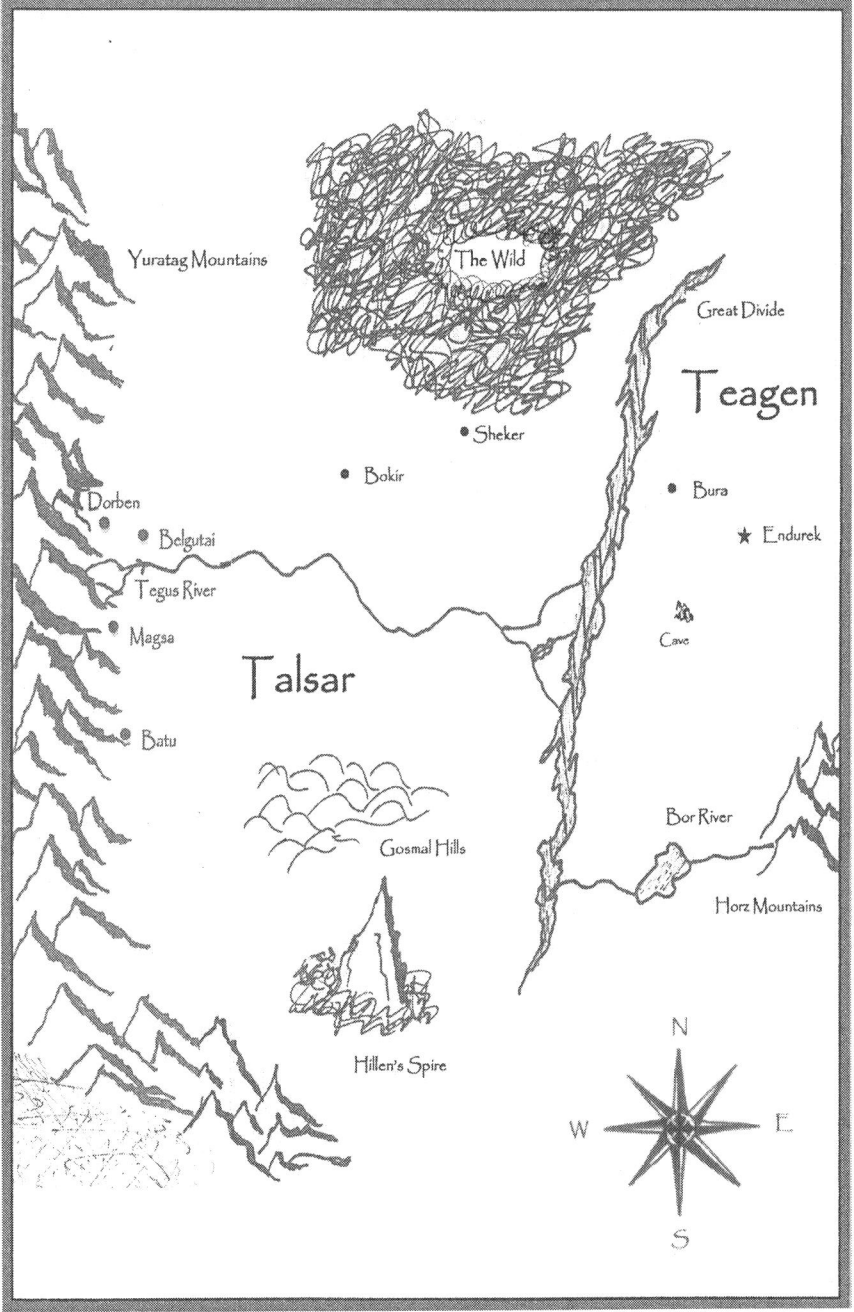

Yuratag Mountains

The Wild

Great Divide

Teagen

Sheker

Bokir

Bura

Dorben

Belgutai

Endurek

Tegus River

Magsa

Cave

Talsar

Batu

Bor River

Gosmal Hills

Horz Mountains

Hillen's Spire

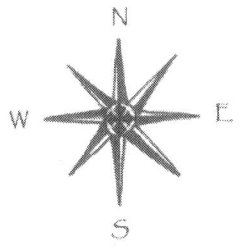

N

W   E

S

Contents:

Chapter 1
Freedom

A ball of anger rumbled in Dash's chest. From the ladder, he peeked up into the sleeping loft. Late afternoon rays filtered in through the small windows set into the stone walls of his family's farmhouse.

Running his fingers through his dark, spiky hair, he watched his brother, Dalan, shove a kerchief into his pack before kneeling to peer under the bed.

Dash climbed down the ladder and stomped into the kitchen where Ma kneaded bread dough.

"Why can't I go?" he demanded.

"That's the tenth time you've asked today, Dash. What's Papa to do if you leave? With Ariyuna already in the capital with the queen, and Tabin arriving any minute to take Dalan there, Papa will need help. We've got the sheep to care for, and the harvest just a step away." She smacked dough into little balls and dropped them on the baking sheet as the oven pumped heat into the already sweltering kitchen.

Dash glared at the dough balls. Resentment flared. Why couldn't he go? Why did he have to stay behind and do all the hard work? They had left him out of the last adventure as well, but he'd followed anyway.

He flung the kitchen door open and trudged out to the barn.

"It's just not fair!" He kicked at a pile of hay. "I'm old enough. I've already gone all over Talsar and even fought tarch."

Dugur, the large old ram, poked his head around a post into the last shafts of daylight making horizontal lines in the dusty air.

"What are you looking at?" Dash kicked hay at the stubborn ram. "You don't care if you stay here or not, but I..." He stopped and glanced into the stall behind Dugur.

Doechin, the pony, swished his tail.

The tendrils of an idea crept into his mind. Did he really have to stay? What if he didn't? Following would only result in being brought back.

But what if he went a different direction?

A black bird fluttered out of the stall and perched on a window ledge. Its sleek feathers glowed in the sunset. Cocking its head sideways, it fixed Dash in a stare.

"Go away." Dash grabbed a dented cup from the ledge and flung it at the bird. With a squawk, it flew off.

Dash leaned over to rub the pony's nose and whispered, "How would you like to go on a trip with me?" He glanced around the barn, but didn't see anyone.

Hope nudged at Dash's anger for the first time in weeks. The pony tossed his head as Dash turned to leave. Back in the kitchen, he peeked in the oven. "What are the rolls for, Ma?"

"Just to eat, and for the trip tomorrow. Keep a watch on them, won't you, so they don't burn?"

"Sure." Dash pulled up a chair and mulled over the blossoming idea. He surveyed the land in his mind. The road wouldn't do once he'd left the farm. He'd have to take trails through the woods.

If he skirted Belgutai and cut across the plain toward the east, he could possibly make it to Bura in a few days. Tabin and Dalan would be heading west over the mountains.

The unfolding freedom sent a faint shiver of anticipation down his arms. Soon he would be away from the farm, from all the work, and from all the nagging. He closed his eyes to soak in the fullness of this thought.

Smoke seeping out of the oven pulled him back to reality. He jumped up and snatched the burning rolls out of the oven.

Dalan stepped into the kitchen and laughed. "Learning to cook like Ma?"

Dash glared at him. "They're for your trip. I wouldn't want you to miss home too much."

"Thanks. I didn't know you cared." Dalan leaned over to look at the rolls. "Not too bad. Only the ones at the back are black. But the rest—"

"You watch them next time." Dash stomped toward the door. "Oh, I forgot. You won't be here. You'll be enjoying the leisure of Temyulun while I slave away to bring in the harvest." He slipped out of the kitchen, whispering, "Or not."

Up the ladder in the sleeping loft, he pulled his pack off the shelf and stuffed in a pair of trousers. He grabbed a clean tunic from the shelf and added that as well.

His brother's mountain knife lay on the bed next to an already full pack. Creeping to the ladder, he glanced down. The room below was empty. He snuck back toward Dalan's bed.

Dash stared at the knife for a moment. When he turned sixteen he'd get one just like it. But two years was a long time. He needed one now. With a quick reach, he seized Dalan's knife and stuffed it in his own pack under the trousers.

"Come for dinner," Ma called from below.

Dash hid his pack under the bed and headed down the

ladder. Dalan set out plates and cups around the rough wooden table, while Ma brought in burnt rolls, sausages, and fruit.

"Is that all?" Dash asked.

Ma sighed. "Your brother is leaving in the morning. We've all been busy helping him get ready. There hasn't been much time for food. Dalan, don't forget to set a place for your uncle Tabin. He'll be here any moment."

The door swung open, and Papa marched in with a big smile on his bearded face. "Evening, everyone."

A tall man with unruly curls and a long brown cloak followed him into the room.

"Tabin!" Ma reached out her arms in greeting, dropping a bandaa apple on the floor. "I'm so glad you made it. Oh!" She peered at the small furry creature beside him, no taller than Tabin's elbow. "And who is this?"

"I smell yummy food." The orange oostai beside Tabin sniffed and grinned, showing a row of pointy teeth. Stretching up onto his tiptoes, he eyed the table.

"This is Taag," Tabin replied.

The little oostai bowed and then bent further to pick up the dropped apple. His eyes twinkled as half the apple disappeared into his mouth with a crunch.

"Oh, it's Taag. I have heard stories about you. Welcome to our home. I'm glad to finally meet you."

Tabin patted him on the head. "He'll be traveling with us to the capital. Not much can entice him away from Temyulun's banquets."

Papa laughed. "Taag here enjoys a good meal."

"Well, it won't be anything fancy, I'm afraid." Ma glanced at the sparse table.

Taag smacked a few times and swallowed hard. "Oh, it is just fine, Madam Cook. I love to eat anything." He glanced at the table again. "And sausages are very good."

Chairs scraped the floor as they all sat. Papa asked a blessing, and Taag dived in. Ma scurried back and forth from the kitchen to the table, bringing out bits of leftover this and that while the oostai devoured all within reach.

"So." Tabin looked over to Dalan. "Do you have the Enk Taivaan packed?"

Dalan put his hand on his chest. "Right here. Where I usually wear it. You said Queen Baiyanarah wanted to see it. But I have no idea if it will work again, or what it will do next time. It still hums faintly, but it's a different tune than when I put it together at the Battle of Temyulun." He glanced up with a slight frown on his brow. "Is Zovlon planning something new?"

Tabin shrugged. "Not that I know of. There have been rumors that he's in Endurek, the capital of Teagen, but our relationship with the High Prince of Teagen isn't the best right now. The prince is very old. He could die any day, and we probably wouldn't even know. I'm not sure what the queen has in mind. She just wanted us to come."

Taag slumped back in his chair and patted his bulging stomach. "That, Madam Cook, was a good meal. A very good meal."

Ma smiled. "Thank you." She rose and laid a hand on Dalan's shoulder. "You have an early morning tomorrow. Better go finish packing. Dash can help me with the dishes."

Dash groaned. There it was again. He had to do all the hard work, and Dalan got the adventures. He shuffled off to the kitchen and started washing up, while Ma made honey cakes for breakfast the next morning.

Just as the first whiffs of smoke caught Dash's nose, she snatched the cakes out of the oven. "Ma, do you have to burn everything?"

Dalan stood in the doorway, grinning. "Nice save, Ma. By the way, Dash, have you seen my mountain knife? I thought I left it on the bed, but it's not there now."

Dash ignored him.

"It will show up." Ma looked over the honey cakes. "I have some village cheese left. Do you want to take that tomorrow?"

"Sure. I wonder if I took my knife out to the barn." He grabbed a honey cake.

Ma slapped his hand. "Those are for tomorrow."

"They taste great!" Dalan mumbled, spitting crumbs on the floor as he scurried for the door.

Shaking her head, Ma sighed. "Off to bed now, Dash. It's an early morning for all of us."

"But, Ma-"

"No arguing. Off you go."

Dash surveyed the remaining food in the kitchen. All the rolls had been eaten. A small bowl of grayish boiled potatoes sat in the cool windowsill, and only two shriveled bandaa apples remained in the fruit bowl. The honey cakes lay in a basket covered by a cloth.

"No dawdling tonight." Ma swept the kitchen dirt toward the door. "I'll see you in the morning, son."

Dash climbed the ladder and pulled his pack out from under the bed and glanced into it. After tucking the few coppers he'd saved into a side pocket, he looked around. "What else should I take? What's Dalan taking?" He peeked in the bulging pack on his brother's bed, but saw only clothes. "Got those." With a shrug, he shoved his own pack back under the bed.

When Dalan came in a little while later, Dash pretended to sleep. The box under Dalan's bed slid out and then back in. He could hear the covers of the bed rustle around, then knees crawling about on the floor. A thud was followed by a muffled groan, and Dash suppressed a smirk. Finally, he heard the creak of the bed as his brother climbed in.

The moon rose higher into the sky, and Dalan's heavy breathing joined Papa's snores. From down in the visiting room, Dash could hear Tabin's snores as well.

He crept out of bed. Pulling out his pack, he climbed down the ladder with boots under his arm.

In the kitchen, he stuffed honey cakes, the hard remnant of village cheese, and the two shriveled apples into his pack.

Ma's small market coin pouch sat on the window ledge. He grabbed that as well. The sorry-looking potatoes beside it received a glance but remained in their bowl.

An almost full moon hung halfway up the sky as Dash led Doechin down the small mountain trail toward Dorben. In the darkened woods, a black bird cawed and rose into the night sky.

Chapter 2
Gone

Giving the covers a yank, Dalan rolled over in bed. The sun's first rays peeked over the mountains and in through the crack in the curtains. He sucked in a quick breath as a jitter of excitement rumbled in his chest. Today he would leave for Temyulun.

"Time to get up, Dash." He picked up a wadded sock and tossed it over to the bed next to his, expecting a groan from his little brother.

"Dash?" He propped himself up on one elbow and looked over at the empty bed. "Why's he up so early?"

Feeling just a little sorry for his brother, who would have weeks of hard labor ahead, he swung his feet out onto the cold, hard floor. Anxious voices rose from the kitchen. He hurried to the top of the ladder.

"I checked the barn," Tabin said from down below. "There's no sign of him there, and Doechin's gone."

Ma groaned.

"Don't worry, Sarnai." Papa's voice sounded strained. "We'll find him. Better go wake Dalan. Temyulun's going to have to wait."

"I'm up." Dalan fumbled down the ladder to the dark, cold kitchen. "What's happened to Dash?" A cloud of disappointment settled over the excitement of his long-awaited trip.

The sleepy oostai wandered into the kitchen. "Is it time for breakfast?"

Tabin shook his head. "Not yet, furry friend. Dash has run off, and we need to find him. Breakfast will be a little slim this morning." He patted Taag's head between his two small round ears.

"I do not like slim breakfasts, but if we must find Dash, I will be all right. Will we leave right away?"

Tabin glanced out the window. "I'm afraid so."

Dalan ran his fingers through his mop of hair, trying to tame it. "I'm all packed and ready to go. Except for my mountain knife."

Ma glanced frantically from Tabin to Dalan. "But... but..."

"We need to go, Ma." Dalan rubbed at his still sleepy eyes and yawned. "We need to find Dash."

"I suppose so. But this is... leaving... too soon. Oh, I hope Dash is all right." She scurried across the kitchen to the bread basket. "The honey cakes are gone! And the cheese, too." She threw open the pantry door. "He took everything!"

Taag's ears drooped. "Do you mean me, Madam Cook? I do like to eat, but I do not steal yummies anymore."

"No, no." Ma hurried back out of the pantry. "Dash. Dash took the food. What will you take to eat? At least Dash won't go hungry today."

"Do not worry, Madam Cook. We will find something, but this is very sad news." His stomach growled. The two grayish potatoes on the windowsill caught his eye. He took one with each hand and sniffed. "May I?" He bowed just slightly to Ma.

"Of course, and I'll make some more honey cakes." Ma threw some flour in a bowl and grabbed the box of eggs. One dropped out onto the floor.

"We don't have time for that, Ma." Dalan turned toward the ladder. "I'll dress and grab my pack."

Tabin headed toward the visiting room. "Taag, I have a few crusts of yarcen bread left from yesterday. It'll have to do for breakfast."

The oostai followed. "That will be just fine. I guess."

Dalan scurried up to the loft, dressed quickly, and swung back down the ladder with his pack to where Tabin and Taag waited by the kitchen door. "I'm ready."

Papa walked with Tabin, Taag, and Dalan out into the fresh morning air. "I'm wantin' to go along with all my heart, but I can't just up and leave the harvest to rot in the fields. It would make for a very hard winter."

Putting a hand on the farmer's shoulder, Tabin faced him. "Don't worry, Jaren. We'll do all we can to find Dash and bring him home. You tend the fields so there'll be something to come back to. It may take some time, though. If I know Dash, he'll be far ahead, and with a pony, he can travel fast. Don't expect us back before snow's fall."

Papa nodded.

"He may have left tracks. I'll be right back." Tabin's form shifted and shrunk down to that of a yuratag cat. He sniffed delicately at the air and the ground, then trotted down the road.

Papa shook his head. "Still gives me the curlies to see him change like that."

"I think it's kind of amazing." Dalan watched Tabin disappear into the trees. "I wouldn't mind being-"

"Don't be wishing for more than you are, son." Papa patted him on the back. "I'm glad you're not a... well, I'm thankful for you the way you are."

Dalan glanced toward the kitchen door. "Looks like Ma isn't coming to see me off."

Papa shook his head. "That woman is bound and determined to make more honey cakes to send with you. I'm sure she'll be out shortly."

A bright grin dawned on Taag's face, but not on Dalan's. "We don't-"

"Oh, she knows there isn't time. But it's all she can think to do right now."

Tabin strode up the path. "It's no use. There's been a heavy rain since he left, and the scent is gone. We'll have to make our best guess at where he's headed, which I believe is toward Dorben. Dalan, you ready?"

"Bye." Dalan gave Papa a hug.

"Take care of yourselves, now." The burly farmer rubbed his nose. Then he pressed two coins into Dalan's hand. "It's all I've got right now."

By their weight and size, Dalan could tell they were silvers. "Thanks," he squeaked out.

Ma's head, dusted with flour, poked out of the kitchen doorway. "You can't wait for the cakes?"

"Not today, Sarnai," Papa called back.

"Bye, then, I guess." She sniffed, wiped her face with her apron, and waved a large wooden spoon in the air.

"Bye, Ma." Dalan ran to her and gave her a hug before heading down the trail toward the village of Dorben. He wished Dash hadn't made this departure so rushed.

Flour from Ma had smudged the front of his tunic. He left it as he trotted forward, trying to keep up with Tabin's long strides.

Taag skipped ahead, singing softly.

"Honey bees flit and honey bees float,
A honey bee lands on the head of a goat.

But he isn't a boat, and he hasn't a coat,
So he ends up deep down in the mad one's throat."

The tall trees hung heavy with moisture. A rustle in the bushes startled Dalan, but it was only a black bird.

Taag pulled out a cold, gray potato and hummed while he munched.

"We'll start in Dorben," Tabin said after a bit. "Then I think we'll try Belgutai."

"Dash mentioned something about Endurek the other day," Dalan offered.

"Did he?" Tabin trudged on for a few strides. "If that's where he's headed, he may skirt both Dorben and Belgutai and head north toward Bokir, but I doubt it. I suspect he'll stick closer to the places he knows. He could have decided to head west over the mountains toward Surtak or Temyulun, but those roads start in Belgutai."

"What about the tunnels from Baiyanarah's house?"

"No." Tabin shook his head. "I don't think he'd try those. Too easy to get lost under the mountain, and he knows it. Besides, he wouldn't have enough food for that."

Dalan nodded and followed his uncle through the tall trees. "I wish I had my mountain knife."

"You didn't pack it?"

"No. I couldn't find it. I'm sure I left it on my bed next to my pack, but then it wasn't there. I searched everywhere, but it's gone."

Taag reached into his shoulder pouch for the other sorry-looking potato. "The sneaker must have it. Mmmm. Your ma makes good food."

Dalan sighed. "You might be right."

"About the cooking?" The oostai grinned up at him.

"No, Taag. Ma's cooking is terrible. About the knife. Dash has been bugging Papa to get one before he's sixteen since I got mine a few months early. But I heard Papa mutter something about mountain knives being for men and that sixteen might be too young for Dash."

It felt strange to be traveling without the slosh of Elch's bottle. He had carried that fish all over Talsar the last time. Now he knew he could talk to her whenever and wherever he needed to. Warmth spread through his chest. He smiled, glad to know the voice of V'Arah, the creator, was only a thought away.

They arrived in Dorben just as the morning bustle lurched to life and asked everyone they met if they'd seen Dash.

"No sign of him," the baker replied.

An old farmer scratched his head with the handle of his walking stick. "Can't say that I've spied the young fellow." He hobbled on.

After an hour, Tabin sat next to Dalan on a bench outside the dressmaker's shop. "I don't think he came this way. Let's go back up the trail and see if we can find pony tracks. Where's Taag?"

Dalan pointed to the pastry shop across the narrow street where the oostai stood on tiptoe, peeking in the window and sniffing loudly.

Tabin laughed. "He really does have just one thing on his mind."

"I'm surprised he isn't as round as a ball. And anyone who thinks Ma is a good cook must have stunted taste buds."

Tabin pulled out his coin pouch and removed a copper. "Taag, catch!" He threw the coin across the road. The oostai leaped high into the air, caught it, and scurried into the bakery.

He returned with a large parcel in his paw and jam smeared across his face.

Plopping himself down beside Tabin, he grinned. "Here's one for you, Mr. Dalan, and one for Mr. Tabin." He sighed deeply. "Now, this is a very happy breakfast." His tongue reached out for the jelly on his cheek before he bit into another pastry.

"I hear you've been a-lookin' for Dash."

Dalan glanced up to see Otgo, the dressmaker, standing in the doorway of her shop.

"I haven't seen him this mornin'." She leaned on the door frame. "But the other day he was askin' quite a many questions about Endurek. If'n that's helpful. I hope you find the little scurrier. He's one to get hisself into a snag, that one."

"Thank you." Tabin stood and bowed to Otgo with his fists crossed on his chest. "That's very helpful. Would you like a jims roll?" He took one from the parcel in Taag's lap and held it out.

Taag's wide eyes followed it.

"Why, thank you, I would." She smiled. "You're a good man, Tabin. I hope you'll be a-findin' Dash soon."

A little girl ran up to the shop. "Madam Otgo, Mama's needin' some blue ribbon."

"Come right on inside, then. We'll be a-findin' it for her. Good travels to you all." She turned and entered the shop with the girl.

"We'd better be off." Tabin looked down the road. "I think we'll go straight to Belgutai. If Dash has Endurek on his mind, he may try the trade road along the Tegus River. It's been a long time since I've traveled that way."

The day stretched on, hot and tiring. They reached Belgutai as the sun sank low along the horizon. Dalan watched the flood of people in dismay. "Where do we start?"

Tabin pushed his way through the crowd. "The Grainfield Inn. Just past the market. And we might even run into someone on the way that's seen Dash. Keep a lookout for farmers from Dorben."

Taag's eyes widened to match the breadth of his grin. "The market means food. I will keep a lookout for that."

"Of course." Tabin headed off through the busy streets.

Taag followed with a trot in his step and a hum on his lips.

When they reached the market, Dalan saw a large crowd gathered around a stall nearby. Angry voices rose from the merchant as well as the throng of people.

He shoved his way through to the front. One man, dressed in clothing far more elaborate than Dalan had ever seen, stood facing the merchant with a defiant look. The black feathers in his hair fluttered in the wind.

The merchant wagged his finger at the man. "I will not be-"

"No, because I'm leaving now!" The well-dressed man pushed through the crowd and hurried down a small alley.

The crowd dispersed, talking loudly about the altercation.

Dalan turned to watch the stranger go.

But as the man entered the deeper shadows, Dalan saw him touch his finger to his forehead. His form shrunk down to that of a black bird, which quickly flew off into the orange sky.

Chapter 3
Unexpected Company

Dash looked down the steep slope that hung over the grassy plain. He had struggled through the rough underbrush of the forest all afternoon, dragging the reluctant Doechin behind him. Itchy sweat ran down his face and neck.

"We're almost there." He reached back to stroke the pony's soft nose as a hot summer wind ruffled his collar. "Just down this last hill, then it will be flat until we find a place to camp." He climbed onto the pony's back and managed to get him moving forward.

A lone black bird circled overhead as Dash and Doechin fought their way down the incline. Prickly shar bushes pulled at Dash's trousers, but he kept urging Doechin onward.

They reached the flatter land where swaying grasses replaced the thorny bushes. Dash and the donkey rambled across the plain until the sun touched the horizon.

He pointed the pony toward a large rocky outcropping. "That should be a good place to spend the night. And there's a stream next to it."

A ribbon of water wound around tall, weather-worn rocks jutting out of the rough grass. Dash dismounted near the stream and bent down to splash cool wetness over his head and neck. After a long drink for both of them, he tied the pony to a large shar bush near the rocks.

He took off the pony's nearly empty packs and set them next to the bush before digging in his own pack for something to eat. A deep rumble emanated from his middle.

He devoured two honey cakes and had picked up a third when he remembered the long journey ahead. "Better not eat everything in one night."

Doechin grazed as a black bird landed beside Dash. One of its beady, black eyes fixed Dash in an unblinking stare.

"What do you want?"

The bird tipped its head a little more but didn't look away.

Dash broke off a crumb of honey cake and threw it toward the black bird. "There. Now bug off. I don't have anything more to share with you."

The bird snatched the crumb and swallowed it in one gulp.

Glancing to where the sun had left its last faint line of light across the sky, Dash put the cakes away. He then pulled his blanket out of the donkey's pack. With a boulder at his back, he curled up and closed his eyes.

❖

Loud squawking woke him early the next morning. A stiff chill penetrated to his bones. He rubbed his arms and squinted in the pale light.

The black bird hopped around in the grass nearby.

Dash looked toward the stream and the shar bush but didn't see the pony.

Tightness squeezed at his chest.

"Doechin?" He scrambled up, pulling the blanket snugly around his shoulders. "Doechin!"

Only a broken stub remained of the shar bush where Dash had tied the pony. Scrambling around the rocks, Dash called again but saw no sign of him. He returned to the stream and noticed tracks headed back toward home on the other side.

"Aw, stomp! Why did he have to go and run off?"

Dash slumped down next to the pony's packs. "What do I do now? I can't go back. They'd all just make me feel stupid like they always do."

The black bird hopped a little closer.

"I guess I could keep going and see where things take me." He glanced at the large bird. "Why am I talking to you? Maybe I've lost my mind already. Shoo! I don't have anything for you this morning."

Stuffing a piece of cheese into his mouth, he dug in the pony's pack. The fire box, the old black pot, and the spoon fit into his own pack, but he didn't have room for the rest of the things he'd found in the barn. He tucked the pony's packs in a crack between the rocks, hoping they'd still be there if he ever came back.

He lifted his pack with a grunt. Heavy, but that couldn't be helped. Swinging it onto his back, he headed out across the plain in the direction of the road. Up ahead and to his right lay the thick forest known as The Wild. Most folks avoided the area. Those who did venture in came back with strange stories of mysterious creatures and yawning black pits. The tales made the hair on Dash's arms stand up. He would skirt it and hopefully arrive in Sheker in a few days.

The black bird followed, circling up above for a short while, before flying off into the forest.

As he traveled along the dusty track, Dash tried to ignore The Wild by thinking of Endurek. The persistent restlessness in his chest reached its uneasy tendrils into his mind. Would he ever find a place where he could just be himself and be happy? He walked on at a faster pace. It had to be out there somewhere.

In the wispy clouds, another black bird tilted and soared in the rising winds. Or was it the same one? He couldn't tell.

Dash's pack grew heavier. His ankle, broken by the tarch several years ago, ached with each step. It reminded him that danger could lurk anywhere. The thought sent a faint thrill of excitement through his chest as he trudged on. This was his very own adventure. One he didn't have to share with his siblings or with anyone else.

The sun dropped lower in the sky and darkness crept over The Wild. Up ahead, a small village on the edge of a narrow river came into view. Gray smoke hung like a blanket over the cottages with wisps trailing off across the plain in the dying wind.

Pulling out Ma's thin leather purse from his pocket, Dash counted the small, dirty coins. A twinge of guilt at stealing it chafed in the tension of his shoulders, but he shrugged it off. A hot meal sure would be nice. His stomach felt hollow and pinched.

The choking smoke almost drowned out the enticing smells that reached Dash's nose as he entered the town. He followed the rough cobble stones of the main road. A little farther on, he found a sad, drooping inn. He limped inside and slid onto a stool at the counter. His ankle throbbed.

The large bowl of stew cost more than he had expected, but he ate hungrily.

At a table nearby sat a well-dressed man with black feathers and gold ribbons in his hair. Each ear had several silver rings. Heavy jewels encrusted his fingers. His rich flowing tunic reached down to the most elaborate trousers Dash had ever seen.

He remembered stories that Papa told about the people of Teagen. The most powerful lived in the capital, Endurek. Dash stared at the man, who glanced at him with dark, piercing eyes.

Dash turned quickly back to his bowl and finished the last few bites. He handed back his empty bowl. "Thank you."

The innkeeper bowed his head. "Are you sure you don't want a room for the night?"

"No." He didn't want to use up all of his coins so soon. A group of trees he'd seen just outside the village, close to the stream, would do for tonight. He wished it was farther from the dark forest.

"He should have a room."

Dash turned to see the well-dressed man slide a whole silver toward the innkeeper's hand. "The one next to mine. And bring him another bowl of stew. I'm sure he's hungry."

The man's small eyes studied Dash. His arms made an elaborate welcoming gesture. "Come sit with me while you eat, boy. Someone your age shouldn't be out on his own." He glanced quickly around the room. "Strange things can happen on the edge of The Wild."

The man headed back toward the table he'd been sitting at. His long, colorful cloak swirled across the floor. Intricately embroidered scenes of forests, black birds, and mountains covered it from shoulder to floor.

A fine golden cord created an impressive border, and though it dragged on the dirty inn floor, it didn't show any sign of smudges or tatters.

Dash stood rooted by the counter.

"Well, go on." The innkeeper gave him a shove. "He's paid for your room and supper and more. At least give him the pleasure of your company."

Tripping on an uneven board, Dash stumbled over and sat down across from the stranger.

"What's your name, boy?"

"Dash."

A faint smile crept up the side of the man's face.

The innkeeper placed another large bowl of stew and chunk of yarcen bread on the table. The enticing smell of vegetables and meat in a rich broth filled the air.

"Thank you." Dash smiled nervously at the stranger.

"Go ahead and eat, boy." The man took a long drink from his mug. "My name is Karakul. I'm from Endurek, the capital of Teagen, and I'm heading home after a not-so successful trading excursion to Belgutai. But never mind that. Where are you headed?"

Dash swallowed a large bite. "I'm not sure. Anywhere but home."

"Ah. A runaway. Well, it just so happens that I'm in need of a boy to help with the cart and goods. Maybe we can be of assistance to each other."

Dash nodded. Something about this pretentious stranger intrigued him. Besides, riding on a cart would be far better than walking, especially now that his ankle hurt so much. He took several more bites of stew.

"So, tell me about your family."

Dash thought for a moment while he swallowed. "There's not much to tell. I have an older sister, Ariyuna, and an older brother, Dalan. My Papa and Ma make me work on the farm all day, while my siblings get to go on exciting journeys. It's just not fair." He shoved another bite into his mouth.

"So, you're off on your own journey now?"

Dash nodded.

"Well, if you'd like to travel to Endurek. I can offer a ride and reasonable pay if you will come with me as my assistant. Work well, and I may take you on as an apprentice. I like your spunk, and I think you will benefit me... eventually."

Dash nodded again and finished up the last bite of stew.

"That's settled then." Karakul stood. "We'll start at first light tomorrow. Your room is next to mine. Follow me."

Dash grabbed his pack and hurried after Karakul, up the stairs, and into a small room at the back of the inn.

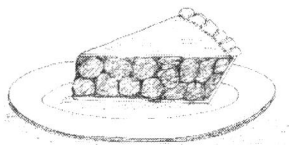

Chapter 4
Pit

"Did you see that? He turned into-" Dalan glanced toward Tabin's pale tight face. The bustle of the market went on behind them as if nothing unusual had happened.

"Come. We shouldn't discuss this here." Tabin strode off across the market toward the Grainfield Inn.

Dalan grabbed the oostai's hand and followed with Taag sniffing at every food stall along the way.

Once inside the inn, Tabin paid for a room. "We'll drop off our packs and then have something to eat in the dining room."

Taag trotted up the stairs behind Tabin. "Eating is a very good idea."

The large room held four tall beds. Several chairs faced an inviting blaze that crackled in the fireplace along one wall. On a small table by the door sat a basket of fruit.

Tabin closed the door, marched over to the hearth, and plopped into one of the overstuffed chairs.

"Ooh!" Taag crunched into a bandaa apple and reached for another.

"Was that man an orlolak like you?" Dalan ventured, making his way over to the hearth.

Tabin slumped further into the chair. "It would seem so. He had the clothing of a merchant from Teagen, probably even from the capital, Endurek. I've never heard of shape changers from there, though it is a country steeped in dark sorcery. And a black bird. Not a good sign."

"That doesn't change our plans to find Dash, does it?"

"No." Tabin sat up straighter. "I just don't like it. All the orlolaks I know have no outward sign of their other shape when they're not in it. But this man had unnaturally dark eyes."

Dalan thought of the numerous black birds he'd seen on their travels so far. Talsar usually didn't have very many. Could the man from Endurek be following them? He put the thought aside. No use getting worked up about nothing.

Tabin drew in a deep breath. "Well, I guess we should eat and then see what we can find out. Checking all the inns might be a good place to start."

"Eat?" Taag's ears perked up.

Tabin laughed. "Yes, eat. Come on."

After a quick supper, they visited all the inns in Belgutai, but found no sign of Dash. Walking back to the Grainfield Inn, they passed the alley where the man from Endurek had disappeared.

Tabin turned down the narrow lane and looked around.

"Here's something." Dalan picked up a shiny black feather.

Tabin took the feather and examined it before stuffing it into his pocket. "Night is coming. We'd better get back."

As they entered the inn, Taag veered to the left toward the dining room. "I smell," *sniff, sniff,* "pie." He pushed the door open a crack. "And Mr. Gan!"

Flinging the door wide open, Taag pranced across the dining room to where Gan sat at a round table.

Dalan followed, waving to his sister, Ariyuna, seated on one side of Gan. On the other side sat her friend Naiyan from the Altan Forest, one of the queen's chief advisors.

"Flittering yak dibbits!" The short, bald man stood up so fast, his chair tipped over. Tassels swung from his wrists and waist. "I am over the haystack to see you, my highest oostai. Where's your partner? Ah, Dalan. And there you are, Tabin. I thought your assemblage was to meet the queen in Temyulun."

The eagle tattooed on his bald head shimmered in the lamplight as he scurried around giving Dalan, Taag, and Tabin hugs. "So good to see the cluster of you."

"It's good to see you, too, Gan." Tabin nodded toward Ariyuna and Naiyan with a smile before gathering a few extra chairs. "We've run into a bit of a problem. I'm glad we've met up with you."

Dalan flashed a smile at his sister and bowed with fists across his chest toward Naiyan, then sat down across the table.

Tabin plunked into a chair. "Our little mess involves Dash."

"What's he done now?" Ariyuna leaned forward, concern settling onto her forehead.

Dalan fiddled with the fork in front of him. "Only run off with Doechin. We don't know where he's gone, but Otgo, the dressmaker, thought he might be heading for Endurek. I guess he'd been asking questions about it, anyway."

"Endurek?" Naiyan ran his fingers through his blond, spiky hair. "That's a treacherous place. It's nice enough on the surface, but underneath..."

Sitting forward, Tabin pulled out the black feather and twirled it in his fingers. "We ran across a merchant from Endurek today that ducked down an alley and turned into a black bird."

"Endurek doesn't have orlolaks." Naiyan frowned. "But lately, the ambassadors from there have had a much stronger aura of sorcery about them. More than I've ever noticed before. I've also heard rumors that Zovlon may be in Endurek. That could explain things."

Gan shook his head. "This news is as weighty as an aching walrus flipper. Well, we must unearth Dash before Zovlon does. That boy is prone to snap a worthy cord if it suits his fancy."

Leaning back in his chair, Taag sniffed at the pie being placed on the table next to theirs.

Tabin beckoned to the waiter. "Could you please bring a piece of pie for everyone here, and two for the oostai."

"Oh, you are a very good man, Tabin." Taag grinned broadly and wiggled in his seat.

"I'm very thankful we've met today." Naiyan glanced over at Taag. "We're in need of your help with little Buren, the new orlolak. He's been asking for his papa, and you seem to be about the only one who can get him to control those bear claws of his."

"Buren needs his papa?" Taag stuffed half a piece of pie in his mouth. "I woo goo if oo."

"What?" Dalan asked.

Taag swallowed hard several times. "I will go with you, but not with you, Mr. Dalan. I will go with Mr. Naiyan and whoever else is going to Surtak. The baby bear needs his papa, and that is me."

"Then it's a chip splitter." Gan shook his head. "Ariyuna, you and I should go with the Dash hunters. Tivver-Taag and Naiyan, you two can sap over the mountains and salvage the bear, or Tailaal. She's caring for the little roarer and may be quite shredded by now."

"Wait a minute." Ariyuna looked around the table. "As much as I want to go looking for Dash, I know Baiyanarah's waiting for me, and she really needs my help. I can't be in both places."

A frown burrowed into Dalan's forehead. "What's with the queen?"

"Baiyanarah's been weak and tires easily since the Battle of Temyulun," Ariyuna replied. "The wound from the disk Zovlon threw has never completely healed."

Gan patted her hand. "We will be swift as honker snaps at finding your brother. Go to the queen in Temyulun with Naiyan if you feel that's where you're needed, and don't flitter your bob about your brother. Taag is more than proficient to scooch over to Surtak and rescue Tailaal from the bear-boy."

"I suppose." Ariyuna refolded her napkin and looked at Dalan. "I'll come join you as soon as I can."

Naiyan pushed his empty plate toward the middle of the table. "Does everyone agree with this plan?"

"As long as I can eat pie, I will be happy." Taag shoved his whole second piece of pie into his mouth at once."

Early the next morning, Dalan, Tabin, and Gan said their goodbyes and set out. The old trade road between Belgutai and Endurek ran along the Tegus River. Gan had arranged horses for them, which made for a very pleasant trip. The late summer warmth mixed with the cool breeze blowing off the river and across the plain.

Dalan breathed in the savory air. But deep down, worry for his brother's safety sucked away his enjoyment of the beautiful weather.

Several days of travel brought them to a place where thicker woods grew along the river bank. As evening approached, they stopped by a large grove of mod trees and set up camp. Dalan collected wood, while Tabin started a fire.

"I think we'll need just a few more logs," Tabin said as Dalan brought another armful of branches. "See if you can find some bigger ones that aren't too wet."

Dalan nodded and headed back into the trees. He searched, but found only small dry branches or bigger ones drenched in mud from the river. Then a short broken log caught his eye. No bigger around than his leg, it leaned against a large fallen trunk. After several pulls, Dalan had it free of the entangling vines.

He lugged it back to the camp and dropped it by the fire. "How's this?"

"Perfect." Tabin hefted the log onto the smoldering fire. "This should be plenty for cooking supper." Using another stick, he shoved it farther over the flames. "Are you sure this one's dry? It's really heavy."

Dalan shrugged. "It looked dry when I found it."

Gan unloaded the horses, led them to the water's edge, then hobbled them while Tabin unpacked food.

"Mmmm. Indeeeed," whispered in the breeze.

Dalan turned toward his uncle. "What did you say?"

"Nothing." Tabin pulled out a pot from one of the packs.

"Mmmm. Indeeeed."

"Either you're saying something, or I'm imagining voices." Dalan peered into the bushes.

"Hot. Yes, hot. Indeeeed. Pit."

"Did you hear that?" Dalan frowned. "Someone's talking."

Tabin set the pot by the flames.

"Mmmm. Pit, pit. Very hot."

"I think it's coming from the fire." Dalan peered at the flames reaching around the log.

"Dalan, get back!" Tabin shoved him aside and yanked

the log out of the fire.

A face with protruding eyes blinked up from the middle of the log. "Very, very hot. Indeeeed."

Dalan grabbed a blanket and whacked the flames that surrounded the talking wood until only smoke drifted up from it.

"Mmmm, better. Pit. Pit. Just throw me over by that tree, if you don't mind. Pit."

Tabin picked up the log and flung it toward the nearest tree. The face disappeared and then blinked out from the tree trunk. "Ahhh. Much better."

"How?" Dalan looked from the log to the trunk and back again. "Who?"

"Well, since you can't seem to talk, I will. Pit. Pit. My name is Moochir, and now I am yours. Indeeeed."

"What's pickering?" Gan asked. "Are either of you watching the flit flames?"

Dalan pointed to the tree where two bulging eyes glanced in slightly different directions. Under them lay a flat nose and a long chin formed out of bark.

"Ramming plank hogs! Don't talk to him." Gan rubbed his bald head vigorously. "It's a woodpit. He'll fasten himself to you, and it'll take a zatting froggit to get rid of the pest."

Dalan managed a weak smile. "I think it's too late."

"Oh, yes. Pit. Pit. Too late, indeeeed."

Chapter 5
A New Master

Inside the inn's small room, Dash lay on his bed, watching the moon rise. A stir of excitement grew in his chest. This could be the beginning of a new life, far from all the meaningless farm work he hated. One where he'd be appreciated for his brains and wit.

What had Karakul said? I like your spunk. For the first time in months, the persistent restlessness subsided a little. His eyes closed, and he drifted toward sleep.

"Wake up, boy."

Dash opened his eyes. Only the first faint hints of light shone in the window of the dark room.

"Up, up. No time for sleeping in today."

Karakul stood in the doorway, dressed and prepared to go.

Dash sprang from the bed. "I'll be ready in just a minute."

"Meet me in the stables." Karakul headed out the door.

Dash fumbled down the hall in the semidarkness to the washroom. After splashing water on his face, he slurped in a quick drink and hurried back to the room. He grabbed his pack and stumbled down the dark stairs to the barn.

Karakul already had the horse harnessed to a cart filled

most of the way with trunks. A small area at the back of the wagon bed was clear.

"Let's be on our way." Karakul climbed up and grabbed the reins.

Dash hopped into the back.

"Not there, boy. Up here."

Feeling unsure, Dash hesitated before jumping out of the back and clambering up to the seat beside Karakul.

The cart rumbled out of the smoke-shrouded town and along the dusty road.

As Dash bounced along beside his new master, he watched the first sliver of sun glow above the horizon.

Karakul held out several bread rolls and a flask. "Better have some breakfast, boy."

"Thanks." A corner of Dash's mouth crept upward. Free food and a ride were a great improvement over walking and scrounging. He glanced sideways at the stately form of Karakul on the seat next to him. The black feathers in his hair fluttered in the breeze. His stern, proud face exuded power.

Dash's smile grew. Ariyuna and Dalan thought they were so special, hanging out with the queen of Talsar. Well, he would show them. He had Karakul. With a little hard work and cleverness, he might become a man of power, too. Someday.

The morning sunlight warmed his face. With a deep breath, confidence filled Dash's chest. Somehow he knew all this would lead to good things.

The afternoon stretched on. Dash curled up in the back of the cart to sleep, thoroughly enjoying the ride and the chance for his ankle to rest.

When he awoke, he realized the cart had stopped and

dusk had settled over the grasslands.

Karakul had already set up camp and was starting a fire. "Come along, lazy bones. You've slept the afternoon away, and now we need some food prepared."

"I'm sorry!" Dash scrambled out of the wagon, chiding himself for not being more diligent. This wasn't a good start to his new position. Taking a large pot, he hurried to the nearby stream for water and lugged it back toward the fire.

"You rest, master." He placed the pot over the flames. "I'll have supper in no time."

Karakul smiled and stretched out on the grass while Dash worked quickly, hoping to make up for his nap and leave a good impression.

Several days passed. Dash worked hard and avoided naps. He cared for the horse, cooked all the meals and even drove the wagon while Karakul rested.

With each day, a sense of freedom blossomed as the Yuratag Mountains grew steadily smaller behind him. Up ahead, the plain became rockier, with large stony pinnacles protruding like pillars out of a flat grassy floor.

One evening around the fire, Karakul stood looking up at the moon. "Dash, what do you see up there?"

"An almost full moon, master. It will be full tomorrow night."

"Stay with the wagon and don't leave until I return." He walked off in the moonlight and around an outcropping of rocks.

Dash waited for him to emerge on the other side, but he didn't.

The stillness of the night pressed in.

Only the flutter of wings broke the silence as a black bird flew off into the darkness.

Dash cleaned up what remained of supper and lay down by the fire, his blanket over his shoulders. But sleep didn't come quickly.

A longing for Ma snuck into his mind.

He shoved it aside.

His master's disappearance bothered him as well. He wondered if Karakul was mad at him, or if he'd even made the right decision to become his assistant.

No, Karakul's actions were his own. If his master returned displeased, Dash would worry about it then.

Toward morning, Dash woke. The light of the moon cast its cold, pale glow on Karakul who lay on the other side of the ashy coals, wrapped in his rich cloak.

Where had he gone?

Dash glanced at the horizon. The sun would be up soon. Wanting to please his new master, he rose and went to the wagon to find something to cook for breakfast.

Lifting the tarp covering the load, he stood back and surveyed the tightly packed chests. What filled them? Was it gold? Treasure? Things that could be exchanged for the comforts of life? He hadn't dared ask Karakul what kind of goods he traded, but from the contents of the wagon, he must be prosperous.

Dash wondered what it would be like to wear a flowing cloak like Karakul's.

Then he noticed a tiny chest, no bigger than a brick, set loosely to one side. Had that been there before? With a quick glance toward his sleeping master, he reached in and picked it up.

Intricate carvings decorated the outside. But along the

front, instead of a plaque where a keyhole should be, the box had five bronze discs imbedded in the wood.

His heart thumped. This was the most amazing box he'd ever seen.

Faint letters glowed across the arched lid. He held it up in the light of the fading moon, and the writing became a clearer.

By ... of ... mo...
Five di ... pla... grant
... odds... even ... will
When ... tur ... give ...

The first trace of sunlight touched the sky, and Dash held the box a little higher. He hoped the brightness would show more of the writing, but the words faded in the new light.

With a sigh, he tucked the box back where he'd found it and grabbed supplies from the sacks at the back of the wagon.

He coaxed the remaining embers into a fire and started breakfast.

When Karakul finally roused, Dash had porridge and tsai ready.

"Well, you've been up for a while."

"Yes, Master." He scooped porridge into a bowl and handed it to Karakul, then poured a cup of tsai for him.

"Thanks."

"I..."

"What is it, boy?"

"Well, it's just that when I was looking for the breakfast food, I found... oh, never mind."

"Found what?" Karakul poked at the fire.

Dash swallowed hard. "A box. A small silver chest with

carvings on it."

Karakul laughed. "And you're interested in it, but afraid I'll be angry with you for snooping." He took a sip of tsai and stared intently at Dash. "That box is very special. A gift from Prince Kasiret, the High Prince of Teagen. What it holds may eventually be yours, but you must first prove yourself worthy."

Dash straightened his shoulders and drew in a more confident breath. "I saw words on it, or parts of words anyway, in the moonlight."

"Very good." Karakul took another sip. "It's a moon box. Only the light of a certain kind of moon will reveal the means to open it. This one may open at the full moon."

Dash poured himself some tsai. The full moon. That would be tonight. And Karakul somehow had contact with the Prince of Teagen. Maybe he'd get to meet the prince someday. But he didn't want to seem overanxious, so he buried his face in his cup.

"Well." Karakul stretched. "I have received word that I am wanted in Endurek. Eat up, and we'll be on our way."

Dash gobbled his porridge and gulped down the rest of his tsai. Endurek! The capital of Teagen. He'd always dreamed of going there. With a burst of renewed energy, he cleaned up.

A small black feather lay beside the fire. Dash picked it up. He glanced over at Karakul. Maybe someday he would have fancy do-dads in his hair as well. Tucking his find into his pocket, he finished the cleanup and hitched the horse to the wagon.

"Nice work, boy." Karakul climbed onto the wagon. "Let's be on our way. We'll be just outside Sheker tonight. No reason to hurry. We can stop there for a day or so to sell wares, and we'll reach the Deep Divide a few days later. After crossing the canyon, we'll be in Teagen."

"Is that what you do for a living? Sell things?"

"Yes. I'm a merchant. I specialize in objects of power, but I sell other things as well. I don't usually travel this direction, though. The prince sent me on a special mission to Belgutai, and I've used it to gather supplies along the way. We'll try the markets in Sheker and Bura before we head to Endurek."

A trill of anticipation quivered inside Dash. The life of a merchant had always intrigued him. He glanced over at Karakul. How had he become so lucky as to meet this man and become his assistant?

Chapter 6
Moochir

Dalan looked at the face in the tree trunk. It grinned back at him, blinking first one eye, then the other. He'd never seen anything like it, or even heard of woodpits. They certainly didn't have any in the woods around Dorben.

"Dalan, my boy, tell me you haven't chattered with this... this..."

"I might have said a few words."

"Gast it all." Gan plopped down beside him and threw a handful of dry grass at the fire. "Blimmer blast that... that... pit."

"I'm sorry," Dalan said. "I didn't know."

"Oh, it's an eagle's slam away from being your fault, my boy." Gan patted Dalan on the back. "Pits will leech onto you, and you can't get a respectable article out of them. They're just a bunch of spongy sucker, parasitic, idler-bidlers."

"Oh, come now, small man. Pit. Pit," the trunk said. "We are not all so bad. Indeeeed. I would have left the boy alone, except that I've become so exceptionally bored with this bunch of trees. I need some excitement in life. Pit, pit."

Tabin sat down on the other side of Gan. "What exactly do you mean by pits attaching themselves to people?"

"Precisely that. A pit can't travel on its own, so they clobber snag someone to skip around with. Regrettably, they can only inhabit wood. Dalan, wander over that way, past the fogger fire."

Dalan walked away from the tree, but before he'd gone far, something yanked him backwards, and he fell onto his back in a pile of leaves. "Ow! What was that?" He sat up and rubbed his elbow.

"That's your snapper attachment to this... this... pit."

"I think he said his name is Moochir," Tabin offered.

"Even worse!" Gan groaned. "If he's given you his pipper name, you'll have to get him to do a loaded whip of valiant acts before he'll release you. And pits are so lazy, you can't even get them to do a lamb's lick."

Gan stood and paced around the fire, muttering. "Pit... sluggish mashers... squash... pit... snapper dag mitts..."

Dalan sat next to Tabin. He watched as Moochir's eyes followed Gan marching back and forth and kicking the dry leaves.

Tabin sighed and whispered, "Probably best to just get supper going. When Gan gets upset, it always takes a while for him to settle down. I haven't seen him this angry in ages, not even when Zovlon's been acting up."

"Why don't you like woodpits, Gan?" Dalan pulled out food for the meal. "Besides the fact that they're hard to get rid of."

Gan stomped his foot. "When I was just a little paper flap, I ran into a woodpit. It took me four pecker slog years to get rid of the thing. The sluggish, galling prankster wouldn't give me a split pea of peace."

He marched off toward the horses.

Dalan pulled a leaf out of his hair. "How are we going to leave here? If I'm attached to that tree, I'm stuck."

"I'm not sure." Tabin poked at the fire. "Gan will know. We just need to ask him once he's simmered down some."

"Indeeeed."

"Nobody asked you," Dalan snapped at the tree, feeling trapped by this bug-eyed creature. "Wait a minute. How did you move from the log to the tree?"

"Mmmm. Just like this. Pit. Pit."

A faint brown blur stretched from the tree to the log. Moochir's face grinned out of the half-burnt log for a second and then zipped back to the tree. "Indeeeed."

Tabin shoved several sausages onto sticks. "Here. Cook your supper." He held one out to Gan as he stomped by and gave one to Dalan.

Dalan took the stick. "If he can move into something smaller, we could take him with us."

"Pickersome stick wickets... pit bother!" Gan sank down next to Tabin and shoved his sausage into the flames. He muttered to himself until the sausage caught on fire. After waving it violently in the air, he whacked it several times on the ground. "Of course we'll have to take the twig viper with us. No choice... no blink batter choice."

He pointed the burnt sausage at the tree. "I'll be watching you, mooch-monster. If you do anything but butterfly softerness, I'll burn you out in the middle of the plain where you'll have to disperse into the grass roots for a kick's age."

"Uuh, indeeeed." The tree blinked several times, and Dalan thought his smile drooped just a little.

Dalan ate his sausage and roasted another, glancing at the tree from time to time. "So, if we can find a smaller piece of wood, one we can carry, we'll be able to keep going?"

Gan nodded. "That is, if you can get this barking blighter to move to something small. They usually prefer extra space." He glared at Moochir.

The tree blinked and smiled. "Pit. Pit. We shall see."

"How about this one?" Dalan held up a large branch.

"Oh, no. Much too small. Indeeeed."

Tabin picked out a larger branch from the pile by the fire. "Would this one do?"

"Certainly not. Pit. Pit."

Dalan stood. "I'll be right back." He strode toward the trees, but just as he stepped into the woods, the attachment yanked him backwards.

Gan jumped up. "Attachments can stretch much farther than this thorny brush pickle is allowing. He's being as difficult as... as a woodpit." He marched off into the trees. "I'll find a blicker log."

The first one Gan brought back had too many branches coming out of it. The second was too wet. The ninth was missing bark on one side, and the fifteenth had no branches and a bug crawling along it.

Dalan faced the woodpit. "Do you want to leave these trees, or not?"

"Oh, yes. I do want to leave. Pit, pit. But only in proper style."

Gan returned with another and another.

Tabin sat by the fire, stifling a smirk that grew larger with each bough. Finally, he said, "We could camp here for a week with this woodpile you've made."

Gan dropped a log by the tree and glared at Tabin. "If I get one any plumper, Dalan won't be able to lug-pug it." He pulled a flaming stick out of the fire and waved it toward the tree. "We could build a cracker flash around the tree and see if that will help you decide."

"You know. Pit. Pit. That last one may work." A faint brown blur stretched from the tree to the log.

Dalan watched Moochir's face emerge for a brief moment then disappear.

"Pit. Pit," came from the tree trunk.

"What's wrong with this one?" Dalan kicked a log.

"Nothing, indeeeed."

"Then why are you back in the tree?"

The tree blinked slowly. "Uuh. Indeeeed."

"I can't believe this." Dalan stomped away, but didn't go too far. He began to see why Gan disliked woodpits.

By the time night descended on the trees, Dalan's exhaustion took over, and he drifted off toward sleep, wrapped in his blanket.

After breakfast the next morning, Gan gathered the horses' packs and loaded them with the meal's leftovers. "I think it's time to flop onward. Mooch-Lick, you need to make a choice. You pick one of these here lap logs, or I'll scorch you out."

"Pit. Pit. No need to be so rushed."

Gan threw a pack to the ground and marched over to the tree. "We are in a vast hurry. Dash has scamper squirreled away, and we must find him before the snapper Zovlon does. No time to fritter-snit"

"Ooh. Pit, pit. An adventure. It has been more than a century since I went on an adventure. Indeeeed."

"Then pick a smack log."

"Will we ride horses across the desert? Pit, pit."

"No," Gan replied.

"Will there be sword fights and pirates? Pit."

"No."

"How about a beautiful princess? Pit. I like princesses-"

"No!"

"In distress. Pit, pit. This adventure needs a princess in distress. Indeeeed."

"Aaah! No!" Gan stormed off toward the horses.

Tabin leaned over to the tree and whispered, "We've got a boy to find, and if you're coming along, I'd suggest you listen to Gan and make a choice quickly. He can be quite stubborn sometimes."

Moochir let out a long, loud sigh. His face disappeared from the tree and blinked out of a log in the middle of the pile Gan had gathered.

Dalan dug through to find the right one, but Moochir kept moving. "This... no, indeeeed. But this one... could be. Pit. Ah, now this one..."

Dalan stood with arms crossed. "Will you just pick one?"

"Possibly." His face flitted to another log. "Yes. Indeeeed. I could be comfortable in this one."

"Is that it, then?"

"I believe so. Pit. Pit. Fairly comfortable."

Dalan picked up the small log and tied it onto the top of his pack. The added weight pinched his shoulders. He moved it to one of his horse's packs.

"Not too tight now, pit, pit. We have a long journey together. A long journey, indeeeed."

Dalan mounted and rode down the dusty path behind Tabin. How had Gan survived four years with a woodpit? Making friends with Moochir might be his only way to avoid going crazy.

"Eep, eep, eep, eep," Moochir chanted to the rhythm of the horse's steps.

Dalan clenched his teeth. "Stop that."

"Eep, eep, eep, eep."

"I can't listen to that the whole way to Endurek."

"Is that where we're going? Eep, eep, eep, eep."

"Yes. Will you stop with the eeps?"

"Could be. Eep, eep, eep, eep, eeuuuh. Indeeeed."

"Gan," Dalan called ahead. "How do I make the woodpit keep quiet?"

Gan shook his head. "That answer is incalculable, my boy. And if I knew, I would tell you as fast as a blithering newt flack."

"Eep, eep, eep, eep..."

Chapter 7
The Moon Box

Dash jerked awake as he felt himself sliding off the wagon bench and grabbed the edge of the seat. With a shove, he seated himself again.

The darkness of night had crept over the plain and the warmth of the day faded. "Are we going to stop soon?"

"Yes." Karakul pointed straight ahead. "See those lights? That's the town of Sheker, but we'll stop before we get there. We don't want anything to interfere with the moon's light. In fact, this might be a good spot."

He pulled the drooping horse to a halt near a narrow stream. Crickets chirped in the grass, and the heavy scent of tsagan flowers mixed with the crispness of the evening air.

Looking up, Dash couldn't see the moon yet. Several dark clouds floated through the sky as he unhitched the horse and led him to the water.

The horse finished his drink, and Dash tethered him out in a grassy spot. The nearby trees produced plenty of wood for a fire. He soon had a blaze going and made a stew out of sausage and vegetables.

"What's Endurek like?" Dash stirred the large pot, trying to imagine the capital of Teagen. Would it be anything like Temyulun?

"More amazing than you could even imagine." Karakul

grinned. "I think you will like it after life on a farm. The bustle of the market, the glitter of the courtiers, and of course there's the palace. Things have improved significantly since Prince Kasiret took over the throne, and that was only about a year ago."

Dash handed Karakul a bowl of stew.

He took a bite. "Mmmm. Tasty. I think I might keep you around. For a while, anyway."

Emotion stirred inside Dash. He hoped it would be longer. He'd already benefited from hanging around with this unusual man.

The night grew dark, and the moon rose large and orange over the mountains.

Dash waited for Karakul to say more about the moon box, but his new master sat by the fire for a long time, smoking his long, carved pipe. Dark clouds floated by, but never completely obscured the round disc of light rising into the sky.

Finally, Karakul rose and stretched. "Well, I suppose we should take a look at that box, if you're still interested."

Dash nodded and hurried over to the wagon. As he pulled the box out of the back, he could see the faint outline of words glowing on top.

"Bring it over here," Karakul called, moving a little way from the fire. "It will work better where it's darker."

Dash carried the box over and tipped it so moonlight shone directly on the top. Bright words shone out and Dash read:

> "By the silvery light of the rounded moon,
> Five digits placed will grant a boon.
> When odds are even, one will do,
> When evens turn odd, I will give two."

Karakul leaned over for a closer look. "Well, there you have it."

"What does it mean? Am I supposed to do something?"

"Follow the instructions, of course. Five digits will grant a boon."

Dash didn't know what a boon was or what five digits meant. Was that five numbers, and if so which ones?

He noticed again the five bronze discs across the front. Maybe this had something to do with the five digits.

Rubbing a finger over one disk didn't produce a number. He tried the other discs, but they felt smooth as well.

"Try putting all your fingers on at once," Karakul suggested.

"Oh." Dash nodded. "Of course, digits as in fingers. But what's a boon?"

"Something that will benefit you."

Dash could see Karakul smiling in the pale moonlight, his intense black eyes more piercing than before.

Dash put a finger on each disc. As his thumb touched the last one, the box whirred. With a clink, the top popped open.

Inside, a round wrist band rested on a bed of purple velvet.

"What's that?" Dash asked.

"It's a moon band. Take it. It's for you."

"For me?" Dash picked up the band and held it in the moonlight. Etched silver patterns swirled around the golden circle. On the inside of the band, Dash noticed more inscriptions that glowed just like the moon writing on the top of the box.

He twisted it and read aloud as he went:

"Wealth is happiness sucked from a well that leaves you

ever thirsting for more."

Dash looked over at his master. "I don't get it. Is that the boon? Wealth?"

The tall man smiled. "For that, we'll have to wait and see what the future brings. Moon bands are powerful, and this one is stronger than any I've seen before." He reached a long finger out toward the moon band. "Very powerful."

A twinge of uncertainty shifted through Dash's mind. "What does it mean by thirsting for more?"

"Wanting more wealth is a good thing. The more motivated you are, the richer you will become. You want to be rich, don't you?"

Dash nodded. Riches were definitely a good thing. Queen Baiyanarah had offered his family a better life, but Papa loved the farm even though very little income came from all the hard work. Dash didn't understand that at all. Less work and a comfortable life made more sense.

Karakul took the box from Dash. The lid closed with a clink. "Go ahead. Put it on."

Excitement filled his chest as Dash slipped the band over his left hand and onto his wrist. It shrunk to a perfect fit. Holding his arm up to the moonlight, he smiled. "I like it."

"Good." Karakul patted him on the back.

Dash glanced at the top of the box. "'When odds are even, one will do, when evens turn odd, I will give two.' I wonder what that means."

"I guess we'll find out next time we open the box." Karakul placed it back in the wagon. "Time for sleep now. We have a big day of trading ahead. Sheker's market is a busy place."

Dash lay sleepless, watching the fire die down and the moon rise higher in the sky. Thoughts of riches, along with the power they brought, filled his mind. The moon band rested comfortably around his wrist, and he smiled to himself every time he glanced at it.

✦

In Sheker the next day, Dash helped Karakul set up his stall of fine linens, silver trinkets, and rugs.

Karakul chatted with potential buyers who came from all over the area.

Dash kept busy running back and forth from the wagon parked down a nearby alley. He hauled trunks, sorted merchandise, and helped customers.

An old farmer came looking for a kerchief for his wife. Karakul bargained and haggled until he extracted a silver from the farmer for a lace-edged one.

Karakul nodded toward a young woman approaching. "You try this one."

"Is there something you are looking for, Miss?"

"Yes. Do you have earrings?"

Dash dug in the trunk by his feet and produced several pairs of silver earrings. "Any of these would look very nice on you."

"Oh, they're not for me. My sister is getting married next week."

Dash held up one pair, then another. He chatted and bargained. A smile grew on her face and his nervousness calmed down. By the time she decided on a pair, Dash had settled the price at one gold coin.

The woman left, still smiling.

"Well done!" Karakul sat down on a trunk. "Those earrings weren't even worth a silver. I think you have a knack for this sort of work."

Dash smiled. "That was fun. Can I try the next one?"

"You may try all that come our way."

The sun descended toward the horizon. Villagers packed up their stalls, and Dash sank onto a closed trunk. "I'm tired."

Karakul looked at him with penetrating black eyes. "Yes. We've had a very successful day. All the better to be as far from here as possible before we rest for the night." He surveyed the market square. "Here, take these trunks back to the wagon and lock them in."

Dash groaned as he stood. His back ached from all the lifting and hauling. But picking up one trunk after another, he situated everything back in its place in the wagon.

He retrieved the horse from the stable, hitched it to the wagon and they headed out of town with the setting sun at their backs.

"You have done well today." Karakul threw his money pouch to Dash. "Count it out, boy."

Being careful not to drop any coins, Dash counted. "There are sixteen golds, seven silvers, plus some bronze and coppers." He replaced the coins in the pouch and handed it back to his master.

Karakul laughed. "Very good. I couldn't have done nearly as well without you. The moon band may have had something to do with it. Now, here's your reward for the day." He handed Dash a large bundle, wrapped in crinkly brown paper.

Dash held the package for a moment, almost too excited to open it. Finally, he slipped off the string and unwrapped the paper covering.

In it lay a soft, dark gray cloak, edged in gold and embroidered with black birds. "Wow." He flung the cloak around his shoulders and smiled as the warmth and weight of it embraced him.

Glancing down at the moon band, he noticed a glint of red along one edge. But maybe it was just the light of the setting sun.

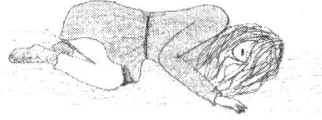

Chapter 8
Distress

Dalan clenched his teeth.

His head ached.

Everything in him wanted to whip the log off his pack and fling it down into the Deep Divide. Moochir had talked to him for two days straight, even waking him in the night to say annoying, stupid things.

The night before, they had made their camp not far from the edge of the Deep Divide. Now they headed down the steep slope into the canyon that separated Talsar from Teagen.

The trail zigzagged downward, through stunted bushes and brown tufts of grass. An occasional rabbit or lizard scurried off the path. Overhead, a black bird circled before flying north along the ravine.

"Eep, eep, eep, eep," Moochir chanted to the rhythm of the horse's steps.

Dalan tried hard to ignore the senseless noise coming from the log.

"Dry and dusty. Dusty, indeeeed. Eep, eep, eep, eep..."

Pulling the front of his tunic up over his nose and mouth, Dalan attempted to block out the dust from Gan's and Tabin's horses. It hadn't bothered him until Moochir mentioned it.

"Hot, hot sun. Pit, pit. Very hot sun. Indeeeed. Eep, eep, eep, eep. I met a man once who had been burned by the sun.

Eep, eep, eep, eep…"

Dalan pulled his hood farther over his head.

At midday, they reached the bottom where a shallow stream meandered along the sandy ground.

"Some shade would be nice." Dalan pulled bread and apples from one of his horse's packs. "I should have thought of this before, but do woodpits need to eat or drink?"

"Certainly not," Gan replied. "They endure like portly hogs on air and sunlight."

"I suppose Moochir would have let me know if he needed something."

Gan snorted. "You can bet your pink flower britches on that."

The horses drank and Tabin fed them oats.

After dumping water over his head, Dalan filled cups from the stream.

Gan surveyed the canyon. "It's going to be a stretched climb back up the other side."

Dalan tipped his head back to take in the steep, striped rock walls of the Teagen side.

"We must ramble north for a flea's hop or two before we get to the path upward." Gan brushed a fly off his neck. "Then it's a climb up the elephant's flank."

"Pit! Pit!" Moochir shouted. "She's coming! Fast! Fast indeeeed! Pit, Pit!"

"Who's coming? What are you talking about?" Dalan looked around, but saw no sign of company.

Moochir's eyes bulged out of the log, his voice high and pinched. "The princess is coming. Coming, indeeeed!" His face faded into the bark, but Dalan still saw the faint outline of it.

"Is he trying to hide?" Dalan asked, leaning over the log.

Gan shrugged. "Any piece of peace is welcome."

A loud pop sounded from across the water. The noise echoed off the canyon walls. Sand on the other side of the stream wavered. With a bang, a huge patch of it exploded into the air.

Clumps of sand peppered the stream as well as the rock wall.

The horses whinnied and bucked.

"What was that?" Tabin held tight to the panicked horses' bridles.

"Pit. Pit. She is here. Pit. Princess in distress. Indeeeed."

Dalan stared into the dissipating cloud of sand. The vague outline of a person stood for a moment and then collapsed.

"Someone *is* there." Dalan splashed across the shallow stream and cautiously approached. The woman's fine clothes were smudged and burnt, and long hair draped over her face. She lay crumpled on her side, not moving.

The shiny rod clutched in her hand looked familiar.

Dalan gasped.

The woman held the staff of the ancient kings that Els Edzyn had given to Queen Baiyanarah.

Gan followed him across and together they carefully rolled her onto her back.

She groaned.

"Ripping snore squeezers!" Gan brushed a wisp of hair away from her face. "It's our very own buzzer bee."

"Ariyuna?" Dalan kneeled down beside her. "Ariyuna!" He patted her cheeks, but got only a groan in response. "At least she's alive."

Tabin secured the horses and leaped over the water. "How did she get here?" He brushed more hair away from her face. "She's got burns on her forehead and hands, and she's holding the queen's staff. Dalan, quick. Get a cup of water."

Dalan ran back across the stream and grabbed his cup out of the sand. Rinsing it in the stream, he then scooped up cool, clear water.

With help from Gan, he propped Ariyuna's shoulders against Tabin's knees and offered her a drink.

She took several sips, but most of it dribbled down her chin.

Tabin pried the staff from her hand. "Gan, can you take this?"

"I will not catch that grandy stick."

"You don't have to keep it. Just put it in my pack for now."

Gan nodded and trotted off with the staff.

Lifting Ariyuna into his arms, Tabin stood. Concern etched his face as he carried her across the stream. "We need to get some help." With Dalan's assistance, he placed her in the saddle of his horse.

"Hang on to her while I get up." Tabin climbed on behind and propped her limp form upright in front of him. "Let's go."

"Grave distress. Indeeeed."

Dalan ignored the pit. He threw the remains of lunch into his pack and secured Moochir's log to the saddle before following Tabin. Gan and his horse trotted behind. They traveled at a swift pace northward to the ascending trail. Half way up the other side, Tabin traded horses with Dalan to keep the horses from tiring too much.

Moochir said nothing, and Dalan, glad for the break from his constant chatter, kept silent as well.

They reached the grassy plain on the other side and continued east. The flatness stretched out as far as Dalan could see. "Where are the towns? Ariyuna needs help."

"The village of Bura should sneaker up in a lizard blink." Gan urged his tired horse onward. "It's sunk into a dipper dot and hard to see until it jack-jumps you."

Tabin nodded and kept going, still holding up the limp and groaning Ariyuna.

Dalan followed. The sun, well on its way to the horizon, beat down on them with unyielding heat. His stomach felt pinched and tight. First Dash and now his sister. *Is she going to be all right?* he asked Elch.

The fish didn't reply.

"There it is," Tabin called from up ahead.

Squinting into the distance, Dalan could see dull red roofs parallel with the plain. He hurried his horse on.

A steep road descended into the town built below the level of the plain.

Along the main street by the market stood a stable willing to take in their horses.

"Is there a healer here?" Tabin asked the stable master.

The man pointed down the street. "Beck. He may be able to help." He looked sideways at Ariyuna. "But then again, maybe not."

"Thanks. We'll give Beck a try." Tabin shifted Ariyuna in his arms so that her head rested on his shoulder before heading down the street.

Gan knocked and a broad-shouldered man answered the door.

When he saw Ariyuna, he opened the door wider. "Come in."

The home had few windows, and a musty smell filled the air. Shelves lined every wall with books and strange objects covering most of them.

"I'm Beck." The healer bowed but didn't lower his eyes. "You may place her on the sofa."

Tabin complied, but stood close by.

A quiver of uncertainty settled over Dalan.

"Tell me what happened." Beck looked her over, felt her forehead and examined the burns on her arms and face.

"We really don't know." Tabin shifted uneasily on his feet.

"So you don't know how this happened?" The healer looked suspiciously at Tabin.

"Not exactly. She, well..."

Ariyuna lay on the sofa, limp and unresponsive.

"I can do very little for her." The healer stood. "Except for these burns, there's really nothing physically wrong."

"What do you mean, there's nothing wrong?" Dalan paced the room. "She won't wake up. That's wrong."

"Unless you tell me more, I can't help."

Tabin shuffled his feet. "She... well, it may have something to do with this." He pulled the staff of the ancient kings out of his pack. "She was holding this when we found her."

"Whoeew!" The healer stepped forward and took the staff. "I've never seen anything like this." He turned the staff over in his hands, looking at every side. "Is this a magical item?"

Gan rubbed his head and frowned. "Oh, this is as heavy as a moose hook. We haven't had any tickle that it might be magical, but we don't know much more than a tumble."

The healer held the staff up to the light. "I don't believe my skill will be sufficient. You'll need to take her to see Zibek in Endurek, the capital. That's where the prince keeps all those who have knowledge of magical items."

He handed the staff back to Tabin. "You might want to

keep that away from untrained eyes. From the little I know, this looks like an object of power from Talsar. My guess is the young lady tried to use this object improperly and ended up injuring herself. Her body appears to be fine, but her mind is in a charmed sleep."

Dalan knelt beside his sister. "Ariyuna, please wake up." He shook her shoulders. Her eyelids fluttered but didn't open. She breathed in deeply before a frown dug into her forehead, and she groaned again.

"Are you sure you can't do anything?" Dalan felt a lump rise in his throat.

The healer hesitated. Shaking his head, he turned away.

Chapter 9
Crossed Paths

Dash hurried to the wagon for the trunk he'd just repacked. It had been a busy day at the market in Bura. The setting sun glinted off the rooftops, tinting everything pink, and smoke from the day's fires hung heavy in the air.

"Don't dawdle, boy," Karakul called. "This gentleman is waiting."

The trunk felt heavier as he lugged his burden back to the stall and flung it open. The bag of silver baubles lay on top.

"I think we have just what you're looking for." Karakul pulled several rings out of the sack.

Dash surveyed the dwindling crowd. The vegetable sellers were packing up what remained of their produce. The blacksmith across the square swept dirt from his shop into the gutter. Only the baker had a line of customers.

Dash smiled to himself. This might just be the life for him. Traveling all over, making a bucket of money in each town and wearing fancy clothes. He fingered the edge of his new cloak.

On the far side of the market stood a house with a dark sign that read *Beck's Herbs and Healing*. Three people emerged from the doorway.

Dash sucked in a quick breath before diving under the

stall. What were Tabin and Dalan doing here? And Gan, too?

He peeked around the side of the stall. Tabin carried a girl in his arms. Ariyuna? But her head rested on his shoulder, her long hair hiding her face.

Karakul haggled with the customer over the price of two silver rings and finally came to an agreement.

Dash peeked out again. Tabin and the others headed toward a tall brick building with red framed windows and doors that matched the roof. *Travelers Repose* in gold lettering stretched over the door.

Karakul kicked Dash. "What are you doing down there?"

"I..." He pointed across the square. "That's my uncle and brother, and Gan, who's the magistrate of Surtak. I don't want them to see me."

"Who's the girl?"

A flicker of concern pressed in. "I don't know. Might be my sister."

"She doesn't look well."

The girl's head flopped back, and Dash saw her face. "It's Ariyuna. The girl is my-"

"Shhh." Karakul busied himself with putting things away, but watched the group until they entered the inn.

"Clean up quickly, boy, and we'll see what we can find out."

Surprised by his master's concern, Dash shoved boxes and bags back into trunks and dragged them to the wagon.

"There's only one inn here." Karakul stuffed a decorative pillow into one of the bags. "We'd better wait to get a room until your family is out of the way."

He finished securing the trunks. After a glance out over the square, he nodded to Dash and marched across to the inn.

Dash scurried after his master, slipping inside just before

the heavy door closed.

"We'd like a room for two with a view of the street." Karakul slid a silver across the counter. "And food brought to our room."

The older woman behind the counter smiled, taking the coin. "I think we can accommodate you." She slid a large key across to Karakul. "The Emperor's Lounge. Up the stairs. First room on the left." Her smile showed yellowing teeth with several missing in the front.

Karakul bowed and headed up the stairs. "Come along, boy."

Glancing back, he saw the woman examining the silver, the smile still fixed on her face.

Once inside the room, Dash flopped onto one of the beds. "I hope Ariyuna's all right."

"You'll have to make a choice." Karakul dropped his satchel onto a chair. "But if you return to your family now, you will need to leave the moon band behind."

Dash twisted the band on his wrist as he considered the choice. If he could only know if his sister would be all right. But thoughts of all the late summer farm work edged forward, and he cringed. He liked this life better. His new cloak's warmth and comfort encircled him. "How much did we make today?"

Karakul smiled. "Twenty golds, eight silvers, plus the trade for that jeweled necklace. The owner didn't know the worth of what he had." His smile widened. "We made a very good trade on that one."

Dash thought he saw two eyes blink out of a dresser drawer, but when he looked closer, they were gone. Must have been his tired mind imagining things.

With a sigh, Karakul eased himself into a chair by the fireplace. "We can find out how your family is and still leave without them knowing we were here."

"I really want to stay with you."

Karakul pulled out his coin pouch and flipped three golds through the air toward Dash. They landed on the bed. "For your help today. I've not done so well in years, and I'd be grateful if you and your moon band would stick around for a while."

"Thanks!" Dash picked up the coins.

"Here's something else." Karakul held out a small pouch decorated in gold swirls and cords. "You'll need something to keep your money in."

"Really?" Dash jumped off the bed and took the money pouch. He slipped the three golds in and added the dirty coppers from his pocket. He smiled at Karakul. "This I could get used to."

Karakul stood and hummed as he unpacked a few things.

Tension seeped out of Dash's shoulders. If Karakul wasn't worried, why should he be? He jingled the coins in the pouch before attaching it to his belt. "So, where do we go from here?"

"If your relatives stick around, we'll head on, but if they leave in the morning, we'll try another day of trading here. I have a good feeling about this place. And with you present, we could do quite well."

He stopped and crossed his arms, looking sideways at Dash. "We may need to find a way to trick the box into giving you another band before the next full moon."

Dash glanced down at his wrist. A red line edged the band, and several of the smaller dots looked bluish. "There's more color now."

He held his arm out for Karakul to see. "It used to be a bit big, but it fits perfectly now."

"Ah, very good. You are learning its lessons quickly."
Karakul pulled the moon box out. "There must be someone in
this town who would know about these sorts of boxes." He
pulled the cord to call for the messenger boy.

Moments later, someone knocked. "You rang, sir?"

Karakul opened the door, pulled the boy inside, and
closed the door quickly behind him. He pinned the boy against
the door with his piercing stare. "Is there anyone in town that
knows about magical objects?"

The boy screwed up his face. "Beck the healer might
know of someone, sir."

"Fetch him."

The boy left quickly.

Dash fidgeted with his band. "Forcing the box to open
won't mess things up, will it?"

"Will it change the moon band's powers? No. We just
need to find a way to make the box think there's a full moon
and open sooner."

Karakul paced back and forth in front of the window as
they waited.

Finally, a knock sounded at the door.

"Get that, boy."

Dash scurried over and unlatched the handle.

The healer entered, closing the door behind him, but
stayed by the entrance.

Standing back, Karakul studied the man. "The messenger
boy said you might know someone that deals with magical
items."

"I am the one to help you. Beck, at your service." The
healer bowed. "That is, I know some things, but not as much as
others. So far I've been able to avoid being conscripted by the
prince, despite my considerable skill. And I'd like to keep it that

way."

"Fair enough." Karakul bowed his head. "If you help us with our little problem, we'll be sure to say nothing of your skill. If you can't help us, there will be nothing to tell. My name is Karakul." He bowed his head.

Dash sat on a bed and watched, feeling a little uncertain about Karakul and what he might be capable of.

Two eyes blinked out of the bed post. Dash jumped. But on second glance, he couldn't see anything.

Beck stayed by the door. "So, what would you like help with?"

"This." Karakul held out the moon box.

"Ah. I haven't seen one of these for a long time." He took the box and examined all sides. "You've already opened it once."

Karakul nodded. "And we'd like to open it again. Before the next full moon."

"A little impatient? I can understand. This is a very potent box, at least what's inside is."

Digging in the satchel over his shoulder, Beck pulled out a small bag with greenish powder. "Sprinkle this on the box. You will still need some moonlight, but even a little will do." He handed the bag and box to Karakul.

Karakul gave the healer a gold from his money pouch.

Eyeing the box warily, the healer backed toward the door. "This has certainly been an interesting day."

Dash sat forward. "Did you see a girl earlier? Is she all right?"

"The girl was rendered insensible from a close encounter with something extremely powerful from Talsar. I was unable to help her. Moon boxes, on the other hand, are simple compared to that."

The healer watched Karakul's reaction closely.

Karakul turned toward Dash. His dark, beady eyes narrowed before a bent smile crept up his face. "You'll have to tell me more about your family at some point."

Chapter 10
The City of Endurek

"He's gone." Dalan held out the log, then glanced around the inn's room for any sign of movement in the wood fixtures. "Moochir's gone." A hint of freedom stirred inside.

"I would say good riddance to Hagery Faz. Don't wish him back, my boy." Gan plumped a pillow and shoved it under Ariyuna's head. "But don't expect the mooch-mangler to let you go that easily. He'll stretch the attachment to an eel's drag if it suits him."

"Did you miss me? Pit. Pit." Moochir blinked out of the door frame. "I've just been listening in on conversations. Very interesting conversations, indeeeed."

Dalan glared at the woodpit. "I really don't care what kind of eavesdropping you've been up to. What we need is a way to help Ariyuna." He dropped the log onto the floor beside his pack.

Tabin strode to the door. "We'll leave first thing in the morning. I'm going out. We're running a little low on supplies, and we'll need a wagon."

An hour later, Tabin returned with several large baskets of food.

Evening stretched into night, and Ariyuna remained listless.

"Come on, Ari." Dalan held a cup of water to her lips.

"You can do this."

Ariyuna swallowed several sips.

"That's it." Dalan tried a piece of bread, but she wouldn't take it, so he gave her more water. "Well, at least she's drinking."

Gan rubbed his head. "She won't be able to keep that up for more than a rat's tail. See if she'll take some milk."

Ariyuna drank half the cup Dalan offered. "I think that's about all I'll be able to get into her tonight. Maybe we should try some thin porridge in the morning."

Dalan cradled his sister's head in his lap as the first rays of sun shone over the distant horizon. Gan had hitched two of their horses to the rented wagon that now bounced along the road toward Endurek.

Tabin rode a little ahead on the third horse.

The day dragged on in dreary stillness. Heat from the summer sun pinched Dalan's neck. That night, they camped beside a very small stream and continued on in the same tedious way the following day.

Dalan kept watch over his sister, who drank, slept, and mumbled at times, but never opened her eyes.

Elch, Dalan called out with his mind. *Is she going to be all right?*

No reply came.

"Moons." Moochir blinked out of the side of the wagon. "Pit. Pit. And a box. Moons, indeeeed."

Dalan frowned. "What are you talking about?"

"Just moons. Moons and boxes. Pit. Pit. You know there was someone in that town way back yester-yesterday. Pit. He looked a lot like you. Yes, like you, indeeeed."

"You saw someone at the market that looked like me?"

"No. Pit. Pit. Not at the market. At the inn, when I was listening. Yes, listening about moons and boxes. Pit."

"What does that have to do with anything?"

"I don't know. Pit. Pit. Just thought you might want to know. But younger. Yes, indeeeed."

The thought landed in Dalan's stomach like one of Ma's honey cakes. Maybe Moochir had seen Dash. Should they go back? The wagon hit a pothole, and Ariyuna's head bounced in his lap. No. They needed to get help first.

A deep sadness settled over him. What was he going to tell Ma? Would he be the only one left from this misadventure?

Out across the plain, a city came into view. "Is that Endurek?" Dalan asked.

"Yes, my boy. The whip gagger city of Endurek." Gan drove the wagon along the bumpy dirt road, directing the horses around the larger potholes.

Dalan studied Gan. "You don't seem happy to see it."

Tabin, riding beside the wagon, shook his head. "We'll all be happier with Endurek behind us. It's a corrupt city. You'll need to watch yourself every moment. Friendly on the surface, though."

"Yes." Gan rubbed the eagle tattoo on his head. "And fancy dressers. But the welcome is only as thick as a cutworm's flapper."

As they approached the city, the road improved, but the crowd thickened. Tall, imposing walls surrounded the capital. Guards in bright yellow and blue stood at the gates.

"Will we have any trouble getting in?" Dalan asked, noticing the guards up on the walls as well.

"We shouldn't." Tabin glanced down at Ariyuna. "It's getting out that can be tricky."

"Pit. Pit. Now this is something to see. Indeeeed."

Gan turned quickly toward the woodpit. "You need to keep as silent as a rotten barrel poke. Not a pit out of you or someone will fling you into a fire."

"I'm touched. Pit. Pit. You do care about me."

Gan glared, and the woodpit's face faded into the bark.

The guards at the gate glanced into the wagon and waved them on into the crowded streets.

"This way." Gan steered the wagon to the left. Banners hung from tall buildings, and gold paint accented the carved bricks. Flowers and trees lined streets paved in swirling patterns of red, gray and purple flagstones that glowed in the setting sun.

"Wow," Dalan whispered. "This is incredible."

Gan grunted. "Don't be slurped in by the bangle-tangle. If my memory is punching correctly, there's a jammer snap inn down this curvature. And it's near the healer's alley. Tabin, be a pintail and slip ahead. See if Zibek still has his shop near the Dragon Fish Inn. We'll meet you there in a flick."

Tabin nodded and rode ahead while the wagon made its way over the decorative cobblestones. Whiffs of smoke hung in the air, along with a perfumed pungent tang that Dalan didn't recognize.

Ariyuna groaned and rolled over as the wagon hit a small bump.

A stable across from the inn took in the horses, and Gan hired a boy to drive the wagon back to its owner in Bura.

Dalan looked up at the carved green sign hanging outside the Dragon Fish Inn.

"Don't worry, my boy." Gan staggered forward, carrying Ariyuna. "It's a plush packer place. But let's get a room squeaky zip. This girl is as substantial as a boulder."

With a quick reach and a thank-you, Dalan grabbed the key from the girl at the counter and hurried up the stairs. He heard Gad trip and grunt behind him.

"You all right?"

"Just hurry, my boy!"

"This is it." Dalan fumbled with the key to the room before swinging it open.

Gan stumbled in and flopped Ariyuna on a large bed covered in a white spread. With a stretch of his back, he looked around with a smile. "This should serve us as good as any split bucket. It's not extravagant by Endurek's whopper-ways, but it's clean and spacious. Our dandelion dreamer should do well here."

The faint light of the moon glowed into the room as Gan lit the lamps.

The door swung open, and Tabin stepped in.

A tall man followed. His long, flowing cloak, embroidered with fish and other water creatures, swirled around his feet.

Dalan noticed that the intricate black bird clasps on each shoulder had red jewels for eyes that winked in the lamp light.

Ribbons and feathers hung in his hair, and silver shoes inlaid with gold clicked on the floor as he entered and bowed low.

"Greetings. I am Zibek, at your service. I received word from the healer in Bura that you would be arriving."

Dalan frowned. "How-" but clamped his mouth shut again.

"And this must be the girl." Zibek strode over to the bed, felt her wrist and lifted her eyelids, but Ariyuna didn't stir.

Still holding up her wrist, Zibek placed a hand on her forehead with his hand. "No fever. Can you tell me what happened?"

"We found her." Tabin shifted his weight from one foot

to the other. "She appeared out of nowhere, holding... a staff. We haven't been able to wake her, but she has been taking water and a little porridge."

"May I see the staff?"

Gan looked sternly at Tabin who shrugged.

"This injury is not physical." Zibek dropped her arm back onto the bed. "She is in a charmed sleep. I will not be able to help if I cannot examine the object that caused it." His piercing dark eyes fixed Tabin in a hard stare.

Tabin sighed, dug in his pack, and pulled out the staff. It glinted and shone in the drab room.

Zibek's eyes widened. He reached for the queen's prized possession. "May I?"

A ball tightened in Dalan's stomach as the healer took the staff.

"Pit. Pit," came a whisper near his ear. "Gone. Gone away. Indeeeed. Pit. Both gone. Poof!"

A smile etched up Zibek's face. He placed the staff on Ariyuna and slipped his arms under her.

A flash of blinding light filled the room.

"Gone. Pit. Pit. Yes, gone."

Dalan gasped and lunged forward.

"Dragging kick roaches! They've vanished!" Gan ran to the bed and whacked at the place Ariyuna had been only moments before. "Staff and butterfly, snatched from right under our snort muzzles. Oooh, this is inexcusable."

Chapter 11
Moonless Cheats

Excitement surged in Dash's chest as they approached the imposing walls and wooden gates. "So this is Endurek?" He tipped his head back to take in the scope of the massive stone walls that looked reddish in the late afternoon sun.

Karakul laughed. "This is Endurek, the magnificent city of princes. Have you ever seen anything as impressive?"

"Temyulun is big, but not as fancy. It's kinda plain and boring. Everyone is grumpy, and it smells bad. 'Course the queen said she was going to change all that, but I don't know if she has yet. I haven't been there since she took over."

"You've met the queen of Talsar?"

"Yeah. She and my sister are always together, scheming things."

Karakul urged the horse farther into the crowd. "Is this the sister we saw in Bura?"

Dash nodded. "She's supposed to be in Temyulun with Baiyanarah right now."

"Ah, so you're on a first-name basis with the ruler of Talsar."

"I guess you could say that. She used to live in the mountains just up from our farm."

The guards nodded to Karakul as he drove his wagon through the gates.

"Do you live here?" Dash gazed wide-eyed at the splendor that now surrounded him.

"Yes." Karakul pointed toward the center of the city. "I live near the market, up against the wall of the grand palace." He lowered his voice. "I've even been given the secret to a small door that lets me into the palace cellars, but I must use it carefully."

People bowed and waved at Karakul as he drove through the city. But some glanced at him fearfully and slid into the shadows between the buildings.

Dash sat taller and straightened the cloak on his shoulders, basking in the power of Karakul's influence.

They followed the wide cobblestoned street until it ended at the market. Driving the wagon around the stalls, Karakul stopped in front of an impressive stone house. Large, open arches adorned the walkway across the front. Trees and bushes surrounded the walled garden where flowers bloomed and rivulets of water babbled along their designated paths.

A black bird perched on the stone wall and watched with beady black eyes as servants unhitched the wagon.

"Come along, boy." Karakul led Dash into the house to where low, comfortable-looking chairs faced an indoor fountain. "Have a seat."

Gingerly, Dash lowered himself into the unfamiliar chair. A servant handed him a cool drink.

"Now the fun begins." Karakul took a sip. "I've gathered some interesting articles on this trip, and with your help, we should do well."

"Will we sell at the market?"

"Yes and no. We will be at the market, but not like the

commoners. We'll contact those who might be interested and push them to pay the highest price possible. Invitation only."

"And what about the moon box? Do you think we should try Beck's idea soon?"

"Of course. We may even try tonight, if the moon shows itself. So, tell me more about this sister of yours."

"There's not much to tell."

Karakul set his cup down and leaned forward. "She's in the council of the queen of Talsar. I believe there is something to tell. How did this come about?"

"Oh, they've been friends since Ariyuna was about ten and started herding the sheep up the mountain. That's when she found Baiyanarah and would visit her all the time. I don't know why. Old people are boring."

The servants brought in a supper of fish, fruits, spiced potatoes, and lots of other dishes Dash had never seen before.

"Don't be shy, boy." Karakul loaded a plate with food. "How did this boring old woman become the queen?"

"That's a long story."

"Good. I like long stories." Karakul sat back. "We have to wait for the moon to rise, anyway."

Dash told of Ariyuna's first journey over the mountains as best as he could remember it. By the time he finished, the sun had sunk below the horizon.

"So you've never been on a journey before?" Karakul asked.

"Oh, I went on one, but I wasn't invited." He told about Ariyuna's second trip with Dalan and how the Enk Taivaan had stopped the war with Zovlon. The story grew as he emphasized his part in the journey. For once someone wanted to hear what he had to say, so he might as well make it good.

With eyes fixed on Dash, Karakul listened until Dash sat

back in his chair and said, "Well, I guess that's all there is to say about that."

Karakul drew in a long slow breath. "This bracelet, the Itgel. Does your sister still have it?"

"Yes, but she only has three stones right now. And my brother still has the Enk Taivaan, but I don't have anything. Not from Talsar, anyway." He ran his fingers along the edge of the moon band.

"It seems to me that you come from a very interesting and powerful family."

Dash scrunched up his nose. "They're not so special once you get to know them."

Karakul glanced out the window. "It's dark now. I'll get the moon box, and we'll make an attempt at opening it." He stood and stretched. "I can see why you're not content to become a simple farmer." With a swish of his cloak, he strode from the room.

Dash stood and looked around. Glittery objects beckoned to him from every corner. Vases sparkled from carved wooden stands, and gold-bound books, interspersed with enticing trinkets, lined decorative shelves. The damp scent of blossoms and evening coolness drifted past sheer, flowing curtains.

A bubble of satisfaction expanded inside. Dash smiled as he took in more of the room. This was how he wanted to live, not in some stinky farm house. But how to go about getting it? He would need money and power.

His fingers touched the coin pouch on his waist. It was a start, anyway, and Karakul had said something about doing well at the market tomorrow.

The moon band on his wrist tingled, and his desire for this kind of life intensified.

"Come along, boy." Karakul stood in the doorway

holding the moon box. "Let's try the roof, and hope the neighbors don't have torches burning." He swung around and headed up a circular stone stairway.

A servant carrying a lamp followed as Dash climbed the twisting staircase. Torches attached to the walls with iron bands sputtered in the breeze that flowed downward, casting dancing shadows all around. Up ahead, Karakul's boots echoed off the walls.

At the top, gusts blew over the houses, catching Dash's long cloak. But he didn't mind. The cloak made him feel important and grown up.

Karakul placed the box on a small table and looked up for the moon. "There." He turned the box to face the moonlight. "It's not full, but it may work. Here's the powder. You may as well hang onto it." He held out the packet of green dust. "Go ahead. Sprinkle some on."

"Me? I... well..."

A cloud drifted near the moon. Dash waited, staring up at the sky. When the cloud passed, he opened the packet. Taking a pinch, he sprinkled some over the top of the box. Faint letters glowed, but he couldn't quite read them.

"Try a little more."

Dash dusted the top of the box with another pinch. The letters glowed brighter. Squinting at the writing, he read:

"Untimely gifts may trick you,
Deceivers, thieves, and moonless cheats.
But power does not change with whims
Nor fail to reach the heart it meets."

"That's different from last time." He glanced at Karakul, who nodded.

Dash's heart thumped as he placed his fingertips along the five bronze plaques on the front of the box. With a faint whir, the lid lifted.

Chapter 12
Pulled

"What do we do?" Dalan looked around frantically. "We have to find Ariyuna!"

"Gone. Pit. Pit. The princess is gone."

"Oh, shut up!" Dalan glared at Moochir. "She's not a princess. And if you want to be helpful, either tell us where she's gone, or go find out."

"As you wish. Pit. Pit."

Moochir's face disappeared from the bedpost.

With a sigh, Dalan raked his fingers through his tangled hair. "I shouldn't have lost my temper."

Gan patted him on the back. "We'll search the whole sogger city for her, even if we have to flip every fool whacker."

A tug pulled at Dalan's back. "Hey, what... ow!" The tug yanked him toward the closed door.

Tabin swung the door open just in time to keep Dalan from slamming into it. "I think Moochir's taking you at your word. You'll have to follow him."

Struggling to keep his balance, Dalan staggered down the stairs. Did the woodpit have to move so fast?

Tabin and Gan thumped down the stairs behind him.

Once out in the darkened street, Dalan grabbed a nearby tree to keep from falling over. With a jerk, the tug pulled him toward the gate, but then turned and wrenched him in the other direction. Lamps set at intervals gave light to streets damp from the drizzle.

Tabin ran after him. "I think we're heading toward the market now."

"Thrusting badger spigots. Moochir could sally our Dalan to the stitch bottoms. I told you woodpits were a burn shave."

Staggering from one side of the street to another, Dalan lurched through the city with Tabin and Gan close behind.

A little boy watched him wobble and turn in a circle. "Mama, what's wrong with him?"

The woman walking with him grabbed the boy's arm and hurried away. "I don't know, but let's go visit your auntie."

Dalan bumped into several trees and crashed through empty stalls at the deserted market. Moochir finally stopped in front of a small mansion surrounded by a stone wall on the far side. A decorative iron gate separated the street from the peaceful garden surrounding the home.

Only Moochir's mouth protruded from an overhanging branch. "Pit. Your twin is here. Pit. Pit." With a blink, his face faded.

A brief thought of Dash rose in Dalan's mind, but Moochir jerked him violently to the left.

"Whoa!" Dalan staggered back through the market and down the same street they had just come up.

He grabbed a lamppost to steady himself. "What twin? And I'm going to be covered in bruises if you don't stop." He rubbed his arm for a second before being pulled sharply forward.

A little farther on, Moochir stopped again. This time in front of a healer's shop.

Tabin came panting up behind. "This is Zibek's place."

"Yes. Pit. Pit. Zibek's, indeeeed. But the princess is not

here. Zibek is not here." His face disappeared, and Dalan, breathing hard, faltered down an alleyway.

"Moochir?" Dalan called, but the woodpit didn't reply. A splash of water hit Dalan's legs, and he looked down just in time to see that he'd stepped in a big, muddy puddle. "Aw, pickles. Oof!" His hands flew up as a strong yank sent him flying face first toward a massive stone wall. "Ow! I can't go through this, Moochir!" he called out, his hands stinging from the collision.

"Pity. Pit. Pit. We will have to go around. Around, indeeeed."

The woodpit traveled along the vines covering the seemingly endless wall. He turned a corner and continued to follow the imposing barrier.

Breathing hard, Gan trotted behind. "This is the stretch mountain fortification around the grand palace."

Dalan struggled to stay upright as they approached an elaborate, golden gate guarded by soldiers with tasseled helmets. A crowd holding torches had gathered outside, and Dalan bumped his way through the mob only to be dragged farther along the wall.

After several more turns, the woodpit's pull loosened.

Dalan could see the same fancy mansion they had stopped in front of before, with the market nearby. "How did we get back here? I'm all turned around."

"Couldn't tell you." Tabin bent over to catch his breath. "I don't know the city that well."

"Moochir!" Gan called, leaning back against the stone wall that surrounded the home.

The woodpit blinked out of a tree trunk. "The princess is inside the palace. Pit. Pit. But this house is the only sneaky way in."

"What about the golden gates we passed?" Tabin

straightened up.

"Pit. Pit. Too many guards. Too many, indeeeed."

Gan crossed his arms. "So you want us to garbage slip through this abode?"

"Yes. Into the palace. Pit. Pit. She is inside."

Dalan peered through the iron gate at the mansion beyond. "Servants are everywhere. How are we supposed to get into the garden, let alone the house?"

One of Moochir's bulging eyes looked toward the mansion, the other scanned the dark sky. "That is not my problem. Not mine, indeeeed. Pit. Pit. That is for you to figure out."

Gan stamped his foot. "You will slug-slither in there and find out. And don't come back until you've learned the pinky-green about this house and its sly cracker connection to the palace."

The woodpit blinked several times before his face vanished.

"Well." Gan sighed. "This is a mule's knot of a problem."

Dalan felt the tug again. "Oh, no." The pull dragged him toward the gate. He hit the bars face first. His cheek pressed painfully against an iron rod. Convinced that significant bruises would be blossoming soon, he tried to peer into the garden through watering eyes.

The tug grew stronger. "I hope no one notices me. Ow!"

"This is flat dog unnecessary." Gan tried to pull Dalan back away from the entrance.

"Ow!"

"Sorry." Gan patted his arm, but frowned toward the house. "That dollop of pit bother knows he can stretch the attachment farther than this. He's just being a rock pest."

Among the plants and flowering bushes, Dalan could see

two servants talking.

"You go ahead," one said. "I thought I heard something over by the gate. I'm going to check it out before I come in."

The other nodded and headed toward a large shed.

"Someone's coming," Dalan whispered.

"What?" Tabin leaned closer.

"I said, someone's coming. Thought he heard a noise. What do I do?"

Tabin shrugged and pulled Gan out of sight along the wall beside the gate.

"What are you doing here?" A mild breeze ruffled the servant's dark blue tunic.

"It's such a beautiful garden."

"We're not going to let you in, so move along."

"I most certainly will." Dalan tried to smile, but the iron bar across his face made it feel more like a grimace.

"Then go. Shoo!"

"As soon as I can, I'll go."

"Make that now."

Dalan tried to push himself away from the bars, but couldn't. He mumbled to himself, "Be quick, Moochir."

The tug yanked him sideways for a brief moment before pulling in the opposite direction, making his face jostle against the iron bars.

"If you really think you'll squeeze through by wiggling, then you're sadly mistaken." The servant grabbed a stick and poked him in the stomach.

"Ow! I said I'd go. I could use a little help, you two."

Gan and Tabin stepped out from beside the gate.

"Good evening." Tabin bowed with his arms crossed on his chest. "I see you're having a little trouble with my friend here."

The servant stood with his stick pointed at Dalan's chest. "Get rid of him before I call the master's guards."

Gan bowed, then bounced up and down as he chanted:

"A stick in the mud,
A pole in the suds.
Wind in the whipper dunk,
Skunks in the sleeper bunk.
What shall we do with the boy on the gate?
What do we say to the mouse in a snake?"

Gan danced around. The tassels on his wrist and waist wagged, and his short legs kicked out in random directions.

The servant lowered his stick just a little and watched. A puzzled frown sat on his face as Gan continued.

"Hold on tight, little mouse,
We'll find a new house.
The stick and the pole,
Must find a new hole.
And what do we do with the boy on the gate?
All we can do is wait."

"Wait for what?" The servant raised the stick again.

Dalan felt the tug loosen. "For this." He pushed away from the bars and fell backwards onto the street, right into another mud puddle.

"Ha! Cricket poppers, Dalan, my boy. As good as a flip squirrel's jig."

Tabin bowed to the servant again. "Sorry for the inconvenience. We won't bother you anymore." He reached down and pulled Dalan out of the puddle. "Let's go while we can."

Dalan stood, dripping. "I hope we *can* go. Where's Moochir?"

"Pit. Pit," came from a nearby tree. "That house is as tight as a sea casket. Pit. And soaked in enchantments. You must forget about the princess. She is locked away, deep. Deep, indeeeed."

Chapter 13
A Fat Donkey

Dash held his breath as the lid of the moon box opened. Inside, he saw not one but two moon bands. Did using the powder mess things up? His cloak fluttered as another gust of warm breeze blew across the roof of Karakul's mansion.

"Very good, boy. Very good!" Karakul reached toward the box but then withdrew his hand. "I believe those are for you."

Dash stared at the bands. "The first time we opened it, the writing on the box said something about giving two when evens were odd, or something like that. Do you think cheating the box made it give us two?"

Karakul shrugged. "Could be, but it's hard to know with moon boxes. Sure, we cheated a little. That could have changed the way the box reacted, but it won't change the fundamental power of the bands."

"They have power?" With eagerness, Dash placed the box on the table and gently lifted one out. Triangular designs encircled it.

"Of course. That's the point." Leaning over, Karakul stared.

With another pinch of powder, light from the moon illuminated the inscription inside the band. Dash held it up. "It says, 'Rich friends are an elaborate veneer that can mask the flaws within.'"

"Ah, this could be very good. We will be meeting with very wealthy, powerful people tomorrow, to sell our wares. What does the other one say?"

The next band had cheerful faces engraved around the outside. Dash read, "'Humor may conquer enemies, but deep character doesn't change with a laugh'."

A broad smile crossed Karakul's face, and torchlight danced in his dark eyes. "This is perfect. Just the help we'll need for tomorrow. Are you ready to bring in lots of gold?"

"Of course. Do you think we can?"

"Put the moon bands on, boy, and we may see wonders."

Dash slipped the two new bands onto his wrist. They shrunk a little, but still felt big. The original band fit more snugly.

"Don't worry, you'll grow into them." Karakul squeezed Dash's shoulder. "Now, off to bed. We have a big day ahead of us." He handed over the moon box. "Put this in a safe place. Follow Serik over there, and he'll show you to a bedroom."

The servant, standing quietly by the top of the stairs, bowed.

Dash took the box and started down the steps. The rush of wings caught his attention, and he turned for one last glance at the roof. Karakul had disappeared. A large black bird rose into the night air with a caw.

Taking several steps back up, Dash scanned the rooftop but saw no sign of his master. He shrugged and headed down again.

The moon bands weighed on his arm, and a little of the old restlessness gnawed at his mind, but he pushed it aside. If Karakul's hopes for tomorrow worked out, the farm would be a distant memory.

He smiled to himself. What would Dalan say about his success? He'd wait until he was as rich and powerful as Karakul. Then he'd show the whole family he'd been right to leave that pointless drudgery behind.

Serik led him to a comfortable room with a large window and a soft rug on the floor. Weariness descended like a thick blanket. Dash didn't bother washing up before collapsing on the wide, canopied bed.

The sun rose with an orange swath across the sky. Dash rolled out of bed, smoothed his clothes, and swung his cloak over his shoulders. The weight of it sent a thrill of expectation through him. He fingered the embroidered black birds and thought about all the times he'd seen black birds lately. In fact, whenever Karakul disappeared there seemed to be one around.

Glancing in the mirror over the dresser, he noticed his hair sticking out in multiple directions. After draping his cloak and tunic over a chair, he washed, combed his hair, and cleaned his teeth. The mirror told him his hair had improved, so he pulled a clean tunic from his pack and settled the cloak back on his shoulders.

"Much better," he said to himself as he examined his reflection. "Now I'm ready for the market."

"Boy!" Karakul called from below.

"Yes?" Dash hurried out to the top of the stairs.

"Hurry, boy. The Master of Acquisition will meet us in the market very soon."

Dash rushed down the stairs. "I'm ready." Catching the bread Karakul tossed to him, he followed his master out the front door to where the wagon waited.

"We'll have more to eat once the market is in full swing."

Dash nodded and climbed onto the seat.

The trip to the market took only a few minutes. Karakul's servants struggled along behind, carrying poles, canvas, and rope. Karakul yelled directions and insults, and in no time, the servants had an elaborate tent set up in a secluded corner of the market square.

Karakul dug through the trunks. "Now, where is that jeweled necklace we picked up in Bura?"

"I believe it's in this one." Dash opened another large trunk. He dumped several bundles on the ground before pulling out the gray box that held the necklace.

"Ah, very good. That's what we will offer this morning."

A trumpet sounded from across the now bustling plaza. Dash peeked out between the tent flaps and saw an enormous square umbrella moving across the market toward them. Four servants held up the supporting poles, and under it strode a man with a billowing red cloak. His golden trousers and an extravagantly embroidered tunic sparkled in the morning sun. Feathers of every color fluttered in his hair.

A haughty smile twitched across his face as he stared at Dash.

Quickly closing the tent flaps, Dash held them tight in his hand. "Someone's coming."

Karakul kept digging in one of the trunks. "Yes. That would be His Excellency, the Lord Temir, Master of Acquisition. He collects objects of magical power for the High Prince Kasiret. A most remarkable and influential man."

"Who? The prince or the acquisition guy?"

"Both, actually." He closed the trunk and moved toward Dash. "But I was speaking of Prince Kasiret, who is powerful beyond imagination and worthy to rule this fair land. I hope you will have the chance to meet him someday. Place your words carefully with Lord Temir, and you may."

Right outside, the trumpet blared again, loud and piercing.

Karakul tugged the tent flaps from Dash's tight grip and opened one side. A servant opened the other.

Dash stumbled back.

"Please come in, Your Excellency." Karakul bowed. "We have been expecting you."

"I should hope so." Lord Temir advanced into the tent. "And I hope you won't be wasting my time with worthless trinkets."

Karakul bowed again.

Unsure what to do next, Dash picked up the gray box and turned with a bow to the Master of Acquisition. Unfamiliar words tumbled out of his mouth. "I doubt your lordship will find this trinket a waste of time. It circles the imagination and glows with potential that only a fat donkey could overlook." Heat burned in his cheeks. Had he just called Lord Temir a fat donkey?

A faint flicker of a smile etched up Lord Temir's face.

Dash shifted his feet. "Since you are far from being a fat donkey, would you like to see it?"

Eyes wide with horror, Karakul glared at Dash.

But Lord Temir chuckled. "And who are you, brazen boy, to talk to the highest counselor to Prince Kasiret like that?"

"Just a farm boy, who has sojourned with the queen of Talsar and found her to be an uninspired flat cake who rules a boring kingdom."

A pang of disloyalty shot through him. He really did like the queen, but the fun of entertaining this powerful courtier overcame his guilt.

Lord Temir's laughter filled the tent. "I like you, boy.

Now, show me what's in the box, and I will tell you who the fat donkey is. If you... well, let's see this trinket of yours first."

Not quite understanding where the words had come from or why Lord Temir found them so funny, Dash opened the box. A faint glow shone out from the two new moon bands on his wrist. They had shrunk slightly, fitting his wrist better.

"Ah." Lord Temir picked up the necklace with a smile. "Now this is more like it, Karakul. Where did you find this?"

Karakul bowed. "In Bura, my lord. I acquired it at great cost, knowing you might be interested."

"Of course I'm interested." He fingered the necklace and held it up to the sunlight streaming into the tent. The cobalt center jewel nestled into the palm of his hand glinted. It's beautiful, but is it really... as fascinating as you say?"

Karakul stood off to the side, his hands clenched together.

Lord Temir fixed him in a hard stare. "I'll make you an offer. But I will need to examine this back at the palace before I part with any gold."

Two tiny black birds engraved on the clasp of the necklace caught Dash's eye. "My lord, we would accept no less than fifty golds for the worthless trinket before it leaves my master's tent, or I am the fat donkey."

"And I would be the fat donkey to accept your offer." Lord Temir laughed. "But since I like you, I will give you forty-nine, and let you have the honor of being the donkey. But surely you'd be a scrawny one."

Dash looked at Karakul, who nodded vigorously.

"Very well." Lord Temir snapped his fingers.

A servant pulled out a large money pouch.

The clink of coins made Dash's insides dance. With some effort, he kept his face from showing his excitement as the

Master of Acquisition counted the golds.

"Better keep that boy close." Lord Temir handed the pile to Karakul "He may bring you fortune of one sort or another."

Glancing down, he reached for Dash's wrist. "There is more to you than I expected. Moon bands. Of a very interesting variety."

Flipping open a large rounded ring on his finger, Lord Temir pressed it against Dash's forehead. "To bring you good luck."

The ring stung his skin and the hair on his arms stood up. He wanted to rub his forehead, but kept his hands down. Giving offence now might reduce the number of golds in Karakul's hands.

Lord Temir turned to leave, swinging his heavy cloak behind him. "We may meet again, boy. You intrigue me."

Chapter 14
Where?

Ariyuna blinked into the dim light. She lay on a hard, wooden bench, barely wide enough for her. Bookshelves stuffed with old volumes lined the room, and filtered sunlight streamed down in a dusty shaft from a tiny window by the ceiling.

A nasty taste lingered in her mouth.

Using her tunic, she wiped powder from her lips and grimaced as bitterness assaulted her tongue.

Where was she? She tried to sit up, but a throbbing headache forced her back down onto the solid bench.

Rubbing her forehead, she attempted again, more slowly, and this time managed to sit. The room spun, then came back into focus.

A wave of fright coursed through her. She reached for her wrist and felt the comfort of the Itgel. At least she still had the bracelet. Its three stones glowed and swirled in the semidarkness.

Grains of sand had wedged themselves between and around the stones. She rubbed each one clean, remembering the lessons that had brought the stones.

The green one came from the shores of Lake Kassar after a wild ride on turtles. The violent storm over the lake had made it hard to trust Elch, but she'd gone anyway. She smiled.

Els Edzyn had given her the purple one after a long, hard trek across the plain when no one wanted to follow her. The sand lord had complained bitterly about traveling in a large flower pot to meet up with her. Her smile widened.

Red pulsations coming from the third stone brought back painful memories. War with Zovlon. Beltreg's death and the loss of so many others. Her smile faded.

Then she remembered that Elch had been a faithful companion. And through the fish, she had found strength to face each hardship. She reminded herself that this wouldn't be any different, but tension still squeezed her shoulders as she scanned her surroundings.

The stuffiness of the room pressed in.

Thirst nagged and her tongue stuck to the roof of her mouth.

She noticed a pitcher and cup sitting on a stand at the end of the bench, and scooted over.

Bitterness from the remaining powder on her lips flowed with the water as she drank, but the wetness soothed her parched throat.

With a creak, the door on the far side opened. A man entered. Ornate jewels flashed on his fingers, and a gold clasp fastened his long, black cloak at his shoulder. He stood proud and unyielding. "I see you've finally managed to wake up."

The deep voice sounded vaguely familiar and unpleasant. But Ariyuna couldn't place it. "What do you want with me? And why are you keeping me?"

"Questions, questions. But you will find few answers. I am Prince Kasiret, and you are in no position to make demands, my dear."

The room wobbled. Ariyuna gripped the edge of the bench and stared at him. The words "my dear" chafed. Formless fear and anger churned inside. *Elch,* she called out in her mind. *What do I do now?*

Be still.

Ariyuna wanted to say more, to spit out strong words that would chase away the daunting man standing before her. Instead, she swallowed the venomous phrases that rose in her throat. Where did these emotions come from?

"May I interrupt?" Another elaborately dressed man entered and bowed low.

The prince swung around. "Ah, Lord Temir. What do you have for me today? I hope it's something interesting."

"For you, Prince Kasiret, I have purchased a jeweled necklace." The man bowed again. "It's not much, but I thought you might be interested. The fool who sold it to me had only an inkling of its value, but the young boy with him..." His gaze intensified. "Well, he was wiser, and looked a little... like you." He stared hard at Ariyuna. "This boy did not appear to be from around here. Talsar, perhaps."

Renewed pounding squeezed Ariyuna's head. How could she be outside Talsar? She had just been in Temyulun with the queen.

Lord Kasiret laughed. "So you bought these jewels from Karakul?"

"Yes, my lord."

"Very good. The boy is far more important and valuable than this trinket. Keep an eye on him. But I am curious to see the adornment you've obtained. Shall we go?"

"I have it in my examination room." Lord Temir bowed.

With a swish of his cloak, Prince Kasiret swept past Lord Temir, out the door.

The other man followed, flashing a quick, curious glance toward Ariyuna.

Pushing up with her hands, Ariyuna tried to rise. Her voice came as a croak. "Wait!"

The door closed with a thud, followed by a click of the

lock.

She slumped back onto the bench, letting out a deep breath. Questions bombarded her mind. Had Lord Temir been talking about Dash? Where could she possibly be? The men were dressed like the ambassadors from Endurek. No, that would be impossible.

Her mind drifted back to the palace in Temyulun. The last thing she remembered was standing in the throne room. The queen had asked her to take a closer look at the staff of the ancient kings.

"So you think there's something more to this staff?" Ariyuna asked.

The queen turned it in her hands. "Yes. We have two of the three gifts from the Storyteller, the Itgel and the Enk Taivaan. But we don't have the Zavtai. I had a strange dream the other day that the Zavtai took the form of a stick, and I thought of the staff. I don't see how it could be. But no one seems to know what the Zavtai looks like or what it does. Not even Gan. So I suppose it's possible."

Ariyuna took the staff from Baiyanarah. "This is when we could use Dalan to help solve the mystery." She studied it and noticed that some of the raised designs wiggled. At the bottom, a ring separated the rounded base from the rest of the staff. With a grunt, she twisted the base... and woke up in this stuffy library room.

Where could the staff be now? Maybe this Prince Kasiret knew. But would he tell her?

She drew in another deep breath. Her head didn't hurt quite as much now.

Motes of dust danced in the thin shaft of light that illuminated the faded carpet. Very slowly, she stood and shuffled to the door. The lock held tight.

Keeping one hand on the wall for support, she wandered over to one of the bookshelves. The leather cover of an old volume crumbled when she pulled it out. Carefully, she placed it back. The next one looked newer. She let it fall open in her arms. Ancient writing scrawled across the pages. From the few words she could make out, the book held notes about politics and kingdom rules. This must be a palace of sorts, but where?

After pulling out another tome, she found records of court cases from hundreds of years ago. Several more books held similar records from the land of Teagen. This must be Endurek.

Elch, what now?

Follow, the fish replied.

An uncomfortable tingling sensation traveled down Ariyuna's arms and intensified in her fingers. When she held a hand up to the book bindings, the tingling deepened. *Is there one you want me to look at?*

The fish didn't reply, so Ariyuna let her fingers drift lightly along the spines of the books.

She found a dusty one about V'Arah that reminded her of home. Some of the text sounded similar to the Onon Book, but with subtle differences.

She moved her fingers farther along the shelf, letting them bump from one book to the next. The unpleasant tingling grew stronger and then ebbed away.

Closer to the window, the feeling diminished significantly. Ariyuna tried moving her hand back along the book spines, but the tingling returned.

Moving upward made it almost go away. She then found a spot where the tingling disappeared completely. A large book with a gold title caught her eye. She reached for it, but the book sent a sharp shock up her arm.

Not that one, I'm guessing.

Elch remained silent.

The one beside it also gave her a shock.

Then she noticed a slim, brown booklet sandwiched deep between the two bigger volumes. Carefully, she reached out a finger and hooked the top of the binding with her nail.

Slowly, the booklet slid out. She kept expecting another shock, but none came.

The cover had small gold letters that read: *Secrets of the Zavtai: Gift of the Storyteller.*

Ariyuna's heart beat hard in her chest as she stared at the little book. Rubbing her finger along the top, she took off a layer of dust.

"How did you know?" she asked aloud.

But instead of Elch answering, a deep voice behind her said, "How did I know? Because I told my servants to bring you here."

Chapter 15
A Stinky Way In

Muddy, bruised, and discouraged, Dalan flopped down onto his bed in the inn. "So, how do we get Ari out?"

Tabin muttered something from the bed on the other side of the room, and Gan slumped into a chair and groaned, "I have not a rat's toenail of an idea, but we must find some way to slip our sweet rose leaf out from that smoker palace."

From the bed post, Moochir blinked into the room. "I did find the way in, indeeeed. Pit. Pit."

"Yes, you did, you hairish warthog." Gan scrunched up his face. "And in the process, you made a ground pigger out of Dalan."

Moochir's face disappeared, and Dalan didn't bother to look where the woodpit had gone. Every part of him hurt, especially his face where the bars had dug in. He knew he needed to get up and wash, and if he didn't do it soon, he'd never move again.

With a grunt, he heaved himself up and staggered to the washroom with an armful of clean clothes and a towel.

But when he arrived, a wooden nose stuck out of the mirror frame.

"What now?"

"I have more ideas. Pit. Pit."

"Like what?" Not sure whether he really wanted to hear these ideas, Dalan threw his clean clothes onto a bench.

"There are many servants in that house. Many, indeeeed. And they come and go without anyone bothering about them. Pit. Pit."

Dalan filled the large wash tub with hot water, made a pile of his muddy clothes, and eased himself in. Cuts all over his body protested, but he sunk down into the water anyway. "Go on."

"I also know where the secret door to the palace is located. Pit, pit. I could lead you there. If you dress as servants, you may get in unnoticed."

"Why are you helping us?" Dalan reached for the soap.

"Why, indeeeed?"

Squinting at the mirror, Dalan couldn't see Moochir's face anymore. He closed his eyes and soaked in the soothing warmth of the bath. After a good scrub, he looked for the pit but still couldn't find him, so he dressed and headed back to the room.

Tabin sat in a cushioned chair with his head resting back and his eyes closed. Gan lay stretched out on the floor, staring at the ceiling.

"Gan." Dalan rubbed his wet hair with a towel and sat down on the edge of his bed. "Moochir thinks he can get us into the palace."

"Ah, the woodpit wants to draw us into another swiller pail."

"I don't know. When I talked with him in the wash room, he seemed... well, willing to help even if he didn't want to."

One of Moochir's eyes peeped out of a dresser handle. The other appeared on the handle below.

"Don't trust a woodpit. They are as polished as an old maid's broom handle and sharper than chicken teeth."

"But what choice do we have?" Tabin sat up a bit. "We do need to help Ariyuna."

"Very well." Gan sighed. "Did the burnt splinter have any ideas bigger than a flea pick?"

"He said we should disguise ourselves as servants, and that he could lead us to the door into the palace."

Sitting up on the edge of the chair, Tabin scratched his head with both hands. "I need to clean up, but it may be worth a try. Gan, do you think you could get us some servant's clothing?"

"With a few fing cloppers, I think that could happen. You go find yourself under all that duck dust, and I will find zazzer duds. Moochir?"

The woodpit appeared in the bed post again. "Pit. Pit."

"Ah, there you are." Gan narrowed his eyes. "What kind of flip servants do we need to correspond to?"

"You are not as kind as Dalan. Indeeeed."

Dalan sat forward. "Please, Moochir. If you don't help us, this may end in disaster."

"For you, Dalan. Pit. Pit. I will do this for you because... because I just might possibly like you. Pit."

He turned both eyes to stare at Gan. "Fish. Pit. Pit. Fish delivery, indeeeed. But you must wait until tomorrow. There are no clothes to buy in the middle of the night. Deliveries are made in the afternoon, and in the afternoon, the master of the house will be gone. Pit. Pit." His face disappeared.

"Thank you, Moochir," Dalan called, but heard no reply.

The soft bed covers encased Dalan as he stretched out. He closed his eyes and rested while Tabin and Gan bathed. But even though his body longed for rest, thoughts of his sister in the hands of a sorcerer kept him from sleep for a long time.

From the sunlight streaming in the window, Dalan could tell the day had begun long ago. His muscles, stiff and sore, protested every move. Tabin sat by the fireplace, reading.

"Where's Gan, and what time is it?" Dalan rolled out of bed.

"Gan's off to buy our disguises, and it's lunch time. There's food over on that small table, if you're hungry."

Dalan dressed and had a bite to eat before Gan returned with a bag of clothes and three baskets of fish.

"What *is* that smell?" Tabin sniffed the air and scrunched up his face. "Really, Gan? You had to get rotting fish?"

"I was in a hipper hurry. And they were as cheap as pebbles."

Leaning over a basket, Dalan gagged. "Can we at least put them out in the hall?"

"If you insist." Gan laughed. "They can't be older than a grasshopper's span."

Dalan tried on the clothes Gan had bought. "Even the servants here dress better than we do." He glanced down at the tunic embroidered with gold leaves.

"I have also found slap slippers." Gan tossed a pair of shoes with curly toes in Dalan's direction. "Well, let's go see if we can angle our way into the point palace."

Tabin dressed. "Where's Moochir?"

"Over here." The pit peeked out of the door just above the round handle, giving him an "o" for a mouth. "You might want to hurry. Pit. Another guest has just descended the stairs to complain about your fish."

With the baskets, they followed Moochir out of the inn, along several alleys, and between elegant homes.

Finally, Moochir stopped at the small service entrance to the fancy house just off the market square.

"Are you sure there's a way into the palace from here?" A tinged of tension rippled through Dalan.

"Indeeeed."

Gan knocked.

The door opened and a servant bowed, motioning them to enter. "You know where to go?"

Gan and Tabin both nodded and entered.

From the far side of the hall, the faint outline of Moochir's face winked out of a wooden pillar. Gan headed toward him.

The servant left down a different hallway, muttering something about displeasing the master with decaying slop.

"Well, well." Gan hoisted his basket of fish onto his head, wafting the nasty odor into the hall that had smelled like spring flowers a moment before.

When he reached the pillar, Dalan couldn't see the woodpit, but he could hear footsteps echoing down the corridor.

He slipped into a small, curtained alcove beside Gan and Tabin.

Peeking around the corner he glimpsed several servants walking toward them. "Wouldn't it be better to pretend we're delivering fish and not hide, or get rid of the fish and just hide?" In the small space, the smell of the rotting catch instantly became overwhelming. "This is going to be hard to explain if they find us."

"Too late now." Gan whispered. "We've crisscrossed our donkeys and ducks, so we'll just have to hope for good turnips."

The footsteps drew nearer and slowed. "Master won't be back until meal time," one said. "And he'll be hungry after a day at the market. We need to have plenty of food for the boy as well."

The maid with a dirty apron nodded. "Yes, Overseer. That shouldn't be a problem. Where did the boy come from, anyway?"

"Talsar, I suppose. His clothes are quite boring, and if I'm not mistaken, his features are like those of the Gahzar tribe near Belgutai. I believe that's where the master went on his last journey."

"Dash?" Dalan whispered.

"Shhh." Tabin pinned Dalan against the wall with one arm.

The man stopped and sniffed the air. "What have those mangy dogs been up to today? The house smells like rotten fish. These servants have to be watched constantly. See that the stench is gone before the master gets home."

The maid bobbed her head again.

The two passed by the alcove and on into another room. Tabin's arm still pressed Dalan against the wall.

"But they know about Dash," he hissed.

"One rescue at a time. Where's Moochir?"

Dalan pulled the curtain open enough to see out, then pointed to an ear on the doorpost of an unlit stairwell leading down in a tight spiral. "Over there."

The footsteps faded, and Gan scurried toward the stairs with Dalan and Tabin following.

Heading down the darkened steps, Dalan heard Moochir. "Best close the door at the top. Pit. Pit."

Dalan climbed back up, hauling his basket that dripped fish slime down his leg, and closed the door. "Now I can't see." Groping around, he found the hand rail and cautiously headed back down into the blackness.

"There is some light at the bottom. Yes, indeeeed," came

from somewhere below.

Dalan muttered to himself, "I could probably follow the stench if my basket didn't smell just as bad."

"Do not disparage the smackers." Gan's voice echoed in the tight stairwell. "They bought us entrance into this camel's pouch of a home." Several loud thumps followed. "Stumbling dag backers!"

"Are you all right?" Tabin asked.

"As good as a flying pancake. And there is a little light coming from down this corridor."

They reached the bottom. A bracket in the wall held a very small torch that sputtered its feeble light into a stone passageway.

"Pit. Pit. Not much wood down here." Moochir's face blinked out of the torch's handle. "Go down this hall, and I will meet you at the next light."

"But what about Dash?" Dalan protested.

Tabin pulled the torch out of its holder. "Ariyuna is in greater danger right now. We can come back for Dash, if that's even who they were talking about. There are many boys in Belgutai." He headed down the narrow hallway.

From up ahead, Moochir called back, "I smell enchantments. Indeeeed. I'll make one more jump ahead, but watch out for-" A shock of splinters stood out from his face in mid-air before he disappeared.

"Ooof!" Gan yelped. "Bang smack it! That's a solid undetectable fortification."

Dalan caught up to where Gan stood with his hands placed against the invisible barrier.

"How do we get through that?" Tabin kicked at the wall.

Gan rubbed his forehead. "I don't know." He closed his eyes. "With weasel dust, I believe. Yes, weasels. Definitely. But not dust. No. Yes. No, powder. Weasel powder."

"What's the difference?" Dalan pressed both hands on the unseen wall.

Gan's eyes fluttered open. "Too turtle dawdling to explain now." He dug in his satchel and pulled out a small pouch. Steam rose as he threw deep red powder against the barrier.

Soon a small hole appeared. A faint brown blur slipped though, and Moochir blinked out of an extinguished torch farther down the passage.

The hole widened.

"That should prosper our travels well enough." Gan ducked through.

Tabin glanced over at Dalan and then back at the small hole. "Um, Gan. We're not as compact as you."

"Jamming flap skinks. I'm so very sorry." He threw on more powder, making the opening bigger.

Once on the other side, Tabin ventured cautiously forward. "We'd better be very careful. I doubt that's the only enchantment."

"What's that?" Dalan pointed ahead to what looked like a large puddle.

"Just splisher drainage. Nothing to stretch your bean about." Gan barged ahead. As his foot hit the water, he let out a yelp and dropped feet first into a wet sink hole. As his head disappeared, fish from his basket bobbed to the surface along with a shower of bubbles.

"Gan!" Dalan peered into the pool. "Gan!" But the small man and his basket had vanished.

Chapter 16
The Best Day Ever

Dash dug a hand mirror out of a trunk and examined his forehead where Lord Temir had pressed his ring. The small inky mark of a black bird adorned his skin. Outside the tent, the noise of the market hummed on.

Karakul sat in a corner, counting the money again. The clinking of coins blended with his mirth. "Well done, boy! Very well done." He grabbed a large handful of golds and held them out. "For you. I only paid two silvers for the trinket, so here's your share of the profits."

Dash took the coins and added them to his money pouch. The fullness sent a thrill through him. "Maybe we can do well all day if you'll let me lead." He twisted the new moon bands on his wrist.

"Most certainly. And with Lord Temir's mark, you should do exceptionally well." He pulled out a bag of fruit, rolls and cheese. "Here's some more breakfast, if you're hungry."

"So, what will we try to sell next?" Dash bit into a pear.

Karakul shrugged. "I think you'd better decide that yourself." He glanced out over the market and groaned. "Oh, no. Here comes Akmat. Be careful. He has cheated me too many times to count."

The moon band with happy faces tightened a little on Dash's wrist, sending a surge of confidence through him. "Don't worry. I'll talk with him." He quickly swallowed his bite and set the pear down.

"Be very careful, boy, or Akmat will leave with your money and your shoes, and you'll still think you owe him something."

Dash nodded, opened a trunk and dug through it. He found two large, matching coin pouches, delicately inlaid with gold and silver designs. Placing the bags on top of the trunk, he turned to see Akmat standing at the entrance.

The man's lanky arms moved erratically as he strode into the tent, and he almost tripped over a small trunk. "Karakul, you dog. I have not had the pleasure of doing business with you lately. Where have you been?"

Karakul scowled and clenched his teeth, but said nothing.

Hiding one pouch in his hand behind his back, Dash stepped forward. "You must be Akmat. I have heard of you and your skill at procuring bargains."

With a laugh, Akmat put his hands on his hips and tilted his head. "Then you have heard well, boy. And who are you?"

"I am Karakul's voice and hands today. Beyond that, you need not worry about an insignificant boy like me." He fingered the pouch behind his back. One of the moon bands tingled slightly. Dash smiled. "I think I have something that will interest you. A fair piece of work at a fair price on a fair day."

A reluctant smile twitched at the corner of Akmat's mouth. "Why would I have any interest in what you have to offer, boy? But since you have Lord Temir's mark, I'll listen." He shifted his feet awkwardly but kept his eye on Dash.

A small crowd gathered to watch the transaction.

"Ah. It will delight you. Unfortunately, it will cost you

one silver to play the game." This time Dash smiled.

A frown settled on Akmat's face. But he dug a small, brown coin pouch out of his pocket and threw a silver onto a trunk before sliding it back into his pocket.

"Very good, my fair sir." Behind his back, Dash slipped the new coin bag up inside his sleeve. Then he quickly reached out and plunged his hand into the pocket of Akmat's cloak.

"What-"

"Shhh." Dash held a finger to his lips and pretended to dig around. He waggled his hand a moment. Then, with exaggerated movements, he extracted the new bag, along with Akmat's small coin pouch. This he quickly hid in a pocket.

Shaking his head, Dash stared at Akmat. "Not good. You have already stolen my wares." He held up the fancy pouch. "The price of silence will cost you a gold, unless you'd like me to call for the palace guards." Dash scratched at his forehead, right beside the imprint of the black bird.

The watching crowd burst into gasps of amazement.

Akmat glanced up at Dash's forehead. "What... how... I didn't steal..." He surveyed the laughing crowd and glared at Dash.

Waving the inlaid coin pouch in front of Akmat, Dash snapped his finger. "This fine bag is of a much larger size than your stingy little one." He pulled out Akmat's small pouch and then tossed it back to the astonished courtier.

The crowd roared with laughter, and Dash couldn't help smiling. "For only two golds, this new pouch would brag of your abilities much better than the old brown sack you now carry. The one that is barely willing to stay with you."

Turning swiftly, Dash grabbed the second one off the trunk. "And for the pair, I would pare the price down to only three gold coins." He reached sideways to where the fruit sat. "I would also throw in this delicious juicy pear."

The crowd hooted and started chanting, "Buy them both! Buy them both!"

Akmat looked around. A bewildered scowl dug into his brow. Grabbing both of the glittering bags, he flung three golds onto the trunk.

The crowd cheered.

"Just one moment, my good Akmat." Dash leaned closer and whispered. "You also owe me a gold for silence. You wouldn't want to be branded a thief."

Akmat flung another gold onto a trunk and stormed out, yelling back as he went, "I'll make you pay for this, boy."

Half of the crowd followed Akmat, while the rest swarmed around the tent, wanting to buy whatever Dash pulled out of the trunks.

After half an hour of frantic bargaining, the crowd thinned.

Karakul slumped down onto a trunk with a big grin on his face. "I haven't had such a good day in all my life. And it's only midmorning." He held out another large handful of golds to Dash. "Now you are the one that needs a new coin pouch."

Digging in a trunk, he pulled out one larger and more ornate than those Dash had sold to Akmat. "For you. May the rest of the day be even more profitable."

"Thanks." He emptied the coins into the new pouch and turned to greet the next wave of customers that had heard of his encounter with Akmat.

Just as the bargaining reached a fevered pitch, a very well-dressed woman pushed her way to the front, followed by several servants. One held an umbrella over her, and another waved a large red and green feathered fan. Several more waited nearby.

"Ah, Lady Idana." Karakul rose and bowed. "You are

truly more beautiful than the sun today."

The lady nodded her head. "I have heard of the excitement you're creating, and I've come to see for myself." She glanced at Dash. "Your assistant has gained notoriety and prestige." Pointing to the black bird on her own forehead, she winked very slightly in Dash's direction. "So, do you have anything for me today? I would love to be counted as part of this day's thrills."

Dash stepped forward and bowed. "I believe I can find something for you, but you must play my game to earn the privilege of buying it."

"I don't..." Karakul began, but then smiled at Lady Idana. "Go ahead, boy."

"One moment, my lady." Dash dug through several trunks before emerging with a complicated hat adorned with a pink and green feather and purple ribbons.

"Oooh! I love it. How much do you want for it?"

"Not as much as you may think, but first you must play my game."

The lady smiled and wiggled in anticipation. "Very well. I do like games."

A cry rang out through the market place. "The guards are coming!"

Many of the merchants began frantically packing up.

Lady Idana leaned over to Dash and pressed a small purse into his hand. "I'll take the hat and play your game another time."

Across the plaza, Dash could see Akmat scurrying in front of a line of guards headed right toward him.

"Very good, my lady." Dash bowed. "I look forward to seeing you again." He handed her the hat and quickly shoved the purse deep into the far corner of a trunk along with his new one.

He looked up just in time to see a captain of the palace guard burst into the tent waving a short sword. The moon bands on his wrist tingled.

Chapter 17
Frippery with Dinner

Ariyuna whipped around at the sound of the imposing voice, slipping the thin book about the Zavtai behind her back.

The handsome Prince Kasiret bowed. "And now I'm-"

"I'm here to meet the new visitor." A piercing giggle came from a girlish young woman in a large, ridiculous hat covered in purple ribbons. It's pink and green feather fluttered as she moved.

A maid stood beside her, suppressing a silly grin behind her hand.

"Be still, Lady Idana."

But the young woman gushed on. "When Prince Kasiret told me he had a beautiful prisoner hidden away in his private library, I just couldn't resist a peek." She winked at Ariyuna.

"I came across Lady Idana and changed my mind about your accommodations." Prince Kasiret inspected Ariyuna from head to toe. "You won't be staying here. Lady Idana will help you prepare for dinner, and tomorrow is the tournament."

Turning to the lady, he continued, "She will need to visit the wardrobe. I'm sure you will find something suitable for dinner. And she can stay there tonight."

Ariyuna scowled. Would they leave her in a closet? The library would be much more interesting. *Elch*, she called out in her mind.

Go, came the faint reply.

Really? A wardrobe?

The fish didn't answer.

"Oops!" The maid dropped her fan, then accidentally kicked it toward the door.

Ariyuna took advantage of the giggling distraction to work the book under her tunic and into the waistband of her trousers. Forcing a smile, she stepped forward.

"That's more like it." The prince held out his hand. "First we will get you out of those drab clothes and into something more appropriate for the court." He turned to Lady Idana. "And don't forget gloves."

His charming smile melted a sliver of the resistance within Ariyuna, but she pretended not to see his offered hand.

"One more thing, Lady Idana." The prince withdrew his outstretched hand.

The giggling returned. "Yes, Your Highness?"

"I need to see Lord Temir about a necklace. I'm trusting you to escort our visitor to the wardrobe."

"Me? By myself?"

"Yes. I think you can handle that without getting distracted. After all, dressing up is your specialty."

Lady Idana blushed and nodded. "Of course. Shall I return her here once she's dressed for dinner?"

"No. Bring her to my dining room. And don't lose her, or you will lose your head along with that... hat you just bought. Remember, she's still a prisoner. But as long as you keep her within sight or in the wardrobe, I don't mind."

"You noticed my hat!" She leaned over and whispered to Ariyuna, "I got it from the new boy wizard in the market."

She raised her voice slightly. "He outsmarted Akmat and has Lord Temir's mark of the black bird on his forehead, like mine." She casually brushed her hair back to reveal the mark.

With a giggle and an iron grip, Lady Idana seized Ariyuna's hand and dragged her along corridors, up stairways, and through rooms with walls inlaid in gold. The maid scurried behind.

Eventually, Ariyuna entered what appeared to be a dressing room. The enormous space held more clothes than the market in Belgutai. Rack after rack filled the entire space.

With a sigh, Ariyuna turned to face the sea of glittering, shimmering garments. "This is worse than when we first arrived in Temyulun," she mumbled to herself.

The maid bowed. "I'll go fetch some help." She hurried out of the room.

Lady Idana grinned and squealed as she ran back and forth, pulling out possibilities for Ariyuna to try on. Dresses, tunics, and hats fluttered to the floor, while a pile built up on a sofa by the fireplace.

Soon three maids assisted Lady Idana, but even with hurried steps, they failed to keep up with the growing mess.

With difficulty, Ariyuna managed to keep the Itgel hidden from the lady and the maids as she tried on the first dress. Then she spotted a wide, lacy garter. Grabbing it off the armrest of the sofa, she slipped it onto her wrist over the bracelet.

Nothing good would come from them seeing or touching the bracelet. If it burned someone, she could be thrown in the dungeon. Did they even have a dungeon here? Her underlying mistrust of the prince vouched for its existence.

The sun sank low in the sky before Lady Idana finally voiced her satisfaction.

Ariyuna stood before the mirror wearing a pink gown covered in dark red lace roses. Green ribbons drizzled from the shoulders and waist. Her hair, piled on her head, had several red feathers dangling down her back.

"Well, what do you think, my dear?"

Ariyuna sighed for the hundredth time that afternoon. "It's amazing." She forced a smile. "Can we be done now?"

"Most certainly. And we need to head to dinner. Oh, I can't wait to show you off."

"Is this how you treat prisoners here?"

"Of course not. You're not really a prisoner. Well, maybe just a bit." She lowered her voice. "I know your little secret. You're actually a princess from Talsar, and you're an honored guest." Lady Idana sighed deeply. "I'm hoping I can get Prince Kasiret to let me dine with you. He's so handsome."

Ariyuna opened her mouth to protest, then decided it might be better to play along. "Do you have somewhere I could put my old clothes?"

"Oh, just leave them there." She waggled her hand toward the sofa and wrinkled her nose. "I don't know why you want them. I could have the maids burn them for you."

"No. I'd rather keep them for now. If you don't mind." Ariyuna scooped up the clothes Ma had lovingly made, with the slender book hidden inside. She barely had time to tuck the bundle down beside the sofa before Lady Idana grabbed her hand.

"Oh! I forgot to give you gloves."

A maid ran to fetch a pair, and Lady Idana shoved them on Ariyuna's hands.

"What's this doing here?" She yanked off the garter that had slid up her arm ahead of the advancing glove. "Oh, never mind. Come along or we'll be late."

She whipped back around toward the maids. "You three. Clean up in here. But don't touch the prison clothes." She lowered her voice to a loud whisper. "You don't want to upset the princess."

The three girls nodded and bowed.

Nervousness grew as Ariyuna traveled through the enormous palace. She tucked the Itgel farther under her glove as she hurried along. *Elch,* she called out. *I don't know if I can do this.*

In her mind, the fish sang a simple song:

Don't be afraid,
Though the river runs wild,
Though the water draws nigh,
I'll be with you...

Ariyuna smiled. *That's the first song you ever sang to me.* She remembered the cave under the Yuratag Mountains from her first journey. It seemed so long ago.

V'Arah does not change. The song is still true.

The doors to a small but extravagant dining room swung open. Soft candlelight glowed from golden chandeliers. Crisp white tablecloths covered the few, small round tables. The center one had two place settings.

Ariyuna took a deep breath and entered.

The prince stood in the middle with only servants waiting around the edges.

"Ah. You've arrived." Prince Kasiret came over to her and kissed her gloved hand. "I am delighted that you will dine with me tonight."

"But Prince Kasiret." Lady Idana flashed a beautiful smile. "You don't want to be stuck alone with a prisoner, and I was hoping I could dine with you as well."

"Be gone." The prince waved a hand at her.

Her smile faded, and her eyes darkened as she sulked

away.

"Come." Prince Kasiret led Ariyuna to a small table on the far side of the room.

Pulling out a chair for her, he bowed. "Please be seated. I want to dine with you alone tonight. I have learned a few things about you, and I have a great desire to learn more. You fascinate me, and I'm sure there are treasures to be discovered."

"But-"

"No arguing, my dear. I'm sure that our meeting was meant to be." He smiled as she sat down.

Again the words "my dear" grated.

A servant filled a glass and set it on the table.

She took a sip and watched the prince giving directions to the servants. On the surface, he appeared to be the epitome of perfect behavior, but something deep inside her prickled.

The drink held fruit juice of some sort, with a faint bitter tang she didn't recognize.

An image of Naiyan's face drifted through her mind before the room spun. She squeezed her eyes closed to clear her head, and when she opened them, she couldn't quite remember what she had been thinking.

Prince Kasiret sat across from her. "Are you well?"

"Yes, just a slight dizzy spell."

A servant placed a platter of delicious-smelling fare in front of her. Fluffy sweet rolls, steaming vegetables, and succulent meats sat next to plates of fruit and cakes.

"Go ahead. Don't be shy. I intend this to be a pleasant and informative evening." His hand rested heavily on hers and his voice gained an eager edge. "For both of us."

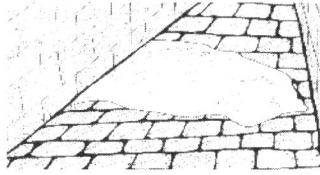

Chapter 18
Into the Palace

More bubbles popped around the floating, rotten fish as Dalan stared with horror into the depths of the enchanted pool. Where was Gan?

Next to him, Tabin dug in his pack and pulled out a thin strong rope. "As soon as I've changed into a cat, tie this around my waist."

The surface of the puddle rippled, and small splashes appeared.

"Wait." Dalan leaned over. "I think that's Gan's basket."

The edge emerged again, and Dalan could see a bulging eye along the rim.

"It's Moochir!"

Wooden lips sputtered in the muddy water. "Help! Pit. He's heavy!" A few incomprehensible words gurgled out before the basket dipped under.

Stretching out on the floor of the corridor, Dalan couldn't quite reach. "Almost."

He scooted farther over the puddle. "Hold my legs!"

Tabin knelt and pressed Dalan's legs onto the floor.

With the next reach, Dalan's fingertips brushed the edge, but the wicker slipped out of his reach. With the third stretch, he hooked the basket and pulled.

"Pit, pit. Indeeeed!" Moochir gasped.

"You weren't kidding. The basket *is* heavy." Dalan slithered away from the edge, barely able to hang on. He could see a white hand gripping the other side. "It must be Gan. Hurry!"

Tabin reached and together they heaved. "Something's pulling him downward."

"Yes. Indeeeed. I am a strong swimmer, but this enchantment is almost too much for even me. Spit, spit."

Gan's head emerged with a gasp, then went under.

Dalan staggered to his feet, his toes splashing the edge.

"Hold on!" Tabin shifted his hands to a better grip on the edge of the basket.

"Pull together," Tabin panted. "One, two, three!"

With another gasp for air, Gan reemerged only to go down once more.

"Again!" Tabin called.

Dalan's arm ached as he and Tabin fought against whatever was pulling Gan under.

After several more tugs, the basket, along with Gan, finally flopped onto the stone floor of the passageway.

Gan coughed and gagged, spitting water in all directions. "Swillering slog twisters," he gasped out. "I thought that sucker had my last shoe string." He eyed Moochir, whose face tipped sideways to drain water out of his spiked ear. "Thank you, pit master. Your spot of help saved this floundering rock dropper."

A faint smile tickled the pit's mouth. "Enough water for one day. Indeeeed. I will meet you at the next torch." His face faded.

Dalan glanced at the fish floating in the water. "Should we take them?"

"Might be good to keep up the disguise. Although, we're so wet now, we look less like servants delivering fish and more like fishermen who fell out of the boat." Tabin shoved a full, reeking basket toward Dalan with his foot. "For you."

"Thanks." Dalan grimaced. "Just what I wanted."

Gan staggered to his feet.

"Are you sure you're strong enough to keep going?" Dalan held out his hand to help the small man balance.

"As right as a rumpus dunker." Gan picked up his empty basket, staggered to the edge of the puddle, and bent over the water to scoop a few fish out.

Dalan grabbed his arm. "Careful!"

Straightening up, Gan peered into the bottom where several rotting fish lay. "This should do in a nip. I suppose we should bluster onward."

A narrow strip of stone flooring edged one side of the puddle. Dalan pressed himself against the wall and sidled past.

Following Moochir from one small torch to another, around numerous bends and twists, they finally stood before a peculiar wooden door.

"A fine pillius puzzle door." Gan set his basket down. "This may take a while."

"A puzzle door?" Dalan asked. "What's that?"

"Just what it sounds like." Tabin held his torch closer to the small wooden barrier covered in intricate carvings set on rounded discs. "You have to move the parts into just the right spot at just the right angle for it to open."

Each circle held a piece of a woodland scene. But certainly not in the right order. The sun was down in the left corner, while an upside down tree lay just above the handle under the shore of a lake. Empty spots lined the border.

Gan placed his hand on a clump of flowers along the edge and slid it sideways. Nothing happened. He grabbed a carved black bird, then slid it out and as far up as he could reach. Still nothing.

A wooden mouth protruded from the lake. "I could-"

"No!" Gan emptied his few fish into Dalan's basket, then flipped his own upside down and stood on it to reach the top.

"Let me help, I'm taller. You might not want to smash your basket." Dalan stood and put his hand on the bird. "Where do you want it?"

"Hurry." Tabin squinted back down the passage. "I don't want to get caught down here. Our fish won't be enough of an explanation."

After several minutes of frantically moving pieces around, Gan stepped back. "I just don't know. This cavernous enigma is bogging my stumper."

With a step back toward the door, Gan moved several more pieces. "Take that one to the pop top, Dalan."

Parts of the door twisted and slid as Gan tried one combination after another.

He placed his ear to the door.

"Hear anything?" Tabin asked.

"No. We could be at this for a gaggers stretch. But I suspect this wing pecker is flapperly vital." He grabbed the large carved black bird and shoved it to the left, then up.

Tabin sat with his back against the corridor wall and watched.

The stinky basket of fish next to Dalan made his stomach churn. He gave it a shove. Out of the corner of his eye, Dalan watched a cow's head morph into the pit's face.

"Hey, Moochir," Dalan called.

The pit faded and resurfaced in the frame.

"Is there any way you could go inside and figure out the combination? Please?"

"For you, Dalan, yes. But for anyone less polite, well, pit,

pit, indeeeed." His face disappeared.

Gan stepped back.

The torch in Dalan's hand burned low. Without light, they could be in trouble. He glanced at the back of his hand. Several years ago he'd received a thumbprint from Odgerel, the strange old woman from Dundaad. If he rubbed the spot, it would glow. But the print had faded away.

Muffled "pit, pit" sounds and "indeeeed" came from within the door. Then the carved discs slid up, down and sideways in rapid succession.

Gan stood back and stared. "Well, down my glog mixer. That pit is actually being helpful. Again."

"Not there. Pit." Moochir's muted voice came from the upper left corner. A moment later, petals of a flower changed into his eyes. "This is a hard one, but I'll get it." The eyes receded and the sun carving shot to the top.

A faint clunk echoed through the hall. The door now had a complete woodland scene with the sun shining down on the large black bird.

Moochir's lips protruded right above the handle. "Try now, Mr. Dalan."

Dalan took it and twisted. It budged slightly with a grind, then stuck. "I don't think we're quite there."

"Indeeeed." Moochir retreated. With another faint clunk, two small pieces at the bottom of the door traded places and the woodpit returned. "Try again. Pit."

Once more, Dalan turned the handle. This time it moved smoothly and, with a soft click, opened inward.

Giving the door a push, he stepped into a short stone tunnel with another door not far away. Thankfully, this one wasn't a puzzle.

His stomach tightened.

What if the puzzle was on the other side?

Dalan glanced back, grabbed his basket and walked to the next barrier followed by Gan and Tabin.

Moochir's face protruded from the center, large and unblinking.

"Thanks for solving the puzzle, Moochir. Is this one going to be a problem, too?"

The pit's face softened, and he blinked. "You are very polite, Mr. Dalan. I might like you. Pit, pit. And I haven't liked anyone in hundreds of years."

"How old are you?"

Gan shoved his way past Dalan. "Oh, stop blibbering like a pick hen and get us through." He pushed his shoulder against the handleless door.

Moochir frowned. "You are not so polite, Mr. Gan."

"That's because I spent a turtle's journey with Seerchir, who... who... oooh! He muddled me to complete goat barmy."

"My cousin Seerchir? You know him?"

"Excessively well." Gan shoved with his shoulder again.

"But you didn't like him. Pity, pity, indeeeed." Moochir's face dissolved, and the door suddenly gave way.

Gan stumbled into a large chamber. Torches burned in sconces along the stone walls. Stacks of barrels and crates lined the area, and two stone staircase led upward, one from each side of the room.

"Follow me," Moochir called from a crate near stairs to the right.

Dalan extinguished his sputtering flame, tossed the stub into a corner and, with caution, crossed the mostly empty room.

"Faster, Mr. Dalan. Someone approaches. Indeeeed."

Taking two stairs at a time, Dalan hurried after the woodpit, who jumped from one torch to the next. Fish slopped out one side of his basket and left a line of slime up the stairs.

Behind him Gan muttered something about stinker pudding.

At the top, a wooden floor covered another storeroom. The clatter of dishes and pans emanated from a kitchen to one side, but Moochir blinked out of a torch leading down a hall to the right. "Leave the fishies here," he said before heading on.

Dalan gladly set his basket aside and followed the woodpit, with Gan and Tabin close behind. Down several more corridors, and up a rickety wooden staircase, he stumbled along. Tiredness pull at him and his arms still ached from hauling Gan out of the enchanted puddle. At the top lay a very small landing surrounded by walls.

"It's a dead end," Dalan whispered.

Moochir nodded. "Indeeeed. Look down." His eyes pointed to the wall on the right.

Through a long, narrow slit running horizontally, Dalan peered down on an eating area much too small to be the main dining hall.

Gan, standing on tiptoe, peeked down as well. "Blazing sack widgets! That's... that's... and he's dining with our flitter mitten!"

"Shhh!" Tabin hissed.

Dalan gulped. Ariyuna, dressed in some obnoxious flowery gown, sat across from a handsome man. Turning his head sideways, Dalan pressed his ear against the slit to try and catch the conversation.

The man's voice drifted upward, smooth as cream. "I have a great surprise for you, my dear."

Since when did this creep get to call Ariyuna "my dear"? Dalan pressed his ear harder against the wall.

"A surprise?"

Dalan heard a waver in her voice that made everything in him want to swoop down and rescue her.

"Yes. Tomorrow you will be an honored guest at our yearly tournament. I would like you to sit up on the royal stage with me and be my guest. Having a princess from Talsar at my side would honor me greatly. What do you say?"

"I have a choice?" Ariyuna asked.

Dalan wanted to yell down that she did. She needed to get away from this man.

But fast footsteps thudded up the stairs.

Dalan turned to see the point of a spear inches from his chest.

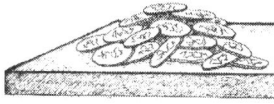

Chapter 19
Clothes for a Prince

Dash staggered into Karakul's home. The hectic pace of his day at the market had left him exhausted to his bones.

Karakul placed a hand on his shoulder. "Tomorrow we will go shopping and find some suitable clothing for you. Maybe we could try our hand at more bargains if time allows. You have done exceptionally well, boy. I may have to promote you, but we'll talk about that more another day. We won't have a full moon tonight, but do you want to attempt the moon box?"

"No." Dash's foot caught on the edge of a rug, and he stumbled forward. "I'm really tired."

"Very well. I'll see you in the morning."

Following Serik, Dash climbed the stairs to his room.

Serik opened the door, pulled down the bed, and took several clean towels out of a closet. "Is there anything you would like, young master?"

"No. Just some sleep." He yawned.

After a quick wash, Dash collapsed onto the soft bed and stared up at the stars through the open window. A warm breeze blew the sheer curtains gently back and forth, and the sweet smells of the garden drifted in. Cricket chirps lent their music to the night air.

He couldn't believe the day. After Lady Idana had purchased the hat, palace guards arrived.

Karakul successfully convinced them that Akmat had

paid a fair price for the coin pouches. The large crowd attracted by the guards quickly became interested in anything he pulled out of the trunks. Almost all the wares they'd brought to the market sold in a matter of hours, and Karakul had to send servants back to his house for more.

Dash fingered his new coin pouch, stuffed to the top with golds, silvers, and coppers. Seventy-six golds in all. He'd never even dreamed of being this rich. "Ha! Papa and Dalan will have to listen to me now." More money sat in his coin bag than Papa earned in several years of scratching out a living on that stupid farm.

A black bird flew by the window.

Still clutching his coin pouch, he closed his eyes as sleep pressed in.

When the morning sun filtered through the curtains, Dash groaned and rolled over. Coins dug into his back.

Pulling the pouch out from under his shoulder, he stretched and remembered the previous day at the market.

The memory triggered a smile.

A knock sounded at the door.

"Yes," he called out.

"Master Dash, it's time to wake up. Master Karakul is waiting."

"I'll be right down." Dash rolled out of bed and landed with a thump on the floor. The coin pouch followed him over the edge and spilled out onto the thick patterned rug with muted jangles.

He put the coins back in one at a time. Each clink sent a pulse of happiness through him. How much would he need for the day's shopping? Slipping six golds into his pocket, he stuffed the still bulging money bag into the top drawer of the dresser. A small dark knob at the back of the drawer caught his eye. He would have to check that out later.

A quick glance in the mirror showed that the black bird mark on his forehead remained. He smiled as he dressed, swinging his cloak over his shoulders, then yanked a comb through his disheveled hair.

Taking the stairs two at a time, he followed his nose to the kitchen. A plate of fresh braided rolls sat on a counter. He snitched one, along with a large piece of cheese.

A servant held out a glass of juice. "Better hurry to the storage room beside the stables."

Dash guzzled the juice.

The servant shoved another roll into Dash's pocket. "Go. Master Karakul is waiting."

Dash nodded and ran.

The side door stood partially open. He squeezed in, tripped over a large box, and fell sprawling across the floor. "Who put this-"

"I did," Karakul replied.

"Oh, sorry, Master." Dash picked himself up and dusted off his piece of cheese. "I was just... they said you were waiting."

Karakul laughed. "I suppose as a farm boy you haven't learned much about dignity. Well, we can fix that. The first thing to remember is that rich men never hurry. Others must hurry to serve you, but you are far too important to rush around."

"Yes, Master."

"Well. Let's get you dressed to match your new status." He strode out of the stables, and Dash followed, wolfing down his roll.

When they arrived at the market. A crowd pressed in.

People reached out to touch Dash or give him a pat on the back, keeping their distance from Karakul.

Dash's chest swelled at the thought of his new popularity. A moon band tingled.

"This way, boy." Karakul managed to grab his arm. "Out of the way!" he called out to the crowd. Almost immediately, the throng parted. "Come along." Karakul strode ahead to a clothing shop on the far side.

Dash scurried after him into the store.

The shopkeeper closed and locked the door behind them to keep the multitude outside. He bowed to Dash. "What may I help you with, most honored guests?"

Karakul nodded his head slightly. "We are here to dress this young gentleman in clothing that fits his station."

"That we can certainly do." The shopkeeper measured Dash and bustled around the shop pulling out trousers, tunics, cloaks, and vests. He shouted orders to underlings who scurried to comply with his orders. Most items he discarded, but some he placed on a separate rack.

After several hours, Dash stood gazing at himself in the long mirror. Regardless of the angle, he hardly recognized the farm boy from Dorben. The finery that adorned him rivaled that of Lord Temir, and he liked it. Especially the two black feathers in his hair.

The clothes were a little on the baggy side, but Karakul insisted that he should leave some room for growing. He couldn't imagine growing that much so soon, but he wanted to please his new master.

"What should I do with my old clothes?" Dash picked up the tunic and trousers Ma had made for him during the long winter evenings.

"Leave them here to be burned."

Dash's fingers lingered on the simple embroidered collar before he slowly set them back down. "How much do I owe you?"

"Mmmm." The shopkeeper pulled out a counting board and slid beads back and forth. "That will come to five golds, exactly."

Karakul stepped forward. "He may look like a gullible farm boy, but he is a prince of Talsar and will not be swindled by a commoner."

Prince of Talsar? Dash mulled over the new title and liked it. He knew Queen Baiyanarah, but he certainly wasn't related. Ah, what did it really matter?

Dash dug into the pocket of his old trousers and pulled out the coins. A reluctance to part with any of his money tugged. He knew he should barter for a lower price. But then again, he could earn more.

The verse from the first moon band came to mind. Wealth is happiness sucked from a well that will leave you ever thirsting for more.

Karakul had said that wanting more was a good thing. It would motivate him to reach for his goals. So the feelings couldn't be bad. Again, he wondered if he should bargain, but decided against it. "I'm feeling generous." The coins clinked into the shopkeeper's hand. "Besides, there's more where this came from."

Karakul shrugged.

The first moon band pinched, and Dash slid it down his wrist to where it fit better.

"Thank you so much, your graciousness." The shopkeeper bowed low. "It has been a pleasure serving you. I'll have the remaining goods delivered to your home very shortly."

With his head held high, Dash strutted out across the

market square. His clothes drew the attention of the crowds, but they backed off when Karakul called out, "Make way for the Prince of Talsar!"

A skinny man dressed in brilliant reds pushed through the throngs. He bowed to Dash. The feathers in his hair fluttered in the wind.

Karakul whispered, "A palace messenger."

The courier held out a gold-edged envelope.

"Go on, boy. Take it."

Dash plucked the envelope out of the messenger's hand, opened it, and pulled out a decoratively embossed card. "It's an invitation to a tournament at the palace."

The messenger continued to bow in front of Dash.

"Is he waiting for something?"

"Your reply. Will you attend the tournament?"

"Oh, well, sure, I guess. If that's okay with you." He glanced up at Karakul who nodded his consent.

The messenger smiled and headed back through the crowd.

"What's a tournament?"

"Ah, you are in for a treat, boy. This tournament is a yearly event and will include many sporting competitions, as well as some surprises. I think you will enjoy it immensely. Besides, I believe the High Prince Kasiret will be there. So will most of the important palace residents."

Dash smiled. The ball of happiness inside grew, and he scratched at the three tingling moon bands.

"I believe we should spend some time reorganizing after yesterday's chaos, rather than attempting the market again. I have more items in storage that can be retrieved in preparation for another day."

Dash followed his master to the storage room. The

afternoon soon filled up with unpacking and rearranging items as servants brought in more trunks and boxes.

By evening, Dash's stomach rumbled. Several snacks throughout the day had held him over, but a gnawing hollowness filled his middle.

The meal, served in the cool freshness of the garden, satisfied his hunger with the most delicious foods he'd ever tasted. He ate until his stomach begged him to stop.

As the sun dipped below the roof tops, Karakul stood and stretched. "I have some business to attend to. Shall we try the moon box again later tonight when I return?"

A jolt of expectation brought a broad smile to the surface at the thought of another band. "I would like that."

Chapter 20
A Slow Fade

Ariyuna poked at the food on her plate, trying to remember all that had happened in the last day or so. The memories came slowly, and Prince Kasiret kept looking at her with a strange glint in his eyes.

In one corner, a group of musicians played soft music.

Refocusing, she reached back with her mind. She'd been in Temyulun with Baiyanarah, holding the queen's staff. Then she'd woken up in this strange palace, with a nasty white powder on her lips. The queen's staff. Where could it be, now? She searched for a memory but came up empty. Something else, something very important, lurked just beyond her grasp. A library... books... a book... the Zavtai. A book about the Zavtai. Where did the book end up?

Elch, why am I having such a hard time remembering?

Silence filled her mind.

She went back to retrieving memories.

After the dressing room ordeal, she'd been brought here. Where was here? Teagen. She remembered that from the library. This must be the royal palace in Endurek. A memory drifted to the surface. The book lay wrapped in her clothes in the dressing room.

She sighed and picked at a gaudy flower on her dress.

Across from her sat the prince. With effort, she focused on his words. He was saying something about being an honored guest at a tournament.

She studied the prince. He seemed respectful and charming, but he aroused deep-down, indistinct feelings of dread.

Muffled voices and thumps came from high up behind the wall to her left. One of the voices held a lilt of familiarity.

She glanced up but couldn't see anything except a thin slit. "Did you hear that?"

Prince Kasiret's brow furrowed. "Don't worry about the servants. They can be very clumsy sometimes." He pointed directly at a server, who scurried forward to fill her glass. "So, my dear. What do you think?"

"About..."

"About coming with me to the tournament. As my guest."

She took a sip of her drink. Again dizziness swam before her eyes. "I'm not sure. So much has happened I don't know what to think."

Elch, what should I do?

Her gut told her to go along with the prince. She suspected he could turn ugly if she refused.

Elch?

Under the table, she slipped her fingers inside her glove and twisted the bracelet on her wrist. The three stones from the last struggle against Zovlon glowed softly.

Well, Elch could be trusted to protect her and change her mind if needed. She would accept his offer. For now.

She forced a smile. "I would be happy to go with you. May I make one small request, though?"

Prince Kasiret beamed. "Of course! Anything for my

princess."

My princess? Had it come to that? A tendril of fear coiled in her chest. But taking another deep breath, she continued. "Could someone other than Lady Idana help me dress for the event?" She pulled at a green ribbon on her gown.

The prince laughed. "Is that all? I would have given you... well, never mind that. I will gladly accommodate your request, although I think you look lovely tonight. You would look lovely in anything."

Elch? Some help would be nice.

Still the fish remained silent.

"By the way," she ventured. "When I woke up, I had nasty powder on my lips. What was that?"

"Only residue from the tonic needed to wake you. A deep, charmed sleep is always tricky. Thankfully, Zibek figured out the antidote."

She nodded.

"Eat up, my dear." The prince piled more delicacies on her plate. "I'm sure you're famished from your long slumbers."

Ariyuna tasted the food and discovered a deep hunger. How long had she gone without eating?

Eventually an empty plate sat before her, and she leaned back into the chair. Her middle felt pleasantly full, but her mind still chafed against the fog.

"How did you like the meal?"

"Delicious." Glancing up, she saw Prince Kasiret pointing at a servant carrying a large tray. "Don't bring the dessert yet, you fool. I'm not ready for it. I will signal when it's time."

The servant, pale with fright, backed away, his hands visibly shaking.

An insistent thirst pulled at Ariyuna. She took several gulps from her glass, then squeezed her eyes shut to steady the spinning room. Could this be left over from her charmed sleep? But she didn't have any dizziness in the dressing room.

With a smile, Prince Kasiret turned back to Ariyuna. "I am so sorry for that unpleasant interruption." He took hold of her gloved hand as she let go of the glass. "We are going to have such a good time at the tournament. My favorite events are the horse races, but you may enjoy something else. I'm curious to see how you like the festivities."

Ariyuna tried to pull her hand away, but the prince held tight.

Her heart beat faster as she remembered when Zovlon had grabbed her hand so many years ago in Surtak. But this was Prince Kasiret.

His handsome face smiled. "Let's dance."

Her defenses melted as he continued to hold her hand. Maybe this wasn't all bad. He was attractive, and he had been kind.

Before she could protest, he raised her from her chair and led her away from the table. The musicians played louder.

At first, she tried to resist as Prince Kasiret twirled her around the room. But her struggle faded. Somehow her feet followed his complicated steps even though she didn't know the dance. His hand around her waist guided her along with a firm grip. She felt herself giving in to the flow of the dance and to Prince Kasiret's control.

Time disappeared.

When she finally sat down again, she was out of breath.

"Now I think we are ready for some dessert." Prince Kasiret waved his hand, and the frightened servant brought out plates of sweetcakes and fruit. From a silver pitcher, a servant filled her glass.

Ariyuna brushed stray strands of hair away from her face

and drained the newly filled cup. How long had they danced? Why had she even consented to dance in the first place? What would Naiyan think? The unspoken understanding that she and Naiyan would marry someday prickled against the prince's forwardness.

She grasped the table to steady the spinning room, then looked up to find the prince staring at her. Heat rushed to her face.

"You are a wonderful dance partner." The prince smiled. "We will have to do that again sometime. But tell me, what do you like to do? What makes you happy?"

Ariyuna blinked several times. No one had ever asked her that before. She had always done what others expected of her. "I don't really know."

"Come, now. You are a princess of Talsar. A member of the ruling house. You must have things you do for enjoyment. Obviously you are rich and doted on."

"Well, not exactly. I *am* acquainted with the queen."

"Now you are just being modest. I believe you are more powerful than you're letting on. You arrived with a marvelous staff and the jewels you wear on your arm and neck are very unusual."

Ariyuna gasped and slipped her hand under the table. She tucked the Itgel further under her glove. "How do you know about the staff?" Bothersome thirst drove her to take a few more sips.

"I make it a point to stay connected." The prince nodded to the servant holding the pitcher. "You intrigue me greatly, and I know there is more to you than you let on. But I must say that you do a convincing impression of a clueless farm girl."

Uncertainty scratched. Ariyuna reached for the necklace that held the clear almas stone from the Altan Forest. Her gift from... from Naiyan. Vagueness filled her mind as she strained to remember one of her closest friends. Why couldn't she picture his face? And how did the prince know about the necklace and the Itgel? What had happened while she slept?

Fear tugged, but the cloudiness of her mind swallowed her concern, despite all her efforts to fight it.

The prince beckoned to a servant, who once again filled her glass.

She sipped the sweet liquid.

"Come." Prince Kasiret stood. "I want to show you the moon over the city. The Gray Tower has the best view, although it *is* a bit of a climb." He pulled her to standing and held her close. "I think it would also be a good place to talk about this staff of yours. I'm sure you know all about it."

She tried to resist, but her arms went limp. A haze washed over her thoughts.

The moon.

Yes, it would be nice to see the moon over the city.

She smiled and allowed him to lead her out of the dining room.

Chapter 21
Separated

Dalan stared down the shaft of the spear pointed directly at his chest. Four palace guards stood with weapons ready.

Gan let out a faint squeak.

A guard glared at Tabin and whispered. "Go. Quietly. You first."

Gan and Tabin headed back down the dark, wooden stairs.

Dalan followed last with a guard poking a spear tip into his back. Had the pit led them into a trap, or did he want them to see Ariyuna? He decided to give Moochir the benefit of the doubt. At the bottom of the stairs, they entered a long corridor. He could see an ear sticking out of a torch handle on the wall.

So far, Dalan hadn't noticed any windows. Could the whole palace be underground, or so secluded from the outside that no natural light was allowed in?

The guard in front of Dalan glanced back and wrinkled his nose. "You stink like rotten fish and you're soaked. And what were you doing up near High Prince Kasiret's private dining area? Who are you, anyway? How did you get into the palace?"

Another guard scowled. "How can he answer if you

pepper him with all those questions?"

"Fine. Let's start with the first one. What were you doing up there smelling like fish?"

"I... uh... the fish were for..."

"Fish for the tournament?" The guard laughed. "Since when did we need fish for the tournament? Fish for the festival, yes, but not for the tournament. And where are the fish now? You didn't leave them up by the dining room, did you?"

"No, they're by the kitchen. We didn't know where to go...."

Elch, help! Dalan called out in his mind. He didn't want to lie, but this had turned into a stickier situation than he'd expected.

The taller guard with a lance pressed into Tabin's back glowered. "Maybe it's a new event. You know how Prince Kasiret is sometimes. Very unpredictable."

"But rotten fish?" The first guard asked. "What would he do with rotten fish?"

"I don't know. I suppose that's his concern, not ours. And I'm not sure I'd *want* to know, if it involves fish that smell this bad."

The first guard poked the tip of his spear into Dalan's back. "To the kitchen. You can explain the fish, and then you'll get an extended tour of the dungeons. We'll ask Prince Kasiret what to do with you once the tournament is over."

"But we've got to-"

Gan gave Dalan a sideways kick in the shin.

"Ow!"

"You've got to ow?" The guard lowered his weapon as confusion settled on his face.

Once again, Dalan's mind reached out to Elch. *We need to save Ariyuna. And what about Dash?*

A comforting warmth pulsed in his chest. *Trust the pit.*

Dalan searched every piece of wood he could see. No part of the pit showed as they marched down the hall toward the kitchen. Their baskets of fish were gone. Someone must have had enough of the smell. He certainly had.

Just as they reached the vestibule by the kitchen where their baskets of fish had been, a crowd of servants burst out of the galley. They carried large trays, platters, and baskets. Delicious smells of freshly baked breads and succulent meats filled the air.

"Mmmm!" The tall guard sniffed the air. "The tournament banquet. Let's get these three taken care of so we can join in before all the good stuff's gone."

Dalan's stomach rumbled. The food smelled amazing.

In a blink, all the torches and lamps in and around the windowless kitchen sputtered out. Even the fires at the far back of the cooking area died down to dark coals.

A collective cry rose from the staff as trays and silverware clattered to the ground. Plates crashed and glasses shattered.

In the confusion of bodies and food, Dalan tried to make his way to the edge of the room. His foot collided with something hard. He then stepped on someone who grunted.

A wet, sticky hand grabbed his leg, but Dalan managed to escape the grasp.

From the other side of the room, he heard, "Gripping flag bottoms! I could spy more in a barrel of brackish ferret spit."

Off to his right, a familiar voice pierced the cacophony. "Follow me. Mr. Dalan. Pit. Over this way. Indeeeed. I can't keep the torches out for long."

Dalan found the wall with his hand. "Where are you?"

"Over here. Pit."

Keeping his hand on the stones, Dalan gingerly followed

Moochir's voice. The edge of the room didn't have as many servants, but a kitchen maid yelped and slapped him on the shoulder when he stepped on what he guessed was her foot.

"Keep coming. Pit, pit."

Kitchen workers yelled and tussled. Something small and round rolled in front of Dalan's feet, and he almost fell.

Up ahead, he heard Moochir. "Keep coming. Pit, pit. Down this hall."

A cool breeze brushed Dalan's cheek as he turned a corner. "Where are the others?"

"They are fine. Faster, pit. Faster, indeeeed."

Dalan stumbled forward in the dark, one hand on the wall and the other stretched out in front. The corridor curved again, and he could see the bright outline of a doorway at the end.

"What's on the other side?"

"Light. Pit, pit. And safety. Keep coming. I will find a place for you to hide."

At the end of the hall, Dalan fumbled for the knob. "Are you sure this is safe?"

"Yes. Pit. But not for long."

Dalan opened the door and blinked down another long hallway. This one had lights at frequent intervals. Moochir's face protruded from a torch on the wall.

Dalan ran as quietly as he could, hoping Tabin and Gan would somehow escape as well.

The woodpit moved to the open door at the end.

Past the heavy wooden barrier, Dalan found himself in a dim, musty library. Half expecting to encounter someone, he hesitated.

Moochir's voice drifted across the room. "Keep coming. Pit, pit. No one is here. They are all preparing themselves for the banquet. We must hurry. Soon the hallways will be crowded. Crowded, indeeeed."

The woodpit led Dalan at a run through numerous chambers and down well-lit corridors.

A servant turned a corner, and the pit ducked into a glass-enclosed room.

Dalan followed and found himself surrounded by the palm trees, leafy plants, and gurgling rivulets of an indoor garden. Sunlight streamed through the glass ceiling, and Dalan lifted his face to the warming rays. Deep breaths of the vegetation's freshness filled him to the core with renewed energy.

"Hurry. Pit."

"But we need to find Ariyuna. Do you know where she is?"

"Possibly. Pit, pit. She may still be at dinner." Moochir's lips protruded out of a palm trunk then disappeared. "Wait." The woodpit stuck his nose out of a planter toward Dalan and sniffed again. "Does she smell like you?"

"How would I know?"

"Indeeeed." Moochir sniffed some more. "You reek of fish. This way. Pit."

He led Dalan back to where they had entered the indoor garden, and took a different hall away from it. Every so often, Moochir stopped and sniffed again.

Dalan glanced around nervously as he followed. So far, they'd seen only the one servant. No sooner had the thought of the empty palace crossed his mind, when he heard scurrying feet coming toward him.

No doorways opened off the hall, but a lone torch cast shadows along the stone wall. Moochir's chin protruded slightly from the torch handle.

Behind Dalan, a long shadow fell across the floor.

Quickly, he stepped back and felt the familiar pinch of a shadow dive. He hadn't tried in so long, he hoped it still worked. Either the people walking toward him would keep going, or he would be very obvious, standing against the wall, thinking he was invisible when he wasn't.

Dalan held his breath and waited.

Two servants hurried by. "I can't believe we had to deliver that fruit," one said. "Now we've missed the beginning of the tournament banquet."

"Next time, we'll get that new little kitchen brat to do it. Ugg. This hallway stinks like fish."

The servants disappeared around a corner.

Dalan let out his breath. It had worked. Taking a step forward, he emerged from his shadow.

Moochir's face popped out of the wooden picture frame right next to him.

"Very impressive, Mr. Dalan. You are a person of hidden talents. Pit. You'll have to explain that one to me at some point."

"It's called shadow diving, but right now we need to find a place to hide before the banquet creates crowds. By the way, you don't have to call me Mr. Dalan. Just Dalan is fine."

"Indeeeed." Moochir vanished and soon blinked out of the doorway at the end of the hall. "We're almost there."

"Almost where?"

The pit dissolved into the wood without answering.

Dalan followed to a series of ornate doors.

"This one," Moochir said. "I smell her in this one, though she herself is not here."

Slowly Dalan opened the door and entered. The late evening rays filtered past sheer curtains, leaving a golden glow in the air. But the room, filled with racks of clothing, befuddled him. What kind of place could this be?

"Hurry," Moochir urged.

Dalan closed and locked the door. "No one's here."

The pit nodded. "But your sister *was* here. Pit. And her clothing still is."

Along one side, almost completely covered in piles of dresses, lay a small couch. Dalan rifled through the mound, but found only ruffles and ribbons. In the corner, he spotted a different looking bundle. "These are Ari's clothes." He picked them up and felt a book.

Outside in the hall, he heard voices.

"Hide in here. Pit, pit." Moochir blinked above the handle of a small closet door.

Giggling, and fumbling steps echoed in the corridor. The latch wiggled. "Who locked this?" The shrill voice of a woman penetrated the door. "I'm the only one who should lock this."

A key scraped in the keyhole.

Dalan snatched up the book and ducked into the closet just as the door banged open.

Chapter 22
The Fourth Band

Dash looked up to see his new master standing in the doorway of his room. He jumped off the bed.

A fiery glint sparkled in Karakul's eyes. "Are you ready to give the box another try?"

"Sure." Dash glanced out the window. "But the moon's only half. Will that work?"

"With the powder and what you've learned, it should. We won't know until we try."

Dash eagerly grabbed the moon box and followed Karakul to the roof. What would the next band bring? He couldn't imagine more than he'd already received, wealth, powerful friends, and an ability to use humor better than he'd ever imagined.

A quick glance down at his new clothes brought a smile. Leaving home was the best thing he'd ever done.

Setting the box on a small table, he looked into the sky. The large, dark yellow half-moon hung low on the horizon, but no clouds blocked it.

From his pocket, he pulled out the bag of powder. "What do you think the box will give us tonight?"

"Us?" Karakul placed a hand on his shoulder. "I believe

the box and the gifts are yours. Let me see what you've already received."

Dash held out his left arm with the three moon bands. The first one fit snugly around the smallest part of his wrist. Its designs and words glowed a faint blue. The others were a little looser, but they, too, glowed in the moonlight.

"Impressive." Karakul nodded. "Yes. Very impressive for such a short amount of time. It takes most people months and sometimes years to get even one band out of a moon box. But you have managed three in a matter of days. Mastery of one band is usually necessary before the box will grant another one."

"I did have you to help me." Dash held up the bag. "And this powder."

"Yes, but you wear the bands. And you're the one that needs to learn the lessons of each one."

"How many bands does a moon box hold?"

"Typically six, but this one is different. It came directly from Prince Kasiret himself." Karakul turned the box so it faced the moonlight. "Let's try it and see what happens."

Dash sprinkled a pinch of powder over the box. Words glowed on the lid, but some letters remained dim.

"Try a pinch more." The merchant leaned over and squinted at the writing. "And tip it toward the moon."

Dash complied. The words glowed brightly, and he read aloud:

"Vagrants misled in a heartless world,
Will force results through lies and woe.
Half-moons deceive, half-hearts receive,
Deception deep from a hidden foe."

The verse didn't sound good. Dash glanced up at

Karakul. "Do you think we should open it? Is it safe?"

Karakul's laugh rang out over the rooftops. "Don't mind the box. Moon bands can be corrupted and used for evil, which will bring about bad results. But you are using them to gain good things, are you not? Go ahead, open it."

Dash thought about his new clothes, his bursting money pouch, and Lord Temir's mark on his forehead. Yes, the moon bands had brought good things.

He placed his fingers on the five bronze discs, curious to know what kind of band or bands lay inside. His master had been right before, so if Karakul thought the warning could be ignored, then he'd try to forget it.

The lid popped open, and one moon band lay on the rich purple velvet. He stared at it, somehow reluctant to pick it up. The verse on the top of the box bothered him. "Can moon boxes lie?"

"No." Karakul leaned over to look at the band. "They are always truthful, but there can be many interpretations of the riddles they give."

Dash picked up the band. It felt heavier than the others. He sprinkled powder on the inside and held it up to the moonlight.

"Great strength and might will bring vast gains.
Fickle admirers flock to the façade of a hero."

Uncertainty gurgled inside. Could this really be a good thing? The words "fickle" and "façade" didn't sound encouraging.

Karakul slapped him on the back. "Congratulations! This is perfect timing. The tournament starts at noon tomorrow. We'll enter you in some events." The merchant's smile widened.

"The crowds will love it! The Prince of Talsar will be the new hero of Endurek."

Dash smiled. He liked the sound of that. Both the prince part and the hero part. Turning the band, he looked it over. Moonlight glowed on the outlines of sporting events and the writing. He slipped the new metal circle onto his right arm and held it next to the other ones on his left. They did look impressive.

"So, you think I could compete in the tournament? What events?"

"Most of them. The wrestling, the horse races, nayza throwing. There are so many more." Karakul paused and his forehead furrowed in thought. "Maybe zodoj, but we can wait and see what the morning brings."

"But I haven't trained for any of them. And I'm not very strong." He held out a scrawny arm. Both Papa and Dalan had strong, muscular arms, but he hadn't even started to fill out yet.

"Not to worry." Karakul grinned widely. "You won't need training. With that new moon band, you'll be able to do anything."

Dash twisted the metallic ring encircling his wrist. It had already tightened to a comfortable fit.

"Very well done, boy. Now I'm going to bed. I'll see you in the morning. Serik will wake you in time for the tournament. We don't want to be late." He strode away, his cloak following with a swish.

Closing the moon box, Dash held it up in the dim light. Some of the letters on the top had faded, but he could still make out most of the words.

Vagrants misled ... heartle... world,
W... force results ... ugh lies a... woe.

148

Half … ons deceive, half hear… receive,
Deception dee… a hidden foe.

Deception and a hidden foe. Dash thought about the words. What did they mean? Karakul said the box wouldn't lie. Half-moons deceive. He glanced up at the partial moon climbing into the star speckled sky. He didn't understand that either.

Serik waited by the stairs.

Dash sighed. He'd better go to bed soon in case Karakul followed through with entering him in every competition tomorrow. And he'd have to keep his eyes out for a hidden foe.

Back in his room, he headed straight for the dresser. After pulling open the top drawer, he loosened the drawstring of his coin pouch.

The golds glinted in the lamplight, and he smiled. He let a few coins run through his fingers. The first moon band glowed with more color. He twisted it and then remembered the strange knob he'd found inside the drawer.

After pulling the dresser drawer almost all the way out, he peered at the back. The knob was no bigger than the end of his thumb. He yanked on it. Nothing happened.

Twisting it to the right, he pulled again. Still nothing. He tried twisting it to the left. This time a tiny compartment slid out. In it lay an intricate black key, only as long as a shar caterpillar, hanging on a thin silver chain.

He picked it up by the chain that glistened in the lamplight.

Dash checked the moon box, but it had only the five bronze plates along the front. No keyhole.

Grabbing the lamp, he searched the walls. Nothing.

He ran his fingers along the baseboards, but still couldn't see a keyhole.

The bed. He hurried over and checked every surface of the carved structure.

Finally, he went back to the dresser and stood, jiggling the key on its chain.

There had to be a lock somewhere.

Chapter 23
An Unexpected Companion

Ariyuna followed along as Prince Kasiret led her through the palace and up a painfully long, winding staircase. The dark, musty smell of the tower pressed in. Ariyuna stumbled on several stairs, but the prince kept a tight grip on her elbow.

The heavy fog in her mind refused to lift. A headache pounded.

She steadied herself on the stone wall as they kept climbing. Ariyuna took several deep breaths, trying to clear the fuzziness away, but it didn't help. Apprehension wrestled toward the surface.

She glanced at the prince. What if she *could* become a princess of Endurek as he had suggested? What possibilities would that hold?

After a long climb, the stairs gave way to a small circular room with heavy stone arches on all sides that were open to the night sky. The half-moon hung low, huge, and orange.

She walked toward the arches. The prince followed, keeping a firm hold on her arm.

"Wow," she whispered. "This is magnificent." City lights blinked into the night, and a warm breeze drifted by. The rich aromas of damp earth and flowers reminded her of summer on the farm.

Her head cleared slightly at the memory. Did the captivating smell come from the circle of spiky, potted plants in the center of the tower space, or from a garden below?

"It is magnificent." The prince turned to face her. "Now, princess. Tell me about the staff you brought with you."

His words pulled her drifting mind back to the present. The struggle within intensified. She knew better than to divulge information, but what did she really know about the staff, anyway? In the back of her mind, she knew it would be better not to say anything even though there were no secrets to hide. But unbidden words rose to her mouth. "Oh, it's nothing, really. Just Queen Baiyanarah's staff that she got in Vachir. Els Edzyn gave it to her."

"It's far more than that, Princess. And you know it. What does it do?"

Forced words that had been on the verge of spilling out dissipated into the vagueness of her mind. Ariyuna scratched her head, wishing her mind would clear. "It... it doesn't do anything. It's just a pretty do-dad."

Prince Kasiret's eyes turned stormy, and his hold on her tightened. "Don't lie."

"I'm not!" Ariyuna tried to pull her arm away. "I don't know anything more. We, that is Baiyanarah and I, were trying to find out more about it right before I arrived here. As far as I know, it's simply a well-crafted, ancient artifact."

Prince Kasiret glared at her before his grip loosened, and he sighed. "I suppose that *is* all you know. I was hoping for more, but this room won't allow falsehoods." His piercing eyes bored into her. "You will tell no one about the staff or our visit here."

Ariyuna swallowed hard. Fear clutched at her throat. How did the prince have so much power over her?

He led her back the stairs and through the palace. Rooms and hallways passed by. Servants scurried out of their way.

They arrived back at the dressing room. Prince Kasiret's grasp didn't loosen until she entered.

Standing at the door, he once again stared directly at her, his charm gone. "You will not leave this room until I call for you. Understood?"

Again, Ariyuna's throat tightened.

Prince Kasiret turned with a swish of his cloak. The door thudded closed, and she heard the scrape of a key in the latch.

As soon as she was alone, dread filled her chest. What had she just done? How had he controlled her? Had she said things she shouldn't have? It was all a blur. Something about dancing and a tower room. An uncertain memory of the moon flickered in her mind. Hadn't the prince said something about the circular room not allowing falsehoods? Had it been an enchanted space?

She scanned the dressing room. Would she spend the night here? No bed presented itself. Her comfort would be the last thing to concern Prince Kasiret, and selfishness absorbed Lady Idana. She sighed.

Naiyan came to mind. How could she have forgotten Naiyan? Had his memory been blocked? She reached for the slender chain around her neck. If only he were here with her now.

Elch! she called out.

A faint scuffle from the closet to her left made her jump. "Who... who's there?" She backed away.

On a small table, she found a lamp and managed to light it with the matches lying nearby. Holding the feeble light up, she scanned the room. She noticed her pile of clothes in the corner.

"The book," she whispered, and ran to the pile. Setting

the lamp on the floor, she rifled through her garments and groaned. "It's gone."

"Ari?"

She whipped around and held up the lamp. "Who's there?"

"It's me. Dalan."

"Dalan? How...?"

She watched her brother emerge from the closet. Dropping her clothes, she ran to hug him. "I'm so glad to see you! Wow. This is just what I've needed. How did you get here?"

"I came to Endurek looking for Dash. Well, you already know that. The rest of it is a long story."

"How did you get into the palace? And why were you in the closet?"

"An obnoxious woman and her servants left a few minutes ago. I had to be really still and quiet while they were here and almost fell asleep."

Ariyuna sniffed the air. "What's that nasty fish stink? Is that coming from you?"

"Yep. We used fish to get into the palace as servants, but Gan got rotten ones."

"Gan's here too?"

"And Tabin, but I lost them down by the kitchens. I hope they're all right."

"Knowing Gan, I'm sure they'll be fine. Especially if he's with Tabin." She gave Dalan's hand a squeeze. "Wow, I can't tell you how relieved I am. I just had dinner with Prince Kasiret. He was very anxious to know more about Baiyanarah's staff, but I can't remember much. Things are a bit muddled in my brain."

She scrunched her eyes closed.

"We can talk about it later." Dalan glanced at Ariyuna's pile of worn clothes lying in the middle of the room where she had dropped them. "I have your book." He held out the thin volume.

Ariyuna released a long breath of relief. "I did remember the book. I was looking for that, and thought maybe Lady Idana or one of the maids had pinched it." She took the book her brother held out. "Elch led me to it when I was locked in a library somewhere in the palace." She scanned the room and lowered her voice to a whisper. "I think it has something to do with the Zavtai. Are we alone?"

"As far as I can tell. I think most of the palace people are at the tournament banquet."

"Pit, pit. Yes, they are. Indeeeed." Bulging eyes blinked out of the wood paneling.

Ariyuna jumped back and held her lantern higher. "Who said that?"

"A woodpit." Dalan pointed to the gnarled face. "This is Moochir, and he's attached to me. So far he's been a help. Most of the time, anyway." He rubbed a large bruise on his arm.

"Attached?"

"I have no idea how it works, but somehow this pit is bonded to me. I can't go very far before he yanks me back. Very annoying. But Moochir did lead me to this room where your stuff was. And he can jump from one wooden object to another."

"Pit. You smell better than your brother. Indeeeed."

Swallowing hard, Ariyuna stared at the bug-eyed creature.

"He won't hurt you." Dalan took the lantern from her and hung it from a hook on the wall. "Maybe we should sit and put together all the pieces of what's happened so far. It'll make more sense that way, and it might help us figure out what to do next."

Ariyuna nodded and shoved several piles of dresses off

the couch onto the floor. "We may not have much time. If Lady Idana comes back, we'll be in trouble. She can't find you here, or the book." She flung the flounces of her dress around until she was able to sit comfortably, but still felt half drowned in ribbons and red flowers.

"Who's Lady Idana?"

Ariyuna sighned and described the courtier.

"She doesn't sound like someone I need to meet." Dalan plopped down onto the couch. "I guess I'll tell my part first, but a shortened version." He recalled the main events since they parted ways in Belgutai, including how they had found and lost her along with the staff.

"So." Ariyuna studied Moochir's face in the wall. "You're attached to Dalan?"

"Yes, indeeeed. Pit."

She nodded, still unsure if she could trust such a strange creature. But if Dalan trusted him, she could tell her story.

Running footsteps echoed in the hall.

"Quick!" Ariyuna jumped up and pulled her brother to his feet. "Get back in the closet."

Dalan ran for the narrow door and shut it behind him.

Someone fumbled with the lock. Finally, Lady Idana stumbled into the room, giggling. "Ah, there you are." She hiccupped several times. "You missed a fantastic banquet. *Hic.* But I guess Prince Kasiret probably provided an even better one. Well, you can sleep in here tonight. I'll be back in the morning to get you dressed for the *hic*-tournament."

With a silly grin and a wave of her hand, she closed the door and locked it.

Ariyuna sank back onto the couch. Exhaustion pressed in on her fatigued mind. Questions about the queen's staff, Gan and Tabin's safety, and her own interactions with the prince swirled in undefined chaos.

Chapter 24
Secrets of the Zavtai

Dalan waited until the he heard the sound of the door closing before peeking out of the closet. Over on the couch, Ariyuna sat slumped with her head back and eyes closed.

He made his way quietly across the room. "Ari? Are you all right?"

"Yeah. Just really tired, and I don't know why. Maybe we should get some sleep." Her eyes drooped.

"What about the book? And you haven't told me what's happened since you came to the palace." He held the book up to the lamplight and his gaze landed on the title, *Secrets of the Zavtai: Gift of the Storyteller.*

"Really?" Dalan ran his fingers over the imprinted leather. Excitement pulsed. Could this possibly be a whole book about the last of the three main gifts from the Storyteller?

Ariyuna sat up. "I haven't had a chance to look at it yet. All I remember is that I woke up in a library, found the book, and then Prince Kasiret showed up with Lady Idana, the one that stopped by just now. She brought me here to get dressed for dinner with Prince Kasiret."

A frown settled on her brow. "Dinner and a strange drink. They kept filling my glass, and I kept drinking it and... and we danced. Ugh! I can't believe I danced with him. My brain was all foggy, and I can't remember much. After dinner, he took me to a tall, stone tower. I do remember that." She bent forward with her face in her hands.

"So what happened in the tower?"

She looked up. "He asked me about the staff and said something about the room not allowing lies. Anyway, he then brought me back here. That's about all I can remember. And tomorrow, I think I'm supposed to go to the tournament with him."

"Well, I guess our next step is to see what the book says. Are you up for that?" Glancing sideways at his sister, he wondered if they should wait until morning.

A yawn stretched across Ariyuna's face. "We can start. I don't know if I'm up for the whole book."

The binding opened stiffly. The leaves crackled with age. "What?" Dalan held the book at arm's length. A grinning face blinked out of the first page. "Books, too?"

"Yes. Pit. Paper is made of wood. Indeeeed."

"Fine, but I can't read the words with your face all over them." Moochir faded and reappeared in the armrest of the sofa.

"So, here goes." Dalan ran his hand over the first page and read aloud:

"The Zavtai is one of three gifts from the Storyteller. Like the other two, the gift has been missing for generations. This book contains all we know at this time. The Zavtai was the first gift to disappear after the Storyteller left Talsar. King Ganzorig was the last recorded keeper, and it is believed he hid it. The following is a collection that has been passed down regarding the Zavtai."

Dalan read through half the entries out loud. Some contradicted ones they had already read. One talked about the staff transforming into the king's pet frog, another said the Zavtai had become a robe the king wore. Still others suggested the gift had been buried, burned, melted down into another object, and even ground up and eaten by the king.

"Eew!" Ariyuna scrunched up her face. "Who would do that? You can't keep something safe by destroying and eating it. I don't think I believe any of those. And I was hoping this book would be key in finding the Zavtai, especially since Elch wanted me to find it."

"It is," Moochir said. "This I know. Indeeeed."

Ignoring the pit, Dalan glanced down at the book. "There's only a few entries left. Should we finish it up?"

"I guess so." Ariyuna stifled a yawn.

"All right. This next one's really short. According to Ganbatter, great-great-great-grandson of the king's scribe, the Zavtai remained with King Ganzorig. Wow. Those names are going to be easy to mix up."

Dalan paused as his eyes scanned farther down the page.

"This might actually have something to it. Listen to this. Ganbatter said the Zavtai was and is what it has always been. But the knowledge of it has not been passed along. When King Ganzorig died, he gave the Zavtai to his son but died before the gift could be fully explained.

"It then became one of the most valued possessions of the Kings of Vachir. Every ruler of Talsar that reigned from the throne of Vachir held and benefited from it, without recognizing its true identity. The gift brought stability to the country as well as freedom to its inhabitants."

Ariyuna sat up straighter. "Is there a description?"

"No." Dalan turned the page. "But the passage says the

Zavtai always stayed by the throne, and the kings held it up when they needed guidance. But that's all."

"There really might be something to this story, but it's obvious that this guy's great-great-whatever grandfather knew more than he said. The Zavtai is small enough to be held." Her face wrinkled in a look of concentration. "I wonder..."

Dalan waited. Ariyuna seemed on the verge of discovery.

She finally let out a long breath. "I don't know. There's so many possibilities, and that was so long ago, and my brain hurts." She pressed fingers to her temples. "I wonder if we'll ever find it again."

"You will, indeeeed." Moochir had moved to the other side of the sofa. "This is very true. Pit."

"What's true?" Dalan asked. "The story, or that we'll find it?"

"Yes. Indeeeed. Both."

"How do you know?"

"We woodpits are as old as our parents, the tarlan trees. We know many things."

"So," Ariyuna ventured. "Do you know what the Zavtai looks like?"

"Indeeeed, but we are forbidden to talk of... of certain subjects. Pit!" He blinked and disappeared.

"Great." Dalan slumped back onto the sofa and slammed the book shut. "He knows, but he's as stubborn as Dugur the ram back home. We won't get anything out of him unless he offers it, or we trick him into telling."

"Don't bother." Ariyuna pulled a silk pillow out from behind her and set it against the armrest. "We have Elch to guide us. Is there anything else in the book?" She curled up with her head on the pillow.

Dalan skimmed over the remaining three stories. "The

rest are a bit ridiculous. One says it never existed, the other two pretty much just say it got lost. And there's a poem in the old language that neither of us can read, so not much help there."

Elch, he called out in his mind. *Is the poem worth looking into more?*

A warmth pulsed in his chest.

Ariyuna yawned. "I don't think I can keep my eyes open much longer."

"That's fine." Dalan stood and draped a long, flowing, velvet skirt over her. "You sleep here. There are enough clothes here to make a bed, but I should probably find a more secluded spot. Maybe in the closet. I think there'll be just enough room to stretch out, and hopefully no one will come snooping too early."

Dalan walked to the far end of the room. "Hey, there's a washroom back here. I could get rid of some of this fish smell. It's been stuck in my nose too long."

"Sounds good," Ariyuna mumbled sleepily.

In the washroom, he found several enormous barrels of cold water, soap, and a few smaller wash tubs. He couldn't find a towel, so he borrowed a thick shirt off the rack. The quick immersion and scrub left him chilled but smelling better. He donned some borrowed clothes and wrapped a thick cloak around his shoulders before heading back to the cramped closet.

Stretching out on his lumpy, makeshift bed, Dalan's mind churned with unanswered questions. Where did Tabin and Gan end up? Would they ever find Dash? And what about the Zavtai?

"Indeeeed," resounded in his ear. He lifted his head to see one of Moochir's eyes, his nose, and part of his mouth protruding from a line of wooden buttons.

"Hey, what do you know about the Zavtai?"

"Many things," the pit replied as he faded away.

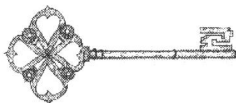

Chapter 25
Bird Paste

As the fresh night breeze blew in the open window, Dash rubbed the tiny silver key between his fingers. He pulled each drawer all the way out, searching for a keyhole, but found nothing.

Maybe the lock wasn't in the room. As his mind mulled over the problem, he took his coins out and jingled a few in the palm of his hand, then stacked them on the dresser and tried spinning one.

The night outside grew deeper, and a cloud covered the moon. Dash sighed, hung the key around his neck, and put the coins away. He would look some more tomorrow if he had a chance. Right now, he needed to get some rest. He wiggled into his old clothes from home that he now used as pajamas.

Before falling asleep, his brain kept busy speculating where the lock could be.

The morning sun cast bright rays over Dash's face, making him squint and sit up. His clothes pinched. He tried to stretch, but a seam in his tunic popped.

Swinging his legs over the side of the bed, he blinked and rubbed his eyes. Were those his legs? Where had all the muscles come from? He sat staring at his lower limbs, now bulging with strength.

He turned his foot in a circle. The ankle that had been broken by the tarch during the Battle of Temyulun moved without pain or stiffness.

The moon bands squeezed his wrists, even the new one. Real muscles existed where scrawny boy arms had been. He held them out and whistled his astonishment.

Standing up, he fell flat on his face. He had used too much effort and knocked himself over. "Ha!" He easily pushed himself onto his feet and took a few wobbly steps toward the dresser, tripping on the rug as he went.

This new body was going to take some getting used to. After pacing back and forth across the room a few times, he moved more freely. It wouldn't be good if he was strong enough for the tournament, but too clumsy. Then he remembered his new clothes. Would they still fit? But they wouldn't be appropriate for a sporting competition.

He pulled the cord for Serik and practiced walking as he waited, kicking the crumpled rug out of the way.

Serik opened the door and stepped in, holding a tempting tray of breakfast. "You rang?" His eyes took in Dash from head to toe as an expression of surprise dawned on his face.

"Um, yes. I was wondering what I should wear for the tournament today."

"I have appropriate attire ready." Serik set the tray down and brought in a pile of comfortable-looking athletic clothing along with a large mirror from just outside the door. "I can help you dress if you like."

Dash looked over the stack. Each piece had a small black bird embroidered on it.

"What is this symbol?" He pointed to one of the birds.

"That is the mark of the royal sorcerers. A very powerful mark, young master. Our High Prince Kasiret is the chief sorcerer. Lord Temir and Master Karakul are two of his confidants."

Dash nodded. The thought of Karakul as a sorcerer scared him, but it made sense. Perhaps someday he could become as powerful as his master.

Whipping his ripped tunic off, he flexed his arms again. He was bigger and stronger than Dalan. And Papa thought he wasn't ready for a mountain knife. Now he could get whatever he wanted. He resolved to buy the best, most impressive knife the next time he went to the market.

He tried on the clothes and found that they fit his new body well.

Serik didn't say anything about Dash's new appearance as he propped up the mirror. "What do you think?"

"I could live with this."

"Yes, young master. I believe you could participate in the tournament. I will be there, cheering for you. The crowd will be most pleased to have a prince of Talsar competing. If there is nothing else, I will go."

"Wait. How will I know what events I'll be in? And when do we leave?" Dash took another look at himself in the mirror.

"I will come for you very shortly to help you prepare."

"That sounds good."

"And I will leave this here for you." Serik straightened the mirror, bowed, and left.

Dash examined himself, flexing his muscles and posing. A grin spread across his face.

His stomach's complaints drew him to the breakfast Serik had left. He hungrily devoured several pastries from the tray, then adjusted the mirror so he could see himself better.

If he didn't want to make a fool of himself, he'd better practice moving. Walking back across the room, he kicked the rug again, sending it sliding to one side. First he tried strutting across the room several times. When that felt more natural, he ran a few steps.

Soon he was jumping as well. Needing more room, he shoved the bed against the wall and kicked the rug under it.

A glint from the floor caught his eye. He bent down to investigate and found a tiny keyhole embedded in the floorboard.

His heart thumped in his ears as he took the key from around his neck. It looked like it might fit. He slipped the key into the lock and turned it.

Click.

A square outline the size of an apple crate appeared in the floorboards. Dash reached down, but it didn't have a handle to pull, and he couldn't get his fingers under the boards enough to lift them. He tried pushing, but the floor was solid.

A loud "Caw!" filled the room.

Dash looked up just in time to see a black bird lift off from the windowsill and fly into the pale morning sky.

He shifted his attention back to the loose floorboard. He needed something strong and flat.

In the second drawer of the dresser, he found a long, thin piece of metal. He hurried back with it. Pulling up with the key, he managed to slip the metal under the loose section of floor just enough to get his fingertips under the edge.

"Yes," he whispered. With a shove, he opened the trap door. Dust drifted in the shafts of early light filtering sideways into the room.

Just underneath the floor lay a second set of boards. The rough planks had a hole in the center, and nestled in the hole was a metal disc.

He reached for it and pulled. The disc turned out to be a lid attached to a tall, skinny jar. The second layer of boards shifted as he pulled. After setting down the jar, he hooked his fingers into the hole and lifted. The boards came out easily, revealing a narrow shaft heading straight down. A flimsy rope ladder dangled along one side. Cool, damp air drifted up, carrying a hint of mustiness.

Dash picked up the jar. Which should he investigate first? The shaft descended too far for light to reach. He needed a lamp.

The container in his hand tingled.

Turning the jar over, Dash couldn't see anything written on it. He twisted the lid. Inside was a thick, black paste. He sniffed and scrunched up his face. Horrible!

"It's got to do something important," he muttered to himself. "If only it had a label." No writing showed when he examined it from every angle. A subtle thought coalesced in his mind. "Moon box powder." He whispered as he jumped up. Taking a pinch of it from the bag, he sprinkled the jar.

With a sizzling sound, letters appeared. "Bird Paste" lay across the lid in large letters. Smaller letters on the side read, "Place a smear of paste on your forehead. More paste will last longer."

Dash opened the lid again and took a very small amount on his finger. He walked over to the mirror and rubbed the paste over the fading black bird on his forehead.

The mark grew dark. A painful crush squeezed for a brief moment.

"Well, that didn't do much." He looked at himself in the mirror, but only the reflection of an ordinary black bird stared back. He turned around to find the feathered creature and noticed that the bird in the mirror moved at the exact same time.

A survey of the room didn't reveal a bird. He hopped toward the mirror and cocked his eye at the reflection. "Couldn't be!"

He raised his arms and jumped around. The black bird flapped its wings and hopped in imitation of Dash's moves. Looking down, he saw bird claws instead of feet.

"Ha, look at me!" He flapped his wings again and lifted a short distance off the floor. "This is great!" After a few clumsy starts, he managed to fly around the room and came back for a tumbled landing in front of the mirror.

Then he remembered the tournament. "Oh, no! How am I supposed to compete if I'm a bird?"

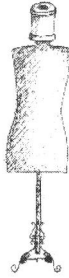

Chapter 26
Dressed in Finery

"Wake up! Pit, pit. No time to sleep longer!"

Ariyuna rubbed her eyes and peered into the bright room.

"Who? What?"

"Time to wake up. Indeeeed. It's late."

Ariyuna squinted and finally found Moochir's face on a wooden footstool near the end of the sofa. "The sun is already up."

"Yes. Indeeeed. Very late. Pit. And you must get ready for the tournament. Lady Idana is already on her way to dress you."

"Oh, no." Ariyuna leaped off the couch, tripped on a pile of clothes, and fell with a thump. "I've got to find something sensible to wear before she gets here. Prince Kasiret promised someone else would help me."

She rummaged through the pile she'd tripped on and found a pair of flowy, light blue trousers. "These might work, if I can find something to go with them."

"I am no expert on fashion, pit, but if you look on the third rack from the back, about in the middle, you might find a tunic to match." Moochir's solemn eyes blinked slowly in the morning light with a mournful droop.

Ariyuna laughed. "Why so sad?"

"Pit, pit. I have never had the chance to get dressed."

"I think I might be able to help with that. Give me a minute to throw something on."

She pounded on the closet door. "Dalan. Time to get up. Palace people are on their way."

A groan emanated from within.

She hurried to the rack Moochir had suggested and found a simple, dark blue tunic that matched the pants. Wrinkles covered it from shoulder to waist, but there wouldn't be time to find something else. She ducked into the washroom, splashed her face, changed, and took a long drink, wondering if she would get any breakfast. And if she did, how could she sneak some to Dalan without giving him away?

"How much time do we have?" She came back out, smoothing the tunic down with wet hands to get rid of wrinkles.

"We have a few minutes. Pit, pit. I checked on Lady Idana, and she's decided to change her clothes for the fourth time. Indeeeed."

"Good." Ariyuna dragged a wooden dress form from the back of the room.

"No, it is not good. She has chosen poorly. Indeeeed."

"No, I mean it's good that we have a minute or two. Now what would you like to wear?"

Moochir's eyes widened. "Me? Pit, pit."

"Yes, you silly. This is wood... oh, it needs a head." She ran back and found a huge wooden spool with the remnants of ugly brownish ribbon wrapped around it. "Eew! This is horrific." She unwound the ribbon and threw it in a corner, then propped the enormous spool on top of the dress form.

"Formal would be nice. Pit, pit. Nice indeeeed."

Ariyuna soon found trousers with a matching tunic and

belt. She wrestled them onto the dress form. Stepping back, she shook her head. "Needs something more."

"A cape, perhaps? Pit."

"Yes!" She hurried between two racks she hadn't perused and found a long red cape. She threw it onto the form and ran to grab the mirror.

Moochir still stared out of the wall.

"Well, aren't you going to see what it looks like on you?"

"Pit!" His face vanished from the wall and then blinked out of the wooden spool.

Ariyuna held up the mirror.

"Oh, my. Oh, my, indeeeed. Pit, pit!"

Ariyuna peeked around the mirror to see the grinning face of Moochir. "Very handsome, I would say. It's just missing shoes."

His wooden face beamed. "I can go without them. You are a very nice girl, indeeeed."

Footsteps echoed in the hall. Moochir blinked and vanished.

"Dalan," Ariyuna called. "They're almost here."

A muffled reply came from the closet. "Do I have time to go to the washroom?"

"I don't think so."

The footsteps grew louder.

"Not good." Dalan thumped around in the closet. "Let me know when it's safe to come out. I've really gotta go."

"I'll try."

"Hurry!"

Without a knock, Lady Idana unlocked the door and burst into the room, followed by servants.

Ariyuna couldn't believe what stood before her. Lady Idana wore layer upon layer of bright green gauze that fanned out from her waist like a gigantic pile of encroaching moss. The skirt, if it could be called that, extended into a lump of a train behind. From her shoulders, cascades of purple and pink ribbons flowed down to the floor, accenting the most hideous dress Ariyuna had ever seen.

Lady Idana's sing-song voice echoed through the room. "Good morning. I'm so excited! Today is the tournament. You certainly got plenty of beauty rest."

A servant, carrying fruits and bread rolls on a tray, slipped past the overflowing courtier and set the breakfast on a small table.

"Ooh, we have work to do." Lady Idana's painted face scrunched into disgust. "You can't wear that to the tournament."

Ariyuna glanced down at her simple blue trousers and tunic. Stubbornness bubbled upward. "Yes, I can. I am a princess of Talsar, and I can wear whatever I like."

A look of shock froze on Lady Idana's face.

Ariyuna supposed not many people directly contradicted this woman and lived.

The courtier's astonishment faded into a forced smile. "But the prince. You must look nice for the prince."

"There is another man that is more interesting to me than your Prince Kasiret." The thought of Naiyan sent a wave of warmth toward her face and a pinch of loneliness through her chest.

Alarm returned to Lady Idana's expression. "But-but-"

"I'll be fine in what I'm wearing." Ariyuna smoothed out more wrinkles from the tunic. "I do need some shoes, though." She held out a bare foot. "Can you help me find some? I didn't see any in this room."

Lady Idana drew in a sharp breath and let it out slowly.

"Of course." She fiddled with her flounces. "Over this way." She flowed across the room like a big fuzzy slug tangled in ribbons.

Fear exploded. Were the shoes in Dalan's closet?

But the courtier opened the door right next to Dalan's.

A soft thump sounded in the wall.

"Oh!" Lady Idana jumped back. "What was that? If there are rats, I'm going to scream. And why do I smell rotten fish?"

"I spent the whole night here and didn't hear or see any rats. Let's just find some shoes and be done." Ariyuna pushed past her into the room lined with racks of shoes.

Lady Idana nodded and followed. Her shoulders visibly relaxed, and she managed a fragile smile. "Blue," she whispered. "We need blue shoes." Scanning the shelves closest to the door, she pulled dark blue boots off the shelf. They sparkled in the light of the lamp a maid held up. "Too plain." She shoved them back and pulled out another pair with tall, spiked heels.

"No." Ariyuna quickly found several pairs of small, flat slippers. Bending over, she slipped the first pair on her feet. Too tight. She tried another. They fit well, even if they sported a few ugly silk flowers. "These will be just fine."

"Oh, no-"

"Oh, yes," Ariyuna interrupted. "Now, let's go."

Lady Idana's eyebrows raised and her mouth opened, but no words came out.

Ariyuna strode back into the main room. "We don't want to keep the prince waiting, do we?" She managed to give Dalan's closet door a quick thump. "We might discover that there are rats after all." Then in a slightly louder voice, she added, "But we're leaving now, right?"

"Rats? In my palace?" The man's voice carried across the room.

Ariyuna whipped around and saw Prince Kasiret standing

in the doorway. Her gut tightened, and she forced herself not to take a step back.

Lady Idana squeaked and bowed low.

"Ah, just what I need." He strode over to the dress form with the spool for a head. "A red cloak will be perfect." Swinging the cape off the mannequin and onto his own shoulders, he stopped to stare at the wooden spool. "Hmmm." Tilting his head, he examined it more closely. "Very interesting. Well, never mind."

The cloak swirled as he turned. "We have a tournament to attend. But before we go, I have a gift for our lovely guest from Talsar."

From the pocket of his vest, he took a small, delicate fan and held it out for Ariyuna with a seductive smile.

Her fingers tingled uncomfortably as she took the ornament. Her gut rebelled. Did she dare drop it? But what punishment would she face if she rejected the prince's gift?

"Thank you." Several bobbled tassels hung from the center hinge. She spread out the fan to reveal the image of a black bird in chains.

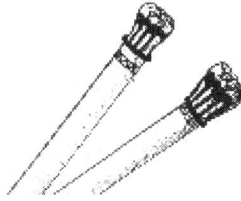

Chapter 27
The Tournament

Dash flapped frantically around the room. How was he going to explain this to Karakul? Fluttering down in front of the mirror, he peered closely at his reflection. Between his eyes was a dull patch of black. The paste. Could he rub it off? He bent his head and tried with his wing, but nothing happened. Another try still left him with a bird's reflection staring back.

Maybe mind power could reverse the transformation. Concentrating hard on his human form, Dash scrunched his eyes closed. A painful squeeze flared in his legs. He popped his eyes open and saw his feet almost appear before black bird claws returned.

He tried again. This time the squeeze traveled all the way up his body. Dash held on to the concentration for as long as possible. Finally, the pinch dissipated.

He opened his eyes, hoping for a human reflection in the mirror. What he saw made him smile. It worked.

But when he reached up to rub the paste off his forehead, the squeeze caught him again.

"Drat." A black bird stared back at him from the mirror. Once again, he closed his eyes, focused on his human form, and felt another agonizing squeeze.

This time, he used his sleeve to wipe off the black paste.

Thankfully, no change happened.

Leaning forward, he studied the imprint on his forehead. The dark image almost glowed. A smudge of the paste remained. Touching it gingerly with his finger, he transformed once again into a bird and back again. This time the change came more easily.

"Woo hooo!" he shouted. "I'm an orlolak, just like Tabin, except I can fly!" He ran toward the bed and, forgetting his new strength, threw himself onto it. Instead of landing softly, he crashed into the opposite wall with a loud thump. "Ow!" He rubbed the back of his head.

Footsteps rang out in the hall. The anxious voice of Serik called through the closed door. "Are you all right, Master Dash?"

"Yeah. I'm fine." He gave his elbow a quick rub.

"It's almost time for the tournament. May I come in and explain your competitions?"

Dash sat up on the edge of the bed. "Sure." Then he remembered the open trap door. He quickly closed it with his foot before scooting the rug mostly over the opening.

Serik entered, bowing. In his hands he held a large roll of parchment.

"What's that?" Dash discreetly moved the rug farther over the trap door with his toes as he stood.

"This is a copy of the ancient scroll of the tournament. It explains the different events and the rules of the games." He placed the scroll on the desk and unrolled it. Bright pictures of races and competitions filled the parchment.

One event, using two large staffs, caught Dash's eye. "What's that?"

"Ah." Serik smiled. "I thought you would like that. It is called Zodoj. It's a one-on-one competition of strength and skill. The winner shouts 'zodoj!' when he defeats an opponent."

"*Zaw*-dawj?"

Serik nodded. "Yes. Zodoj."

"I want to try that one." Dash felt the new moon band tingle, but he ignored it. "Is there a prize for this competition?"

"Oh, yes." The servant's eyes glinted. "The biggest prize of all. Gold, honor, and the losers become slaves of the winner. I thought you might like to try this competition, so I brought these." He scurried out the door and grabbed four staffs from the hallway.

As big around as stout branches and half Serik's height, the rods were adorned with gold banding and carved ends. "These are called ohstans."

"Wow." Dash reached for one.

"You'll need two." He handed Dash a second one.

The staffs felt balanced and comfortable in his hands. Serik showed him pictures and demonstrated different defensive and offensive moves.

"Let's give it a try. Are you ready?" Serik picked up the remaining two ohstans and took a defensive pose.

Dash attacked, and within a few strikes, the servant had lost one.

A few whacks later, Serik stood defenseless, but a wide grin glowed on his face. "You have deceived me. You are a zodoj master. Prince Kasiret and all of Endurek will be more than pleased to watch you fight."

Dash looked down at the staffs in his hand. How had he known what to do? Where had the strength come from?

The new moon band felt tighter on his wrist. All the moon bands had tightened, but maybe that came with his overnight growth. He wiggled them into more comfortable positions.

"Well done!" Karakul entered, his cloak flowing out

177

behind him. He slapped Dash on the back. "Those moon bands have certainly done their work, and you look magnificent."

He took a few steps back to examine Dash better. "You are taller as well." Leaning in for a closer look at his forehead, Karakul smiled. "Very well done. Now, I believe it's time to leave for the tournament."

"But I've only learned one sport."

His master slapped his back again. "You won't need to learn others. You can sit them out, but I suspect you'll learn them quickly enough if you want to join in."

Dash grabbed the ohstans and his cloak, and followed his master down to a waiting carriage. Four servants clung to the outside of the coach as it rolled out of the gate.

The market square stood empty except for a few flocks of birds pecking at the cracks in the pavement. The carriage clattered over the stone street. As it entered the narrow alley on the far side at a frightening pace, they almost ran over a small boy.

Dash basked in the growing feeling of pride in all that he'd accomplished. If only Papa could see him now.

No, he had farther to rise. He would wait until he so overshadowed anyone in his family, they would all have to bow to him. A half smile crept up at the thought of his family groveling.

The image of Ma's face flitted through his mind, and a brief sense of shame jabbed at his desire to rule over the family. Pushing all thoughts of them aside, he concentrated on the fight ahead.

Soon they arrived at the stadium. Karakul's servants jumped down and cleared a path through the noisy, excited crowds to a golden gate.

Past the entrance, they found a place to stop. Karakul

climbed out of the carriage. "Let's find out when your event will take place. Follow me."

They walked swiftly through several stone archways and out onto a green field encircled by tiered seating packed with spectators.

Karakul held up his hand. "Wait here." He darted up a stone staircase that led to what looked like the seats of honor. Dash watched him bow to the man in the largest, most ornate chair and tell him something. The man nodded, and Karakul hurried back down.

As Dash squinted up, he saw someone very similar to his sister Ariyuna. But it couldn't be. Why would she be here?

Karakul arrived back on the lawn. "Prince Kasiret is pleased that you are here and has commanded that your competition start the tournament. It is a great honor to be first."

A twinge of nervousness passed through Dash as he surveyed the field. What had Serik said? The losers become slaves? There seemed to be little choice now but to go through with this. "Where do I go?"

"Just out to the center." Karakul pointed. "They will send out opponents for you. And don't worry. Serik is a zodoj master, and you defeated him easily." He patted Dash on the back. "You can do this."

Trumpets rang out and from somewhere he heard a loud voice. "Victory belongs to the strong!"

The crowd roared.

Dash took a deep breath, held the ohstans tighter, and headed out to the center of the field.

His first opponent marched out to great cheers and whistles. The well-built man stood a whole head taller than Dash. Muscles bulged out of rips in his tunic.

On Dash's wrist, the most recent moon band tingled.

Strength flowed through his arms down to the sticks.

The roar of the crowd grew as his opponent approached. The clamor drowned out the loud voice whose announcement included "Dash", "Talsar", and "Master Balta".

Shouts of "Hail, Balta!" rang through the stadium. The heartless crowd obviously wanted a fight. They didn't care that the defeated contestant would lose his freedom forever.

Whack!

Dash felt the power of Balta's wallop reverberate down his ohstan sticks and into his arms. He retreated.

Whack!

Another blow barely missed his hand. He couldn't just stand there and take blows, so he stepped sideways.

The unfamiliar movements of his arms and complicated steps startled him at first. But giving in to them produced a flow that surprised even his burly challenger.

Dash's sticks struck with accuracy and force.

Balta stepped back.

He struck again and managed to get through Balta's defense for a definitive blow to his chest.

The pair traveled the length of the field with Dash pushing his opponent backward. The sticks clacked and thumped as the two sparred. Dash tried not to think about his moves. His arms and legs knew what to do.

With a clatter, one of his opponent's ohstans flew into the stands. Fury boiled in Balta's eyes. He grabbed his remaining stick with both hands, bellowed, and charged at Dash.

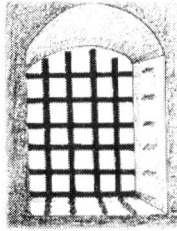

Chapter 28
Shhh!

Dalan waited in the dark closet until the noise dissipated. Even then, he lingered for several minutes. With the slit of light creeping in under the closet door, he could vaguely see Moochir's face on the inside.

"Is it safe now?" he whispered.

Moochir disappeared. Dalan heard his muffled voice. "All clear. Pit, pit. You may come out now."

With caution, Dalan opened the closet and peeked out. Disheveled piles of clothing lay on the floor with hangers sticking out at odd angles.

Once back in the main room, he noticed Moochir's face blinking out of a large wooden spool perched on top of a dress form. Dalan smiled. "You look handsome."

The woodpit beamed. "Your sister dressed me. Pit, pit. I even had a beautiful red cape. Beautiful, indeeeed. But the prince snitched it."

Dalan's bladder made him dance, and he ran for the washroom. "I'll be right back." After, he took a drink and splashed water in his face. Feeling relieved and refreshed, he wandered back out toward the window, glancing around for the pit. A remnant of rotten fish stench followed him like a clinging mist. Would he ever get rid of it?

"So where do we go now?" Outside, Dalan could see the bright sun rising higher in the cloudless sky. "I suppose the tournament is today."

"Yes, but not until noon. Pit, pit."

Dalan's stomach rumbled. "I suppose there's no hope of breakfast."

"Ah, there is breakfast. Indeeeed. Your sister didn't eat all of hers, and the small tray of rolls and fruit was left behind by the servants. Pit. It will make a sad breakfast, but not as sad as no breakfast."

The comment reminded Dalan of Taag. Sometimes he really missed that ravenous fur ball. He sighed and glanced over at the woodpit. "But what about you?" Dalan found the tray with rolls and bits of fruit that he didn't recognize. He stuffed a pastry in his mouth. "Wha do oo eat?"

Moochir's eyes bulged more than normal. "Me? Me, pit, pit, indeeeed? No one has ever asked me that. No one has ever cared if I was dressed or if I..." His face scrunched up as if he might cry.

Dalan stopped mid-chew. How should he react to a blubbering woodpit? "Um..."

Moochir sniffed and blinked several times. "So, pit, pit. We must find a way to get you to the tournament."

"Yes." Dalan swallowed. "I should probably find something that's suitable for the occasion. I wouldn't want to stand out too much. And I don't think anyone will notice if a few pieces of clothing are missing from this room." He stepped over a pile as he headed toward the racks.

"I will find something. Pit, pit. Something suitable for a tournament." Moochir's eyes traveled along the wooden rods, scanning the options.

"Nothing too fancy."

Moochir blinked approvingly. "You and your sister are much alike."

◈

"This way. Pit," Moochir whispered from out in the hall as Dalan inched the door open.

Holding up the edges of the blue cape Moochir had insisted on, he followed the pit out of the dressing room.

Empty corridors followed vacant rooms. Dalan entered each with caution, his heart pounding in his ears. "Everyone must be at the tournament."

Moochir nodded. "Stick close. Pit, pit. I will find a way to the others and hide you."

After many twists and turns, Moochir led Dalan into a deep tunnel. "This is good. Good, indeeeed."

Musty air filled the dark, narrow passage, and Dalan felt cold water seep into his shoes. "But I can't see, and it's wet."

"Put your hand on the wall. Pit. Oh, dear. Oh, dear, indeeeed. No wood."

Dalan stopped.

"I must stretch for a long distance. Very long, pit. Can you run?"

"In this darkness?"

"Put your hand on the wall and run. Pit. Go!"

The tug of his attachment yanked Dalan forward, and to avoid falling face first, he ran.

"Slow down," he called as loudly as he dared. "I can't keep up." But the relentless tug continued. His hand slid across the rough stone of the walls, and his feet splashed through shallow puddles on the floor.

Dampness soaked through the fancy shoes Moochir had

picked out. His cape flapped behind, dragging in the puddles and slapping its wet edges against his legs. Now he'd smell like stagnant puddles as well as fish. But the thought didn't linger as he tried to navigate the darkness at a rapid pace.

Finally, Moochir slowed, and Dalan came to a splashing halt. Sunlight filtered through a grated window in the wall in front of him. Overhead, more grates created checkered shadows on the stone floor. The cheers of a large crowd filled his ears.

Dalan drew in several quick breaths. "Was that really necessary?"

"Shhh. Pit. Look."

Dalan crept forward and squinted through the opening in the wall. An enormous green field spread out before him, with a stadium surrounding it. In the center stood a muscular boy with a familiar face. "What? Is that Da-"

"Shhh," the woodpit hissed in his ear. "It is your twin. Pit, pit. But look up."

Dalan took a step back. Glancing through the grates above, he saw a platform. Several rows of feet with intricate slippers led to glittering trousers. Taking a few steps sideways, he could see faces. A woman sat next to a very distinguished man.

Dalan started, "Ari-"

"Shhh," Moochir hissed in his ear, again. "It is your sister. Pit, pit. But you must be hushed. Indeeeed. That's Prince Kasiret, the High Prince of Teagen."

"You're talking more than I am." Dalan turned to scan the field.

Dash held two gilded sticks, and a massive man swung a similar stick at him. Or *was* it Dash? The boy looked bigger and stronger, but the face was definitely his brother's.

"That doesn't make sense," he whispered.

"Shhh," the pit replied.

Dalan watched as what appeared to be Dash deftly forced the brawny giant backwards. "Couldn't be."

"Will you keep quiet? Pit."

"No one can hear us over the roar of the crowds."

Moochir glanced up. "That one might."

Dalan followed the pit's gaze to the feet of Prince Kasiret, and whispered, "Fine." He refocused on the field just as Dash's opponent attacked with astonishing speed. His brother stumbled backwards. Double-handed blows from his opponent's remaining stick rained down.

The throng erupted with shouts of "Balta, Balta."

Just when Dalan thought his brother must be defeated, Dash swung around and did a back flip. Using both sticks, he hit the challenger across the knees. The man fell, his stick spun into the air, and Dash caught it.

A deafening clamor rose from the stadium. Dash bowed.

Bellows of "Talsar, Talsar, Talsar," filled the air.

Once again Dash bowed.

Prince Kasiret stood, and the shouts died down.

Shifting his position to see better, Dalan watched through the upper grates.

A regal voice from above echoed out over the field. "Let the winner approach."

Dash strutted across the grass. An arrogant expression of elation glowed on his face.

"Well done, Prince of Talsar."

Dalan frowned. Since when was his brother a prince of Talsar? He turned his attention upward.

"You proved yourself to be a zodoj master and have acquired a slave in a very short amount of time. I believe the crowd would like you to continue. If you win this next round, I would like to confer on you the right to be considered a noble of

Endurek." He leaned over to whisper in the ear of a servant beside him.

"No," Dalan squeaked out. "Don't do it."

"Shhh." Moochir's face appeared in the board right beside Dalan's head.

Prince Kasiret glanced down with eyebrows raised and a half-smirk on his lips.

Dalan froze hoping the darkness of the passage would hide him from view.

Standing on the edge of the field, Dash crossed his fists on his chest and bowed again. "I would like that very much, Your Highness. And I would be more than happy to try another round." He marched back out to the center of the field.

"Very good!" The prince raised his hand and pointed to a door on the far side of the stadium.

The multitude responded with roars of enthusiasm.

Dalan clenched his fists. "The little traitor."

In his ear, Moochir whispered, "We need to leave. Now. Pit. We've been spotted."

Chapter 29
Dash's Betrayal

Ariyuna leaned back into the large seat beside Prince Kasiret's. The most honored place in the stadium had a fantastic view.

Horses and chariots waited on the far side of a large field surrounded by a tiered stadium. People, dressed in bright colors, filled the seats.

The first round of the initial competition of zodoj had just ended, and the noisy crowd cheered and yelled. But fascination with the boisterous multitude had drawn her attention away from Prince Kasiret's address to the crowd and the winning contestant.

Her ear caught the word "Talsar" as the crowd chanted. Could one of the competitors be from Talsar?

She shielded her eyes against the bright sunlight illuminating the field. The younger contender had the body of a man but a face no older than fourteen winters.

Ariyuna squinted to take in his features. Familiarity flared. "Dash?"

Prince Kasiret laughed as he sat. "Yes, my dear. It's your little brother from Dorben, grown strong through the influences of Endurek."

She studied her not-so-little brother. How had Dash changed so much in just a few weeks? What on earth had he been up to?

Her brother strode back to the center of the field for the next round. What would Ma think? Ariyuna wanted to jump up and save him from the fight, but now Dash's words to the prince came back to her. He said he was happy to go another round. He *wanted* to fight.

Servants brought trays of baked delicacies and cheeses. Ariyuna's middle rumbled. She had taken a few bites of a roll in the morning, but Lady Idana hadn't given her time to eat much and she wanted to leave some for Dalan. Now the sun had reached the top of the sky.

"Please, help yourself." Prince Kasiret held up a tray.

She selected a berry pastry that melted into sweetness in her mouth. As she finished, her mind wobbled, but the sensation flitted away. She must be hungrier than she'd realized.

"I'm so glad you can be here with me." The prince offered another tantalizing roll. "Now all of Endurek will see that we belong together. I think you would make a wonderful addition to our nobility as well." He paused and sniffed the air. "Do you smell rotting fish? The cleaning obviously wasn't done properly." He glanced down through the floor grates. "Those responsible won't remain to make that mistake again."

Ariyuna shrugged. She did catch a hint of nastiness, but the fish smell made her think of Dalan. If he could be nearby, she didn't want to give him away.

Prince Kasiret patted her sleeve. "But how could I let something like fish bother me when I have you by my side?"

Ariyuna didn't trust herself to reply, so she surveyed the field instead. A wave of dizziness rolled through her mind. She squeezed her eyes shut.

When she opened them again, the inviting pastries drew her, and she took another.

Out on the field, Dash waited, twirling his staffs to entertain the crowds.

"You have to admit the game of zodoj is very exciting." The prince sat forward. "A true contest of strength and skill. What makes it even better is that the loser becomes the slave of the winner."

Apprehension chilled Ariyuna. How would they rescue Dash if he became a slave? But he did win the first round. How could that have happened? He didn't know zodoj any more than she did.

Roars erupted from the crowd.

"Here come two more opponents." The prince shifted in his seat with excitement. "We've never had two against one before. I thought the people would enjoy that."

Ariyuna gasped, drawing away from him. "They're twice Dash's size!"

The thwack of wood against wood rang out over the noise of the throng.

Her mind, which had cleared overnight, pinched and tightened again. Why couldn't she think clearly? She selected a dainty sugared roll from the small table between her and the prince. She tried shaking her head to clear the fog, but it didn't help.

The pastry stuck in her throat. She reached for a flask of juice, but fogginess squeezed in.

For a few minutes, Dash did well, but then his opponents attacked from opposite sides.

The crowd screeched and cheered.

She didn't want to watch but remained glued to the action. Just when she thought her brother had lost all hope, he flipped low to the ground, and one muscular rival toppled.

The other man, with sticks raised, crept up from behind.

"Watch out!" She inched to the edge of her seat. With a quick breath, she realized Dash couldn't hear her above the din.

Prince Kasiret laughed. "So you do care. I was beginning to wonder. These games really aren't much fun unless there's a personal investment."

Ariyuna released the iron grip she had on the armrests of her chair and wiggled her fingers. She wanted to deny her anxiety but couldn't.

She picked up a fourth pastry and flopped back in her chair. Her full stomach protested, but something about the delicate rolls enticed her to take a bite.

With a resounding whack, Dash disarmed his second rival. Relief washed over Ariyuna. At least her brother wouldn't become someone's slave. She pressed her fingers against her pounding temples.

Beside her, Prince Kasiret stood and addressed the crowd, but Ariyuna's dampened mind struggled to registered the activity around her.

Dash approached the base of the stairs leading up to where she sat.

The prince raised his arms. "Come forward to recite the oath."

Oath? What oath? He couldn't! Down at the base of the stairs stood her brother. A wide grin spread across his face.

"No, Dash. Don't!" she called out.

He waved. "Hi, Sis!"

At her protest, something cold slithered across her wrists. In her lap, the fan's tassels had grown into tendrils that wrapped their coils around her arms, fastening them to the armrests of the chair. No matter how hard she pulled, they didn't budge.

What now? Her dampened mind struggled to respond.

"Prince Dash of Talsar." The prince's voice boomed out over the field. "Do you swear allegiance to the throne of Teagen?"

Dash bent at the waist. "I do."

"And do you swear to uphold all that is good for Teagen, making any threat to it your personal enemy?"

"I do."

"Very well. Come take a seat, Dash, Prince of Teagen, Lord of Endurek."

Thunderous applause and cheers filled the air.

Ariyuna slumped back in her chair with a groan. This was all so confusing.

She pulled, but the fan still held her arms tight.

The prince smiled down at her. Something in the shape of his mouth tweaked bad memories. But as his hand rested heavily on her shoulder, a vague contentment washed over her mind.

"You worry too much, my dear. Sit still and enjoy the games. Besides, we now have a guest to keep us company."

A small niggle inside Ariyuna wanted to protest, but the prince's words fell soothingly on her mind as it drifted toward pleasant nothings. He had called her "my dear." She couldn't be angry at someone so handsome and fascinating.

Dash took the stairs two at a time.

"Go!" The prince flicked a hand toward the courtier on the other side of Ariyuna.

Dash took the vacated seat.

"So." He grinned at Ariyuna. "What do you make of me now? Not just a little scrawny farm boy any more. And I don't plan on going back."

Reprimands lingered incoherently at the back of her

mind, and she heard herself say, "That's very nice, Dash."

His gaze drifted down to the bonds that held Ariyuna to her chair, and his hand moved to touch the silver bands inlaid with colorful designs. "Did you come to find me and take me home?"

"I suppose. Right now I'm spending time with Prince Kasiret. We are becoming very good friends, I think."

"Naiyan won't like that." Dash grinned.

"Naiyan? No, I suppose not. But that's what I'm doing. I don't need Naiyan when I have a prince for company." Why did her mind feel so dull? And somehow the words coming out of her mouth sounded silly and flippant.

As the last of her resistance died away, the fan retracted its tendrils. Ariyuna rubbed her wrists. "Well, that's better." She opened it and smiled at the chained bird picture. "Prince Kasiret, this is a very interesting gift you gave me. I like interesting gifts."

"I'm glad you do." He reached for the tray. "Would you like another pastry?"

Chapter 30
Down Through the Trap Door

What a day! Dash squinted into the setting sun and rubbed his arms where he'd received several hearty blows. But the bruising had faded and little soreness remained. With a grin, he rested back in his chair next to the High Prince of Teagen, taking several deep breaths to soak in all that had happened in such a short time.

He'd woken up stronger than he'd ever dreamed. The paste from the trap door had helped him turn into a black bird. He'd also won a tournament event and three slaves. He now sat in the place of honor with High Prince Kasiret and his own sister, who babbled nonsense and was somehow trapped by her fan. A brief pang of concern dissolved into a smirk. For all her time with the queen of Talsar, she wasn't navigating this brush with real royalty very well.

His mind almost couldn't believe his luck. Reaching for his coin pouch, he remembered that it was safe back at Karakul's. But the memory of its dense jingle reminded him of still further power.

The prince held out a coin pouch. "Well done, Prince of Talsar. Here is part of the prize for winning."

"Thank you." Dash bowed his head as he accepted it.

"Would you be interested in participation in any more games?"

"Not right now." Dash straightened. Out on the field, horses lined up for a race around the stadium. "If Your Highness doesn't mind, I'd like to watch. I've never attended a tournament before."

His hand drifted to the moon bands that now glowed even in the full sunlight. No way could he have come this far without them.

In the back of his mind, the last verse from the top of the moon box nagged.

Vagrants misled in a heartless world,
Will force results through lies and woe.
Half-moons deceive, half hearts receive,
Deception deep from a hidden foe.

Yes, but all worlds were heartless, weren't they? Especially home, where he hadn't been appreciated. But what about "vagrants" in the first line? He didn't consider himself a vagrant, but perhaps he could be considered a wanderer now, with no permanent home.

Had he forced results through lies? Well, maybe. Not lies, but forced? Possibly. Karakul saw no problem with using the powder to open the box early. And his amazing new strength had been a gift. So had the other benefits of this new life.

What about the deception from a hidden foe? He smiled. The only one deceived sat between him and Prince Kasiret. His own sister had fallen into a trap. Ha. Served her right for trying to keep him squashed into the farm dirt and preventing his rise to power.

His gut told him he now stood on the cusp of greatness,

and he resolved not to be taken in by any hidden enemy. What had the moon band said? Something about great strength bringing vast gains and something about flocks of admirers. Nothing bad in that. He smiled. Everyone loved him, and he had three slaves.

"Would you like something to eat?"

Prince Kasiret's voice pulled Dash out of his contemplations. "Sure."

A nod from the prince brought a servant scurrying over with a small table and tray of fruit and cheeses.

Dash reached for a banda apple. "Thank you."

"Karakul tells me you have many talents. I would be greatly interested in getting to know more about you."

"I would like that." Dash eyed the tray.

Prince Kasiret reached across and took a banda apple as well. "Then I'll arrange for you to move to the palace where we can more easily continue our interactions." He bit into the fruit.

A blast of excitement shot through Dash. "Of course. When should I come?"

"No need to delay. The tournament will end in a few hours. I will have the guards return with you to Karakul's home to retrieve your belongings."

"Guards?" Dash leaned forward. "Do you think guards are necessary?"

Prince Kasiret laughed and pointed out over the crowd. "How do you think you would travel undisturbed through this city now? All these citizens know you as the zodoj hero of the tournament, Lord of Talsar and Prince of Teagen. You will be the topic of conversation around every table tonight."

"What about the three men I defeated this morning? They could guard me."

"Yes, eventually. At this point, they are angry that you

conquered them and are mourning the loss of their freedom. Perhaps in time they will be useful to you. But right now, you are too valuable to be left in their care."

Dash's heart filled up his chest. Too valuable. The words settled, warm and comfortable. He bit into a piece of cheese as horses thundered by.

Several strength competitions followed. He almost agreed to try one of them, but decided that sitting with the ruler of Teagen would serve him better. Besides, none of the other competitions provided slaves to the winner.

The sun descended from the sky and lit up the horizon in a blaze of gold for the closing ceremony.

Dash glanced over at his sister staring off into space as the final cheer erupted from the stadium. She looked dazed and stupid.

"Ah, here are the guards." Prince Kasiret stood and stretched. "A very good tournament. I hope you enjoyed it."

"Very much." Dash stood as well.

"Guards, take this prince of Talsar to Karakul's home and bring him back in time for the feast."

The soldiers clicked their heels and tapped spears on the floor, then escorted Dash out of the stadium.

A golden, royal carriage, pulled by the most beautiful, matching, chestnut horses he'd ever seen, drove him through the crowded streets. They soon arrived at the walled gate in front of his former master's house. Once inside Karakul's gardens, Dash instructed the guards, "Wait here, and I'll return shortly."

Taking the stairs at a run, he hurried to his room. Only minutes remained to explore the opening in the floor before he left.

He locked the bedroom door behind him, stuffed his few belongings into a tooled leather satchel he found in the closet and set it on the bed. His heart thumped. Taking the key out from around his neck, he pushed back the rug, then slipped the key into the tiny hole.

The floorboards came up more easily this time. Quietly, he removed the second set of boards and peered into the darkness. He would need a light.

A lamp stood on the chest of drawers, already lit by a servant against the oncoming night. He grabbed it and climbed down the wobbly rope ladder, being careful not to get the lamp's flame next to the fraying fibers.

The ladder snaked down more than three times his height. A small, musty room that had been dug out of the dirt lay at the bottom. It had a table jammed against the far wall on the right. Stacks of books stood like stalagmites on the floor and table. Large ornate chests lined the rest of the rough walls, and the dark outline of a small, wooden door showed in the wall to his left.

Dash opened one trunk. Jewels of all colors blinked back in the lamplight.

"Wow," he whispered.

He opened another. Rich cloth glittered.

The third held golds.

"Not much time," he reminded himself. He stepped over to the cluttered work table, burdened with ancient volumes and loose papers. A small book lay open with inky scrawls across the pages. A pen and inkwell spilled over onto the wooden desktop.

His eye caught his name in the writing. Following the crooked lines with his finger, he read in a whisper:

"Three moon bands complete. Prince Kasiret is

anxious that all be given quickly, so I must be swift. Dash is growing in power, and if I am to use him to conquer the throne, I must stay one step ahead of him and keep him under my control."

Dash's head spun. Did Karakul write this? He flipped back a page and noticed his name again. How could Karakul betray him like that? An empty darkness filled his chest.

The lamp flickered. He needed to hurry. Slamming the book shut, he tucked it under his arm. A few steps brought him over to the chest of golds. He filled his pockets, including a handful of gems, just in case. He would come back for more later.

With the lamp and book in one hand, he scurried up the ladder, replaced the boards, and slid the rug back over the trap door.

A knock startled him. "Who is it?"

"Karakul."

"Hold on! I'm coming!" In a panic, Dash stuffed the book and the treasure into the satchel and replaced the lamp on the dresser. He shoved the key under his tunic. It wouldn't be good if Karakul knew he had that.

He unlocked and opened the door. "Come in."

"I hear you are leaving me for the palace." Karakul's imposing form filled the doorway.

"Yes. Prince Kasiret invited me, and I don't think I should refuse him."

"No. Best not to make him angry. I'll miss you, boy, but I visit the palace often and will likely see you soon. We have some unfinished business to discuss."

Dash thought of the book and swallowed hard.

"The guards are becoming impatient and are stepping on my flowers. You'd better go."

Dash nodded. "Thank you for everything." A lump stuck in his throat. Karakul had helped him in so many ways. But now the trust had shattered.

Chapter 31
Splashed and Sacked

"Where to now?" Dalan took one more glance up through the grate at his sister sitting next to Prince Kasiret.

Moochir's eyes blinked out of a support beam near the soggy tunnel. "It's a long jump. Pit. Are you ready?"

"What about this?" Dalan picked up the very short end of a torch from the corner, obviously too short for a flame. "Can you transfer to this so we can go together?"

"Most certainly. Pit."

Only Moochir's lips protruded from the side of the torch handle, between Dalan's fingers. "But hurry, indeeeed."

Dalan reached out to find the wall and ran, splashing down the passageway as fast as he could manage. But something large caught his foot. The scrap of wood flew out of his hand, and he fell with a splash. "Yuck! This water tastes worse than it smells." He sputtered and spit, then felt around in the thick darkness for the torch handle.

Somewhere behind he heard, "Keep going. Pit."

He stood and wiped his mouth on his tunic, but that was soaked as well. Fumbling around, his hand found the wall, and he sped up to a trot.

Only a short distance farther, he felt his attachment pull backwards. "Moochir! Where are you?" He stumbled back a step

200

only to be jerked sideways and then forward. "Not so fast!" He almost fell again as the pit yanked him along.

When the pull finally eased up, he saw Moochir blinking out of a thin wooden door frame.

"That was far. Pit, pit."

"Too far," Dalan agreed.

"I smell another... indeeeed."

"Smell what?" Dalan sniffed, but only filled his nostrils with the stench of nasty water and rotten fish.

"The short, rude one. Pit. Follow me."

"You mean Gan?"

Moochir didn't answer.

Dalan crept along several passages and down a flight of stairs. He grabbed a lit torch off the wall and held it out to see where Moochir might appear next.

"Not far now. Pit, pit."

"Are we back by the kitchen?"

"Yes. Indeeeed."

"You know there are a lot of servants down here."

"Yes. Pit. And the short one."

Up ahead, Dalan saw a storage room filled with sacks, crates and barrels.

"In here. Pit."

Moochir's face bounced from crate to barrel and across burlap sacks so quickly his nose blurred. Finally, he stopped near a large, lumpy sack. "This one here." He pointed with his gaze. "The short one is in this."

Dalan knelt beside it and poked.

A grunt emanated from within.

"Gan?"

A muffled voice came from inside that sounded like "Abbub uff ibots. Et ee ou uh ere."

Dalan tried to untie the sack but couldn't loosen the knots. Wishing his mountain knife hadn't disappeared, he looked around and found a tarnished, notched kitchen knife. With some effort, he sawed through the string.

Gan tumbled out, hands bound, a thin strip of cloth tied around his mouth.

It took several moments to release him and help him up on wobbly legs.

"It's about time. They kept me in a closet for a beet's growth, then set me in here to germinate. I've been trussed up like a skamper wippet for what seemed to linger toward days, though it may have only been more like a shroom hogs wallow." He clapped Dalan on the shoulder. "Good to see you, my boy. We'd better remove our skins from this danker stink before anyone comes spying."

"Where's Tabin?" Dalan poked at another sack.

Gan reached out to steady himself on a barrel. "Pickered off to spank knows where. I'm sure we'll find him in a slick spit."

Gan's legs shook and almost collapsed before Dalan could ease him onto a crate.

"I'll be strong again in a milliwig. My walkers simply need a few stretcher strides. You lead the way."

"Are you sure you're all right?" Dalan held out his arm to the short, wobbly man. "Let me find something for you to eat and drink. Sit here, and I'll be right back."

Peeking out of the storage room, he watched the kitchen servants. "I don't think this is going to work," he whispered to Moochir, whose eyes bulged out of the door frame.

"Wait a little longer. Pit. The short one still needs some time to recover. Indeeeed."

A servant hurried out of the kitchen with a tray and small

pitcher, but hadn't gone far when someone called him back.

"Really?" he complained. "I can't carry everything." Setting his tray and jug down on a crate nearby, he headed back to the kitchen.

"Perfect." Dalan slipped out and grabbed several meat rolls and the pitcher before bolting back to the storage room.

"Here. Have this first, and then we'll get you out of this place."

"You are as fabulous as a rainbow cow washer, Dalan, my boy. This is just what the pig farmer asked for."

Gan wolfed down the meat rolls and drained the jug.

Out in the hall, Dalan could hear the servant shouting about the missing food and jug. "I suppose we shouldn't have stolen it."

"Take this." Gan held out a silver. "Slip it onto his desolate platter if you can."

The servant had stormed back into the kitchen, so Dalan placed the coin on the tray and returned the empty pitcher.

Gan tottered out into the hall, and Dalan hurried over to take his arm. "Moochir? Can you get us to the dressing room?"

The woodpit blinked and jumped ahead.

Dalan followed. Back by the kitchen, he heard a scream and loud chattering about a ghost taking food and leaving coins.

Following a long circular route, they arrived at the room full of clothing. Gan headed straight for the washroom muttering about fishery glop-goobers.

"I'll wash up when you're done," Dalan called across the room as he sank onto the floor near the sofa. He didn't want to spread the stench of his sodden clothes onto the only piece of furniture. A crust of bread still sat on the armrest. He took a bite of the stale roll and leaned his head back as he chewed.

"Moochir? What do we do now?"

203

When he didn't hear a reply, he lifted his head but found no sign of the woodpit.

Ariyuna's pile of clothes from home still lay on the floor next to the sofa. Dalan pulled out the book about the Zavtai.

Gan hummed as he washed, while Dalan opened the ancient book. He reread some of the stories before coming to the poem they'd puzzled over before.

"Gan, can you read the old language?" he called.

"Only a little, my boy. Just enough to squeak at a bulger bat."

Dalan studied the poem. Queen Baiyanarah and Naiyan could have read it easily, but they were far away. He sighed and studied the unfamiliar words.

The humming grew louder as Gan finished his wash. He emerged dripping and grinning with most of his clothes discarded. "Peppering flag glitters! I didn't detect the fillings of this room. I must inspect its splenderous holdings." He bustled around between the racks, holding up tunics and trousers.

A thick shirt became a towel to dry off with as the magistrate of Surtak continued his rummage through the clothes. Once satisfied with his selections, he flung a light green cape around his shoulders before consulting the mirror.

"Um, Gan. Maybe we should be looking at this instead."

Gan stopped. "If it will rally round the weasels, then we must. Now, what did you flap about the old tongue?"

Dalan held up the book.

With one hand, Gan took it while cleaning out his ear with the other, using the corner of a stray tunic. "Washeries are a pleasure, my boy." He sat down with a bounce.

Dalan stood. "That's why it's my turn now." He headed for the washroom.

"Ooh. A puzzler." He held the book up, tipped it

sideways, and shook it.

As soon as Dalan had removed as much of the stink as he could, he dressed and headed back to where Gan slumped on the sofa.

"Ah, you're done." He sniffed. "And fresh as a doorstop. Thankfully this doodle is only a three-line squirt on the page. But it's a rhymer and will sound wearisome once translated. There are several words that pop. 'Vachir.'" He pointed to a word on the page. "And that one is 'Zavtai.'"

Dalan leaned in closer. "Can you read any of the others?"

"This one here is... is mujific, no, mujetis... oh paddle gumps! Mmm... ah... jes... yes! Majestic. Majestic Zavtai. This is going to take a stretched figgy jib or four. What is this book, after all?" He flipped it closed, using his thumb to hold his place.

"Hooee, my boy. A sparkle fling of a find." Gan flicked the book open to the poem again.

While Gan muttered to himself about gifts from the Storyteller, Dalan stood and wandered around the room. He pulled out the small box that held the Enk Taivaan. Its shiny black surface felt smooth and comforting in his hands.

"Storyteller!" Gan yelled. "Another word cracked."

Dalan kept pacing. He opened the Enk Taivaan box and pushed the three small silver wedges around on their bed of red velvet. What was the real purpose of it anyway? He'd used it to end the battle of Temyulun. The Enk Taivaan's song had transformed some of the violent tarch back into peaceful shimeg and forced the attacking army into a frantic retreat.

No battle had presented itself here in Teagen yet, but Dalan wondered if the Enk Taivaan could be used in other ways.

Elch, he called out in his mind. *Could this help to save Dash? And what about Ariyuna?*

If the gift can be of any benefit, you will know when to use it, the fish replied.

A peaceful confidence filled his chest. He smiled, closing the box.

"Flaring pox daggers. This is hard." Gan wiggled in his seat. "I need Tabin. There's definitely a mind scratch to this jot that could be indispensably important."

Chapter 32
A Proposal

Ariyuna stared out at the field. Her mind swam in docile ignorance.

"Come, my dear." Prince Kasiret stood next to her with an outstretched hand. "The tournament is over and everyone is going home. Follow me."

Darkness had crept over the stadium. Lamps sputtered in the twilight. She took his hand. Her pudding mind tried to remember what events had taken place out on the field, but she couldn't quite recall. Something about Dash. And horses, lots of horses. Sword fights as well and... and...

She sighed. "I guess it's done." Pushing up on the armrests of her chair, she swayed to a stand before flopping back down with a grunt.

"I think you ate a few too many pastries." Prince Kasiret pushed the small table aside and pulled her upright. "But that may fit well into my plans."

"Oh." Ariyuna smiled. "You have plans?"

"Yes. Wonderful plans. Don't forget your fan."

Ariyuna's fingers fluttered down to the seat where the gift had fallen. "No. Mustn't forget that. It's a very interesting trinket. From you. So very considerate to give me a fan on a warm day. Where are we going now?"

"We will return to the palace." The prince led her to his carriage.

Once back at the royal citadel, the coolness radiating from the stone felt soothing on Ariyuna's hot skin. "Why am I so toasty?"

"That, I can't say. The day turned out to be warm, but mildly so. Come this way. I would like to have a chat with you."

Her mind floated in swirls. The pastries had left a bitter imprint on her tongue and in her mind.

Dash. She had to... to save Dash. But Prince Kasiret didn't concern himself with that, so-

"This way, Princess. Here, you can rest on this bench."

Ariyuna plopped down. "Where is Dash?"

"I'm not really sure. I've invited him to stay here at the palace with us. He will be very comfortable and well taken care of."

"Oh. That is very nice. He'll be close by, then."

The prince sat beside her. "I've been thinking more about you, little princess, and the idea of joining the royal families of our two countries."

"Would that lead to better lives for everyone? But I'm not really a princess." Her mind strained to reach the depths of the conversation.

"You are close to Queen Baiyanarah of Talsar, though, and that practically makes you royalty."

"I suppose you could look at it that way."

"Of course. And the easiest way to expand our kingdoms and help each other would be your hand in marriage."

"Mine?" Ariyuna held up her hand for inspection, turning it from front to back. "To whom?"

"To me."

Surprised, Ariyuna shifted her gaze to the prince. He

certainly was handsome. And polite. Except for something about the fan that she couldn't quite remember. She spread it out to reveal the chained black bird.

Her other hand drifted up to the jewel around her neck. Naiyan had given that to her. Naiyan. A distant, warm memory wavered and then dissipated.

"What do you think?" The prince drew her hand away from the necklace and held it. "We could rule both countries together."

A negative thought sparked. Someone else had tried to convince her to marry, to rule together. Zovlon! In Belgutai. No, she couldn't give in to that. But this was Prince Kasiret of Teagen.

The uncomfortable thought grew. Bits of the fog lifted only to resettle in another part of her brain. If she could only focus on Naiyan. She concentrated, but couldn't bring an image of his face to mind.

What about Elch?

Elch, help. She called out.

A bubble of clarity expanded and then shrank.

Elch!

She tried again to bring up an image of Naiyan. A memory of walking with him in the gardens at the palace in Temyulun formed a fuzzy picture. Her mind latched on to it.

She could feel his hand holding hers.

No, wait. Prince Kasiret held her hand.

She pulled it away.

A golden fish swam through her thoughts, and her mind followed it. Circling out from the small bubble of clarity, it expanded the lucid spot that threatened to collapse at any moment.

One word surfaced. Faint, but repetitive. *Yield.*

Closing her eyes, she rested her head back. Yield, but how? And to whom? The prince?

No. To Elch.

In her mind she grabbed on to the fish's tail. Round and round it swam, pulling her in a sweeping motion that slowly cleared the fog in her brain.

Prince Kasiret kept talking, but she didn't listen.

Memories of other times with Naiyan passed by. His face became more coherent, and her dependence on his strength and friendship grew more articulate.

Elch, what's happening?

Focus on me.

She tried to relax both her mind and body, allowing the fish complete control.

The deep voice of the prince droned on. But the fish offered the only sense of normalcy in the haze, and she kept focused on Elch.

The bubble expanded. Warmth and comfort filled in the space that confusion had tangled.

Oh! I've been drugged. Again.

The thought hit with a thump, sending shock waves of clarity through her mind. But the vague blur still pressed in from the edges.

The fish smiled.

I need to get out of here.

That would be good, Elch replied.

With a limp numbness, her whole body wobbled to a stand. She forced her eyes open wide and stared at Prince Kasiret.

"Is something wrong, my dear?"

Her reply sounded stiff and unconvincing to her own ears. "Yes." She tried again. "Yes. I need to go. Now."

A frown settled on the prince's brow. "Now?"

She nodded.

"Where?"

"To a restful place."

"Very well. We'll continue our conversation over dinner. I'm sure you will enjoy the food. The kitchen staff have prepared something special for you."

Ariyuna smacked her mouth several times. The lingering bitterness of the pastries made the blur in her mind reach in. No. No more special food.

Go. Now!

The command forced her feet to take several steps away from the bench.

Prince Kasiret stood as well and snapped his fingers at a servant by the door. "Aidos. Take the princess to my personal dining room. We will have dinner shortly."

The tall servant bowed, extending an arm to indicate the direction Ariyuna should go.

Down numerous dark halls and through a large atrium, Ariyuna followed Aidos. The farther she went from Prince Kasiret, the more her mind cleared. Strength returned to her limbs. Had he been using mind control as well as the pastries? Maybe she hadn't noticed it because the pastries made her so docile.

Clearer thoughts bombarded her. Where were the others? Had Dalan stayed in the dressing room the whole day? The dressing room. If she could just make it back there, she could rest.

Looking to her left, she recognized a corridor, and her thoughts connected with Elch. *This way?*

The fish nodded agreement.

Taking a quick turn, she slipped behind a large potted

palm tree. Up ahead, Aidos kept walking.

She tiptoed into the long hallway, and after a few quiet steps, she ran with stiff, stilted paces. The dressing room couldn't be too far away. The thick, rich carpets muffled her footsteps some, but between the rugs, her shoes rang out on the stone floors.

A quick glance behind showed no sign of Aidos, so she kept running. A servant stepped out of a room and stifled a yelp as Ariyuna barely missed ramming into her.

To the right, a dark, carved door looked familiar. She turned down another passage and darted for the door of the dressing room.

Something stung the palm of her hand. She slowed just enough to glance down. A faint yellow light pulsed warmly through her fingers, and she could feel the smooth roundness of a stone.

Why? Her question shot out to the fish.

Surrender. When you no longer had anything to fight with, you surrendered completely. Nothing else could have pulled you out of the fog.

Thank you. Ariyuna placed the pulsing stone onto the bracelet. With a flash of golden light, it stuck next to the red one. She now had four colored ornaments on the Itgel.

Just ahead, she saw the dressing room door. She darted for it, but the handle wouldn't budge.

"No." She rattled and pushed to no avail. "Please open. Please, please."

Down the long corridor, Aidos ran toward her, waving his arms in the air and yelling, "Wait for me, My Lady. You're going the wrong way!"

Using her shoulder, she turned the handle and shoved as hard as she could.

The door suddenly gave way.

She tumbled into the room and landed face first on the floor.

The door closed behind her and the lock clicked.
Another pair of fancy shoes landed close to her face.

Chapter 33
Deception Builds on What Is Weak

Dash rested on the plush couch of his room in the palace. Karakul's servants had delivered him and his belongings only a few minutes earlier. Thankful that his encounter with his old master had been brief, Dash mulled over his finds from beneath the trap door. The golds and jewels he'd stuffed in his pockets now occupied several deep pouches in his pack.

Where had all the riches come from? They must belong to Karakul. And the journal. Its entries were up to date, so his master must have been entering the secret room frequently. Had it been through Dash's room, or through the other small entrance? Next time, he would explore the earthen room further.

If there *was* a next time.

He picked up the journal, then set it down again, somewhat afraid of what else he might find. He would read through it for more details later. Right now, he wanted to soak in the warmth of the fireplace and the comfort of the sofa.

A knock and the turn of the handle startled him from his relaxation. The door banged open, and Prince Kasiret stood in the doorway holding a lighted torch.

The dark countenance of the visitor pulled Dash to his feet. "Is everything all right?"

The prince stood with a piercing stare. "Bring the moon

box and the powder. Time to try it again."

"How-"

"Karakul has kept me informed of your excellent progress." A forced smile spread across his face. "I also want to help your advancement continue."

Dash dug in his satchel and pulled out the moon box and powder. "Anything else?"

"No. Follow me." Prince Kasiret turned with a swish of his cloak.

Dash followed to a wide winding staircase. Smoke from the torch drifted down, choking his lungs. Shadows danced on the curved stone wall.

The muscles in Dash's legs burned, but Prince Kasiret climbed upward at a fast pace. Wind whistled through small slits in the stone, causing the torchlight to flicker and sputter.

Just as dizziness drew the walls inward, Prince Kasiret stopped. He opened a doorway onto a circular roof surrounded by a short stone wall and three spires.

"Place it over there." The prince pointed to a small table and set the torch into a bracket on the wall.

Dash obeyed.

The crescent moon hung low over the horizon. "Should I try it now?"

"No reason to wait." Prince Kasiret leaned in hungrily.

Dash took a pinch of powder and sprinkled it over the box. Faint lettering appeared, but he couldn't read it. He tried another pinch, but it did little to clear up the writing. He glanced into the sky. "There might not be enough moonlight."

Picking up the box, the prince tipped it toward the sliver of light. "There. Try reading it now."

Dash moved over next to the prince and read:

"Three times a fraud, three times a cheat,
Deception builds on what is weak."

"Have I opened it three times before?" Discomfort niggled in his belly. Yes, and this would be the fourth. But the first time wasn't cheating. There had been a full moon. But he'd used the powder three times all together.

The bands tingled.

Uneasiness spread onto his shoulders.

His feet felt like clay.

The word deception had shown up again. Did the box have consciousness and remember what had happened? He peered at it suspiciously.

With a deep chortle, the prince clapped him on the back. "Well, are you going to open the box or leave us both wondering what's inside this time?"

Dash managed a smile and took the box. Setting it on the table, he placed his fingertips on the five brass plaques. The lid lifted easily.

On the soft velvet lay another band. It took several pinches of powder and just the right angle with the moon to reveal the script etching into it.

"Adoring attention creates a hollow shell of worth."

Adoring attention. Dash liked the sound of that.

"Of course." With a snap, the prince closed the lid. "You made quite an impression today with your performance at the tournament. The crowd loved it, and now they love you. Your fight against two opponents has taken zodoj to a whole new level. I think you will find it difficult to travel the city for a while. The commoners can't resist a hero, and with this new band, your popularity is sure to grow."

Dash looked at his arms. The left had three bands already. The right had only one. He placed the new one on the right, glad that the skinny boy arms no longer existed. The bands were tight, probably from his new physique. But Dash would gladly tolerate that if his arms remained muscular and strong.

"I believe the box will give you only one more." A glint of greed flickered in Prince Kasiret's eyes. "We can try for that one soon. With the moon waning, it won't be wise to wait long."

"Can we try it tonight?"

"No. The box will open only once a night. Now you need some rest. You've had a long day."

"Yes, Your Highness."

"Tomorrow we can see what this new band will bring. But there's no need to wake up early."

"I hope it brings something good."

"Have they ever disappointed you?"

Dash thought about the different bands. The first one had promised wealth. That had definitely happened. And if he could get back to the trap door in Karakul's house he would be more than comfortable for a long time. Those gems might each be worth a bag full of golds.

The second promised rich friends. He thought of the powerful people he'd met at the market, Lord Temir and Lady Idana. And even now, he stood next to the High Prince of Teagen. Not bad for a simple farm boy.

He glanced at the third. Humor had definitely helped. He hadn't used that one as much. It remained the most comfortable on his wrist, though it did squeeze some.

The physical strength from the fourth had far exceeded his expectations.

The bands' patterns glowed slightly, illuminating their

purposes. Dash twisted the new one on his wrist. "So, adoring attention."

With a hand on Dash's shoulder, Prince Kasiret led him back toward the spiral stairs. "I would like you to be my special guest tomorrow. I will be busy until midmorning, but after that we must become more acquainted. I have been searching for someone to help me rule this land. Someone moldable. And, if Karakul hasn't lied to me, your Talsar connections are impressive and may prove invaluable."

To mask the burst of excitement within, Dash allowed a half smile to creep up the side of his face.

Once back in his room, he sent the servants away and locked the door. In the light of the blazing fireplace, he opened his bag and dug out the gems and golds. Spread out on the table, they sparkled with a rainbow of colors in the lamplight. He stored them away, then opened the journal.

Flipping forward a number of pages, he found the spot where Karakul had first found him.

The narrative followed the events as Dash remembered, but the small manipulative comments regarding his progress with the moon box penetrated like cuts from a knife.

He turned another page and read in a whisper. "'The boy has opened the moon box again and found two bands tonight. His progress is swifter than I expected, and he should be at a very beneficial place by the next full moon. I have yet to decide how I can use him to infiltrate the palace, but I'm sure the answer will present itself. He is quite naive and will do almost anything I suggest, which will be handy in the near future.'"

Had Karakul ever cared? Or had he simply faked affection in order to gain power? He didn't even have the decency to call him by his name when they talked. It had always been "boy."

Anger replaced the excitement the moon box had

generated. He couldn't believe he'd fallen for Karakul's deception. Was this the hidden foe the box had talked about? Well, betrayal this deep would not go unchallenged.

He flipped the page.

"The time is getting closer. I have the boy right where I want him. He will compete in the tournament today. Prince Kasiret has assured me that he would take the boy in if he won. This would give me direct access to take over the throne. Once he has all six moon bands, his power may rival the prince's, but he must never know this."

"Ha!" Dash said aloud. Karakul's plans included treason. If the prince knew about this, Dash could rise to power even more quickly. He could prove his worth and importance to Prince Kasiret as early as tomorrow morning. And if his powers could rival the prince's, then what?

Pulling a blanket around his shoulders, he curled up on the sofa. The luxurious bed sat abandoned to the shadows as Dash mulled over the journal and how he would present it to Prince Kasiret.

Chapter 34
Deciphered

"Not again!" Dalan knelt down on the floor and rolled his limp sister over. "Ari! Are you all right? Please talk to me."

"I'm fine." Her words slurred. "Well, not really fine. Dalan, is that you?"

"Hey, Sis."

"I'm so glad." She lolled her head sideways toward Gan. "And you! This is great. And you locked the door. I'm not very all right. I've been drugged and keep saying stupid things."

"Come rest on the couch for a bit. That'll help." Dalan pulled her up to standing, hoping the effects wouldn't last long. He certainly didn't want her to get trapped in another charmed sleep.

"I'm supposed to have dinner with Prince Kasirct soon." Ariyuna hobbled forward. "But I'd rather sleep. I am so very tired."

Gan helped support her to the sofa. "Then you should rest, delicate butter pudding."

"But Lady Idana will come to find me very soon." She collapsed onto the soft couch.

"Chucking smoke carp. If we can't feduzzle the milkmaid, we'll stuff her up the chimney instead."

"That would be just fine." Ariyuna relaxed back into the

cushions.

"Here." Gan flung off his bright green cape and spread it over her.

"Thank you. I don't think I can keep my eyes open any longer." A smile settled across her mouth. She nestled her cheek into a pillow. "Mmmm. This feels so good." Soon soft deep breaths took the place of her quick shallow ones.

"I think she's out." Dalan allowed his shoulders to relax a little, but worry still tugged. *Elch?*

Comforting warmth filled him. *V'Arah holds her securely.*

Gan let out a deep breath. "Now that she is resting like a squeeze bug cocoon, we should mole out that Zavtai book and pick at the poem some more."

"Indeeeed. Pit, pit."

Dalan searched the area and found a chin protruding from the side of a wooden vase. "Where have you been?"

"Scouting around. Pit. I tried to find the tall one, but I didn't want to stretch too far."

"Did you find him?"

"No, Pity. Pity."

"Should we go looking for him?"

"I think now is not a good time. Indeeeed. The palace has many guests from the tournament, and they are all milling around."

Gan piled clothes to create a seat of sorts and sank into it with the Zavtai book. "Not as comfy as the couch, but our badgered plum needs it more than my timeworn edifice. Come, Dalan. We must cipher more of the rhymer."

"May I see? Pit, pit."

Gan glared at Moochir. "Your kind are as helpful as a rock snack to a drowning fire mouse." He held the book tight to his chest. "Then again, you are old. Old as the tarlan trees."

"And he *has* been helping," Dalan offered. "He found you in the sack, and he's kept me safe. So far, anyway. Can he take a brief look?"

"Against the recommendation of my busted buttons, but I guess so."

Dalan moved a tall, wooden lamp closer to Gan. Its flame puffed out black smoke until he adjusted the wick.

Moochir shifted to it and leaned toward the page Gan held up. Only one eye blinked out of the narrow pole. "Mmmm. I see. Pit. Yes. Indeeeed."

"What does it say?" Dalan asked. "Can you read it?"

"It is about the Zavtai. Pit, pit."

"What about the Zavtai?" Dalan squinted at the words. Anticipation tingled. "Gan figured out a few words like 'gift' and 'storyteller', but they didn't help much."

"Yes, it is a gift. From the storyteller. Indeeeed."

Gan slammed the book into his lap. "We know that already, you gusting brick blighter."

Moochir frowned. "I can help, but not under verbal abuse. Indeeeed." His face faded from the lamp.

Gan wiggled in his clothes-pile seat.

"Moochir, come back," Dalan called. "Can you help us?" He searched the room. A muffled harrumph came from the direction of the closet, and Dalan found the woodpit at the bottom of the door. "Please help."

"I would like to help you, indeeeed. But Mr. Gan does not appreciate me and does not really want my help, so I will leave now. Pit, pit."

"Wait! What about the Zavtai?" Dalan asked in desperation, only half expecting Moochir to answer.

The pit's face had disappeared, but his muffled voice vibrated out of the wood. "I know many things about the Zavtai.

Many things. Indeeeed. As Mr. Gan said, I am as old as the tarlans."

Dalan banged on the closet door. "Moochir!" he called. After searching the whole room, he still couldn't find the woodpit. He turned to Gan. "Moochir could have helped us."

Gan sighed. "You're right. I'm exceptionally sorry for dancing the scuff bicker jig. My youthful scourge left me with smolder memories of a pit's grasp and very little tolerance with their kind. Moochir, if you can hear me, I extend my cavernous regret for my discourteous words."

An eye appeared on the lamp stand.

"Moochir? Is that you?" Dalan strode across the room.

A full face protruded. "Apology accepted. Pit, pit. I am not as begrudging as my cousin Seerchir. I will help." But a slight pout lingered on the woodpit's features.

Gan once again held up the poem. "Every time I've tried to learn the old language it has whipper dunked me. This is as far as I'm acquainted." He pointed to certain words. "Majestic, Zavtai, kings, gift, storyteller, and then at the end, truth."

Moochir blinked. "You have some words. Pit, pit."

Red crept up Gan's face, but Dalan interrupted. "Yes, you are very correct, Moochir. Thank you. We would love to know if you can read any of the other words."

"Certainly. Pit, pit. The in-between words are... the, great, of, humble, with, place, stripes, brings, in, freedom, and through. But not in that order, and with a few more added in. Indeeeed."

Gan's white knuckles gripped the shaking book. "Splitting plank slivers!"

Dalan grabbed the volume from Gan. "Maybe Moochir and I can keep working on this. By ourselves."

"Indeeeed!" Gan spat out as he stomped off toward the

washroom. "I would rather soak in brackish pickle gel than... than... oooh!"

Dalan let out a sharp breath and ran his fingers through his hair before turning to Moochir. "Shall we continue?"

The woodpit smiled at Dalan. "Yes. I like you. Pit, pit. The whole verse says, 'The majestic Zavtai, staff of the great kings of Vachir. This humble gift of the story teller, with all stripes in place, brings freedom through truth.'"

Gan rushed back and grabbed a pen and scrap of parchment. Scribbling fast, he muttered to himself. "Much better. I knew you could pound it out."

"But what does it mean?" Dalan leaned over to read Gan's script.

"Yes!" Gan danced around swishing his pen in the air. "I suspected this fly was in the cabbage soup. The scribbler points to the staff as the star boomer prize!"

"Baiyanarah's staff? Baiyanarah's staff is the Zavtai?"

Gan chanted with each footfall. "Yes. Yes. Yes. Yes!" He pranced around the room.

"But what about this part? It says something about stripes. I don't remember stripes. Could the staff be incomplete?"

Gan stopped in the middle of a pirouette and shuffled over. "Blast it to frog stockings." He reread his translation of the poem. "You are right, Dalan, my boy. We must find out about the streak stripes. Maybe Moochir?"

Looking around, Dalan didn't see any sign of the woodpit. "I think he's gone. Besides, he's already helped a lot."

The door to the room rattled, and a woman's voice called out. "Open up. I can hear you in there, but I don't have my key."

"Who is it?" Dalan shoved the book back among

Ariyuna's clothes.

"Lady Idana. I've come to find Princess Ariyuna." The door rattled harder. "In the name of Prince Kasiret, open this door or you will feel his wrath, whoever you are."

"Princess?" Dalan glanced at his sister.

Gan twirled around in panic. "I must hide. I would not be welcome here." He made a dash for the closet.

Dalan hurried to the door and opened it. "If you're looking for her," he pointed to Ariyuna, "she's asleep."

"And who are you?" Lady Idana glared at him.

"No one of any significance, your most glorious majesty." He bowed low, trying to hide his face.

Lady Idana stomped over to the sofa and shook Ariyuna. "Wake up. We must dress you for dinner."

Ariyuna didn't stir.

"Wake up!"

With a soft grunt, Ariyuna rolled over.

"Prince Kasiret will be very upset with me. And you, if you don't go to dinner." She shook Ariyuna several more times but got no response.

"Oooh!" She stomped her foot. "This is very bad." After storming around the room, she headed out the door, slamming it behind her.

"Is she departed?" Gan peeked out of the closet.

"Yes." Dalan hurried over to the couch. "But I'm worried about Ariyuna."

"If she's taken the prince's dabble zing, she may just need rest."

"I hope you're right."

Chapter 35
Breakfast with Pastries

Ariyuna woke to the morning sun filtering in between fluffy white clouds. Her brother slept sitting on the floor with his head resting on the sofa near her feet. His mouth hung open.

Curled up in a pile of clothes, Gan snored.

Trying not to wake anyone, she slipped off the couch. A quick search of the racks produced comfortable looking trousers and a long flowing tunic, which Ariyuna took with her to the washroom. On the way in, she snatched an extra shirt off the rack to use as a towel.

She scrubbed and splashed, trying to piece together the events of the previous day. The tournament had taken a wrong turn when Dash showed up as one of the contestants. But *had* it been Dash? A very young, muscular man with the face of her brother lingered in her memory.

The pastries. Those weren't right. The more she ate, the fuzzier her brain had become.

Prince Kasiret's calming voice permeated all of her memories. Including... including a marriage proposal? No. He hadn't directly asked, only suggested it. She couldn't remember responding and hoped her muddled words had somehow dissuaded him. Marrying Prince Kasiret was certainly out of the question.

The thought of Naiyan brought a smile to her face as she patted her cheek dry with the extra shirt. She rubbed her dripping hair, then twisted the fabric around her head. One unruly sleeve hung down to her shoulder.

With clean clothes and skin, she looked around for something to brush her teeth with. Finding nothing, she resorted to using the wet sleeve of the shirt hanging down from her makeshift turban.

Muffled voices rose to shouts in the main room. Opening the door, she stepped out.

Dalan ran around, throwing piles of clothes in the air while Gan crawled under the racks.

What are you looking for?" She rubbed her hair.

"Ari! You're safe! Gan, she's over here."

A shiny, bald head popped up from behind a rack. "Smothering honey pickles. So she is. We thought you had been plucked by an angry nut yit."

"I was just washing up."

Dalan stepped over a pile on the floor. "We tried to wake you last night after Lady Idana left, but couldn't."

"Lady Idana? Oh, right. Prince Kasiret wanted me to join him for dinner. I guess that didn't happen. I don't even remember her coming."

"She was angry."

"I'm sure." The mental image of Lady Idana's frustration brought a smirk to Ariyuna's face. "She may be back this morning. I have a suspicion Prince Kasiret's persistence won't let her rest." She held out the hem of her tunic. "I suppose this will be fine if the prince insists on breakfast." As an afterthought, she slipped on a pair of gloves. She didn't relish the idea of touching Prince Kasiret's hand and wanted to keep the Itgel hidden.

"Oh." Dalan turned sharply and scampered over to the

sofa. "I almost forgot. We translated the poem in the Zavtai book. Actually, Moochir did. Then he left, and I haven't seen him since. But we got a little snippy with him, so who knows when he'll be back. He can't be far. The attachment's not pulling."

Gan stood with his hands on his hips. "Now, don't be a humbler bumbler. You soothed the prickle pit nicely while I chomped his twigs. The troublesome slop can all be placed on my platter."

"Here." Dalan held out the scrap of parchment with Gan's scribbled translation. "Read this."

Ariyuna's eyes widened as she scanned the page. "The staff? The staff is the Zavtai?"

"It appears to frolic that path, my petite pepper pie."

"What about the stripes?"

Dalan ran his fingers through his already messy hair. "No clue. Do we have any idea where the staff might be? The last time I saw it, Zibek the healer snitched it. Along with you."

"I haven't seen it, but Prince Kasiret may know. Then again, after two druggings, he can't be trusted. I may have a chance to do some snoop-"

"Guests!" Gan dove behind the couch.

At the sound of hurried footfalls in the hall, Dalan sprinted for the closet.

The key scraped and the handle turned. Lady Idana burst into the room and glared at Ariyuna. "It's about time you woke up. The prince is furious that you slept through dinner, and I got my share of grief over it. I certainly hope you found it worth your while."

"Yes, thank you. I slept well." She slipped the parchment into the pocket of her trousers, making it bulge a bit.

"Well, since you're up, it's time for breakfast. The prince

cleared everyone out of the upper dining hall just for you." Lady Idana scanned Ariyuna's choice of attire from head to toe. "No, that won't do. Won't do at all."

"Yes, it will." Ariyuna skipped over and took Lady Idana by the elbow. "Come. We have breakfast waiting, and I would like you to join us."

Lady Idana's eyes brightened. "Me?"

"Yes." Facing the prince alone didn't set well with Ariyuna, and even Lady Idana's presence might help. "Ooh. I just had an idea. Could we visit the kitchens first? I would love to see where all the amazing palace food comes from."

"I suppose." Lady Idana frowned. "Although I don't make a habit of associating with underlings."

Ariyuna swallowed a biting comment that rose in her throat, and forced herself to choose sweeter words. "What do you think the prince will want for breakfast this morning? I just adored those pastries he served yesterday at the tournament." Ariyuna pranced down the hall followed by the sputtering courtier.

"He always has pastries for breakfast." Lady Idana hoisted the skirt of her orange and green swirled dress and trotted along, trying to keep up.

With directions from Lady Idana, they arrived at the kitchens. The high speed bustle radiated tension. Cooks yelled at younger helpers, while Ariyuna deftly dodged servers with steaming teapots and plates.

"You shouldn't be down here, ladies." A tall, skinny cook hollered over the din. "You'll spoil your nice clothes."

"I told you." Idana pulled at Ariyuna's sleeve. "Let's go. We're just in the way."

"Sure." Ariyuna snuck several pastries off a tempting tray and held them under the flow of her tunic, hoping the frosting wouldn't stick to the fabric. "Which way to breakfast with the prince?"

A smile dawned on the courtier's face. Without hesitation, Lady Idana pulled her along several passages, up stairways, and through an indoor garden.

"Oh, this is nice." Ariyuna reached out to touch the enormous leaf of a towering plant. "Can we eat breakfast here?"

"Certainly not. It's haunted. And if we don't hurry, we're going to be late."

The upper dining hall held only ten round tables, covered in white cloths and decorated with fresh flowers. In the middle stood Prince Kasiret.

He bowed. "I hope you slept well, Princess. I missed you at dinner."

"See," Lady Idana hissed. "I told you."

Ariyuna ignored her. "I'm here now." She bowed slightly to the prince. "And I would enjoy breakfast with you. Especially if my new friend can join us." She slipped her free arm through Lady Idana's.

A brief scowl flashed across the prince's face, replaced by a forced smile. "Whatever you wish. Please, come sit." He swept his hand toward a table in the center set for two.

Servants scurried in with another place setting and a chair.

"Oooh! Thank you, Your Highness." Lady Idana wiggled herself onto a cushioned chair.

A servant pulled one out for Ariyuna. She sat, careful to keep the pastries from squishing as she transferred them from under her tunic to her knee.

Using a passing tray of baked delicacies for cover, she slipped the stolen pastries onto her plate, hoping the difference wouldn't be noticed.

Lady Idana helped herself to three berry rolls and quickly devoured one. She prattled on about their detour to the kitchens and her inability to get Ariyuna to wear anything even remotely close to appropriate.

The prince ate, unamused, listening and watching.

Servants poured hot tea, and Ariyuna wondered if she could risk a sip. The same tea filled Prince Kasiret's cup, so she decided to drink. She didn't want to arouse suspicion.

"Please have another one." The prince held out the tray with pastries.

Ariyuna put on her best smile and manners. "Thank you ever so much, but I'm quite satisfied at the moment."

Next to her, Lady Idana giggled loudly. "I'll take one more."

The prince set the tray down. "I believe you've had enough."

"Oooh. The room is spinning." Lady Idana gripped the table and giggled again. "I never knew breakfast with you would be so exhilarating. Everything is so warm and fuzzy." She tipped sideways, almost falling out of her chair.

Prince Kasiret snapped his fingers. "Take her away."

Several servants hurried forward, helped Lady Idana to standing, and led her out the door. Her loud giggles filled the room.

Pushing past her, a tall man entered.

A genuine smile brightened the prince's face. "Good morning, Zibek. Are you ready?"

"Yes, My Lord." The healer bowed.

"I'm very sorry to leave you, my dear." The prince stood and gave her hand a squeeze. "I have urgent business. Please finish your breakfast, and I will return shortly."

As soon as the two men left, Ariyuna shot to her feet and

pushed in her chair.

A servant rushed forward. His smile rested uneasily. "Miss... uh... Your Highness, please wait here for the prince to return."

"Aidos! So pleasant to see you again. I just want to explore that lovely indoor garden. I've never seen so many plants growing inside. I'm sure the prince can find me there. Don't worry. I know my way." She strode quickly toward the door.

Aidos stood frozen, his eyes wide with bewilderment.

Seizing the chance to slip out from under his watch, she scurried down the hall, following the sound of the two men's fading footsteps. If she could follow Zibek and the prince, she might find the staff.

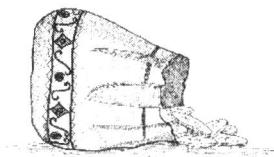

Chapter 36
The Last. The Strongest. The Snare.

Dash woke while the sliver of moon still glowed in the sky. The sun would rise shortly. Picking up the moon box, he settled himself on the window seat.

Prince Kasiret said the box couldn't be opened more than once a day. Was this still the same day, since they'd opened the box before midnight?

Dash ran his hand over the top, feeling the carved surface bump under his fingertips.

Only one more band to go. Somehow he had to stay ahead of Karakul. The last band might also give him the power boost he needed to equal Prince Kasiret and keep his old master at bay.

Impatience grated and grew. The sun lurked not far away. He didn't have much time to debate this with himself. The powder sat on a table nearby. It wouldn't hurt to try. So much had happened since he left home, why not this?

With a pinch between his fingers, he sprinkled it over the box and held the small chest up to the waning moonlight.

Faint letters glowed in the darkness. "Just a little more," he whispered to himself. A large pinch of powder brought the letters to the surface.

The last. The strongest. The snare.

"That's short." Dash placed his fingertips on the bronze discs.

The last. Well, he already knew that.

The strongest. That's what he was hoping for.

The snare. But for whom? If he could ensnare both the prince and Karakul, he could become the ruler of Teagen. So much had already happened since he left home.

The box opened easily, and Dash smiled when he saw the last moon band resting on the velvet.

He had them all.

Sprinkling powder on the band, he held it up and read:

"Looking down prevents seeing what is above."

He read it a second time and whispered to himself, "And what could that mean? I guess I'll find out." As he placed the band on his wrist, a new idea penetrated his mind. He dug out the bird paste and rubbed a little on his forehead.

The squeeze told him the paste had worked. He grabbed the small key for Karakul's trap door in his claw and took a flapping run toward the open window. As he flew off into the fading night, the key dangling from his feet twirled in the wind.

Down below lay the tournament stadium, but the large open area that hosted the market drew his attention. Next to it sat Karakul's house.

After circling twice, he managed to locate the window to the room he'd stayed in. Cautiously, he landed on the windowsill with a clink of the key against the stone. A cool breeze fluttered the curtains through the partial opening. Lingering night shadows filled the room.

Hopping inside, he checked to make sure it really was empty before changing back. The transformations came more easily now. He moved the rug and floorboards, cringing when one board slipped to the rug with a dull thud. He waited and listened, but no new sounds marred the stillness. Quickly, he lit the lamp on the dresser and descended the long shaft to the dirt cavern below.

The stacks of books now lay strewn across the floor, and a dried trail of ink ran from the bottle tipped over on the table. Papers littered the confined space.

Someone must have been searching.

The journal. A smile tugged at his cheek. The power of the journal belonged to him.

Looking around, he found a small empty coin pouch. He filled it quickly from the trunks that sat open, their contents partially spilled onto the floor. Soon even his pockets bulged with gems and golds.

After one last perusal of the books, a nervous tug to leave pulled at him. As a crow, he couldn't carry a book, and his pockets wouldn't hold any more. The pouch would be enough of a struggle.

He extinguished the lantern halfway up the shaft and entered the dark room above. Replacing the floorboards and rug took only a moment. With a quick rub to the forehead, he transformed and gripped the bulging bag with his claws.

Flapping wildly, he finally lifted into the air and headed back to the palace. The first streaks of dawn painted the sky as he crash landed onto the floor of his palace quarters. The pouch spilled across the rug.

Time pressed in. Servants could arrive any moment. He transformed, thankful the smear of bird paste had lasted through all the needed changes. He then dumped the contents of his pack onto the bed and refilled the bottom of it from his pockets, replacing a few items on top to hide his cache.

He had just finished cleaning up the bed when Serik arrived with clean clothes and hot water for washing. He also brought a tray of breakfast that wafted its enticing smells into the air.

"Mmmm. I'm hungry. And what are you doing here? I thought you worked for Karakul." Dash leaned over the tray and breathed in the deliciousness, wondering if Serik could be a spy for his old master.

Serik lifted a low table and set it near the sofa. "I do. Karakul asked me to accompany you to provide some familiarity in the complicated environment of the palace. The prince will come for you in several hours. He plans to dine with the princess shortly, then will meet with Zibek before he attends to you." He poked the embers of the fire into a comforting blaze.

"Would he mind if I take a stroll out in the city while I wait?"

"It may not be safe, young master. The crowds will recognize you." Serik turned his head toward the door to make sure they were alone. "If you would like, I could come up with a disguise and escort you out of the palace for short while."

"Great." Dash wolfed down several bites of sausage and pastries. "Hey, Serik, can we go right away?" He shoved in a few more bites.

The servant nodded, latched the door, then dug in a large closet next to the bed. He emerged with an armful of clothes. "It would be best not to use my name in front of others. That sort of familiarity is frowned upon in the palace."

"What should I call you, then?" Dash finished the last of his breakfast and gulped down the juice.

"Probably best not to say much. Some may recognize you as a person from Talsar, and that could attract unwanted attention." Serik held out a pile of clothes. "These should do nicely. You'll want to blend in with the people."

Dash wiggled into the garments. The brown tunic and trousers contrasted with the bright colored clothes he had purchased earlier with Karakul. What he saw in the mirror solidified his resolve to never be a peasant again.

Serik scooped up the remaining clothes and placed them back in the closet. "You can pretend you are a servant under me."

Dash nodded.

"If you are ready, Master, follow me."

He led Dash down through the servants' quarters and out a small back door. After a few blocks, they reached the market, already bustling with the day's activities.

Dash whispered, "Wow!" Vendor after vendor held out merchandise and called to passersby. All across the market, Dash saw his own face. Painted on plates, woven into small mats, and drawn on parchment.

"The hero of the tournament!" one vendor shouted. "A souvenir to remember the moment. Only two coppers."

"Tunics with the Prince of Talsar's autograph," another called.

"Autograph? I never-"

"Shhh." Serik leaned over and spoke quietly. "This is what I anticipated. You should not venture out in public alone. Come." The servant led Dash toward a stall. "I would like one, please." Placing three coppers on the ledge, he took the hat and handed it to Dash. A parchment picture of himself, tucked into the band, smiled out over the crowd.

Dash rolled his eyes. "Really?"

Serik led him to a small bench in the center of the market that had just enough room for them both to sit. "Listen to the people."

"Can you believe that prince?" one man said.

"I hope he stays in Endurek. We could use some new blood in the palace."

"... the most magnificent tournament I've ever seen."

"Prince Dash should compete again."

"He's so handsome and strong, and a real prince as well."

A grin crept up Dash's face. Every conversation included him, and they all adored him. His face paraded by on fans, shoes, tunics, and umbrellas. Even hair feathers had his name painted on.

The latest moon band tightened to a snug fit on his muscular wrist. Not only did he have the hearts of the masses, he had the beginnings of wealth enough to take whatever he wanted. Someday these people would all be under him.

A tap on his arm pulled him back to reality.

"We should return. You need to get ready to meet with Prince Kasiret."

With several glances back, Dash followed Serik toward the palace. They reentered through the servants' doorway and hurried up to his room.

"These will be appropriate." Serik handed Dash another stack of bright clothes, including a long black cloak with silver birds embroidered along the edges.

Reaching into his satchel, Dash dug out a gold and handed it to Serik. "For your troubles and the hat."

The servant bowed low. "You are very gracious, young master."

"How long will they sell all that stuff?"

"The items with your face?" Serik shrugged. "For weeks, possibly even months if you continue to make your presence known and admired."

Visions of greatness danced at the edge of Dash's mind.

The gap between this and his former farm life caused a laugh to bubble out.

"Is something funny, young master?"

"Nothing in particular. I just thought back to where I came from. I certainly like this life better. I don't ever want to go back."

Serik smiled. "I'm glad you are content. Prince Kasiret should be on his way." He bowed and left.

The reflection in the mirror bore little resemblance to the boy who had left Dorben in search of adventure. In his place stood a strong, tall, young man, dressed in royal finery.

The moon bands on his wrists glinted in the midmorning sun.

Reaching over to the table, Dash picked up Karakul's journal and reread the last few entries. The incriminating words leaped off the page. He should have no trouble overshadowing his former master. The prince, however, might be harder.

Out of the corner of his eye, a face blinked in the frame of the mirror. But when Dash looked again, it was gone.

Chapter 37
Discovery at Spear Point

Dalan stood for a moment with his hand on the door latch. "So, what do we do now? Try to follow Ariyuna? Find Tabin? Stay here?"

"I suppose..." Gan's bald head emerged from behind the couch. "Giggles of gaggles."

"Giggles?" Then Dalan heard them as well. Laughter echoed in the corridor just outside the door. "I can take one giggler, but not a whole herd." He ran for the closet as Gan disappeared behind the sofa again.

The door swung open with a bang, and the laughter stopped abruptly.

A girl's voice broke the silence. "I can't believe Lady Idana has done it again. Every rack, too. And we just cleaned this up last week."

"Can't we leave it for her?" another asked.

"Of course not. We're the servants, and she's the important one. Now let's get to work. We need to have it tidied by lunch time."

Dalan hoped he wouldn't have to stay put that long. More than that, he hoped cleaning up didn't involve putting things away in his closet. It would be a shock for the maids to find a boy hiding in the palace.

He listened carefully for different voices. At least four maids worked on the mess left by their lady. He settled himself in a corner to wait, hoping Gan could successfully keep himself concealed.

Time dragged. The maids sang, chatted, and laughed. Hangers rattled against racks, and brooms swished along the floor.

"Push that sofa back, would you?"

"Ooof. It's heavy."

"No it's not. Here, let me help."

A scraping sound made its way through the closed door. "See. Light and easy."

"Now it is. When I tried the first time, it wouldn't budge."

"It still doesn't want to go all the way against the wall. There must be something behind it."

Dalan crawled forward and put his head against the floor, trying to see under the door. He squinted with one eye and saw feet, a mostly clean floor, and two maids pushing on the sofa.

"Aw, just leave it. I'm sure Lady Idana will destroy this room again shortly. We can clean out behind it then. We're almost out of time. Finish up, girls, we're needed in the dining hall."

A scurry of feet crossed the floor. A maid bent over to pick up a pile by the sofa. "What about these? I didn't see them because they were almost under the sofa. They're not clothes that belong here. And they're very dirty!"

"Eew. Burn them."

The maid with the bundle hurried out of the room.

Dalan's heart raced. She'd taken Ariyuna's clothes and probably the Zavtai book along with them. Should he run after her and risk getting caught? Or had they learned all they could from the ancient book?

He strained to see if Gan had reacted, but the small man remained still behind the sofa.

Blood thumped in his temples. The voices of several girls still drifted through the room. He realized that even if he ran now, he wouldn't know which way the maid with Ari's clothes had gone. The book was probably lost.

"That's all we have time for. Let's go."

Dalan heard the door bang. His heart thumped out the passage of time as he waited a little longer. Finally, the silence stretched on long enough for him to risk leaving his confined hiding place. He stood and cracked opened the closet.

"Blistering dust dumplings!" Gan shoved the couch out from the wall. "Those invaders took the vital jots."

"Should we go after them?"

"No, my boy. Your life is worth more than the scribbles. We must be patient and wait to see what rolls out of the bog next."

Dalan sank onto the cleared sofa. The maids had cleaned thoroughly. All the clothes hung neatly on the racks, and not even a speck of dust remained on the floor. He leaned his head back. "I don't want to wait. That's all we've done so far. We need to do *something* to help."

"But nothing has jumped, so there's nothing to ride."

"We could look for Tabin. He's got to be here in the palace somewhere. And where's Moochir?"

Gan wandered the racks, pawing through the garments. He held up a multicolored tunic. "Quite as splendid as a strutter bird." Pressing it against his chest, he frowned. "No. Too long."

"Will you stop looking at clothes and help me think of something we can do to help."

"I *am* thinking. I am thinking that we should pause and relish the walrus robes while we wait."

Hopeless! Dalan closed his eyes. Ariyuna wanted to find the Zavtai, so she probably wouldn't be back for a while. Dash needed rescuing, but he might be reluctant to leave, especially since he'd pledged his allegiance to Teagen. Tabin could be anywhere. He would feel it if Moochir had gone very far, but the pit was being elusive. And Gan seemed contentedly absorbed in the fashions of Endurek.

That left only himself.

He sat forward. "I'm going."

"Where?" Gan held up a pair of striped trousers. "No, too lengthy and plain as a butter slug." He shoved them back on the rack.

"I'm going to look for Tabin and hopefully find Moochir."

"Very well. But keep your elbows vigilant for pick snatchers. I will perch here and wait for our spring blossom to bound back. If she repops with an inkling about the Zavtai, we may pursue that."

Dalan nodded and slowly opened the door. The corridor echoed with sounds from other places, but he couldn't see anyone. Creeping out, he turned left and followed the empty passageway.

"Moochir?" he called softly. *Elch?*

Neither replied, so he continued through the palace. At one point, he thought he felt the woodpit's pull, but it dissipated quickly.

Frustration churned inside. Several times he had to duck into doorways or behind tall plants to avoid contact with servants. Where would Tabin be? Did the palace have a dungeon?

"Moochir, I could really use some help."

"Is that right?"

Dalan spun around to find two palace guards with their spears pointing at his chest.

"So where is this Moochir?" A very young looking guard jabbed his spear closer.

"I would like to know as much as you would." Dalan took a step back.

"And who might you be?" The older guard stroked his impressively waxed mustache.

"My name is Dalan. Dalan of Dorben, Jarensson."

"That's a fancy name, but it doesn't explain your presence in the High Prince's quarters."

Dalan sighed and swallowed his rising frustration. The High Prince's quarters. He'd wandered right into the most guarded part of the palace. This wouldn't have happened if Moochir had given him some direction.

"We've had a number of intruders lately." The young one nudged Dalan down a different hallway with his spear.

"Hmmm," the other replied. "Could be the tournament."

"Could be. We should keep an eye out for this Moochir gentleman. And it's almost time we returned to our post."

Dalan preceded the prodding of spear points down into the cold, dark regions of the palace. His suspicion that a dungeon existed soon proved true. But where had Moochir disappeared to?

Frustration twirled into anger in his belly. He'd finally tried to do something to help, and now he would be locked away, unable to do anything remotely useful.

They passed numerous barred cells. Dark lumps lay snoring in corners or slumped against the stone walls. Others had gaunt prisoners hanging on the bars, watching the procession. Small fingers of sunlight leaked in through high, grated windows.

"Let's see if these two get along. They're both new to our accommodations. Ha, ha."

"Best not put them together. We do have a few empty cells." The younger guard pointed across the corridor. "He should go in there."

"I make the decisions around here." The creak of a key opened the already occupied cell. The mustached one pulled the door open with a grating squeal.

Dalan clenched his teeth. Not only would he be locked away, he'd have to contend with another disgruntled prisoner.

The guards grabbed him by the arms and flung him in. He landed on his belly in a pile of musty straw.

The bars clanged shut and the guards left.

Dalan got quickly to his knees and looked around. Straw covered the stone floor in a thin layer.

In the shadowed corner, a person-sized lump stirred. "Welcome."

The voice sounded familiar.

"Tabin? Is that you?"

Tabin laughed. "You've come to keep me company, I see. Now we can enjoy the wonderful hospitality of Endurek together." He crawled over and sat near Dalan. "You all right?"

"Yeah." He dusted off his hands. "Just mad at Moochir. If he'd shown up, this wouldn't have happened. But he left me to wander the palace alone. I know he's close by because the bond doesn't let us get very far apart. I hope he realizes that he's almost as locked up as I am."

"Indeeeed."

Dalan searched the cell for any scrap of wood. Near the entrance, a broken board set across several stones made a rudimentary bench. Two eyes protruded from the side.

"Where have you been?"

"Close by. Pit, pit."

"You could have helped me." Dalan clenched his fists. "You could have led me so that I didn't get caught. How am I supposed to help Tabin now?"

Moochir's eyes narrowed and disappeared.

"Come back, Moochir!" Dalan flopped down in the dirty straw and sneezed.

Tabin placed a hand on his arm.

"What's all the commotion?" The two guards stood at the bars with spears poking through.

The younger one gave his companion a shove. "I told you not to put them together."

"You don't tell me what I can and can't do. You're only one step above a latrine grubber."

"Am not! And who took ten years to be promoted to dungeon drudger?"

Their spears turned to point at each other.

Use the Enk Taivaan.

Elch, is that you?

The Enk Taivaan.

This isn't really that big of a deal. Just two guards arguing. Shouldn't I save it for something more important?

Now is important.

Dalan pulled out the box tucked into his tunic and opened it. The faint hum barely vibrated above the shouted insults of the guards.

One of Moochir's bright eyes blinked on the end of the bench, rekindling the anger simmering inside Dalan. What was he so cheerful about?

The thumping of frustration kept him staring at the silver

wedges. He hadn't used the Enk Taivaan since the Battle of Temyulun, but the fish urged him on.

His cold fingers fumbled with the pieces. He managed to get two wedges joined. The hum grew louder. He chased the third piece around the velvet-lined box several times before he grasped it and clicked it into place.

Sweet harmonies filled the air. Dalan sat holding the box. The anger within seeped away. Outside the cell, the guards stopped. Both turned. Gripping the bars, they listened, fixated on the music with faces pressed against the metal.

Elch, does the Enk Taivaan have anything to do with peace?

Warmth spread through Dalan, all the way to his fingertips.

With the tension shattered, Dalan took the pieces apart and closed the box.

"So." The mustached one blinked several times, then grinned at his younger partner. "I believe it's time to collect the noon meal from the kitchen."

"You're right, as usual, my friend. Let's get it over with."

The two guards left, and the pit's whole face appeared in the board.

"I'm sorry I got mad at you, Moochir." Dalan tucked the box back under his shirt.

"You are forgiven. I should have explained. Pit. The only way to get you safely to Tabin was to have you arrested. They immediately kill unexplained visitors in the dungeons before asking any questions, but not ones up in the palace. Pit, pit. Also, your twin is coming."

"Dash?"

"Yes, coming soon. Indeeeed."

Chapter 38
The Queen's Staff

The hems of two cloaks flowed around a corner. Ariyuna followed, thankful for her soft slippers. After giving Prince Kasiret and Zibek time to traverse the passage, she risked a peek around the bend.

They had reached the stairs at the end and were ascending. Their voices echoed in the larger space.

"So tell me what you've learned, Zibek."

"I think it best to show you. It has some interesting properties, travel being one of them, but it's not working well. I've lost several servants. Fortunately, I've managed to snatch it back before they disappeared completely. Who knows where they ended up." He laughed.

Ariyuna strained to hear but didn't dare creep forward until they had climbed higher on the stairway. A heavy door opened with a groan.

"After you, My Prince."

Rushing forward, she reached the base of the stairs in time to see the two men enter an elaborate entrance above. The heavy door swung closed but didn't quite latch.

What now, Elch?

Wait near the door.

Cautiously, she climbed the stairs. By the door stood a

large grouping of potted plants. If she crouched down, she could almost hide behind them. She would be seen easily enough if someone looked directly at the plants, but those hurrying by might not notice.

A chill ran down her spine. If Zibek laughed at the thought of sending servants off into nowhere, she really didn't want to be under his control again. Though the room muffled their voices, Ariyuna picked up bits and pieces of the conversation.

The more she listened, the more Prince Kasiret's voice sounded familiar from somewhere deep in her memory. Even his tone and choice of words rang ominously in her ears.

She thought back to her earlier times with him. He had come across as kind, but on second review, she disliked how he had pushed her to tell about the Zavtai. And why did he want to marry her? Something about joining the thrones of Talsar and Teagen. She couldn't disregard the two times he had drugged her.

Their words came more clearly now. She stiffened. The men must have moved closer to the door.

"And see here, My Lord. Shallow grooves. I believe there are other pieces to this staff. Once those are found, I suspect it might be the most powerful item in your collection. That is, if you have the strength to control it."

The prince's voice turned harsh. "I have the power. Do not underestimate me, Zibek. You may be skilled in discovering objects of power, but using them is my specialty."

Shock pressed Ariyuna against the wall.

She recognized the cruel voice.

Zovlon!

And he had the queen's staff.

Her head spun as she resisted the urge to run. How had

Zovlon become the ruler of Teagen? How would she save Dash from his grasp? The events of the last few days fell into place. If Zovlon controlled Dash and convinced her to marry him, he would have no trouble ruling Talsar as well as Teagen.

She gripped the rim of a pot to steady herself and forced several slow, deep breaths. *Elch!*

Wait.

Yes, but-

Wait.

Fine. But that's not going to be easy.

Doing the right thing rarely is.

I guess I should know that by now.

She sensed the fish smile.

Taking a few more deep breaths, she leaned toward the doorway.

Zibek's voice pinched. "I really don't know what or where the remaining pieces could be."

"Are there no books in the library?"

"I haven't done a thorough search yet, but I do recall a thin brown book of stories that might be helpful."

"I want answers by tomorrow, not stories. Right now I have to deal with a young boy who thinks he's a prince."

Heavy footfalls neared and the door groaned open.

Ariyuna scrunched herself into the smallest ball she could make, thankful for the thick leaves. She ducked her head and held her breath.

Elch, hide me!

A single pair of boots stomped past and descended the stairs. They faded down the lower corridor before she dared pull in another breath.

Zibek remained. She could hear his voice inside the room. Did he still have the staff, or did Zovlon take it with him?

"Sheker," she heard him shout. "Take Bek and search the library for that book."

"I'm sorry, sir, but Bek is gone. He disappeared with the last trial."

"Find someone else then. I need to know how to complete this staff. Botakoz, put this away."

A crash resounded.

"Don't drop it, you fool! Lock it up with the necklace. I need to go visit someone."

"Yes, master," came the shaky reply.

Once again, Ariyuna ducked her head.

The healer clumped down the stairs trailed by two servants.

Ariyuna waited. No sound came from the room. Could it be empty?

Muttered words followed a scraping sound of something heavy on wood. "Left alone again." More grating. "I'll probably be stuck here all day with nothing to do, waiting for them to come back."

Something thumped.

Go in and use your charm.

Now?

Yes.

You're crazy, Elch, but then again, your suggestions usually work.

Usually?

Fine. Always.

Ariyuna stood and stretched her cramped legs. With a timid knock on the door, she called out, "Hello? Zibek, are you there?"

"No, Miss. He's not here." The pock-faced boy, younger than Dalan, rubbed his palms on his frumpy tunic.

"May I come in?" She sauntered forward, trying her best to act like Lady Idana. "Oh, we haven't met yet. I'm Princess Ariyuna from Talsar." A quick perusal of the room revealed only the one servant. "I was hoping Zibek could show me some fascinating items. I really do love to see new and interesting things, especially if they are shiny." She smiled brightly at the servant.

"Like I said, he's not here."

"I bet you are one of his most trusted servants, if he left you here to watch over things. Maybe you could show me instead of Zibek."

"I... I don't know. Well." A twitch of a smile tugged at his cheek. "There is one thing." He slid the staff out from a soft cloth bag. "I need to put it away, but you can look at it first."

"Ah! That's exactly the kind of beauty I came to see. You are so sweet to let me look." She reached out and touched it with one finger. Drawing her hand back quickly, she whispered, "Is it safe?"

"Of course." He picked it up and handed it to her. One thought tumbled over another. Should she run with it? Could she travel with it? No, that might take her far away from Dash. She needed a distraction.

"Tsai!"

"What?"

"I just remembered that it's time for tsai. Would you be a dear and order some brought up here for me? I'm not used to going without, and I am very thirsty. I've just got to have tsai."

"But the nearest call bell is down the hall."

"That close? Very good. Now be a dear, and get that ordered. I'll watch over this magnificent stick."

"It's a staff, Your Highness, and be very careful with it. It's also very powerful."

"Oh, dear!" She held the staff at arms length.

He shuffled sideways to the door, keeping his gaze on the staff. Once out in the hall, Ariyuna heard him run.

She examined the staff as time ticked by. It looked the same as always. A peek into the hall revealed no sign of Botakoz. Where had he gone?

Taking a stroll around the room, she was various strange objects including an unusual jeweled necklace.

After another glance down the hall, she stuffed the staff under her long, flowing tunic and made her way down the stairs in the opposite direction.

That was way too easy, she told Elch. *But isn't this stealing?*

Gifts from the Storyteller cannot be owned. Go back to the dressing room.

If I can find it. The halls all look the same.

She dodged palace staff as she ran, trying not to be seen. But servants came out of nowhere at times. For some reason, no one tried to stop her. She passed through the indoor garden and recognized a hall on the far side.

After what felt like an eternity, she reached the dressing room. The locked door rattled when she tried the knob.

"Open up, it's me." She pounded.

"Smacker waffles!" The lock clicked, and the door swung in.

"Gan! Where's Dalan?"

"He went poking for Tabin, but I'm doubtful as a swamp pig that he'll find him. He's been gone for a pink fly's lifetime."

Ariyuna closed and locked the door. She scanned the immaculate room in amazement, then focused back on Gan. "I got it!" She pulled the staff out from under her tunic. "But I know Zibek will be coming after me. We've got to find a place to hide it."

"Could you use it to bouncer budge to elsewhere?"

"No. The Zavtai is incomplete. I could end up anywhere."

"Then I know just the fog screen." Gan pulled out a small ornamented bag, no larger than the palm of his hand.

"I don't think it will fit in there."

Gan smiled and opened the clasp. "I exposed this last season. It may be a fourth gift from the storyteller, or just a bubble jig of fun." The Zavtai barely fit through the opening, but it disappeared into the depths of the bag. Gan clicked it shut and attached it to his waist.

"We should check the book." Ariyuna looked around. "Where are my clothes?"

Gan hung his head. "I'm dreadfully crushed, my sweet nut patty. The maids scooped them up with the bound doodle and threw them in the flasher flames. But don't stretch your mind over that. You must rest yourself and be ready for the bullish altercation ahead. I will make myself in short supply."

Ariyuna nodded and headed for the couch while Gan ducked behind it.

Heavy boots arrived outside the door, and Ariyuna's heart jumped into her throat. *Elch? What should I say?*

Only the truth.

The door rattled. A key scraped in the lock. Zibek strode into the room, his piercing gaze fixed on Ariyuna. "There you are."

Chapter 39
Deception Deep

Dash threw on his new cloak with the silver birds lining the edges and examined himself in the mirror again. Confidence swelled in his chest.

The moon bands cut into his wrists a little, but that didn't matter. They still looked impressive. Vibrant colors mingled with the silver on each of them.

A servant knocked and hurried in. Holding the door open, he bowed.

Prince Kasiret entered. "Come with me. We need a private place to talk."

Dash dipped his head and followed, grabbing the journal on his way out.

The prince smiled at Dash. "I hope you had a restful night."

"Restful enough."

"We have a few things to discuss." He led Dash down hallways, up stairs and along numerous passages.

Dash gripped the journal a little harder. "And I have something to share with you."

A shadow of surprise flashed in Prince Kasiret's eyes. "I would be most interested to hear it." He swung open a heavy wooden door and motioned for Dash to enter. "This is my own private library."

Several servants frantically searched the shelves. "Out!"

the prince ordered.

"But Zibek-"

"Zibek is a fool. I am the High Prince of Teagen, and you would do well to obey. You can continue your work after lunch. I will not need the library then."

The servants bowed and shuffled out, closing the door behind them.

"So." Prince Kasiret swung around to face Dash. "What's this bit of news you wish to share?"

Dash held out the journal. "I found this in Karakul's home. From his own writings, I believe he plans to take over the throne." He waited for the expected look of shock from the prince, but only saw a spreading smile.

"I already knew that. But I will take the journal as written proof." He held out his hand for the book.

Dash reluctantly handed it over.

"Now, for some news of my own. I would have imprisoned Karakul a long time ago, but I needed him."

"Needed him?"

"Yes. To find you and bring you to me."

Dash felt a purr of importance rumble inside.

"I also needed Karakul to give you the moon box. I am very pleased that he has succeeded in helping you attain all the moon bands I placed in it. A very powerful and unusual set. They have definitely surpassed what I expected. And you even succeeded in obtaining the last one on your own."

Dash glanced down at his wrists. "So the moon box really was from you? Karakul had mentioned that, but I wasn't sure if that could be true."

The prince patted Dash on the shoulder. "You have done well and learned to use them even faster than I expected. Do you like them?"

Dash held out his wrists. "They've been great. But they're getting a little tight."

"Ah. That is part of their nature. As you learn to perfect the gifts, they do become snug. But their true purpose has not been fully revealed yet."

"They do more?"

Prince Kasiret's smile broadened.

Dash wondered just how powerful he could become with these moon bands. "But why did you give them to me and not keep them for yourself?"

Prince Kasiret laughed. "I don't need them. Hold your arms out in front of you."

Dash followed the prince's instructions.

"Now touch the bands together."

The bands pulled toward each other. A blinding light flashed from his arms, along with the rustling clank of metal on metal. Dash blinked several times before his eyes adjusted. The center bands on each side had grown three short chain links that bound his wrists together.

Prince Kasiret's laughter filled the room. "Now you are my slave and will do my bidding. Karakul, too, will learn not to underestimate me."

Dash tried to pull his arms apart, but the chains held him. "Let me go."

"I have made many attempts to take over the throne of Talsar. Your siblings have stopped me the last two times. But with you, I will succeed." His laughter filled the small space. "I've already captured your brother, as well as Tabin. That cat has frustrated me for too long now, but this will end it. All that's left is to get your sister to marry me, and I will have Talsar."

Dash swallowed hard. His mouth felt as dry as sandpaper.

"And in case you're interested, I believe you know me

better by the name Zovlon."

A gasp caught in Dash's throat. He'd only glimpsed the enemy of Talsar from a distance during the Battle of Temyulun, but he now saw the resemblance.

"You're Zovlon?"

"Yes, little princeling. And now I am your master. You have accepted the gifts I offered, and you've pledged your allegiance to me. From now on, you will do as I say, or I will dispose of you."

Deep inside, Dash had resented and rejected his family, but not so deeply that he would willingly join Zovlon. A sudden longing for Ma's warm arms around him and Papa's gruff rubs on his head filled his heart. He'd fallen for Karakul's trap, and now he was Zovlon's prisoner.

His thoughts spun in chaotic confusion. Did Zovlon really have Dalan and Tabin captured? And what about Ariyuna? The bonds that held her in her seat at the tournament came to mind. She had been really out of it, too. Had she been under a spell? He hoped desperately his sister was strong enough to resist the evil prince who stood gloating over him.

Several guards entered. Dash recognized them as the men he'd fought in the tournament. They were his slaves. They would help. "Get me out of these," he demanded, holding out his hands toward Balta, the zodoj master.

They laughed.

Balta tapped the bands with his spear point. "The prince paid us a large purse to let you win. That makes us his, not yours. He defeated us with a pile of gold before you even had a chance at us."

Zovlon gave Dash a shove toward them. "Take the boy below until I'm ready for him."

"Yes, My Lord." Balta grabbed the chain and pulled Dash

forward. The other two tagged along behind with spear points poking his back.

Dark, musty stone soon replaced bright, clean halls. Cold radiated from the masonry, and a foul odor permeated the air. Dash's heart grew heavier with each step he took down into the dungeon.

Two guards met them at the prison entrance.

"Should we put him with those other two?" the younger guard asked.

"Nah. The prince wants him alone." Balta's spear pricked Dash's back with a sting.

"Over here." The older mustached guard pointed.

They shoved Dash into the cell and slammed the bars shut.

He stumbled and tripped, landing in the filthy straw that covered the floor. Only a small shaft of light touched the wall from the high window.

Dash rolled onto his back, with his wrists chained. A tear leaked out and trickled into his ear. Alone. He was alone.

Betrayed.

Locked up in a dungeon.

The money, the fame, the power... all gone. What would the crowds think now? Would Zovlon tell them what he really was?

The bands cut into his muscular arms. He did still have the increased strength. And he still had his cloak.

He remembered the mark of the black bird on his forehead. Reaching up, he rubbed it. But without the bird paste, nothing happened.

Memories of the last few weeks played through his mind. In hindsight, he could see the treachery at every turn. A brilliant plan that had ensnared him from beginning to end.

He propped himself up against the chilly wall. Grabbing a handful of straw, he threw it across the cell. "Why me?"

"You are angry. Indeeeed."

Dash searched for the source of the voice. A face blinked out of the side of a wooden bucket in the corner.

"Who are you? What are you?"

"My name is Moochir, and I'm a woodpit. Indeeeed. And you are Dalan's younger twin."

"You know Dalan?" Dash sat forward, eager to hear anything about his family.

"Indeeeed. He is my attachment."

"Your what?"

"Attachment. We are bonded. Pit, pit."

Dash didn't quite know what that meant, but he didn't care at the moment. "Is he all right?"

"He is frustrated, like you. Pit, pit. But he will be all right. He is talking to Elch."

Dash's anger intensified. Elch. He didn't want to hear about that stupid fish that everyone thought was so special. A fish was a fish. Nothing more.

He slumped back against the wall. "I just want to get out of here."

Moochir blinked several times. "Elch can help. Pit."

"A fish isn't going to get me out of this mess. Where is Dalan? Can you ask him to help me?"

When Dash looked again, blank boards made up the side of the bucket. His hand closed around another handful of straw. Where did Moochir go? And why did everyone think Elch was anything more than a cat's dinner?

He sat for a long time, his mind fixated on his travels with Karakul and the events at the palace. Cold seeped into his back and legs. The image of a fish kept popping up, but Dash suppressed it by concentrating on other memories.

But the relentless fish wouldn't go away.

"Fine!" he called out into the empty cell. "If you really are more than a fish, I could use some help."

Warmth spread from his back, down his legs, and all the way to his fingertips. The pinch of the moon bands eased.

Dash sat up straighter and rubbed his wrists. "So, you are real?"

Of course, came the reply in his mind.

Chapter 40
Dash's Story

All around Dalan the dismal prospects of being helpful in any way radiated in cold, rank vibes. Tabin lay curled in a corner, snoring. Moochir hadn't shown himself in a long time, and the stifled stillness of the prison pressed in.

Several rats scurried by in the meager light provided by the high barred window, but they didn't bother entering the cell. Somewhere off in the distance, a solitary drip reverberated. He leaned his head against the wall and stared at the ceiling.

"You are awake. Indeeeed."

Dalan bolted upright. "Where have you been?"

"Not far. Pit, pit." His stretched face protruded along one slat of the wooden bucket holding putrid water.

"Did you find anything?"

"I stretched as far as I dared, but not far enough to find the short one or the sister one. I did find the twin one."

"The twin? Dash? You know that he's three years younger than me, right?"

"Of course. Pit, pit. He is miserable. Indeeeed."

"What's happened to him?"

"I didn't ask, but I can find out." Moochir dissolved into the wood.

Dalan waited.

His brother must not be too far away if the woodpit could reach him. In the corner, Tabin rolled over but kept snoring.

The splotch of sunlight crept slowly along the top of the wall. He settled himself down onto a slightly thicker patch of straw and closed his eyes as time once again stretched on.

"Psst. Dalan. Pit."

The whistle of the wind outside mixed with the crackle of the straw. He thought someone had called his name.

"Dalan. Pit."

He sat up. "You're back. What did you find out?"

Moochir grinned. "I have your twin's story. Indeeeed. A very sad one."

"I'd still like to hear it. Tabin should, too. Tabin!"

"Mmmmmph."

"Tabin, wake up."

"Why? There's nothing to do here."

"We've located Dash."

Tabin opened one eye. "Dash? How did you do that?"

"Moochir."

"I'm up." He raised himself to sitting, stretched his arms, and yawned widely. "Go ahead. How is Dash?"

Moochir related the basics of Dash's journey, how he left home, lost Doechin, and found Karakul. He recounted his travels, including the moon bands and his rise to power and prominence.

When he got to the part about taking over the rule of Teagen, Dalan laughed. "That sounds like Dash." But the mirth left a bitter aftertaste in his mouth.

"Could be. Pit, pit. His discovery that Prince Kasiret was really Zovlon did not make him happy. Indeeeed."

"Zovlon?" Tabin sat up straighter. "That would explain a

lot. But High Prince of Teagen? Well, I guess we all know he's a weasel. He must have plans to use it against Talsar somehow. We need to get out of here. But if Dash is already locked up with us, that leaves Ariyuna and Gan."

"And me. Pit, pit."

"Yes, and you." Tabin stretched out his legs. "Dalan, how much of a pull can you tolerate?"

"I don't know. I can't tell how far Moochir travels, but I suspect it's not really very far."

"I have tried to find the other two. Pit, pit. But they have been out of reach. Indeeeed."

Tabin wiggled backward until he sat against the wall. "I wish we could talk to Dash, but I suppose yelling wouldn't work, and the guards would put a quick end to it."

"There is a way. Pit. For you, Dalan, since we are connected." A grin crept up his wooden face. "Place your hand on my ear. I will stretch my face to the twin. Whatever you say will come out my mouth."

"Your ear?"

"Of course. Pit, pit."

Moochir turned sideways so that only his ear showed. Three spikes, like little branches, protruded from it. Dalan grabbed the wooden ridge between his fingers. "Do I just start talking?"

"Who said that?" Dash's voice vibrated faintly from the wooden ear.

Tabin shrugged. "I guess he heard you."

"Dash? It's Dalan. I'm talking through Moochir."

"How?"

"I'm not sure, but Moochir and I are bonded. I guess that makes it possible somehow. Are you all right?"

"No. This is terrible. I... I thought..."

"Moochir told us your story. Don't worry. Elch will find a way to get us out. Ariyuna and Gan talk to her all the time."

The silence expanded as Dalan waited for a response.

"Dash?"

"I'm here. I'm just not sure about Elch. I thought I felt her, but she's a fish."

"She's more than a fish, but you have to discover that for yourself. If you trust her, you'll realize that she's pretty amazing."

"I'm not going to trust a fish. We need to find a way out ourselves. Have you thought of anything?"

"No."

"Are you waiting to rot into the nasty straw?"

"No! Look, Dash. We'll get out of this. Moochir said you have moon bands on your wrists."

"Yeah. They're really tight and they hurt."

"So, what are they?" Dalan tried to imagine what they might look like.

"I don't know exactly. Karakul gave me this box that only opened with the full moon. The bands came one at a time."

Dalan's forehead wrinkled. "But you haven't been gone that long. How could you have more than one?"

"After the first time, we used this powder to cheat the box into opening with a smaller moon. I got two bands once, so I have six in all."

"What do they do?"

Excitement reverberated in Dash's voice. "They're amazing! Money, friends, being really strong, lots of things." Then sadness crept into his words. "But that's all gone now."

"So you found Zovlon?"

"Yup. He seemed so nice at first. I won two competitions at the tournament, and he invited me to sit with him."

"I know."

"You do?"

Dalan slid his finger away from a sharp twig on Moochir's ear. "I watched you from a secret tunnel Moochir found. It led to right under the royal seats. I saw Ariyuna, too."

"She acted weird that day, like she couldn't think straight."

"Yeah. I noticed that, too. But when I talked to her later, she thought that Zovlon's food had something in it that made her sluggish and loopy. I hope she's all right. She went to find the Zavtai, and I haven't seen her since. We haven't found her down here in the dungeon, so hopefully she's not in any trouble."

"The guards are coming." Dash's voice wavered. "My cell is near the door. Gotta go. If I can get out, I'll come find you."

Clanking sounds and faint laughter replaced Dash's voice, and Moochir's whole face reappeared.

"Thanks. Is he okay?" Dalan asked.

"Yes. The guards were bringing food."

Dalan scrunched his eyes closed and rubbed his hand over his forehead. "He still thinks he can do everything on his own. Will he ever learn?"

Moochir faded.

Dalan's attachment yanked. "Oh, no. Moochir is reaching."

The tug pulled him to his feet and shoved him up against the bars. His face, body, and arms pressed against the cell door. A bar ran right across his face. "Seriously, Moochir?"

A guard's harsh voice echoed through the stone dungeon. "What's all the commotion?"

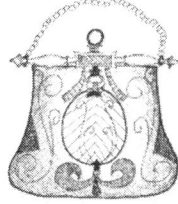

Chapter 41
Only the Truth

Only the truth, Ariyuna reminded herself as she looked up at Zibek. Why did Elch always give such difficult instructions? Lying about the staff would be so much easier, but she decided to follow Elch's directions.

Only the truth.

The angry healer marched toward her with two servants scurrying behind.

Ariyuna sat up straighter on the sofa.

"Did you see the staff?" His stern face radiated mistrust.

"Oh, yes. It's beautiful."

"Where is it?"

"I'm not really sure. It went into a very small bag and disappeared. The staff couldn't really be in the bag. It was way too long for such a small pouch. But somehow it fit."

Zibek frowned. "Did you take the staff?"

"Oh, yes. Like I said, it went into a tiny bag. No bigger than this." She spread out her fingers and held up her hand, realizing how silly she sounded. Was the truth really the right answer?

The healer sighed. "Did you eat pastries for breakfast?"

"I most certainly did. They were delicious. Your cooks

make wonderful food. I took a few from-"

"There's no use asking her any more questions." Zibek turned to the servants. "She's not herself right now."

The men traded knowing nods and smiles.

"Make sure she doesn't leave this room. Have all the food come directly from the servant's kitchen. Nothing special. We'll question her again tonight." He hurried out, his swirling cloak hitting the servant's legs as he went.

Ariyuna waited until his footsteps faded, then smiled at the two servants who remained.

"May I have some tsai? Please? I'm really thirsty. And what are your names?"

They looked at each other.

"I'm Junu and this is Ehrbol." Junu stepped toward the door, with his partner close behind. "I'll get the tsai. You stay right outside and make sure she doesn't leave."

Ehrbol nodded, and the door closed behind them. Ariyuna heard a whispered argument, before one set of footsteps scurried down the hall.

She sunk back onto the couch. "So, Gan. What now?"

"I'm as sure as a blind badger in a stink squirrel's tunnel," came the muffled reply from behind the sofa. "Elch is telling me to linger, so I think I'll simply sit snug bug for a bit."

Outside the door, Ariyuna heard another conversation, but it didn't sound like Junu. Besides, he had just left to get tsai.

Three voices came through the closed door. It opened and a maid entered, followed by a tall man with spiked blond hair.

The maid bowed. "I'm sorry to bother you, Princess, but this gentleman insisted on seeing you."

"Naiyan!" Ariyuna jumped up and ran to hug him. "I'm so glad to see you!" Peeking over his shoulder, she smiled at the maid. "You may go. Please close the door."

The servant girl bowed and left. When the door latched, Ariyuna released her grip. "When did you get here? Why did you come?"

Naiyan held her at arm's length. "When you vanished, the palace guards and I searched Temyulun, then Surtak, the Altan Forest, Dorben, Belgutai. On a whim, I decided to try Endurek. It's taken me a long time, but I'm finally here. Are you all right?"

The couch slid forward, and Gan's head popped up. "Flabbergasting tart peanuts! It's good to see you, Sunshine Boy."

"Gan!" Naiyan scanned the room. "Is anyone else here?"

Ariyuna nodded. "Yes, Dash, Dalan, and Tabin are all here, somewhere, but Tabin's been captured, Dalan went to look for him, and I don't know exactly where Dash is. He's somewhere in the palace."

Bewilderment spread across Naiyan's face.

She laughed. "Maybe we should start at the beginning."

Naiyan and Ariyuna settled onto the couch while Gan leaned over from behind. Between the two of them, they filled Naiyan in on the basics of what had happened.

"So you have the Zavtai?" Naiyan's wide eyes turned to Gan.

"Right here in my pincher pouch." He pulled it off his waist, opened the clasp, and drew out the staff.

Ariyuna shook her head. "I still don't understand how it fits in there."

"A very unmanageable explanation." A brief frown crossed Gan's forehead.

Naiyan held the staff for a moment and then handed it back to Gan. "Better keep it safe. I have some urgent news for you." He let out a deep breath. "The queen is... well, do you remember the wound she sustained at the Battle of Temyulun?"

"Yes." Ariyuna's stomach twisted.

"Well, as you know, it's never healed, and it's slowly poisoning her. She's become quite ill and weak."

Ariyuna swallowed hard to press down the developing lump in her throat.

"Stuffed musher logs. That's serious!"

Naiyan nodded. "You're right. She's not doing well. That's partly why I needed to find you as soon as possible. I also needed to know that you were all right."

He took her hand in both of his. "Now, I think our next move should be to find Tabin, Dalan, and Dash. Then we'd better all leave for Temyulun as soon as possible. Would the guards let you wander a bit?"

"Maybe," Ariyuna choked out. "We could at least try. There's only one guard right now. I sent the other one to get tsai, but he'll be back soon. Let's go right away."

She gave Naiyan's hand a squeeze. "I'm so glad you came."

"I couldn't just leave you to make your way home alone. And the queen really needs your help and comfort."

She walked to the door and opened it. "Hello, Ehrbol. I'm going for a walk. I saw an indoor garden not long ago, and I would like to find it again."

"But Zibek said you must stay in this room."

She smiled sweetly at the guard. "Come with me. Then I'll be just as safe. But I *must* see that garden again."

Before Ehrbol could say anything more, she pranced down the hall.

"Wait for me, Princess." He scurried after her.

Ariyuna glanced back and saw Gan and Naiyan following

at a safe distance.

She took several wrong turns and followed them up with giggled apologies until she arrived at the glass-encased indoor garden.

"Miss! Don't go in there."

"And why not?"

"It's haunted." Ehrbol shuddered involuntarily.

"Oh, that's silly nonsense. Haunting isn't real. You can stay out here if you like and make sure I don't come out. You can guard this room instead of the wardrobe door. That makes things easy enough." She gave him a playful pat on the cheek and bounced through into the room.

"Miss, I...oh...ooh. There are four entrances. I can't watch them all."

Ariyuna smiled back through the closing glass doors and wandered toward the left.

The guard hurried to the entrance on that side. As soon as she saw him leave, she beckoned Naiyan and Gan toward the same door she had used.

Running forward a bit, she made it to the entry on the left at the same time as Ehrbol. She waved and bent over to smell a flower.

Moochir's distorted face popped out of the wooden planter.

"Oh! You scared me. You look a little stretched."

"I am. Indeeeed. I only have a moment. Pit, pit. Dalan, Tabin, and Dash are all imprisoned in the dungeon. I can lead you there, but we must rid you of the guard. Indeeeed."

"Gan and Naiyan are with me. They should be entering the garden any moment now. How do we get to the dungeon?"

Ariyuna glanced to the left. The guard stood with his back to the garden. "I'll try to distract Ehrbol-

"Air Hole?"

"No, Ehrbol. The guard. Which door should we leave from?"

"The one Air Sole is guarding. Pit, pit. By the way, Hair Ball has problems with his hands itching when he gets nervous. They are already bothering him. If you can scare him a bit more, he may leave his post. Indeeeed."

"How do you know that?"

"Never you mind. Pit! Hurry, I can't stretch this far for long. Dalan will be a pancake. Indeeeed."

Ariyuna saw Naiyan and Gan creeping between the palms. She pointed to the direction they needed to exit. When they nodded their understanding, she trotted ahead to where Ehrbol stood and opened the door.

"Um, excuse me. I just saw a face in a planter, and it talked to me. Is that normal?"

The guard's eyes widened. He scratched at his hand. "Oh, no, Miss, I mean, Princess."

"I also thought I saw two men sneaking through the palms. Is that allowed?"

"No, Princess. No one goes in there. Like I said, it's haunted." He scratched at his other hand.

"I would feel better if you came in and checked it out. Or maybe you could find Junu, and he could come with you."

Ehrbol nodded. "Good idea, Princess. Please stay here and enjoy the flowers." He hurried off without waiting for her reply.

Ariyuna watch him disappear down the hall and then slipped out with the other two right behind her.

"This way. Pit." Moochir indicated the hall with a twitch of his eyes. Gan, Naiyan, and Ariyuna pursued him as he jumped from picture frames to planters to window ledges, before descending a steep set of stairs.

Halfway down, the woodpit stopped. "Here is where it gets tricky. We must enter the dungeon, find the keys, and free the others from two different cells without being caught. Or you will be executed. Pit, pit. Any ideas?"

"I thought you had this worked out." Ariyuna put her hands on her hips and tried to catch her breath.

"Oh no. Pit. I ran into you by accident. I have nothing planned. Indeeeed."

"Crabby flap boxes." Gan plunked down on a stone step. "If we get caught, we'll be as much help as puckered hens."

Ariyuna squeezed her eyes shut and rubbed her face. "We can't just walk down there and introduce ourselves."

Naiyan looked around. "We need a place to hide and think this through."

"Wait a moment. Pit. You may not be able to boldly introduce yourselves, but I can. Indeeeed." His face faded.

"Wait!" Ariyuna reached toward the woodpit, but he disappeared.

Naiyan groaned. "This could get ugly."

Chapter 42
The Fish

Dash held out his arms and glared at the moon bands. The splashes of color had faded. A dark tarnish covered the once sparkling silver. In the dim light, he could see flecks of blood along their edges where they dug into his skin. He pulled his wrists apart, but the three chain links still bound them together.

He worked his fingers open and closed to ease the tingling, but that only intensified the painful squeeze on his forearms. There had to be a way to get them off.

A deep, torturing thirst interrupted his thoughts and distracted him.

Sinking to his knees beside the wooden bucket, he lifted it awkwardly. A splash of putrid water filled his mouth and ran down his chin. With a gag and cough, he spit it out and wiped his mouth on his tunic.

He couldn't take this anymore. He needed help, but who?

Trying to stand back up only landed him sideways in the straw. He tried again and pushed himself to standing.

Pressing his face against the bars, he peered in both directions. No one.

Elch came to mind.

Elch. Dash didn't even like the name. Tabin had once

told him it meant messenger or energy. Even that bothered him for no particular reason.

He paced restlessly back and forth in his small cell.

Moochir had mentioned Elch. Ariyuna and Dalan couldn't stop talking about the stupid fish. Could she really help?

Finally, in desperation, he called out into the dank dungeon air. "If you're real, Elch, get me out of these bands."

The moon bands remained, but a soothing warmth wrapped around his arms. The pain eased.

"Oh, yeah, that feels better. Can you help me get them off?"

Only the place of total surrender can remove them, echoed in his mind along with the image of a fish.

Dash shook his head in disbelief. Had that fish actually talked in his head? Couldn't be.

But what if...? "Who's there?" he asked.

I am.

"Elch?"

Yes.

He rubbed a hand over his face. Maybe he was losing his mind. But just to be sure, he tried again. "So, I need to find the place of total surrender? Where's that?"

You will know when you find it.

"But I want them off now. Why'd they get so tight?"

Each one is a good gift. But they can be twisted into a form of slavery. What was the verse for the first band?

"I don't know. Something about wealth being happiness sucked from a well." Dash smiled to himself. "That turned out to be true. Money makes people happy. It made me happy."

Yes, but didn't it also leave you thirsting for more?

Dash ignored the question. "If I could just get the bird

paste from my palace room, I could fly over to-"

The wealth of family and friends far outweighs that of gold.

Dash didn't appreciate the fish's intrusion. He liked the gold. And he'd rather be away from his family, out on his own with no one to boss him around.

What about the second band? the fish asked.

Grudgingly, Dash searched his memory. "Rich friends are an elaborate veneer that can mask the flaws within. That one's good, right? Rich friends can help cover up my mistakes."

Do you think that friends drawn in by riches or power are true friends? Have you made any true friends here in Endurek?

Dash thought of Karakul. No, he'd betrayed their friendship. So had Prince Kasiret. Serik? No, he'd just done his job as a servant. There had to be more. He racked his brain but couldn't think of anyone.

And where are your friends now, at your time of need?

Dash sighed. "Fine."

He paced the cell floor again. Why had no one come to help him? Didn't they care? The more he mulled it over, the clearer it became. He had no friends.

You do have one friend. I am here.

"You're a fish." Dash kicked at the straw. "So, what about the third band? Laughing is good, right?"

Absolutely. Laughter is healing in many ways. But what did you discover about it?

Dash thought back to his time selling in the market. Humor had worked well, but laughter could be cruel and hide the truth.

"And the fourth?" he asked.

Great strength and might will bring vast gains. Fickle admirers flock to the façade of a hero.

Dash flexed his muscles, but stopped immediately when the bands dug in. "I liked that one. And the people all loved me.

You should have seen all the stuff at the market with my face or name on it."

The hero you became was only a false front. Why would they stay loyal to that?

"I *was* a real hero. I won at the tournament. And look, I'm still strong." Dash picked up the bucket and hefted it over his head.

Yes, but where are your admirers now? I don't hear them clamoring for your release.

Irritation roiled within. A sudden weakness made his arms tremble. He threw the bucket into the corner, but not before it slopped putrid water all over his chest. The stench of it assaulted his nose as it oozed down to his trousers.

"Yuck!" Dash tried to wring out his tunic, but a nasty brown film remained.

Stomping around the cell, he kicked at the bucket, but howled as his toes collided with the sturdy wood. A twinge of longing for his solid work boots passed through his mind. "Stupid palace slippers. Completely useless."

Why did all this bad stuff have to happen to him? And Elch was just a meddling nuisance. Why should he listen to a fish, anyway? Fish didn't have all the answers. This whole conversation put everything in shadows.

You are doing well, Dash. You are sensing shadows.

"What use is that?"

Shadows are created by the presence of light.

"There's no light in this. The fifth band said, 'Adoring attention creates a hollow shell of worth.' That's no better than the other one. Being popular was great, but it crumbled."

In his mind, Dash sensed the fish smile.

"It's not funny. I had it all and lost it."

You had nothing. True worth is not found in the temporary.

Dash plopped down. His face landed in his hands. He was frustrated by his conversation with Elch, angered by his imprisonment, and tormented by the pain radiating up his arms.

The last verse rattled around in his head. *Looking prevents seeing what is above.* What did that mean? Elch would probably have some gloomy explanation that would burst his last bubble. He didn't dare ask.

Maybe that Moochir character would give him better answers. "Moochir?" he called. "Are you there?" He wobbled to his feet, retrieved the bucket, and twirled it around. No face.

Exhaustion settled over him. He had no energy left to fight the pain, or the disturbing thoughts that his talk with Elch had left. He sat down and let the tears flow.

The final verse bobbed to the surface again. He repeated it to himself several times but couldn't figure it out.

Elch pressed into his thoughts. *The greatest things in life are often bigger and higher than yourself. You need to shift the weight of your life onto something that will actually hold it up.*

Dash didn't want to shift anything unless it meant shifting himself out of this horrible cell.

The bands have created a far deeper bondage than this cell does.

"Oh, shut up." Dash slumped over into the rotting straw and closed his eyes.

In his half-awake mind, the events of the past twisted and mingled with a horrifying effect. Karakul became a giant black bird that tried to scratch his face. Money poured down from the sky, but the sting of it sent Dash running for cover. Courtiers laughed at him. The people in the market bought everything they could with his face on it, then slashed them with knives. He tried to run, but his legs had the strength of jelly.

He opened his eyes with a start. "What was that?" Sweat soaked his tunic. He rolled over and stared at the blackened, crusty ceiling. "You win, Elch. The last verse says I need to look up instead of down. How do I do that?"

You're in a good place now. Where else can you look when you're flat on your back?

Dash rolled his eyes. Lying in rancid straw on the floor of a dungeon wasn't exactly his definition of a good place.

Chapter 43
Escape

The bars dug into Dalan's face, and still Moochir pulled. He could see the guard running toward him. "Tabin, what do I say?"

The guard pointed his spear at Dalan's chest. "What's the idea? You won't get out that way, boy."

"I understand." Dalan tried to pull his arms away, but they wouldn't budge. "If pressing on the bars got me out, I'd be long gone."

"Don't get sassy with me. Back up."

The attachment pulled harder. "Oof! I would love to. Can't right now. But I will as soon as possible."

Tabin stepped forward. "I'll keep an eye on him."

"Ha! That's no help. What kind of escape plan are you two cooking up? Nobody gets out of this place. Not while I'm here."

The attachment eased for a moment. "Hang in there, Dalan. Pit, pit. I found them."

The guard's eyes widened. "Who said that?"

Dalan backed away from the bars only to be jerked into them again. "Ow! Really?"

"Who said that?" the guard insisted.

With a straight face, Tabin spoke up. "Dalan here said, 'Ow, really,' but a strange creature called a woodpit came to give us a report just before that. He can transfer from one wooden object to another. It's very likely he spoke out of the bench here. Did you see him? He's a very unusual character."

The guard took a step back. His spear shook, and the color drained from his face.

Tabin patted Dalan on the head. "Unfortunately, my friend here is attached to the woodpit who is pulling on him at the moment. The attachment doesn't reach as far as the creature would like to go, so it's rather uncomfortable."

Taking another step backward, the guard whispered, "Ghosts. You're talking to g... g... ghosts."

"No," Tabin corrected. "A woodpit."

The guard turned and ran for the entrance.

Tabin smiled. "It's amazing how effective the truth can be. I guess the fine folks of Endurek are afraid of ghosts."

With his mouth squished by the bar, Dalan muttered, "Doesn't help me out much. I hope Moochir hurries."

From time to time, the pull eased a little, only to tighten again as Dalan waited. "This better be good." Then suddenly, he fell back into the cell.

"I've returned. Pit, pit. Help is coming. Oh, this will be fun. More fun than I've had in years. Indeeeed!" Moochir's face grinned out of the bench and then faded.

"I don't know what to make of him sometimes." Dalan stood and dusted straw off his trousers. "I hope he doesn't make things worse."

Tabin grabbed the bars and glanced in both directions. "Nothing coming so far, but a woodpit having fun is something I've never heard of."

A yelp sounded from down the passageway, and the tall,

younger guard came into view. He stopped right by the cell. "You were serious when you said you talked to someone?"

Moochir's face grinned out of the bench. "Of course they were. Pit, pit. And I'm simply trying to be friendly."

The guard's lip quivered. His trembling spear protruded through the bars toward the bench. "What *is* that thing?"

"That?" Tabin pointed to Moochir's face. "That is a woodpit. Mostly harmless and usually annoying. I wouldn't recommend an attachment to one."

Dalan wanted to add his agreement. Moochir had been more than annoying at times. On the other hand, a good part of him had grown fond of the intruder.

"Hello, guard person. Pit, pit." Mischief danced in Moochir's eyes. "I have one simple request."

"No! Go away! The guard poked at the face in the bench with the point of his spear, but Moochir moved. His face reappeared farther down the plank. The guard poked again and again, but Moochir simply shifted to different parts of the bench.

"You haven't heard my request. Indeeeed."

The guard jabbed.

"Rude! Pit, pit. Didn't your mother teach you not to poke at faces when you're being spoken to? Indeeeed!"

"I don't take requests from ghosts!" The bench now bristled with large splinters, but the guard still tried to harpoon Moochir.

"Stop." Dalan tried to grab the spear and almost got his hand impaled on the bench.

"I can stop this. Pit, pit." His face vanished and reappeared on the handle of the lance. "Much better. Indeeeed."

"Ahhh!" The guard dropped the spear and backed away, his eyes bulging with fear.

"Now for my request. Pit, pit. Drop the keys as well."

Glancing down at the spear on the floor, the guard reached for the ring on his waist with shaking hands. But instead of dropping them, he bolted.

"Pit. I'll be right back."

Scuffles and shouts rang out from down the corridor.

Tabin laughed. "I suspect Moochir will be successful in the end. But I doubt anyone will ever believe the guard's story." He brushed splinters off the bench with a handful of straw from the floor and sat.

Trying to see down the dark hall, Dalan could hear bits and pieces of the fracas as Moochir pursued the guard. Finally, he heard the jangle of metal against stone. "It sounds like he dropped the keys, but how is that going to help us? We won't be able to reach them."

"I guess we'll find out." Tabin stretched himself out along the bench, his knees bent and hands behind his head.

Dalan waited and listened, but silence hung in the air like an oppressive cloud. "I think we're stuck for now." He plopped down on the straw and rested his head against the cold stone wall.

Footsteps rang out in the passage, and Dalan sat forward. More guards? They could really be in trouble now.

"Chilled nose beets. Why are you two just lazing around like dawdle lizards on a sun bake?"

"Gan!" Dalan and Tabin said in unison.

"And Ariyuna." Dalan ran to the bars. "And Naiyan! How did you all get down here?"

Naiyan reached through the bars and gripped Dalan's shoulder. "With Moochir's help. But we haven't found Dash yet."

"I will lead you. Pit, pit," said the bench.

"There you are." Ariyuna bent down and pressed her face into the bars. "Are you all right?"

"Most certainly. Pit. That guard had fear fogging his brain and corrupting his aim. Indeeeed. But we may not have much time."

Gan held up the keys. "Happened to find these pitched on the bitter stones." He winked at Moochir and tried one key after another. "Picking vat turtles. One of these has got to spring the plucked geese." The lock creaked. "Ah, that one's the buster." He swung the door open.

"Indeeeed. This way. Pit." Moochir directed with his eyes back toward the entrance. "I will have to jump ahead."

"Not too fast." Dalan rushed out of the cell.

"Don't worry, my friend. Pit, pit. Your twin is not that far."

They ran back to the entrance, where Moochir blinked out of a small table.

"I will have to jump again. Pit." He pointed his face to the left. "Down this way."

"Dash!" Dalan called.

"Dalan? Is that you?" came the reply.

He reached the cell before he could answer his brother's question. The others came pounding behind him.

"Get me out." Dash held onto the bars with a white-knuckled grip.

Gan produced the keys that fumbled through his fingers and fell with a clatter. "Oh, this is as wearisome as a goat stroll in midwinter." He snatched them off the stone floor and shove in the key he'd used for Dalan's cell. The door swung open.

Moochir cleared his throat. "Um, from here on I have no plan. Pit, pit." His face blinked sideways from the tipped bucket in the corner.

"Not again." Naiyan peered farther down the dark corridor. "So, any ideas?"

"Wait here. Pit, pit. I will return shortly."

After Moochir vanished from the bucket, Ariyuna pushed her way past Gan and Dalan to give Dash a hug. "We've been so worried." She held him at arm's length. "You've grown."

"Yeah. It was one of the bands." He held out his bound wrists. "They started out really good, but now I'd rather be rid of them."

"They look painful." Naiyan placed a hand on Dash's forearm and one below his wrist.

"Ooh. That feels good." Dash smiled weakly.

"It's not much. We need to get the bands off." He took the other arm and did the same.

Dash stretched his fingers several times. "Elch said they would come off in the place of total surrender. Wherever that is."

Gan shrugged and glanced toward Tabin.

"Don't look at me. I don't know either, but we'll find it. Right now we need to hurry. Moochir, can you lead us out of the palace? Moochir?"

The woodpit reappeared. "Indeeeed. Possibly." From the bucket, he stared into nowhere with his mouth puckered. "Pit!" His blank look turned into a smile. "I've got it. Follow me!"

Chapter 44
Eep, Eep, Eep, Eep

Ariyuna tromped just ahead of the others, but found it hard to follow the woodpit. The dungeon had very little wood, and in the dark, the long jumps left her bewildered at times.

"Moochir!" her call echoed down an even darker, damp, tunnel-like passage.

"Not that way. Pit, pit. Over here."

"Drowning sea pigs, Moochir. Are you leading us to the soggy bottoms?"

"Indeeeed."

Ariyuna hurried down the dank passageway.

"Not so fast." Dash, lagging behind, bent over to catch his breath. "My legs are getting really tired. I think my new strength is wearing off."

Tabin put his arm around Dash. "Come. I'll help you."

Naiyan gave Ariyuna's hand a squeeze. "Are you all right?"

"I will be once we get out of here."

"Not far now. Pit. Hurry." Moochir's voice echoed off the stone walls.

The twisting, tortuous route narrowed. The ceiling sloped downward to where Ariyuna had to bend over. Had they traveled far enough to escape? Could these dungeons possibly extend past the palace walls?

The tunnel widened again, and a steep wooden staircase led upward to a narrow door.

Moochir blinked out of a step. "Careful, now, and quiet. Pit. I don't know exactly where this leads."

"Can you find out?" Dalan whispered.

"Indeeeed. Wait here. Better yet, wait at the top of the stairs. Pit, pit. It will give me a little more room to stretch."

Dalan climbed up, and Ariyuna sat down next to him on the top step. Dusty light filtered under the solid wooden door.

She wanted to say something to encourage him, but nothing came to mind.

He sighed. "I suppose we should have asked Moochir to take us past the kitchens. If we can get out of the city, it will be a long trip home without food."

"I have a little money." Naiyan held out a small coin pouch. "But I used most of it getting here."

"Simply blasting Zovlon's stench hole to the background will be enough for me. If we can snicker away with all of us and the Zavtai, I will be as happy as a rooster with a fat spring worm."

Dash sat on a lower step, his head in his hands.

"What kind of slugger indigestions are eating you, Dash, my boy?" Gan patted his arm.

"I don't know." Dash rubbed his knees. "I'm so tired. The thought of walking all the way back home... I don't think I can do it." Scratching at his wrists produced several fresh drops of blood that dripped onto the step below. "I got everyone into this mess, and now I'm putting you all in danger again."

"Nonsense." Tabin sat down next to Dash. "You're family."

Moochir appeared in the door frame and whispered,

"Not good. Pit, pit. There's a small possibility I've led you into an impossible escape."

"Well, tell us the ghastly circumstances, and we'll decide how to bash the bull pusher forward." Gan stepped up until he stood face to face with the pit. "And don't leave out even a mouser crumb."

Moochir cleared his throat and stared, wide-eyed at Gan. "I... well... this... pit..."

"You can just say it." Naiyan put his hand on Gan's shoulders and pulled him down a step away from Moochir.

Gan took a second step back.

"Indeeeed," the pit whispered. "The door opens up behind the throne, and... and the prince is sitting on it right now. Pit, pit."

"Is there any hope?" Panic rose within Ariyuna, and she took a deep breath to quiet it. "Could we somehow sneak past him?"

"I might be able to help. Pit. I'll give it a try, anyway."

Ariyuna pressed her ear against the door.

Angry, muffled voices stopped abruptly when Zovlon's voice dominated the conversation. "Silence. We will continue this discussion later."

"When is later?" Moochir's voice sounded far away.

"What is that?" A shocked voice asked.

"A woodpit. Everyone out!"

Shuffling feet hurried across the floor amid exclamations about ghosts and the power of the prince's sorcery.

Moochir's face appeared suddenly. "Sneak through the door, and run to the left when I give the signal. Pit. There's a curtain along the wall. It will hide you most of the way. Indeeeed."

Dalan stood and whispered. "What's the signal?" But

Moochir was gone.

The pit's voice rang out across the throne room again. "Most exalted majesty. Indeeeed."

"Don't even try that with me, pit. Who are you attached to?"

"Ah, you assume I'm attached. Pit, pit. Maybe I come seeking an attachment. A powerful attachment."

Moochir's face popped into the door frame for only a moment. "Run!"

"Where are you, pit? I know your kind."

"Of course you do. Pit, pit. I'm over here in the picture frame."

Ariyuna opened the door as quietly as possible, but her heart thumped loudly in her ears. The back of the throne left only enough space to squeeze out. Peeking through a split in the curtains that hung along the wall behind the throne, she surveyed the room. Moochir was on the far side, jumping from one frame to the next.

Zovlon followed him intently, striding around the edge of the room.

She dashed to the left behind the heavy curtain, then peered around the edge into the throne room. A gap stretched out to where an ornate doorway opened into a hall.

Moochir smiled. "Would Your Majesty like a woodpit companion? You would make an influential attachment. Indeeeed."

"No! Most certainly not. But woodpits are not found in Teagen. Only in Talsar. Tell me your attachment. You couldn't have come on your own. I know your companion is close by and is from Talsar. Speak up, pit!"

"You are not my master, and I don't feel compelled to tell you anything. Pit."

"Ah! So you are attached. Who?"

Tabin helped Dash and Gan out and they all scurried through the ornate entry.

Naiyan closed it gently behind him, muffling the sounds from the throne room. "Where to now?"

"No flea squasher of an idea." Gan peered in several directions.

Ariyuna hurried to the left, fear driving each stride. "Let's follow this until Moochir catches up."

Tabin glanced out every window they passed. "If I could see the sun, it might direct us east toward the servant's gate." He peeked out another window. "It's noon. The sun's directly overhead and no help at all."

"I can help. Pit, pit."

"Moochir!" Dalan ran to the large flower pot. "Are you all right?"

"I am fine. Pit, pit. But the prince is very angry. Indeeeed. This way." He vanished and reappeared down a side corridor. Zig-zagging through dusty rooms and narrow halls brought them to a small iron gate.

Beyond it, a large garden stretched out. On the far side, Ariyuna could see another gate set into the high stone wall that surrounded the palace. "Across?" she asked Moochir.

He nodded from a tree just outside.

Ariyuna pushed on the gate, but it wouldn't budge. She rattled it again. "It's locked."

Gan and Naiyan both tried.

"Take that twig, Dalan. Pit, pit."

Dalan reached out as far as he could and barely touched the twig. "It's too far."

Overhead, an eagle circled the garden.

Dalan reached again but couldn't grab it.

The eagle circled lower.

Ariyuna thought she heard footsteps in the hallway behind them. "Hurry."

With a steep dive, the eagle plummeted toward the garden.

"Eeek!" Gan squeaked.

Tabin smiled. "Tailaal."

The eagle transformed into a tall, slender woman. Her long black hair, streaked with gray, blew in the breeze. "It's good to see all of you. But I've been flying over this city for two days, and I only have a moment to spare." She pulled a small scroll from her sleeve and gave it to Naiyan. "Come as soon as you can." She turned.

"Wait!" Dalan waggled his fingers toward the twig. "Can you hand that to me?"

Tailaal looked at him with a quizzical smile. "A small request." She picked it up and handed the twig to Dalan. "Goodbye!" She transformed and took off into the sky.

"What does it say?" Dash scooted over.

"No time now." Naiyan tucked the scroll into his pocket. "We'll look at it as soon as we're in a safer place."

"Very good. Pit." Only half of Moochir's mouth showed along the slender twig. "I am the key, put me in the key hole. Indeeeed!"

Dalan slid the twig into the lock. The tiny piece of wood twisted and shook. Then a click rang out.

The gate swung open, and they all tumbled out into the garden.

"To the right. Pit."

Ariyuna ran. Hope bubbled upward, but she pressed it down. Would this really work, or would they be stopped at any moment now?

On the far side, Dalan slid the twig into the lock of the gate set into the stone wall. Soon they all slipped out into the busy street.

"We made it!" Ariyuna took in a deep breath of the city air, tainted with odors of horse and smoke.

"Over here. Indeeeed."

A horse-drawn cart piled high with straw stood along the edge of the lane.

"This is all too convenient." Naiyan eyed the cart.

"Don't just stand there like a slother slug." Gan wiggled his way in until only a brightly colored slipper showed.

Tabin gave it a shove and it disappeared into the straw.

Elch? Ariyuna reached out with her mind.

Warmth spread from her chest. *The driver can't figure out why he stopped, but he won't wait for long.*

Dalan helped Dash into the cart and covered him with straw.

"Hee-ya!" the driver called.

Ariyuna, Naiyan, and Tabin hopped on and wormed into the pile as the cart started down the street.

"I hope he's leaving the city," Ariyuna whispered, not knowing if anyone could hear.

"I hope so, too," Naiyan replied. "I guess we'll have to wait and see."

Through the straw she heard a cheerful "Eep, eep, eep, eep, eep, eep, eep, eep-"

"Will you stop," Dalan hissed.

"I like horses. Horses and carts. Eep, eep, eep, eep..."

Next to her, the straw shook as Tabin tried to contain a laugh.

"What's so funny?" she asked.

"Moochir did that all the way from Talsar. Drove Dalan

crazy."

The cart rattled along the street. Shouts rang out. Ariyuna's fists tightened around handfuls of stubble. She didn't dare speak as the bubble of hope within popped. If the guards discovered them, there wouldn't be a second escape.

The shouting grew louder. "Close the gates! The prince is sealing the city. No one in, no one out!"

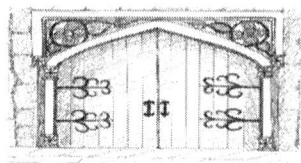

Chapter 45
Zovlon

Heavy boots ran past the cart. A deafening creak filled the air. Dash held his breath as the guard and the driver yelled at each other.

"Back, you filthy peasant! Out of the way! We're closing the gates."

"My horse won't go backwards!"

The cart stopped and shuddered. The horse neighed and stomped.

"Yes, it will." The guard's commanding voice penetrated the straw. "You're blocking the gate. Back up so we can close them. Orders of the prince."

"My horse won't listen to the prince. He doesn't listen to anyone, not even to me. Let me go forward. Then I'll be out of the way, and you can close your stinking gates!"

Dash wanted to make a small hole in the straw and peek out, but didn't dare.

"Back! Prince's orders."

The horse's hoofs clacked on the cobblestones. The cart wobbled and shook before darting forward with a jerk.

"Come back!" the guard yelled. But the horse bolted, bouncing the cart along the stony road.

"Whoa!" The driver shouted. "Whoa! Not that way!"

The ride turned even rougher. The cart jolted and jumped. "Slow down, you senseless beast. Back to the road."

"I knew it." Dash moaned. "I'll never be able to get away from the prince."

"Yes, you will," Tabin replied. "Hush."

Dash slammed against the side of the cart and then bounced back toward the middle. He tried to find something to hang on to, but his hands found only loose straw. The bands dug painfully into his wrists.

"Oof," Gan grunted. "Get your fester foot out of my mumbler."

Tabin yelped. "That's my elbow. And don't bite it."

The cart slowed and finally lurched to a stop.

"I need to get out of this toss bucket before my breakfast rewallops." Gan pushed his way forward.

Dash followed, wiggling until he tumbled out along with a shower of straw.

All around lay a flat, stony land. No sign of the road. Off in the distance, he could see the walls of Endurek, the capital city of Teagen. The excitement of entering the city many days ago with Karakul had completely dissipated. Seeing it so far away left a strand of hope for the days to come.

"Hey!" The driver stood beside the cart. He held the reins with one hand and pointed his whip at the crowd emerging from his load of straw. "Oooh! You're the ones the prince is looking for!"

Naiyan bowed. "Very possible. But as you can see," he spread out his arms to the surrounding nothingness, "you have no one to help capture us out here. We have no intention of hurting you, but we would like to compensate you for carrying us so far and so well." He dug out his coin pouch and produced two silvers. "Here."

The driver took the coins and frowned.

Naiyan dug out another. "Will this help repay you for your services?"

The driver smiled. "I believe it will. Now, since you messed up my straw, and I'm old and you are not, and you need to stay in my good graces, and my horse needs a little rest, help me restack the straw. Then you can be on your way." He dug two straw forks out from behind the bench and handed them to Naiyan and Tabin.

With quick experienced flings, the spilled straw was soon piled back onto the cart.

Naiyan tucked the forks back behind the bench. "Thank you, sir."

"I can't promise my silence." He eyed them suspiciously.

Naiyan nodded. "We don't expect you to be dishonest." Crossing his fist on his chest, he bowed. "Safe travels to you."

The man climbed onto the cart and whistled to his horse. The cart rambled back toward the road.

"Would this be a safe place to look at the scroll?" Dash pulled straw from his clothes. Had everyone else forgotten the note?

"You are a curious wink swimmer." Gan picked a stalk from his hair. "Yes, let's have a look at the scribbler."

Naiyan dug out the scroll and opened it. "It says, 'The queen's condition is growing rapidly worse. Please return as soon as possible.'"

His face pale, Naiyan rolled up the scroll. "It will take weeks to get back to Temyulun."

"And there's that." Dalan pointed off in the distance. A cloud of dust rose up into the air from the direction of the city. "I bet Zovlon's found us."

"I can run much faster as a cat, and I can take one person to the queen." Tabin glanced around at the group.

Gan looked at him in surprise. "You've never carried even a fleece bibbet before."

"The situation demands it." Tabin turned toward the rising dust cloud. "But we need to go now. Who's coming with me to Temyulun?"

"Naiyan, you should go." Ariyuna wrapped her arm in his. "You can heal the queen."

Naiyan shook his head. "I've tried everything I know. You or Gan should go. You could comfort her, but Gan might be able to slow her illness until we can get there. Or, since Dash can't travel fast, maybe he's the one to go. Either way, someone should go. It'll create the diversion the rest of us will need to get away."

The gnawing weakness from the bands kept Dash silent.

"We can definitely provide a diversion. Gan. I think you're the queen's best hope. You coming?" Tabin's form shifted until a yuratag cat stood before them.

Gan climbed on. "Oh! I slipper forgot." He reached into the small bag attached to his waist. Pulling out the Zavtai, he handed it to Ariyuna. "You should take this. If we are snatched, I don't want to have it extracted. We will thunder to the queen and look for you to follow like hornet prickles."

Tabin shot out across the flatness toward the dust cloud with Gan flopping around on his back, whooping.

Ariyuna managed to tuck the Zavtai into the decorative belt of her tunic. "I wish he'd left the bag as well. This staff is heavy. But I suppose Zibek thinks the staff is in the bag. If Gan's captured, he'll be disappointed."

"Wait." Dalan looked around frantically. "Where's Moochir?"

Not a speck of wood lay nearby, and no shrubs grew in the barren wasteland, not even a tuft of dry grass.

"I'm down here. Pit, pit."

Dalan slapped his hand to his chest.

"Ow! That's my face. Indeeeed."

Pulling out the small wooden box that held the Enk Taivaan, Dalan smiled. "There you are."

"Yes. Pit. No other suitable abode around, and this is more convenient for travel. Pit, pit."

Dalan frowned. "You mean you could have traveled there all along, but you chose to make me carry a log and pulled me through nasty puddles?"

A sheepish grin spread across Moochir's face.

With a shake of his head and a sigh, Dalan let the box fall back onto his chest.

"Ow. Pit."

Naiyan pointed toward the descending sun. "Traveling east should eventually bring us to Talsar."

Dalan put his arm around Dash. "Can you make it a little farther?"

"I think so."

As they traveled on, Dash fell farther and farther behind. He stumbled. Sharp, hot pain shot through his ankle, but he pushed forward. "I'm really thirsty. The water in the dungeon stunk."

Dalan shifted his arm to better support his brother. "I don't know if we'll find much water out here, but there's a stream at the bottom of the Deep Divide."

"How far is that?" Dash hobbled forward.

"Don't know."

Off in the distance, the cloud of dust had turned and now seemed to be heading away from them. Dash pointed.

"Looks like Tabin's distraction is working."

Up ahead, Ariyuna shouted something and beckoned.

Dalan tried to sound enthusiastic. "Maybe she's found water."

The thought of a drink spurred Dash on. When they reached the spot, Ariyuna pointed down. "There's a bit of a cliff. We could rest in the shade. Down the slope from here is a ravine that heads east. It might lead into the Deep Divide."

Dash groaned. "I was hoping for water."

"Sorry. None that I can see, but I might be wrong. The ravine looks like it might have been carved by water a long time ago."

Rocks and sand shifted and slid as Dash made his way toward the shady spot, still clinging to his brother. The small patch of shade provided a cool respite. Dash sat with his back against the rock and closed his eyes.

A breeze blew on his face. Pain throbbed in his wrists and ankle. With Talsar still so far away, Dash wondered how they would make it without water or food. At least there would be water once they reached the Great Divide. Maybe even a few berries growing along the Tegus River on the other side.

"Dash." Ariyuna sat down in front of him. "I want you to have this." She pulled the staff out of her belt.

He lifted his head. "Me? Why?"

"I don't know. Elch just told me to give it to you. She insisted." Ariyuna held out the staff. "Do you think you can carry it?"

He nodded, grateful for her trust after all he'd done. "Thanks, I guess." His fingers tingled as they wrapped around the staff. "Are you sure I should take it? I don't know if I can keep it safe."

"Elch will help you."

Down among the rocks between them, a pulsing glow shone out. Ariyuna reached for the blue stone. Then smiled. "Elch says I was right to trust her, and you." She placed the stone on the Itgel, and it stuck with a flash of blue light.

"I got another stone," she called out, holding up her wrist.

The others gathered around.

The wind shifted and blew from behind Dash, as if he sat against a wall of air instead of rock.

Ariyuna leaped up.

One glance back made Dash jump up beside his sister.

The others all stood staring at the cliff. Instead of a rock wall, air swirled, creating vertical spirals of sand.

Dash stepped forward and stuck his finger tip into the vortex. It melted in the wind, but formed again as he pulled it out.

"Whoa! Careful, Dash." Naiyan grabbed his hand and examined the end of his finger.

Ariyuna leaned in toward Dash. "Is it okay?"

Picking up a stone, Dalan threw it into the cave. The rock disintegrated into sand that joined the swirling wall of air.

What is this place? The thought jabbed at Dash's mind.

In his head, he heard Elch. *It's the place of total surrender.*

Dash opened his mouth and then shut it again. *Can you hear what I'm thinking?*

Yes.

Uneasiness settled within. He wasn't sure he liked having someone listening to his thoughts.

He stepped back and surveyed the swirling wall. His heart thumped, flipping between fear and hope. *What happens if I go in?*

To go in, you must give yourself entirely to V'Arah and let him rebuild you.

Will it take off the bands?

A deep voice boomed out from behind. "Very impressive!"

Dash spun around. "Prince Kasiret!"

Beside him, Dalan stumbled backwards, and Naiyan caught him. Ariyuna's grip dug into Dash's arm.

"Oh, you can stop calling me that. Zovlon will do just fine. I see you have found the Cave of Defeat. One of my favorite places. I have dissolved many enemies here. It's a great place to rid myself of bothersome people."

"How...?" Dalan began.

"How did I find you? I am drawn to power. My army is busy chasing Tabin and that clown Gan. But here is where power has gathered. Lovely Ariyuna carries the Itgel. Dash has the staff, which I believe is the incomplete Zavtai. And you, Dalan have the Enk Taivaan. Three very powerful items."

"You can't have them. Pit, pit."

"And the woodpit." Zovlon laughed. "I knew you were attached to someone from Talsar."

Dash's heart beat wildly. His head spun. This was all his fault. He had run away and joined Zovlon's side. And now Zovlon would possess all three gifts from the Storyteller.

Chapter 46
Surrender

Dalan stepped forward. "Moochir is right. You can't have Talsar's gifts from the Storyteller."

Naiyan came to stand next to him. His hand rested reassuringly on Dalan's shoulder.

The sorcerer's laugh of triumph echoed off the rocks. "There's little you can do to stop me. Ariyuna, this is the third time we've met. Last time, the queen's entire army came against me, but you still couldn't defeat me. I survived, and here I am now, the ruler of Teagen."

Ariyuna twisted the bracelet on her arm. The five stones glowed softly. "I still have two more stones to find. The Itgel is incomplete."

"That doesn't matter to me." A sneer curled his lips. "You are far from your home and the friends that have helped you in the past. And you are weaker than you know."

She smiled. "Yes. I am very weak, but I'm not alone. I have family and friends right here with me. Elch, too."

"Don't think you can bully her, Zovlon." Naiyan took a step closer to Ariyuna. "Her connection with Elch is strong."

"Ha. You can't possibly think Elch will help you here. Teagen is not V'Arah's domain. Few, if any, even know of

V'Arah, and none revere him. Elch is unknown."

Dalan bit his lip. They really were isolated out in this barren stretch of land. No army would come to their rescue this time. And not even Gan or Tabin knew where they were.

Ariyuna unlatched the bracelet. The sun, reaching past the shadow of the rock wall, glistened off the silver.

Dalan's heart beat faster. "Put it back on," he whispered. But Ariyuna didn't seem to hear him.

She held out the ancient band. "You've already tried to take this from me once, and it burned you. What makes you think you can handle it this time?" Colorful reflections glinted from the five stones.

Dalan held his breath, hoping his sister wouldn't give in. She trusted Elch and wouldn't do anything without consulting the fish, would she? Uncertainty roiled within. How could she be so calm?

Zovlon reached into a pocket and pulled out tooled leather gloves. "I've come prepared this time. Give it to me, and I'll let you go." He slid his hands into the gloves.

Naiyan tried to lower Ariyuna's outstretched arm. "Your generous offer is empty, Zovlon. All you know is deceit and lies."

"Is that your defense?" The sorcerer laughed. "Childish insults that mean nothing?" He snatched the bracelet. "Thank you, my dear."

"No!" Dalan wanted to grab the Itgel and run, but Zovlon took a menacing step forward that halted his advance.

Ariyuna stood, dazed but still calm. "Don't worry, Dalan. Elch has things under control."

"How can you say that?" Confusion fed into anger that spiraled inside Dalan.

"I would have to agree with Dalan." Zovlon held up the Itgel. It sparkled in the sunlight. "I believe that *I* have control now." Scooping the silver bracelet into a gloved palm, he stuffed it in a pocket inside his cloak.

"Now, Dalan. I believe you have the Enk Taivaan. When I first saw the pieces, I disregarded them as worthless clay. But since that little object did have the power to turn my tarch army into chaos, I've reconsidered."

Dalan's hand went instinctively to his chest.

"Hey. Pit, pit. That's still my face. Indeeeed."

"Sorry." Dalan gripped the box as best he could without squashing Moochir. He considered opening it and putting the pieces together, but how could he complete it before Zovlon snatched it up?

"Dalan. Pit." Moochir whispered. "I may need to leave you. If I do, I want you to know that you have been my favorite attachment. Pit, pit. Indeeeed."

"What are you talking about?" He glanced down at the box around his neck. "You can't leave now."

Zovlon took several steps forward.

Dalan wanted to back away, but something kept him in place.

A malicious smile spread up Zovlon's face as he held out his gloved hand.

Elch!

I am here.

Don't let him take the Enk Taivaan.

The gifts are not nearly as valuable as the connection to their source of power. They are useless without V'Arah.

Is that what you told Ariyuna? Dalan waited, but the fish didn't answer.

Elch's warmth spread through him. *Give him the box.*

Dalan hesitated, clinging to the Enk Taivaan.

Your trust is misplaced.

Dalan sighed as Elch's peace grew. He took the Enk Taivaan from around his neck.

Moochir grinned at him. "You are a good person, Dalan. Indeeeed. I will miss you tremendously."

Zovlon seized the box. "And I get a woodpit along with the Enk Taivaan. The pit may come in handy."

Moochir winked at Dalan.

Zovlon turned. "Ah, little Dash. You held such promise, and then you disappointed me by becoming too ambitious."

"I won't be your slave." Dash gripped the Zavtai with both hands and raised it threateningly. The bands that connected his wrists dug in.

"I've so much more to offer. If you'll let me."

Dash hesitated and lowered the Zavtai slightly. "Like what?"

"Power over your neglectful family, boy. Power over the people of Talsar and of Teagen. Power over the riches of both lands. The worship of your subjects. The list goes on."

Dalan watched with horror, wondering what his little brother would do. Was he listening to Elch or trusting his own wisdom? He wanted to help, but he didn't know how.

Zovlon leaned in. "You could have it all."

Dash glanced at his wrists, painfully constricted by the moon bands. "What about these?"

"You won't need those when you follow me. Those were intended to give you a taste of the life I have to offer."

"Can you take them off?" Dash stared intently at Zovlon.

"Well, that depends-"

"You can't. Elch said they would only come off at the place of total surrender. This is the place of total surrender." With the tip of the staff, he pointed to the swirling wall of wind and sand.

Zovlon laughed. "Go ahead, boy. Step in. You will not return the same, if you return at all. V'Arah will twist and dissolve you. Nothing will remain. I have yet to see anyone reappear." Zovlon stepped toward Dash.

Raising the Zavtai ready to strike, Dash stood his ground. "I'm not giving you the staff. It doesn't belong to you. It's Queen Baiyanarah's."

"Your precious queen is dying. Who will rule then? I fully intend to be the sovereign of both Teagen and Talsar, and you could rule beside me."

Dash stepped toward the vortex, still holding up the Zavtai. "I'd rather dissolve."

"No!" Dalan cried out. He couldn't lose his brother, not to that unknown frenzy of wind and sand.

Ariyuna's eyes widened and her voice cracked. "Are you sure?"

"I can't live with these bands." Dash took another step toward the swirling wall. "And Elch says I should go in."

"Give me the Zavtai." Zovlon fixed his eyes on the staff. A greedy light reflected in their dark depths.

"No. I'm taking it with me." He looked toward his siblings. "If... if I don't come back, tell Ma and Papa I'm sorry and... I really do love them."

Dalan wanted to say something. He wanted to stop his brother. But Elch had said this was where he'd be free of the moon bands. The lump in his throat grew. Why did he have to lose his brother just as he was learning to trust Elch?

"I've got to go in." Tears welled up and several spilled down Dash's cheeks. "Goodbye."

He stepped back into the churning wind.

As he did, Zovlon lunged forward and wrenched the Zavtai from Dash's hands. Holding up the staff before him, his eyes alive with triumph, he crooned. "All three gifts from the storyteller."

His gaze shifted to Ariyuna, Dalan, and Naiyan. "Do you think you can stop me now?"

Chapter 47
Dissolved

Dash felt the Zavtai jerk from his grasp, but he couldn't stop his backward motion. The wall of wind hit him and pulled at every fiber. His body disintegrated, filtering into a drizzle of sand. The particles coalesced into a cloud that moved in a circle around the cave.

Was he dead? He didn't have a body anymore, but somehow he could still think. The squeeze from the moon bands throbbed. That didn't make sense either. He didn't have arms anymore.

In the swirling wind, he saw another cloud of sand. Its shape shifted and moved until the form of a fish emerged.

Elch?

I'm here.

Relief washed over Dash's consciousness. At least he wasn't alone. But how could he see and hear without a body?

A deep power pulsed in the blustery vortex. A power much stronger than Dash had ever experienced. But not an oppressive power, like Zovlon's. A supportive, comforting power that radiated restrained and soothing strength. It penetrated to the core of his being like a warm embrace.

All the things he'd done, the things he knew were wrong, somehow didn't matter anymore. He wouldn't mind staying here forever.

So, is this the place of total surrender?

Yes. The fish moved closer.

Then why do the bands still hurt?

You gave up your old existence to join V'Arah's wind, but you have not loosened your grip on the fleeting things you love.

Dash thought about the bands. The first one had given him wealth. But Elch was right. Family and friends brought a wealth money couldn't buy.

Part of the pain from the bands disappeared.

Dash thought about the second band. Rich friends. Or not. They had all abandoned him. He could live without that sort of friend.

More pain dispersed into the wind.

Humor. He didn't need a band for that.

The physical strength had been nice. But time to grow and hard work would produce the same effect.

The pain from the remaining moon bands dropped to a dull ache.

What about popularity? That had been harder to come by in his old life. But that might have been his own fault. He'd done his share of mean things to others.

That can change, can't it?

Of course. Elch's reply held more comforting warmth.

All right, then. I don't need that band either. Or the last one about focusing on myself, since I'm nothing but a sand cloud now.

The lingering fragments of discomfort vanished. *Are they gone?*

Yes. You are truly free.

So what happens now?

Watch.

The wind pushed him toward the mouth of the cave. No sound entered, but he could see Zovlon dancing with glee, holding up the Zavtai in one hand and the Enk Taivaan in the other. Naiyan bent over and whispered in Ariyuna's ear. As if in a trance, Dalan stood staring into the cave, his back to Zovlon's victory celebration.

"I'm here," Dash called out, but his brother didn't respond.

His perception changed. Now he could hear Zovlon's shouts and Dalan calling, "Dash! Are you in there?"

"I am!"

"I think he's gone."

"No, I'm not!"

Ariyuna came and stood next to Dalan. She grabbed his hand and sent a nervous glance back at Zovlon, still dancing around and shouting. "What do we do now? I'm not hearing anything from Elch."

Dalan said nothing.

"Let's wait." Naiyan put his arm around her shoulder, keeping an eye on the dark sorcerer. "Dash seemed convinced this was the place to become free of the bands."

"You can wait all you want." Zovlon cackled. "No one ever comes out."

"Dalan. Pit, pit." Moochir still peered out of the Enk Taivaan box Zovlon held in his hand. "I will say my final goodbye now."

Dalan spun around, and his eyes widened "No, don't go!"

"Zovlon. Pit. Against my overwhelming inner objections, I choose you to be my new attachment."

"What?" The sorcerer held up the box.

Moochir's face disappeared.

"Where did he go?" Dalan looked around. "There's no other wood."

Zovlon's tunic rustled and a vague face appeared. "It is a

little known fact that woodpits can also inhabit cloth for a short time. It is fibrous, like wood. Pit, pit. Zovlon. This is the end."

The sorcerer's shock turned to horror as his tunic twisted and tightened. Then, stretching out away from the cave, the tunic pulled. He stumbled, yanked along by the woodpit. Just as suddenly, the tunic lunged in the other direction, jerking him back.

Dash watched as the dark sorcerer was pushed, pulled, twisted, and flung around. The direction changes became more violent. With each hurl he swung closer to the vortex.

Ariyuna, Dalan, and Naiyan scattered out of the way of the woodpit's wild tantrum.

"Let go, you miserable pit!" Zovlon shouted, trying to stay upright.

"Dalan knows how far I can stretch an attachment. Pit, pit. Would you like to know as well?"

"No!"

"I can feel some wood a great distance from here. Toward Endurek. Far, indeeeed. Would you like to find it?"

"No! Let me go."

"Pit. Since you don't want to go that way, we will go in the opposite direction. Indeeeed."

Moochir's face blinked out of the sleeve of Zovlon's tunic before the sleeve stretched straight toward the swirling wall of wind.

With the Zavtai and the Enk Taivaan firmly in his grip, the sorcerer stumbled forward at a reckless pace. "No, not in there!" But as he hit the vortex, Zovlon and his shouts dissolved into the wind.

"Moochir!" Dalan called.

A blast of wind blew Dash's cloud of sand up toward the top as Zovlon and Moochir entered.

But the sorcerer's body didn't form a cohesive cloud. A muted cry of agony vibrated though the cave, that died out. Dark sand from Zovlon filtered down to a layer on the floor.

A small cloud formed, and Dash recognized Moochir's bulging eyes and silly grin.

"Dash. Pit, pit. You are free. Indeeeed."

"I suppose. I'm not sure what's happened."

"A good thing has happened. Pit, pit. But I can't stay here. I'm a loose pit now, and V'Arah will send me on. Goodbye, Dash."

The pit's cloud of sand dissipated until it blended with the rest of the particles swirling around the cave. "No, wait. You can't leave." *Elch? Will he be all right?*

The fish didn't answer.

At the entrance, Dalan, Ariyuna, and Naiyan once again stood staring into the cavern.

"We can't go home without Dash." Ariyuna reached out a hand toward the wind, then withdrew it.

"I'm here!" Dash shouted, but no one responded.

"Zovlon may have been right." Naiyan took her hand in his. "Maybe no one ever comes out."

"What will we tell Ma?" Dalan sank to the rocky ground. "We lost Dash, the Itgel, the Enk Taivaan, and the Zavtai. What will the queen say?"

Ariyuna dropped down beside her brother, staring blankly into the cavern.

"We can't stay long." Naiyan sat beside her. "The queen may not be alive when we finally reach Temyulun. We have a long way to go with no food or water. This wasteland may do us in before long."

Deep sadness and a longing for home filled Dash's consciousness. The journey home would be almost certain death, but he wanted to be a part of it. He wanted to be with Ariyuna, Dalan, and Naiyan. He wanted a hug from Ma.

Elch, I want to go back.

Chapter 48
Complete

The wind shifted and grew stronger. Dash's sand cloud pulled together into a tighter mass and began to solidify.

He watched his feet take shape. Legs joined his ankles. A torso formed, followed by arms. He held them out. This wasn't the muscular body the moon band had given him, but his smaller, boyish one.

The grand clothes from Endurek, now soiled and torn, hung limply on his frame. The fancy slippers were gone. Reaching up, he felt an unruly mop of hair on his head.

A golden shimmer caught his attention. Glancing down, he saw an intricate diamond shape glowing on the inside of his left arm. A tooya, like Ariyuna's and Dalan's.

Elch smiled.

The wind slowed, and the remaining sand including grains in the swirling vortex settled to the floor.

"Dash!" Ariyuna rushed into the cave. She slammed into her brother and held him in a tight embrace. Dalan and Naiyan joined her until Dash groaned.

"I'm so glad you're alive." Ariyuna pushed him to arm's length. "And you're back to your normal size. I like you better this way." Wiping a tear from her cheek, she smiled. "The bands are gone."

"Elch was right. No more bands. But my wrists are still a bit sore."

Dalan grabbed his other arm and turned it palm up. "You have a tooya."

Dash nodded and grinned. "Not the easiest way to get one, I suppose."

"What happened? We saw you dissolve." Ariyuna refused to let go of his hand.

"I did, but I turned into a sand cloud. Somehow I could still see and think. Elch was here as a cloud, too. We floated around. I could hear what you were saying, but you couldn't hear me."

"Where are Moochir and Zovlon?" Naiyan wandered toward the back of the cave.

Dash's gaze drifted to the pile of darker sand. "That's all that's left. When Zovlon came in, he screamed and disappeared. His sand didn't turn into a cloud at all. Moochir became a cloud and then said V'Arah was moving him on. I don't know where he went."

Sadness drooped over Dalan's face. "I'm going to miss him, even if the attachment was painful sometimes. He ended up being a good friend."

Dash kicked at the sand. "He did say something about being a loose pit, so maybe he didn't stay attached to Zovlon. I hope we find him again."

Ariyuna nodded. She hadn't spent much time with Moochir, but she had grown to like him immensely. After all, he had helped to free them from the palace and dissolve Zovlon. Although, she suspected the sorcerer would return somehow.

"So now we head home with none of the gifts." Dash sighed.

"We have you." Ariyuna gave his hand a squeeze, then let it go. "That's better than all the gifts together. Besides, Elch basically told me to give the Itgel to Zovlon."

"Me, too." Dalan reached for the place the box had hung. "She *wanted* me to give up the Enk Taivaan. It's strange not to have the weight and bulk of the box around my neck."

Ariyuna used her foot to poke at a shiny spot in the sand. "What's that?"

A silver circle emerged.

"I found something over here, too," Naiyan called. "But it's buried deep."

Dash picked up the ring his sister had uncovered. "It's one of the moon bands."

The shiny silver circle trembled in Dash's hand, jumping toward the edge of his palm. Suddenly it flew across the cave.

"Ow!" Naiyan rubbed his shoulder. "Why'd you do that?"

"Sorry." Dash ran over and picked up the moon band that lay at Naiyan's feet. "I didn't throw it. It just flew over here on its own." The band pulled toward the sand.

Wandering around, Dash looked for more. "Here's another one." As soon as he uncovered it, the band zipped toward Naiyan, skimming the rippled surface until it stopped right by his feet.

"I've found the edge of the third." Dalan kept his hand in the sand. "I'd better hold onto it tight." Using both hands, he pulled the next one out. "It wants to come." The band, hooked on Dalan's fingers, stuck out sideways toward Naiyan.

"Stand back," Ariyuna warned. "Two more are wiggling free, and I don't know if I can catch them both." Her hands reached for the vibrating sand. "I got one."

The other bounced across the cave floor and stopped on top of Naiyan's foot.

Ariyuna transferred the one she caught to Dalan's hand. "So that's five of them. One more. Watch out!"

The last band flew through the air and hit Naiyan in the thigh. "Ow. Dash, I can see why you didn't like these bands."

Ariyuna picked up the three bands by Naiyan's feet and held them tight. "I wonder if there's something in the sand that's pulling them."

Dalan looped his onto her fingers, and Dash added his as well. All six bands on Ariyuna's fingers pulled toward the sand.

"We can find out." Naiyan dug, flinging grainy handfuls to the side. "Hey! I think it's the tip of the Zavtai. But it's buried straight down."

Dalan knelt to help.

The more the Zavtai emerged, the more strongly the moon bands pulled toward it. Ariyuna wrapped the fingers of both hands through them.

Dalan scooped out sand from the hole around the staff. "'The majestic Zavtai, staff of the great kings of Vachir,'" he recited. "'This humble gift of the Storyteller, with all stripes in place, brings freedom through truth.'"

"Dalan, you're a genius." Ariyuna bent down. "The Zavtai's incomplete, right? It needs stripes." She held the quivering moon bands out toward the staff.

Dash frowned. "How could something bad from Zovlon be part of the Zavtai?"

"Maybe they're not actually bad. And maybe they're not from Zovlon." Ariyuna shifted her grip on the vibrating bands. "Zovlon's an expert at twisting good things to fit his horrible plans. Dash, can you tell us more about the bands?"

"Sure." He pointed. "That one helped me make powerful friends. That band brought wealth, and that one was for using humor to get out of sticky situations. This one made me strong, and the last two made me popular and proud of my own accomplishments."

Ariyuna pondered that as she studied the bands. "Wealth, friends, humor, strength. Those could all be used to do good things. So could getting along with others and accomplishing stuff. But I might need to think about that some more."

"Got it!" Naiyan drew the Zavtai from the sand. "We should try one and see if it fits." He held out the staff and scrunched up his face.

Ariyuna laughed. "I won't let them hit you." Carefully taking one band off her fingers, she gave it to Dash. "You'd better try it. I don't want the rest to go flying."

"It looks too big." Dash placed the first band over the top of the staff. As he maneuvered it down the shaft, the band narrowed into a thin circle. Toward the bottom, it shrunk and stuck, filling in a small groove.

They all gazed at the staff in silence.

"Let's try another one." Dash took the next band from Ariyuna. This time, it changed shape quickly and stuck to the top of the Zavtai, just under the rounded end. "I bet they'll all fit."

One by one, Dash placed the bands on the Zavtai. Each changed shape and size to fit snugly onto the staff.

"Wow." Ariyuna took the staff from Naiyan. "In all these years we've had this, we didn't realize anything was missing. Here, Dash. I believe it's yours. You retrieved the bands to complete it."

Dash turned the staff around in his hands, examining the new additions. "I don't know."

"I wonder if the other gifts are here as well." Naiyan poked at the sand with his foot.

"Oh!" A bolt of excitement shot through Ariyuna. "That would be amazing." She shuffled her feet to move sand as she walked around the cave.

"You're not too tired to search some more, are you, Dash?" Dalan asked.

"No. I'm not tired anymore. But I'm not very strong either." He flexed his skinny arms.

Dalan laughed. "You'll get there."

Spreading out, they searched the cave floor.

"I see a string." Ariyuna bent over and pulled on it. "Is that yours?"

Dalan hurried over. "Yep." He dug down, following the cord that connected to the Enk Taivaan box. "I hope the rest of it's still there."

Scratching at the sand, he removed handfuls until a small black box emerged. He opened it. A comforting hum reverberated through the air. "All three pieces are here." The box closed with a click. He looped the string over his head and tucked the box under his tunic.

"The Itgel must be here somewhere." Ariyuna brushed sand off her hands. "But how will we find it, since the Zavtai and the Enk Taivaan were buried so deep? And what happened to Zovlon? Part of me can't quite believe that he's actually gone forever."

Dash grinned. "Would glowing help?"

"Help find Zovlon?" Ariyuna didn't feel at all inclined to have another encounter with the sorcerer.

"No, the bracelet." Dash pointed to the sand at his feet. Tiny, round patches of color ran in a short line.

"That's got to be it." Ariyuna rushed over and dug quickly. Soon the Itgel emerged. She dusted it off and placed it on her wrist. It curved to her arm with its familiar cool metallic embrace.

"Whoo-hooo!" Dash did his best imitation of Zovlon's victory dance. "We have all three gifts!"

"You saw that?" Ariyuna grinned.

"Sure did. And now he's gone, and we have the gifts."

"Hmmm..." Dalan dug out the box from around his neck. "The poem about the Zavtai said the staff brings freedom through truth. Do you think the other gifts have a specific purpose?"

"I've wondered that." Ariyuna held out her wrist. "It seems that whenever I've had to trust Elch with something big, that's when I get a stone. I would say trust is the purpose of the Itgel."

Naiyan made his way from the back of the cavern. "What about the Enk Taivaan?"

"That one's easy." Dash grinned. "It's peace. The song that comes from it makes you feel all calm and quiet inside. Like it did when it ended the Battle of Temyulun. Try it."

Dalan opened the box and clicked the pieces together. As the Enk Taivaan's song filled the cave, a deep serenity settled over Ariyuna. She remembered the battle outside Temyulun and frowned. "I got really angry at the end of the battle. How did that happen if the song brings peace?"

"The song had stopped by then, and maybe you weren't really listening to it." Dalan took the pieces apart. The melody died down, lingering momentarily in the light breeze that swirled around in the cave.

"I think you're right." Ariyuna brushed a strand of hair from her face. "I was probably too focused on my fears."

"Could be." Naiyan's voice held urgency, and he grabbed Ariyuna's arm. "But the wind is starting to swirl again. I think we'd better get out."

Chapter 49
To Temyulun

Dalan hurried toward the cave entrance. Wind pulled at his clothes and sand flew through the air, scouring his skin.

Beside him ran Dash. "I don't want to get dissolved again." His brother's voice held a hint of panic.

They all tumbled out as the opening once again became a swirling wall of wind and sand.

Dalan's stomach rumbled, and his tongue briefly stuck to the roof of his mouth. With so much going on, he hadn't been paying attention to his bothersome thirst. Now discomfort surged to the forefront, but he pushed it aside. He needed to stay focused on getting home.

Naiyan scanned the horizon. "I'm guessing the Deep Divide is that way. We'd better at least start toward Talsar and hope we meet up with someone who can get us there faster."

"Hold on." The tickle of an idea grew in Dalan's mind. "The Zavtai..."

"This?" Dash held the staff up.

Ariyuna looked at him skeptically. "You aren't thinking we should try to use it to travel, are you? It didn't work out so well last time. I couldn't control anything."

"It was incomplete last time." Dalan reached for the

Zavtai. *Elch, should we use this?*

He waited but didn't hear a response.

Elch?

Why didn't that fish respond? He needed some help. Turning the staff over several times, he couldn't see that anything more was missing, but they hadn't realized the staff needed bands before this trip.

You would tell me if I was putting everyone in danger, right?

"What are you thinking, Dalan?" Ariyuna's voice pulled him from his contemplation and he lowered his arm.

"I'm wondering if this will take us to Temyulun, but I can't get Elch to answer me. If travel is completely dangerous, she would tell me, right?"

Naiyan nodded. "Elch only speaks when it's absolutely necessary. If you're not hearing anything, there may not be anything important to say."

"So how did it work last time?" Dalan examined the staff.

Ariyuna shrugged. "I twisted the base. But I have no idea how to direct it."

"You were thinking of me the first time you tried it." Dalan scanned the area. "Maybe we just need to think about where we want to go."

"Let's try a short trip first." Naiyan rested a reassuring hand on Dalan's shoulder. "How about that big rock over there? And we should all hold on to the staff so we stay together."

"Okay." As Dalan beckoned Dash closer, his stomach tightened. The last thing he wanted was to travel back into danger.

With a deep breath, he held out the Zavtai. "Everyone hold on. I'll twist the bottom, and we'll all think about the rock over there. Ready? One, two, three."

The base twisted. Rocks and sand blurred into grayness.

The Zavtai bent his arm down as the ground refocused.

The big rock materialized right beside him. Ariyuna wobbled on top of it, and Dash sprawled at the base.

"We did it!" Dash shouted.

"Why are you sideways?" Dalan reached out to pull his brother upright.

"I imagined tumbling through the air toward the rock."

"And I thought about landing on it," Ariyuna added.

A thread of excitement wove through Dalan. He looked around. "Let's try one more practice. This time no tumbling, and we should all think about landing on our feet just to the left of that patch of sand over there."

Everyone nodded.

He took another deep breath. "One, two, three."

This time, the jump kept them in the same positions they'd started in.

Dash whooped and danced around. "We're going home!"

"Home or Temyulun?" Ariyuna asked.

"Temyulun." Naiyan's voice came out husky. "The queen may not last much longer. We may miss her if we go to Dorben first."

Dash's shoulders slumped. "All right." He reached out for the Zavtai.

"Wait." A zing of fear shot across Dalan's chest. "Exactly where in Temyulun? This thing could tear us apart if we're not specific."

"The throne room in the palace." Naiyan ran fingers through his hair. "Right in front of the throne. No, wait. We might land on people. How about in the back, right corner by the potted tsas tree?"

Dalan nodded. "Everyone ready?" He gripped the staff hard, hoping this wouldn't land them in some strange place or fling them apart. "One, two, three." The base twisted, and rocks blurred.

A haze filled every direction. Even the Zavtai was a vague outline. Coils of fear pulled at his concentration as the emptiness stretched on. "No, think about the throne room. Only the throne room." Saying it out loud helped. So did clenching his teeth.

His stomach lurched, and the throne room of Temyulun blinked into existence. Beside him, Dash looked a bit pale, but they had all arrived.

"We made it!" Ariyuna quickly surveyed the empty room. "Where is everyone?"

Naiyan let go of the Zavtai and strode toward the immense doors. "Probably attending the queen. Come on."

Dalan followed Naiyan through the deserted palace, trying not to make any unnecessary noise. "Even the servants are gone."

"Most have probably been sent home." Naiyan hurried on.

They turned a corner near the queen's chambers and ran into a hushed crowd.

An older servant scurried forward and bowed. "Master Naiyan, I'm so glad to see you! Ariyuna, Dalan, and Dash as well. Oh, this is very good. You must all go in and see the queen at once."

"Thank you, Berke." Naiyan clasped his shoulder firmly before heading toward the queen's room.

Dark drapes covered the windows. The queen's bed sat in the center instead of its usual place in the corner, and a roaring fire burned in the grate. A rack with blankets stood near the blaze.

"It's hot in here," Dash whispered.

"Shhh." Dalan pointed to the sleeping Baiyanarah.

A maid hurried over to them on tiptoe and hugged Naiyan, but said nothing. Dalan recognized her as Naiyan's sister, Sahraa.

She gave Ariyuna a squeeze and waved to Dalan and Dash. Then grabbing a chair, she moved it near the bed and motioned to the other maid to bring more.

Dalan found a stool behind the door and set it beside the bed, while Ariyuna and Naiyan sat on the other side.

Dash spotted a table in the corner with a water pitcher and glasses. He filled and drank three cups before offering some to the others.

Baiyanarah's eyes fluttered open. "Oh, it's so cold."

"Here's another warmed blanket, Your Majesty." Sahraa took one from the rack and tucked it under the already thick pile of covers. "And you have some visitors." She resettled the pillows under the queen's head.

"Oh, I don't really have energy for visitors, Sahraa. Who are they?"

"Ariyuna, Dalan, Dash, and Naiyan."

Baiyanarah's eyes widened as she fought to sit up. "Ari? Are you really here? And Naiyan?"

"I am." Ariyuna leaned over the bed. "Just rest."

"And the boys?"

Dalan stood and took the queen's cold hand. "We're here."

"Dash." Baiyanarah tried to raise her head again. "I must see Dash."

"Hello." Dash managed a small wave from the foot of the bed.

"Oh, I'm so glad you're all right. I had terrible dreams that you joined Zovlon."

Dash hung his head. "Well, I... I almost did. But in the end, I realized following V'Arah was better." He held up his arm with the tooya on it.

A tear rolled out of the corner of the queen's eye, into her hair. "That's more than I had hoped for." She groped around for Ariyuna's hand. "And you, my dear. I was so worried. But this festering wound from Zovlon is finally getting the better of me."

Dash held up the staff. "Um, I think this belongs to you."

The queen looked at the staff with a frown. "It's changed."

"Yes." Ariyuna pointed to the stripes. "Dash found the bands that completed it. We used it to travel back."

"Amazing! Dash, you'd better keep it. I have no use for it now. That way, you will each have a gift from the Storyteller." She closed her eyes and took several deep breaths, followed by a long pause in her breathing that made Dalan's whole body tighten.

With a gasp, her eyes popped open. "One more thing." She paused, struggling for air. Letting go of Ariyuna's hand, she grabbed Naiyan's. "Naiyan, the throne of Talsar... is yours."

"But-"

"No, young man. I've been training you for this ever... ever since I began ruling. All the magistrates... are in agreement."

"I, well, I couldn't do it on my own."

"Then have Ari help you." She took each of their hands and joined them together. "It's what you both want. Isn't it?"

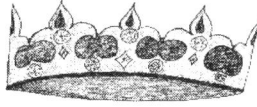

Chapter 50
Two Ceremonies

Ariyuna didn't know what to say. She glanced from Naiyan to the queen, who had closed her eyes again. The topic of her affection for Naiyan had come up many times in conversations with Baiyanarah. But was now the best time for a wedding? Did he even want this? Or was he being pressured into it?

Naiyan squeezed her hand. A genuine smile crossed his face, and his eyes held a tenderness she hadn't noticed before. "It's not much of a proposal, but what do you think?"

So he was going along with this? Her mind spun. "It's all very sudden, and we don't have much time to plan, and, oh, how would my parents get here? And what about Gan and Tabin?"

"So, is that a yes?" He kept a grip on her hand.

Baiyanarah opened one eye. "It's a yes, young man. Now go plan the wedding, and we'll throw in a coronation. I need to rest."

"Are you okay with that?" Naiyan glanced toward Ariyuna.

She gave a small nod. Leaning over, she kissed the queen on the forehead. The smallest hint of a smile emerged.

Satisfied for the moment, she tiptoed out.

Dash scrunched up his face as soon as the door shut behind them. "Are you two getting married?"

Naiyan grabbed Ariyuna's hand and grinned. "Looks like it."

Sahraa stole out of the room and joined them. "I'm so excited for you!"

"Do you think she'll make it until tomorrow?" Naiyan's smile faded. "Or should we do it sooner?"

"I think tomorrow will be fine. Midnoon." Sahraa gave her brother a squeeze. "The queen's been like this for over a week, although today she's somewhat worse. But I suspect she'll be okay until the wedding."

She turned to the boys. "We have so much to plan. Dalan and Dash, can you run down to the kitchens and inform them? After that, you can help wherever you find a need."

The boys hurried off.

"Bossy as ever," Naiyan whispered under his breath.

Ariyuna smiled. "We might just need someone bossy to pull this off." But Baiyanarah's deteriorating condition pressed in on the joy of the new developments. This wasn't how she had imagined her wedding.

"Now." A frown settled across Sahraa's forehead. "We don't have a moment to spare. Naiyan, you arrange the details for the coronation. Ari and I will plan the wedding part." She turned to Berke. "Can we get all the servants back right away?"

Naiyan took Ariyuna's hand and whispered. "Are you sure about this?"

"Yes." The warmth of his hand triggered familiar memories of comfort and support. "I've been sure for a long time."

"Me, too."

A flurry of activity filled the rest of the day. The quiet

palace turned into chaos as servants poured in and messengers ran out. Bright colored flowers and decorations gathered in the throne room. Sahraa scurried here and there, a large scroll tucked under her arm.

In the middle of the chaos, Ariyuna crept back to Baiyanarah's chamber. She settled quietly, into a chair near the head of the bed.

The queen rested, her breathing slow and rhythmic. Ariyuna slipped her hand into Baiyanarah's. Lowering her head onto the bed, she let the tears flow.

She remembered her visits with Baiyanarah as a young girl. The old woman had taught her to knit, read, and make yarcen bread. They had journeyed together all across Talsar before she'd become queen. And after that, Ariyuna had spent so much time with her in the palace. How could she go on without her oldest friend?

Baiyanarah's soft voice cut through the still air. "Don't cry for me, Ari."

Ariyuna lifted her head and wiped her face on her sleeve. "You've been in pain for so long. And I know you're going into V'Arah's depths, which is more wonderful than I can even imagine. But what will I do without you?"

"You are a wise girl. You'll be fine. Naiyan will be your strength, and you will be his. And, most of all, you both have Elch." She paused. "I have one last request."

Ariyuna sat up straighter. "Anything you want."

"Can you select something for me to wear tomorrow? I plan to be there for your big day."

Ariyuna wiped her face again and managed a smile.

"What color would you like?"

"Yellow. For the sun. You have been my sunshine since that first day you discovered me in the mountains."

Ariyuna searched the queen's wardrobe and found a flowing golden gown. She hung it on a hook near the bed.

"Now I need to rest again." She patted Ariyuna's hand. "I would suspect that Sahraa is in a panic looking for you by now. Come see me again before you sleep."

"I will." Ariyuna kissed her forehead and went to find Sahraa.

The sun dipped below the horizon, but the bustle and activity in the palace showed no signs of slowing down.

"There you are!" Sahraa grabbed her hand. "The dressmakers are frantic for you to try on your wedding gown."

"Oh, no!" Ariyuna remembered the ridiculousness of the court fashions in Temyulun. She should have said something sooner.

Sahraa grinned. "Don't worry. I think you'll like it. The dressmakers were rather displeased with my simple directions."

◆

After another quick visit with Baiyanarah in the middle of the night, Ariyuna fell exhausted into bed. Sahraa promised to wake her early in the morning.

What seemed like only a few minutes later, Sahraa shook her. "I have a surprise for you."

"Is it morning already?"

"Yes, Sis. I can call you that now, can't I?"

"I guess so." Ariyuna smiled and rubbed sleep from her eyes. "How is the queen?"

"The same as last night."

Fogginess filled her mind and pulled her back toward sleep. Then realization hit. Her wedding day had arrived! The thought sent a thrill of joy through her. She sat up. "What should I wear?"

Sahraa had clothes waiting, so she got dressed quickly and followed her soon-to-be-sister to the dining hall.

"My little Ari!" Ma jumped up to hug her. Papa waved.

"Ma? Papa? How did you get here?" She leaned over to give Papa a squeeze.

He patted the chair next to him. "Come sit and have some breakfast. Tailaal visited and told us about the queen some time ago, so we thought we'd better come see her. It looks like we've arrived just in time."

Something fuzzy brushed Ariyuna's elbow. An orange oostai grinned up at her, his cheek bulging and a sausage in each hand.

"Taag!" She gave him a hug.

The oostai swallowed hard several times. "It is so good to see you, Miss Ariyuna. Temyulun has very good food and very good friends. I like it here. Oh, I almost forgot." He shoved a small boy forward. The toddler smiled up at her with pointed teeth, and she noticed one rounded, furry ear.

"Buren?"

Taag nodded, stuffing a sausage into his mouth.

"He's grown."

"Yes, and he can control changing into a bear much better now. We will see you later, we must find more breakfast pudding. Ours is gone, and Mr. Dash is waiting for us." The oostai took Buren by the hand and trotted across the dining hall.

Ariyuna could see her brothers on the other side. She waved and settled back into her chair. "Have you talked with Dalan and Dash?"

"Yes." Ma helped herself to another pastry. "We arrived last night but couldn't find you. They told us all about your adventure."

Ariyuna barely had time to eat a few bites before Sahraa dragged her off. The morning drifted by in a blur of activity. She managed to see Baiyanarah several times, but wedding preparations took priority. Her hair was transformed into a work of art. Her wedding gown fit comfortably, and as Sahraa had promised, no obnoxious floof marred the inventive lines.

Before she knew it, she stood at the back of the throne room, filled to the very edges with people. In a reclining chair near the throne, Queen Baiyanarah surveyed the crowd. A hint of a smile rested on her face.

Naiyan stood before the throne as the ceremony started.

She wanted to remember every detail, but the mix of pressing emotions dominated. The crown of Talsar sparkled in the sunlight as the Grand Duke of Dundaad placed it on Naiyan's head.

She felt a tap on her shoulder.

Sahraa whispered. "It's time."

Up at the front, Naiyan glanced back and smiled. Soft music filled the room as Ariyuna stepped forward.

Baiyanarah's half smile lingered, as she closed her eyes and rested her pale head back on pillows.

When Ariyuna reached the front, Naiyan took her hand with a reassuring squeeze. The ceremony progressed with all the necessary formalities. But she kept glancing over at Baiyanarah, torn between the wonder of marrying one of her best friends, while anticipating with dread the death of another.

All too soon, the combined ceremonies came to an end. Naiyan leaned over and kissed her.

A crown was placed on her head as shouts rang out. "Long live King Naiyan and Queen Ariyuna!"

The title surprised her. She'd been too busy to realize that by marrying Naiyan, she was now Queen of Talsar.

As she walked away from the throne with Naiyan, a short man burst out from the back of the crowd.

"Gan!" Ariyuna held out her arms in greeting.

He pushed past her. "Scoured toad nails. We must see to the queen!"

"Which one?" someone shouted, but Ariyuna spun around and hurried to Baiyanarah's chair. The queen's face was deathly white and her chest alarmingly still.

She drew in a sudden deep breath. "Did I miss anything?" The sweet smile on the queen's face grew, and she opened her eyes. "I was trying to soak it all in and must have dozed."

"Not at all," Ariyuna reassured her. "But you should rest now."

"Will you come with me?" Baiyanarah whispered.

"Of course."

Chapter 51
Home

"Dash, wake up!"

Dash opened his eyes, and a form wavered into focus. Dalan? He pulled the covers higher and muttered, "Go away. It's still dark out." His warm bed drew him back toward the comfortable cocoon of sleep.

"Wake up. The queen."

Dash smiled sleepily. "Which one?"

"Don't be a pig head. This is serious. Baiyanarah. She's gone."

The comfort of his bed dissipated. Dash sat up, rubbed his face and reached for clothes. "When did this happen?"

"Just a bit ago. Ariyuna and Naiyan have been with her all night. They wanted you to get some sleep."

When Dalan and Dash reached the queen's chambers, a group of servants milled around the door. Pushing past the crowd, they squeezed in.

Ariyuna came over and hugged him. She wore a simple purple tunic and dark trousers that looked like ones Ma had made. Her wedding gown hung in a corner. She tried to smile, but her red, puffy eyes betrayed her true feelings.

Dash walked slowly toward the bed. Ma and Papa sat off to one side, and Tabin stood by the fire, his back to the room.

Gan rocked back and forth in a chair on the far side.

No one spoke.

On the soft bed, Queen Baiyanarah lay, pale and still.

The tightness in Dash's stomach grew and filled his whole body.

She is not here, Elch reminded him. *Only her shell remains. The Baiyanarah you love has entered V'Arah's depths and is well.*

Is she with Beltreg?

Yes, and a host of others, too many to count.

The tightness eased slightly.

The door creaked open. Burke entered and bowed. "It is time to prepare the queen."

Naiyan nodded. He placed his arm around Dash's shoulders. "Come. I know Taag and Buren are waiting for you."

Taking one last parting glance at Baiyanarah, he left with Naiyan.

All the joyful decorations from the wedding and coronation had been removed and replaced with gray. Silence permeated the palace even though a large number of servants still bustled around. Dash helped half-heartedly.

Taag tried to get him interested in playing boombook with Buren, but that didn't last long. The boy's claws kept surfacing, and after popping six balls, Dash gave up.

As the days to the royal funeral ticked by, Dash's longing for home grew. Inside, he felt tired. His wrists no longer had the tight bands, but a stiffness lingered.

On the morning of the burial, the servants left a gray tunic and trousers for him. He dressed and ate without much thought, then joined the rest of his family in the procession.

Silent crowds, dressed in gray, lined the streets.

Dash. He heard Elch in his mind. *Why are you so sad?*

Beltreg's gone. Baiyanarah's gone. Who's next?

The fish smiled. *The great beyond isn't so bad. But you are left without the love, company, and support of the ones who have gone before you. This life is but a blink. Now that you have a tooya, you too will join them someday.*

Dash thought about that for the space of several blocks.

Is she really in a better place? And Beltreg, too?

A fierce warmth radiated within. The immense power filled Dash so completely that no feelings of sorrow remained. His fingertips tingled, and his body felt as light as air. It reminded him of the cave, only much stronger. Once again, every part of him wanted to immerse himself in this space and never leave.

As the sensation subsided, Dash drew in a quick breath. *Is that what it's like?*

That is only a taste.

A smile crept up his face. He looked ahead to the ornate casket that held the queen's body. The tightness inside him faded away, replaced by a peaceful calm.

After all the requirements of the formal interment of Queen Baiyanarah had been fulfilled, Ariyuna approached Dash. He sat on a long, narrow step in a corner of the still-bustling dining hall.

Nearby, Taag called to a servant for more honey cakes while Buren snuggled in Ma's lap.

"So." Ariyuna sat down beside him. "How are you?"

"Okay, I guess. Considering the circumstances." Dash let a smile peek out. "I've had some talks with Elch."

"That's always good."

Dash's grin widened. "You're the queen of Talsar now. Wow. I never thought I'd be related to a queen. Does that mean I'm a real prince of Talsar now?"

"Yes, but I'm still your big sister." She gave him a playful punch on the arm.

Dash looked around the hall. "I used to love it here. Now all I want to do is go home and stay for a *long* time."

"There's nothing like running into what's wrong to make you appreciate what's right." Ariyuna shifted on the small step. "Ma still can't cook, but I'd take her burnt rolls over the finest palace delicacies any day."

"Her scorched potatoes and soggy dumplings, too," Dash added.

Dalan came and sat with them. "Are we talking about Ma's cooking?"

"Yep." Dash glanced at Ma, who bounced Buren on her knee. "I'm ready to go home. Maybe the haying will make me strong again." He flexed his skinny arms. "Not much there now."

"Just give Papa time." Dalan laughed.

Naiyan swung by and grabbed Ariyuna's hand. "It's settled. We'll leave tomorrow for our wedding trip."

Her face flushed and her eyes flickered with expectation. "We're going to the Altan forest first, right?"

"I don't think my family would have it any other way. They're planning a huge celebration. I've gotta run. I'll catch up with you later." He gave her a quick kiss and strode quickly out of the dining hall.

Ariyuna settled back on the step. "Ma mentioned something about Buren. What's happening with that?"

"Oh, boy." Dalan shook his head in disbelief. "I think Ma's realizing the house can be a bit empty without all of us around as much. When she found out Buren was an orphan, she decided to take him in. Maybe she's trying to make up for rejecting Tabin when he was young and couldn't control changing into a yuratag cat. Something about adopting him came up as well."

Dash picked up a ball that had rolled to his feet and threw it back to Buren. "What about the bear teeth and claws? Can she handle those?"

"Taag's going home with them, too."

Ariyuna waved at the little boy. "That doesn't bode well for Ma's cooking. She'll never improve if everything she makes is gratefully devoured."

"Maybe Taag and I can learn to cook." Dash's eyes lit up with anticipation. "It'd probably be better than Ma's cooking, and Taag could eat all day long. He'd like that."

"Dash, are you sure you don't want to stay here?" Dalan threw the straying ball back to Buren.

"I'm sure. I've been gone from home way too long. In fact, I think we might be leaving soon. Papa's anxious to get back to the animals. But I still have to convince Ma that using the staff for travel is safe. She had a bit of a meltdown about it yesterday. But Taag's excited to try."

"Oh, I almost forgot." Dash unhooked a mountain knife from his belt. "This is yours, Dalan. I'm sorry I pinched it."

"*That's* where it went." Dalan took back his knife and examined it. A slight frown softened into a grin, and he held it out toward his brother. "I'm not really going to need it here in the palace. You can hang onto it for a bit. These knives are handy on the farm."

"No, I want to earn my own. Papa and I had a talk. He said if I work hard, I might be able to get one early, like you did."

"There's one other thing." Reaching down to the floor, Dash lifted up a glass bottle with a narrow neck at the top that expanded into a globe at the bottom. It was filled with clear water, and a small golden fish swam in it. A cork, lodged in the opening, kept the water inside.

Ariyuna smiled and took the bottle. "This is how it all started."

The fish swam around, gulping in mouthfuls of water.

"Who should I give Elch to?" Dash leaned in to peer at the fish.

Ariyuna smiled. "You'll know when the time is right."

Important Characters

Disclaimer from the author: The meanings of some very ancient words, especially ones used for place names, have been forgotten or distorted with the passage of time. There may, however, be a few people out there who remember the old language and can fill in some of the missing information.

Aidos (meaning: moon friend) - A servant in the royal palace in Endurek.

Akmat (meaning: stupid) - A wealthy and influential citizen of Endurek.

Ariyuna (meanings: holy, pure, sacred) - Simple farm girl from Dorben who goes on several journeys through Talsar.

Baiyanarah (meaning: joyful sun) - The old hermit woman who lived in the mountains near Dorben before becoming the queen of Talsar.

Beltreg (meaning: wolf cub) - Tabin's nephew who lived with Gan and died during the Battle of Temyulun.

Buren (meaning: perfect, full) - The youngest shape changer, who can turn into a bear.

Dalan (meanings: embankment, dam, seventy) - Ariyuna's younger brother.
Dash (meaning: good luck) - Ariyuna's youngest brother.

Doechin (meaning: singer) - The pony Dash takes when he leaves home.

Elch (meanings: messenger, energy) - The fish Dalan takes along on the journey, who is the voice of V'Arah.

Els Edzyn (Meaning: sand lord) - Ruler of the Elsen Khelver in the ancient city of Vachir.

Gan (meaning: steel, hearty, steady) - The magistrate of Surtak.

Jaren (meaning: sixty) - Ariyuna's papa.

Karakul (meaning: dark slave) - The merchant/sorcerer from Endurek who befriends Dash.

Lady Idana (meaning: more beautiful than the moon) - A lady in the court of Endurek.

Lord Temir (meaning: iron) - A courtier in the palace in Endurek.

Moochir (meaning: twig) - A woodpit who attaches to Dalan.

Naiyan (meaning: eighty) - Advisor to Queen Baiyanarah. Alban and Sahraa's brother.

Prince Kasiret (meaning: evil) - The High Prince of Teagen, an imposter.

Serik (meaning: support, hope) - A servant in Karakul's house.

Sahraa (meaning: moon) - Servant in the royal palace. Naiyan's younger sister.

Sarnai (meaning: moon) - Ariyuna's ma.

Taag (meaning: lid) - The oostai who follows Dalan on his journey.

Tabin (meaning: fifty) - Ariyuna, Dalan, and Dash's uncle of sorts who helps on their journey.

Tailaal (meaning: interpretation, solution) - Daughter of the previous ruler of Talsar, King Galdak, and an orlolak that takes the form of an eagle.

V'Arah (meaning: short for Elah Sh'maya V'Arah - God of heaven and earth) - The long form of the name has been forgotten by most.

Zibek (meaning: silk) - A healer from Endurek who has strong connections to Prince Kasiret.

Zovlon (meanings: misery, torment, suffering) - The evil sorcerer who tries to find the Enk Taivaan and attacks Temyulun with his tarch army.

Other Places, Objects and People

Altan Forest (meaning: Golden Forest) - A forest on the eastern slopes of the Bat'Uul Mountains that extends into the plain. Where the Setgel tribe lives.

Banda apples (meaning: bench apples) - A light green, sweet apple.

Bat'Uul Mountains (meaning: Strong Mountains) - The range that runs along the western edge of Talsar.

Belgutai (meaning: unknown) - The town closest to Dorben and a major trading hub for the eastern side of Talsar.

Bokir (meaning: unknown) - A small village south of The Wild where Dash meets Karakul.

Bura (meaning: unknown) - A town built into a dip in the plain just east of the Great Divide.

Dorben (meaning: unknown) - The small town closest to Dash's family's farm.

Els Edzyn (meaning: Sand Lord) - Ruler of those who live in Vachir and are able to shape the sand. Used to be helpers to the Timojyn, the ancient rulers of Talsar.

Edurek (meaning: unknown) - The capital city of Teagen.

Enk Taivaan (meaning: complete peace) - One of the three gifts from the Storyteller.

Gahzar Tribe (meaning: Earth Tribe) - The tribe that lives on the plains between the Bat'Uul and Yuratag Mountains.

Itgel (meaning: faith, trust) - The bracelet that Ariyuna is given. One of the three gifts from the Storyteller.

Nayza (meaning: spear) - a javelin type spear thrown toward a target. A sporting event at the tournament.

Ohstan (meaning: unknown) - The staffs used in Zodoj.

Onon Book (meaning: Book of Truth) - the ancient collection of wisdom and stories about V'Arah

Oostai (meaning: to have hair or fur) - Small furry creatures from the Bat'Uul mountains.

Orlolak (meaning: to change) - A person that can change into an animal. Very few exist and they only come from Talsar.

Setgel Tribe (meaning: Soul Tribe) - The tribe living in the Altan Forest.

Shimeg (meanings: to sip, to suck) - The ancient creatures that live under the Yuratag Mountains.

Sheker (meaning: sugar sand) - A town just south of The Wild on the eastern edge of Talsar.

Talsar (meaning: grateful) - The country where Ariyuna, Dalan, and Dash live.

Tarmoor Tribe (meaning: Rake Tribe) - The tribe living on the eastern side of the Yuratag Mountains.

Temyulun (meaning unknown) - The capital city of Talsar where the royal palace is.

Teagen (meaning: desired) - The land to the east of Talsar. The Great Divide is the border between the two lands.

The Great Divide - The deep chasm that divides Talsar from Teagen.

The Wild - A dark forest on the northern edge of Talsar. Few venture in, and no known habitations lie within the woods.

Tsai (meaning: tea) - Tea served with a little milk and a dash of salt.

Tooya (meaning: ray of light) - Mark on the forearm that people receive when they learn to trust V'Arah.

Woodpit - Rare creatures that live in wood and can jump from one piece of wood to another. They form attachments to others for entertainment that can last for decades. Only a few exist, and they live only in Talsar. Their life spans are as long as their parent tarlan trees' lives.

Yuratag (meaning: unknown) - Used for the Yuratag Mountains and the cats that originate from there.

Zavtai (meaning: to be free) - One of the three gifts from the storyteller.

Zodoj (meaning: to beat) - A game of one-on-one combat using large staffs. The winner must disarm his opponent by knocking both ohstan staffs from his hands.

Also available:

Veiled Light
The Land of Talsar - Book 1

The Upside Down Kingdom
The Land of Talsar - Book 2

Watch for:

The Gift Box
A story for Advent

About the Author

Heidi Likins credits imaginative thinking of all sorts with expanding her understanding of God. Her love of adventure started with a childhood in the hot, muddy jungles of Papua New Guinea and continued while weathering the frigid steppes of Outer Mongolia. She now lives near the Rocky Mountains with her husband and kids, and is awaiting the next adventure.

37753145R00220

Made in the USA
Middletown, DE
05 December 2016